Strap In

Lou Morgan writes smart, sexy stories about women finding love across difference. Lou is a Black biracial woman who believes all readers deserve to see themselves reflected on the page. Lesbian books are her passion. In her spare time Lou reads and reviews sapphic romance, pines after middle-aged actresses, and volunteers with the Romantic Novelists' Association. She lives near Glasgow.

LOU MORGAN
STRAP IN

hera

First published in the United Kingdom in 2025 by

Hera Books, an imprint of
Canelo Digital Publishing Limited,
20 Vauxhall Bridge Road,
London SW1V 2SA
United Kingdom

A Penguin Random House Company
The authorised representative in the EEA is Dorling Kindersley Verlag GmbH.
Arnulfstr. 124, 80636 Munich, Germany

Copyright © Lou Morgan 2025

The moral right of Lou Morgan to be identified as the creator of this work has been asserted in accordance with the Copyright, Designs and Patents Act, 1988.
All rights reserved. No part of this publication may be reproduced or transmitted in any form or by any means, electronic or mechanical, including photocopy, recording, or any information storage and retrieval system, without permission in writing from the publisher.
No part of this book may be used or reproduced in any manner for the purpose of training artificial intelligence technologies or systems. In accordance with Article 4(3) of the DSM Directive 2019/790, Canelo expressly reserves this work from the text and data mining exception.

A CIP catalogue record for this book is available from the British Library.

Print ISBN 978 1 83598 334 8
Ebook ISBN 978 1 83598 328 7

This book is a work of fiction. Names, characters, businesses, organizations, places and events are either the product of the author's imagination or are used fictitiously. Any resemblance to actual persons, living or dead, events or locales is entirely coincidental.

Printed and bound in Great Britain by Clays Ltd, Elcograf S.p.A.

Look for more great books at
www.herabooks.com | www.dk.com

For MP, whose unwavering support and encouragement made this book possible. I cherish you every day.

And for RW, who believed in me long before I believed in myself. I miss you every day.

This novel contains depictions of racism, including the use of a slur, and trauma as the consequence of male sexual violence.

Chapter One

Jean perches on a stool, sipping her second martini. She'd held off ordering to begin with – simple date logic. Without a glass in hand, it was much easier to pretend she hadn't arrived at eight p.m. precisely, that she'd simply breezed into Strata seconds before Scott. But then the minute hand twisted inexorably towards quarter past, and the bartender's stares had grown pointed. So, she'd ordered a martini, not yet anticipating it would be the only dirty thing about her night.

Jean is not Scott's first choice. And that's fine – he wasn't hers either, with thinning hair and a paunch not quite concealed by the swing of his jacket. But at least he'd worn a suit. Thought: *this is the image I'll project to the world, the best version of myself.* And so – bored and with an itch to scratch – she'd swiped right.

Her phone pinged with a match twenty minutes later. Long enough that Scott must have deliberated too. And Jean understands it, eyeing herself in the mirror. Even in the bar's soft lighting there's no mistaking her crow's feet. The slackening of the skin around her neck. Her clothes are impeccable, but this dress is tighter than it was even six months ago. Jean drains the glass, plucking the olive from the cocktail stick and popping it into her mouth. She chews slowly, savouring the salty tang.

What she really wants is a side of mozzarella sticks or a basket of wings. Something heavy enough to quash the butterflies. But that would scupper her chances. Fingers greasy, lipstick smudged – no man wants to hook up with that woman. And even if Scott's not coming, there are other... possibilities. Jean hasn't shaved her legs, squeezed into shapewear, and spent billable hours perched on a hard stool to simply call it quits. To go home alone and administer her own battery-powered orgasm.

The door swings open, drawing Jean's gaze. For an absurd, hopeful moment, she thinks: *Scott?* From the corner of her eye she searches for greying sandy hair and a lantern jaw. The jeans and blazer that are the smart-casual uniform of white men of a certain age. And there is a blazer. But nothing beneath it that needs concealing.

A young woman strides into the bar, dark curls bouncing round her lapels. She wears cargo pants, a silken top baring just a sliver of sun-kissed midriff, and an unmistakable air of confidence, even though she's alone.

The young woman draws appreciative glances as she passes. Even the nervous lad clearly out on a date can't resist looking. And Jean can't blame him; not really. This girl is curvaceous with a cinched waist, and warm brown just-back-from-holiday skin. And as she leans against the bar, her blazer rides up to display an ass so tight it's tempting to take a bite. If Jean were a man, she'd want this girl too.

The girl catches her staring. Looks Jean up and down, appraisingly. Then her full lips curve into a grin.

Jean's lips twitch – close enough to a smile that her staring is mitigated, but chilly enough to ward off conversation. Or so she thinks.

'A mojito please.' The young woman nods towards Jean, curls bobbing. 'And another martini for the lady.'

'Dirty,' Jean says, automatically.

The girl turns to look at her full on, eyebrows climbing. 'What?'

Heat floods Jean's cheeks. 'The martini. There was an olive in it, and a dash of juice. That's called a dirty martini.'

There's a playful gleam in her eyes, dark and glittering with mirth. The young woman's gaze never leaves Jean's as she speaks: 'And your dirtiest martini please, bartender.'

There are a dozen things she ought to say to put the girl off. Jean would bet her Rolex they're not in the same tax bracket. But her brain and her tongue can't seem to cooperate. It's ridiculous – she hasn't frozen like this since her first trial, a baby solicitor in borrowed heels, when she'd realised her co-counsel wasn't coming. William Decker's idea of a baptism by fire, and Jean's of a recurring nightmare.

Oblivious to Jean's discomfort, the young woman taps her card against the machine.

The bartender pours gin, vermouth, and a healthy splash of olive brine into the shaker. Ice rattles against metal as he mixes. And it's a sound Jean will never tire of hearing. She can't help but thaw as he pours it into her glass and garnishes it with an olive.

'Go ahead.' Her companion nods to the cocktail glass. 'I'm Ava, by the way.'

Jean lifts the glass to her lips. It's cool and sharp, with just a hint of salt teasing her tongue. She makes a little noise of contentment. And Ava doesn't seem to notice when the bartender delivers her own cocktail. Her gaze is still fixed on Jean. It should be disconcerting, being stared at by a stranger, but the warmth of those brown eyes sets her at ease.

But Jean isn't here to make friends. She shakes her head to break the trance. 'You should drink that while it's fresh.'

Ava blinks, confused. Finds the mojito at her elbow. 'Right.' She holds her cocktail out. 'Cheers.'

Jean clinks their glasses together. It would be churlish not to. 'Cheers. Thank you for the drink, Ava.'

She turns in her seat, facing the bar once more. But Ava doesn't take the hint. She hops up onto the stool beside Jean's, sipping at her mojito. 'You're welcome.' A beat. 'And you are?'

Their eyes meet in the mirror. 'Jean.'

'Nice to meet you, Jean.'

'Likewise.'

They sip in companionable silence, which Jean very deliberately does not break. Sooner or later Ava will get bored – and the sooner she does, the faster she'll saunter off to somebody else. If Ava wants a drinking companion, she won't be short on takers.

'So.' Ava stirs the mint with her cocktail pick. 'What brings you here?'

Jean grasps the stem of the glass, rolling it between her fingers so the martini swirls. She will not share confidences with her dewy-skinned competition. 'Drink.'

Ava's laughter is more musical than the electronic pulse playing through the speakers. 'Do you ever give answers longer than one word?'

In spite of herself, Jean smiles. 'Sometimes.'

'You're a tough cookie, huh?'

'Yes.' The drink is smooth and crisp, just the way she likes it. And Jean's resistance melts just a little. 'I've had to be, in my line of work.'

'Don't tell me.' Ava's eyebrows knit together as she takes in Jean's clothes, her accessories, her bearing. 'You make good money, but you're not boring, so nothing in finance. No doctor has a manicure like that. And you're careful about what you say. Lawyer?'

Surprise buoys Jean past reserve. 'Yes! How did you guess?'

Ava smirks. 'Takes one to know one.'

And Jean sees it then, how it could go if she stays with Ava. Relaxing into the evening instead of thinking constantly about how she's perceived. Bonding over their shared profession. And more of this electric conversation, Ava curious and teasing by turn until Jean forgets to be standoffish. But it wasn't the promise of conversation that lured her to this bar.

'It's not that I don't appreciate the drink,' says Jean. 'But we'd both do better alone.'

Ava tilts her head, birdlike. 'Better at what?'

'Better at...' Jean sighs. Flicks her gaze towards the booth where two young men stare at Ava with naked admiration. 'You'd have a shot with either one of them. Or both, if that's your thing. They haven't stopped looking since you got here. The only reason they haven't come over here is they're worried the reject will get stuck with an old lady.'

'I'm happy where I am.' Ava stirs her drink, smile growing. 'And I don't see any old ladies here.'

Jean rolls her eyes. Nice as it is to be part of the sisterhood, she has no practical use for solidarity. 'You might be,' says Jean, ignoring the compliment. 'But I'll only get results flying solo tonight.'

'And what results might those be?' There's a teasing glint in her eye that tells Jean she knows full well – but it's not like she's laughing at Jean, it's more… an invitation of sorts, to be in on the joke.

But Jean has no patience for deciphering secret meanings. It's gone half past. Even if Ralph Fiennes were to walk into this bar and whisper Shakespearean sonnets into her ear, she'd need time to detect potential serial killer vibes. It'd be ten before they got back to her place, unless he lives closer. And Jean has to be up by five if she's to meet her trainer before work. Time is wasting.

'I'm trying to get laid.' And so far, all she's managed to score is a pity martini. Jean takes another sip, washing away the taste of bitterness.

Ava's smile grows wide, teeth gleaming. 'I could help you with that.'

'But that's my point – you're a hindrance, not a help.' Jean closes her eyes. Only partially blunts the edge of her exasperation. 'I was supposed to be on a date. I came here to meet a man. But he was a no-show.'

'He stood you up?' Ava's voice is loud, carrying. Heads turn. And her look of sudden incredulity is so comical that Jean wonders if she's being had – though what Ava's game is, she can't begin to guess.

'Don't act so surprised.' Her voice has a bite of frost; the tone Jean uses to send her junior associates scurrying. And she means to teach this girl a lesson. 'It'll happen to you too. A lot sooner than you think, let me tell you. They hit forty and start falling for girls who were foetuses in your prime. So, take my advice: make hay while the sun still shines.'

Ava's laughter is bright and sharp, a blade between the ribs. Her scorn cuts deeper than Scott's indifference. Jean hops down from the stool, lifting her handbag.

Ava all but falls to the ground in her haste to block Jean's path. 'Oh! No, no. I'm not laughing at you. It's n—'

'Forget it.' Jean tries to sidestep her, but Ava's in the way, all bouncing curls and big pleading eyes.

'I promise I wasn't laughing at you, Jean. Please don't go.'

Despite herself, Jean is intrigued. But she keeps her voice carefully flat. 'Then what?'

The young woman runs a hand through her unruly mane. And for the first time she seems nervous. 'A man won't stand me up because he won't ever have the chance. And that's not because I'm special. I just... I don't date men.' Her lips twitch, and Jean gets a strong sense Ava's trying not to crack up. 'I thought it was obvious?'

The bartender's cough sounds suspiciously like laughter. Jean glares at him before looking the young woman up and down. The boots are a little on the butch side, and the blazer. But the silky top, the chunky silver necklace, the gloss coating her plump lips... 'Not really. At least, not to me.'

Ava's nose wrinkles. A lone crease lines her forehead. 'But I've been hitting on you for a solid fifteen minutes. I bought you a drink.'

'But you don't look—' Jean's brain short-circuits as she processes this last piece of information. The pity martini... wasn't a pity martini. *Oh.*

Ava rolls her eyes. But – apparently – she's not offended. At least, not enough to give up on Jean. 'Not all lesbians are butches or studs. Stay for another drink and I'll explain everything. The entire gay agenda and a dirty martini – what more could a woman ask for?'

A decent fuck. It's on the tip of her tongue, but then she remembers the young woman's offer: *I could help you with that*. Jean's scalp tingles. Best to avoid all mention of sex. It might not be the night she'd planned, but Ava's company appeals more than her empty house. She's watching Jean, openly hopeful.

'Fine,' says Jean. 'But I'm buying my own. Because this is not a date, or anything like one. And you can stop flirting.'

Ava makes a three-fingered salute. And Jean realises that, while her nails are painted a deep burgundy, they're clipped short. 'Scout's honour.'

'You were never a Scout.'

'They let girls join. Especially the tomboys.' A grin. 'But no, I wasn't a Scout.'

They take turns ordering at the bar. Ava darts off to claim a freshly vacated booth. And Jean goes first, staring down the bartender, whose face remains carefully impassive. He's young, but surely he's heard stranger things in his line of work. He slides her sparkling water across the countertop. If Jean's going along with this, whatever it is, she's keeping her wits sharp.

She weaves between tables and swaps places with Ava, breathing in the spice of cedar undercut with jasmine as she passes. It's a curious scent for a young woman – masculinity softened by subtle floral notes. Something Jean could imagine inhaling from a lover's neck as he moves on top of her.

Jean's hand trembles as she reaches for her drink, condensation blessedly cool beneath her fingertips. It's been too long since her last hook-up, a dismal fumble with a CFO that left her frustrated and him sated. Instinct tells her that Ava is anything but complacent about a lover's pleasure, or lack thereof. Then Ava's sliding back into the booth as if summoned by the thought, carrying a fresh mojito and that same intriguing scent.

'I hope you don't mind,' she says. 'But I ordered us wings. And fries.'

Jean's mouth floods at the thought. She swallows. 'I agreed to one drink, not food.'

'Do you want me to cancel them?' Ava shifts, hovering on the edge of her seat. Ready to call Jean's bluff. 'I can still catch her.'

At that exact moment Jean's stomach rumbles. Late home from the office and with a date to prepare for, there had been no time for dinner. Heat floods her cheeks, but her voice remains steady. 'That won't be necessary.'

Ava's too clever to outwardly savour her victory. She nods in acknowledgement, betraying not so much as a flicker of satisfaction. And Jean sees it – how Ava must catch the opposing counsel off guard.

'Which firm are you with?'

'I'm not that kind of lawyer, Ms Corporate.' Ava smirks, as if she can read Jean's mind. And it's not a lack of intelligence holding her back. Nor – Jean's instincts tell her – talent. There's a sharpness to Ava, a forwardness and charm that can't be taught. Ambition, then, must be what's lacking.

'What kind of lawyer are you?'

Ava scoffs. Then she looks hard at Jean, gaze penetrating. 'Is that *really* what you want to ask me about?'

Jean considers her next words with care. And Ava seems content to let her, watching – always watching – but never pressing. It would be safer to stick to work, certainly. As a senior partner Jean is sure on her feet in legal discussions. Mergers and acquisitions. Advice and crisis management. And she's well placed to offer a junior colleague pointers. In this conversation, Jean would have the upper hand.

But she can have that conversation at any conference or function, where students and interns buzz around her like mosquitos. And it doesn't make her blood quicken. Doesn't leave any part of Jean curious about what's coming next. She's on autopilot then, not anticipating her opponent's next move.

'No, actually,' says Jean. 'It's not.'

Ava leans forward, an elbow on the table, chin perched against her palm. 'Go on, then.'

And Jean almost wishes she'd opted for a third martini, for the gin to burn her embarrassment clean away. 'How do you do it? With women?' Ava's eyes pop cartoon wide, and Jean's tongue trips over her teeth in haste to stop her seizing on this slip. 'Pick them up. Other… females. Date them. Or whatever it is you do.'

She gulps at the sparkling water, draining half the glass in one go. And it's as if the bubbles have entered Jean's bloodstream, fizzing and popping just beneath her skin.

'Apps mostly. I don't have time for much else. Too busy with work – you know how that goes. Sometimes my friends set me up.' A gamine shrug. Then her eyes lock with Jean's, and there's no mistaking Ava's intent. 'Occasionally, once in a blue moon, I'll bump into a woman who steals my breath away.'

'Oh?'

'Doesn't happen that often. But when it does…' Ava trails off, leaving Jean to imagine all kinds of unspoken pleasures.

'How do you know?' Jean clears her throat. 'When it's like that with a woman?'

Ava frowns, considering. 'Being near her is just... this intoxicating feeling. Like the first time I ever tasted champagne. And the closer I get to her, the more alive I feel. It's an ache, only the last thing you want is for it to stop.'

Jean's heart pounds, so loud in her ears it drowns out the music. She's still scrambling for something, anything, to say when the server sets two steaming baskets down before them. And Jean has never been so grateful for a heap of wings.

Ever gallant, Ava pushes the basket towards her first. And Jean plucks a wing from the pile, tearing meat from bone. The crunch of the skin, the tenderness of the chicken – it tastes so good that Jean doesn't care how she looks, reaching for a second even as she chews. There is no elegant way to eat food like this. And it doesn't matter how Ava sees her. Not one tiny bit. Jean drops the glistening bone down onto her napkin and devours another wing.

Ava pops a fry into her mouth, flashing an appreciative smile. 'I like a woman with an appetite.'

Jean doesn't know what to say to that. But she doesn't shoot Ava down, just lets the flirtation stand, which is a response of its own.

'You know,' Ava says, between bites. 'People think of lesbian relationships as being butch/femme. And fair play to all the women living that life. But it's not the only choice. Butches can be with each other. Femmes can be with each other. And plenty of lesbians don't fit into either camp.'

'Okay.' And it is. Jean hadn't considered any of those possibilities, hasn't dwelled on the ways in which women might desire one another. But the thought doesn't bother her.

'Also, you don't have to be a lesbian to want other women. There's a whole spectrum of human sexuality.' Ava grins. 'I just happen to sit very comfortably at one end of it.'

Jean blinks. She's heard of Kinsey and his scale. But it had never occurred to her to question where she herself might sit on it; to imagine any other possibility than the life she's mapped out for herself after graduation. Joining a respectable law firm, marrying a man who could match her ambition, making partner by forty-five. In every respect she's succeeded, except the divorce – but that scarcely matters nowadays, outside of the church, even if it had sucked the wind from Jean's sails.

'You alright?'

Jean nods. Even knowing that Ava is not her competition doesn't make it any more appealing, the thought of exposing this part of herself to a virtual stranger. 'Tell me: is it very different to being with a man?'

A shrug. 'I wouldn't know.'

'Of course. That was a foolish question.'

'No, it wasn't – not every lesbian has only ever been with women.' Ava gives Jean a moment to mull that one over, getting stuck into a wing.

'But if you've never slept with a man, how do you know...' Jean trails off, realising that *what you're missing out on* may not be the most diplomatic way to end her question. She leans back in the seat, wondering when her curiosity outstripped all caution – and manners.

Ava's smile is knowing, as if she can read the thoughts inside Jean's head. 'Do you want the honest answer? Or the PG one?'

'Give it to me straight,' says Jean. And right away she's rewarded with that warm, husky laugh.

'Honestly, my body's only ever responded to women. Back in school I'd kiss boys at parties now and again, so nobody would guess. But there was no spark. No heat. Nothing. Girls, on the other hand?' Ava smirks. 'I realised early on that what they called practice was the real thing for me. The thing that made my heart race and other parts… well. I didn't get how they could just stop as if those kisses didn't leave them aching for more, and go back to their boring boyfriends the next day.'

Mouth suddenly dry, Jean drains the last of her sparkling water. But it doesn't stop her from imagining what makes Ava ache now.

'That was my misspent youth,' Ava says, with an air of studied casualness. 'But tell me. If you've never been with a woman, how do you know for sure that you're not into it?'

She pushes the near-empty basket towards Jean, offering the final wing, not seeming to expect an answer.

And Jean takes a bite, savouring the final mouthfuls. She doesn't know what this is, in that strange liminal space between a date and not. But – whatever it is – this thing with Ava is oddly comfortable. Jean doesn't have to put on the performance of a desirable woman; she can simply let herself be desired.

Her glass is empty, the basket left with only a few crumbs. Jean had agreed to a drink, and has kept her promise – only, she doesn't want this thing with Ava to end. For all the night's electric possibilities to dissipate into nothing. 'You know,' Jean says, 'of all the ways this evening could have gone, I didn't see this coming.'

'Same here. Ordinarily I spend more time bringing women up to speed with the practice than the theory.' Ava's eyes sparkle with mischief, and something else Jean isn't ready to name. 'But for you I'm willing to make an exception.'

'Why?'

Ava raises a single eyebrow, sceptical. Then something unreadable passes across her face. And she looks Jean dead in the eye, says: 'Because you're a total fox. Smart, funny, beautiful – Jean, you're a triple threat.'

Beautiful. The word hits Jean in the solar plexus, so earnest. And the way Ava looks at her, in that moment Jean feels it. Which is why she's bold enough to slide round the booth. To lean into Ava's curls; breathe in that intoxicating scent. 'I've never been with a woman,' she says. 'But I'm starting to wonder whether I've missed out.'

She's close enough to hear Ava swallow. 'Do you want to try it?'

'I—' Jean's cheeks burn.

'Does the idea of it turn you on? Even a little bit?'

'I don't know, exactly – what it is that I'm supposed to imagine.' Beneath the table Jean wipes her palms on her skirt. 'I'm just curious is all.'

Ava tilts back her head and laughs, though Jean doesn't understand the joke. Not until Ava adds: 'I've been with a few *curious* women. Once upon a time they were all I knew.'

Then there's no more resisting it. Jean can't stop herself from wondering what it would be like, to be known by Ava. To get closer still. And the opportunity to find out is within her grasp. 'Would you like to be with another curious woman now?'

'You sure?' Ava pulls back far enough to look at her closely, teasing and not. 'Curiosity killed the cat.'

'Ah,' says Jean. 'But satisfaction brought it back.'

Chapter Two

Jean has her card ready when the driver pulls up outside a tower of flats. She taps it against the reader, ignoring Ava's protests, and steps out into the cool night air. But from there she's lost – Jean hasn't set foot in East London for a decade, and has no idea which block Ava even lives in. And she is still finding her bearings when a pack of young men approach, hoods up, filling the air with obscenities.

The taxi pulls away before she can reconsider. Jean tenses, phone clutched tight in her hand.

And Ava's hand comes to rest in the small of her back. She shouts back at a youth, undaunted. 'You kiss your mother with that mouth, Daniel Avery?'

Daniel kisses his teeth. 'You suck your mother with that one?'

The cacophony of laughter confirms Jean's worst suspicions about that charming little phrase.

'Say that shit to me again and I'll suck *your* mother.' Ava fishes keys from her pocket as she speaks, unhurried. 'I'll suck her *pumpum* so good you'll be my stepson by summer.'

Daniel turns beet red. The group of young men fall about laughing, shoving and jeering at him, whoops echoing long after they're out of sight. And Jean realises they're boys really, for all that swagger, more bark than bite.

'Sorry about that,' says Ava, unlocking the door and holding it open. 'They're harmless really. But if you don't stand up to them, they think they can get away with anything.'

'You've got quite a tongue.'

Ava summons the lift and leans close. 'Stick around and I'll show you what else it can do.'

The pit of Jean's belly goes tight with want. On weak legs she follows Ava into the lift. Its walls are covered in graffiti and – though there are no obvious puddles – the lift carries the distinctive reek of piss.

Catching sight of herself in the fluorescent lighting, pale and shiny-faced, Jean wonders what the hell she's doing here. It's the sort of encounter that might be spun into a funny story for the girls over brunch – except for the sex of her conquest. Jean has no intention of coming out to them over mimosas, or at all.

Though Jean attempts to keep her expression neutral, Ava must read some uncertainty. She strokes Jean's back through the wool of her coat and says: 'Don't worry. My flat's nicer than this. Scout's honour.'

Jean cracks a thin smile. Then the lift lurches to a halt. Though Jean follows Ava out into a corridor, mercifully piss-free, it's as if her stomach remains in the lift, plummeting towards the ground floor.

Then Ava opens her door, painted deep red, and Jean follows her inside. Though she'd never been a Scout, Ava was telling the truth about her flat. They're standing in a tiny living room opening into the kitchen. The smell of spices permeates the air, traces of cooking detectable beneath the warm vanilla of candles.

The walls are cream, adorned with prints by artists Jean doesn't recognise – all of it brightly coloured, and all featuring Black women. There's a compact dining table and four chairs, all painted sunny yellow. Gauze curtains cover the balcony, strips of fairy lights hanging down from the pole, casting a gentle glow over the room. Ava lingers by the door, uncertain, even though they're in her home.

'It's gorgeous,' Jean says, entirely truthful. And the tension melts from Ava's shoulders.

'Thanks!' Ava shrugs off her blazer, folding it over the back of a chair, and holds out a hand for Jean's. 'Would you like some coffee? Or would you prefer a tour?'

A tour can only mean one thing. There are two doors – one must be the bathroom, and the other Ava's bedroom.

Jean kicks off her heels and slips out of her coat, letting it pool on the floor. Takes one step, then another, closing the space between them. Looking directly into Ava's eyes she says: 'Give me the tour.'

Then it's impossible to say who bridges that final gap. Ava's lips are on hers, gentle, searching. And Jean understands what it is then, to be with a woman who steals your breath away. Her lips part as she gasps for air. And Ava's tongue glides against hers.

Jean clings to Ava's shoulders, uncertain that her knees alone can hold her. And Ava's hands are everywhere, stroking her hair, caressing Jean's hips, cupping her cheek. It's as if she's hungry for the feel of Jean, desperate to touch every part of her. Emboldened, Jean pushes Ava towards the nearest door – the one she presumes is the bedroom, and it must be, because Ava takes her hand and pulls Jean through to another room lit by fairy lights.

There's a double bed nestled against the wall, neatly made; an Ikea wardrobe and dresser; a bookshelf rammed with paperbacks and weighty law tomes. It's snug but clean; cosy and comfortable. The best-case scenario for a one-night stand.

Jean's relief lasts until Ava reaches for the light switch. Swiftly, Jean covers her hand. 'Don't.'

A question forms on Ava's lips and Jean kisses it clean away. Then, somehow, they're perched on the edge of the mattress. Ava's hands, slow and sure, skimming the contours of her body. And Jean melts into her touch. Gasps as a thumb swipes across her nipple. Both of them, Jean realises, are rock solid; straining against the lace of her bra. The force of her own want leaves Jean weak.

Then Ava cups her face with unexpected tenderness, caressing the sharp edge of Jean's cheekbones. Her fingers burrow into Jean's hair as their lips meet, again and again. And she pulls the combs free with a gentle, practiced ease. Jean's hair tumbles loose around her shoulders, and Ava looks at her with unguarded desire. Kisses Jean's mouth, her cheek, her throat. Ava's voice is barely more than a whisper, breath hot as a brand against Jean's neck as she says: 'I'd really like to undress you.'

And Jean laughs at her enthusiasm, until she realises it's a question. Ava's hands have stilled their exploration. 'Be my guest,' says Jean.

Ava pulls her close; stops kissing Jean just long enough to pull the dress over her head. Only then does it occur to Jean she's still in her shapewear – ordinarily she'd have excused herself and reappeared in lingerie, preserving at least some vestige of feminine mystique. But there had been no room for any thought in her head except getting closer to Ava.

And Ava doesn't seem to mind her Spanx. Body curled around Jean's, she plucks and circles each nipple. Toying with them until Jean whimpers. An exquisite pleasure so sharp it's right on the border of pain. Jean can't help arching towards Ava's mouth in offering. And Ava eases her down against the mattress, curls spilling silky soft over Jean's arm as she lowers her head.

Ava's lips close around her nipple, licking and suckling, relentless, until Jean's frantic with pleasure. Then, looking up at Jean with darkened eyes, she switches to the other side. Starts the sweet torture all over again. Jean strokes her hair, filled with affection for her surprise seductress. Ava hasn't once reached between her legs, and already Jean's knickers are plastered to the contours of her sex.

Even after Ava pulls away, the wet lace of her bra continues to tease each bud. Her fingers hook around the hem of Jean's Spanx, pulling them down over her belly and kissing a trail across the newly exposed skin. Jean can't remember the last time anyone touched her like this, worshipping every inch of her with hands and lips and tongue. She lifts her hips, obedient; lets Ava pull the sodden scrap of her underwear away too.

At this point the bra does little to preserve her modesty – and anyway, Jean's too turned on to care. She unfastens the clasp and tosses it onto the floor. Then she's naked.

For the longest moment Ava simply looks at her, pale and luminescent in the soft glow of fairy lights. Jean's on the cusp of covering herself when at last she speaks, voice low and husky. 'You're stunning.'

Jean laughs, surprised – and a little uncertain – as Ava settles down beside her. Surely, she has brought home younger, skinnier, more beautiful women. But Ava speaks the words with the intensity of truth. And Jean doesn't know what to make of that at all. She's trembling like a virgin. And in a way, this is a first time.

Ava pulls back, tucking a strand of hair behind Jean's ear. 'You alright?'

Jean can only nod.

'We can stop. I don't want to take anything you're not comfortable giving.'

At this Jean blinks. How many men, over the years, have given her the opportunity to turn back after they'd crossed the threshold of a bedroom door? When she was lying naked in bed? None that she can think of. Not even Henry. And for once the strangeness of this new experience is what makes it reassuring. She leans up, pressing a kiss to Ava's swollen lips. 'I want… things I don't know how to ask for. I want you to fuck me.'

Ava's throat bobs. 'Yes ma'am. You mean with my hands, or… with a toy?'

'A toy.' Ava's silent for so long Jean worries she's made a blunder. 'Sorry, is that an urban legend?'

'Not all lesbians have strap-ons.' She presses a kiss to the curve of Jean's shoulder. 'But you're in luck, because I do. Give me a sec.'

Ava rolls off the mattress and shimmies out of her cargo pants and cheekies. Yanks the blouse over her head so she's standing there in a sports bra. In the half-light and shadow, it's hard to make out specifics. She's slender with smooth skin and toned ample thighs that Jean wants to reach out and touch. But – before she can find the courage – Ava crouches, pulling a crate from beneath the bed. She digs about for a moment and retrieves the strap-on.

It's more complicated than Jean had expected. And she watches, mesmerised, as Ava steps into the harness. Fastens the buckles with nimble fingers. It's obvious she's done this before. Then the dildo's in place, purple silicone that carries the promise of pleasure, curving upwards at a jaunty angle. A pulse gallops between Jean's legs. And the dildo bobs as Ava crawls towards her.

But she doesn't climb on top of Jean – not right away. Ava might be young, but she has finesse. She pulls Jean close, their kisses hot and urgent. The silicone presses insistently against Jean's belly, a firm reminder of what's still to come. Ava strokes her hair, her arms, her breasts, her belly, her thighs, until every part of Jean is alight. Only then does her hand slip between Jean's thighs.

Jean parts to Ava's touch, crying out at that perfect glide. Pleasure sweet and golden as honey builds inside her. Fingertips skate across her clit, knuckles nudge at her entrance... but Ava never lets her reach the crest. She slides her fingers free and licks them clean, eyes fluttering closed as she tastes Jean's desire.

'Give me... Please,' Jean says, incoherent with longing. 'I need... Ava...'

'Shhh.' Ava kisses her forehead, shifting to straddle Jean. So warm and smooth on top of her. 'I'll give you exactly what you need.'

Ava doesn't waste any time delivering on her promise. She braces both arms on either side of Jean's head. And when they kiss Jean tastes herself on Ava's lips, an unfamiliar tang. She opens her thighs, a clear invitation, and Ava slides between her legs. Fills Jean completely.

Her fingers curl against the blades of Ava's shoulders, pulling her closer. Ava's breath hitches. She rocks her hips. And pleasure licks at Jean, slow and relentless. She buries her face in the crook of Ava's neck, tasting the salt of sweat. Breathing in cedar and jasmine – that delicious genderfuck of a scent – and something unnameable that's all Ava.

With every thrust Ava shudders. Jean can't tell where her trembling stops and Ava's begins. And the strap-on must be working for her too, though Jean doesn't understand the mechanics of it. And as she tips towards orgasm, she isn't capable of puzzling it out.

Of their own volition her legs lock around Ava's hips, pulling her deeper and deeper inside. And Ava picks up the pace. Jean can't stop herself from crying out. Each stroke hits some tender spot deep inside, again and again, the ecstasy of it floods every nerve. She's breaking apart, only Ava's arms holding all the pieces of her together.

Ava's cheeks are flushed red with the effort. Then she too is tipping over the edge, eyes rolling back in her head as she slumps. Even at the crest of her climax she's a considerate lover, careful not to crush Jean. Smoothing the hair back from her face.

'You okay?'

Jean nods, breathless. 'That was...'

Ava's smile is tired, and more than a little smug. Her back is slick beneath Jean's palms. 'Good, right?'

'Very.' She can't very well deny it; her limbs still slack with orgasm. And she doesn't want to. Ava's earned a little preening.

She pulls out, slow and careful, rolling onto her back. Unfastens the buckles, clumsy now.

The strap-on is glistening with Jean's wetness. Her own thighs are coated in it. Empirical evidence, proof that she – Jean Howard – enjoyed sex with a woman. With a *lesbian*.

Ava pulls Jean close, stroking her shoulder. 'If you have any questions, now's the time.'

And there are dozens of things Jean wants to ask, so many questions they're crammed against her skull.

What does it mean that I liked sleeping with you?
Do people judge you for wanting women?
How do you say it?

But those are all too heavy for a hook-up. And there's no use asking Ava how she can possibly change the idea of Jean that her friends, her colleagues, have held onto for decades – not when Ava herself doesn't have the first clue who Jean is, even if she has an apparent knack for working Jean's body.

Beside her Ava stirs, propped up on one elbow to look down at Jean's face. 'Are you sure you're okay?'

'Fine.' Jean stares up at the ceiling, the strange interplay of light and shadow. 'Is it always like that? With a woman, I mean.'

The mattress shakes as Ava chuckles. 'No. I'm just that good.'

Jean rolls her eyes, grateful the shadows dim her own smile. 'Be serious.'

'I am. Not just anybody could rail you like this.' She flops back down on the bed – apparently orgasms make Ava playful. 'Think you'll do it again?'

'What, now?' Jean snorts. 'You have the stamina of youth on your side, but I'd ache for it tomorrow.'

'Not now. I mean in the future.' Ava rolls onto her stomach, the length of her body flush against Jean's, long and brown and slender. And a fresh pulse flutters between Jean's legs. 'With other women. Or,' she says, more quietly, 'with me.'

'I haven't—' Jean clears her throat. She wants a glass of water, but there's a domesticity to that which doesn't fit within the parameters of a one-night stand. 'I haven't thought about it yet.'

'Take your time,' says Ava, casual as if it matters not a bit to her. And she'll have no trouble finding other women to take Jean's space in this bed. 'There's no rush.'

'Thanks.' With a film of sweat coating her, the night air brushes cool against Jean's skin. A shiver runs through her.

And Ava, already so attuned to her body, pulls up the duvet. Says: 'Want to sleep here?'

'No.' *Yes.* It would be easy, to sink into Ava's arms and let her eyes close; spend the night being held; wake up to a soft body and a playful smile. But difficult, not to get hooked on the reverence in her touch. And Jean hasn't made it this far by depending on others. 'No, I'd better get going.'

'Oh.' Ava pulls the blankets up over her own body. 'Okay.'

Jean rolls out of bed and retrieves her clothes with all the dignity she can muster. This is the advantage to going home with another person to their place. At any moment Jean is free to gather her stuff and go – no awkward hinting that she prefers to sleep alone, no elaborate story about an early start.

Yet, from the moment her feet touch the carpet, Jean wants nothing more than to get back in bed; to curl up beside Ava until their limbs are tangled like vines. For the first time that night, what Jean's doing feels wrong. But her head knows better than her heart – or her vagina.

Jean finds her phone, summons the first available Uber. Stuffs her panties and shapewear into the handbag. Squeezes back into her dress. Wraps the coat around herself – she'll button it in the lift. Her car is less than five minutes away. And there's nothing here for her, she tells herself; at least, nothing that won't upturn the careful order of her life. Jean steps into her heels, ignoring the pinch and rub.

'Thank you,' she says. The words final, inadequate. 'This was… Thanks.'

Jean turns her back on Ava, but not before she's witnessed disappointment on the younger woman's face. Walks out of the door, away from the yearning to kiss that frown away. Goes down the lift. Steps out into the cool night air.

Chapter Three

In the morning, Jean's loose limbed and pleasantly aware of her own body. And if her bed is empty, at least there are no distractions from the day to come. She throws herself into it with gusto, working up a fresh sweat with her trainer, Grant. But as Jean lunges and stretches there's a delicious ache inside her. And her legs are still a little slack with the echoes of orgasm.

Though Jean keeps the yawning to a minimum, Grant quips about a late night, so she knows he has suspicions about her nocturnal activities. He's spent enough of their sessions entertaining Jean with stories about his own conquests – young men just as ripped as he is – that she's sure he wouldn't judge her, even if he did know the full truth.

But Grant's opinion isn't what matters. His perception of Jean has no bearing on whether she can make that last, glorious leap to managing partner. Even after a quarter of a century with Decker Dennings and Howard, having her personal life fed through the rumour mill now just might be enough to derail everything she's worked for – it's not a chance Jean is prepared to take. Men have the luxury of mistresses, outside children, remarriage when wife number two inevitably discovers number three. But the standards remain different for women, regardless of

HR's regular reminders that DDH is an equal opportunities workplace. Which means discretion has always been the better part of valour, even when she had little to hide.

Still, as Jean showers, scrubbing the sweat from her skin, it's impossible not to think of how Ava had touched her mere hours before. And part of Jean wonders what it would be like, to have stayed and showered with her, pressed together in that tiny bathroom.

She dries her hair, pinning it into her ever-present updo – professional, with just a hint of feminine softness. Slips on sheer tights, a cream blouse, her hunter green tweed suit. Spritzes her pulse points with Chanel. Applies a subtle coat of make-up, the look men take to be natural when it's anything but. Then – always last – her pearls, cool at the base of Jean's throat.

Bogdan arrives with the telepathic sense of timing that saw him promoted to be her personal driver. Ready to face the world, Jean gets into the company car, just early enough that the streets of London are still driveable. Gliding through the City she reads Henshall's latest list of demands, updated since last night; though it's his company's salvation, her client is doing his damnedest to slow the deal, perhaps even sink it. She'll talk to Peter before proceeding – better not to leave a paper trail voicing these suspicions to their managing partner. More straightforward, Jean signs off on Hugo's promotion. Their hungriest intern has earned a seat at the table.

Bogdan slows to a halt, and Jean slides from the back seat, stepping out into the City's heart. And though the arctic breeze chills her legs, cutting through ten denier tights, Jean can never resist appreciating this view. Skyscrapers stretching up between wisps of cloud, DDH a finger pointing straight to the heavens. Glass and chrome reflecting the watercolour blue of a winter sky.

Ava too will be making her way to work, out there under the same pale sunrise. And perhaps she'll spare a thought for Jean. But that's an end to it. They will never be more than a fond memory to one another.

In the lobby, Helen's waiting as always, poised with her tablet and Jean's breakfast – eggs, spinach, and a scalding red eye to launch her into the day. They go over her itinerary on the ride to the top floor, in a lift perfumed only by lavender carpet shampoo. And Jean settles into her office, reading documents as she eats – until word of a client's insider trading yanks Jean's attention from breakfast. Data breaches are an ugly business, confirming the public's worst fears about fat cat financiers crossing any line for profit. But, whatever else happens, DDH will come out of this smelling like roses.

Afterwards, there's no hope for her eggs, but plenty for the firm. Jean brings Alexander's team up to date on the Leonides brief, referring them to frameworks and by-laws drafted for rapidly expanding corporations, designed as a safeguard against every problem they're capable of imagining – and at least a few they aren't.

–

The days that follow are much the same, herding associates and fending off disaster. There was a time when it thrilled Jean – when this was all she wanted. But now it leaves her weary, falling into her king-sized bed by midnight. And when Jean's tired, she's vulnerable to thoughts of Ava.

The memory of her doesn't fade with time. Ava's there when Jean closes her eyes at night. There when Jean opens her eyes in the morning. There when Jean opens the drawer in her bedside table and slips the vibrator down beneath the covers. Shuddering and sticky-fingered, Jean has no resistance to fantasies of *what if*.

Jean's bed has never felt this empty; not since the divorce. And even then, she'd missed the warm bulk of Henry far more than their rare nights of passion. Bearing in mind the old adage – that the best way to get over the last one is with the next one – Jean curls up on the sofa, sips a martini, and swipes through a selection of men. Bankers, executives, civil servants. All her own age and standing. Ideally suited, on paper. But not a single smile intrigues her. Not the way Ava's knowing grin has got under her skin.

Even work can't fully snap Jean out of it. Peter suggests a sabbatical without a trace of irony, asking how their team can take time off for burnout if leadership won't do the same. And Jean makes all the right noises. But inwardly she seethes. Jean's performance hasn't suffered from the temporary madness of her personal life, and she hasn't missed a single step with Leonides. Managing partners don't step back for a few months; they step up here and now. And it's Jean whipping the firm into shape while Peter wines and dines clients; Jean managing the Leonides case, ensuring their investigator – Carl – tracks down everything from the money Leonides shelled out through a subsidiary to prevent a paternity lawsuit, to his high turnover of PAs.

On his way from her office, Carl pauses, asks if there's anything else he can help with. And there's a moment of madness when Jean is tempted to give him a personal assignment. There's not much to go on. Ava, low thirties, ethnically ambiguous. She's some manner of lawyer; lives in a block of flats in Newham. With those details Carl could almost certainly track her down. He's accepted private commissions from the partners in the past, tailing cheating spouses and tracking down a runaway daughter.

He's dealt with the tawdry before, and been nothing but discreet. But the thought of explaining her one-night stand with another woman to the taciturn PI... It's not that Carl would judge. He's seen all sorts. And his daughter married her long-term girlfriend last summer; Jean herself approved the firm's gift of cut-crystal champagne flutes. It's that Carl has only ever known Jean as straight. There was never any evidence to the contrary. And Jean would sooner reach into her own chest and hand over her bloody, still-beating heart than expose that part of herself to an employee's scrutiny.

Still, Jean regrets not knowing more about Ava. A surname; a place of work. With hindsight she realises they'd have tumbled into bed no matter how she'd steered the conversation – red pill or blue, it mattered not. She bids Carl goodbye and returns to her files.

–

After work, exactly one week since Ava railed her (Jean had googled the term and given her vibrator an extra workout as she mused on its meaning), Jean returns to Strata. Bogdan's puzzled by her instructions – there are no meetings in Jean's calendar, and she's not the type to stop for nightcaps. At least, not as far as her driver knows – Jean uses Uber for her dates and hook-ups, scrupulously careful to avoid leaving a paper trail via her account with DDH's car service.

But Jean doesn't give him a backwards glance, striding into the bar and claiming the same stool where she'd sat waiting before. She orders a dirty martini from the young bartender, still struggling to grow his peach fuzz into a beard, scanning the bar as he prepares it. The booths are all full and the tables joined together for a birthday party – Jean peers between balloons, cranes to see past relatives hugging hello, but there's no sign of Ava. No irrepressible curls, no eyes alight with mischief, no teasing smile.

Still, the night is young. Jean waits, sipping her drink and scrolling through her emails. Orders another drink as the family behind her are served their main course. It's possible that night was Ava's first time in Strata too – that she'd never been before, will never return again. There are thousands of pubs in London. And Ava had seemed spontaneous, bold – not necessarily a creature of habit.

The booths are half empty by the time the family are served cake, Jean on her third martini. She watches as two waitresses carry it out, a roman candle fizzing sparks while three generations sing. The light blurs and Jean turns away, blinking until she's regained composure.

The bartender hovers, drying a glass. Clears his throat. 'She's usually here on Wednesdays.'

Jean lowers her martini. 'What?'

'The woman you were… talking to last time. She comes by for Happy Hour.'

Jean gapes, not believing her luck. And the barman must take her silence for confusion – he slides a small blackboard along the counter, times and prices chalked around smiling bottles. And Jean snaps a dutiful photograph. But she doesn't need it. Already the details are branded onto her mind, a plan taking shape.

'Thank you,' she says, sliding a crisp twenty across the counter.

Chapter Four

It's easy enough finding a man who will agree to a Happy Hour date. Cheap drinks, female companionship, and the possibility of sex – what's not to love? Frank doesn't work comparable hours, so he's readily available at six p.m. on a weekday. But compatibility isn't foremost in Jean's mind. At least not with the human shield she has procured – walking, talking plausible deniability. Anything to keep from appearing desperate.

There's no time to go home and change after work – she's leaving early enough as it is – so Jean wears a bottle green dress and tan heels to the office. Paired with a blazer it just about passes as a business look. Helen's the only one brave enough to comment on her outfit, telling Jean she looks irresistible in the lift up. And just this once she's happy to let the familiarity slide.

Even with two whole hours shaved off, the day crawls by. And Jean scarcely touches her lunch, anticipation coiled tight and heavy as a python in the pit of her belly. She dials in to conference calls, proofs the Leonides policy documents, coaxes Henshall into another round of negotiations. Pushes the knowledge that Ava might not even be there to the back of her mind.

At twenty-past five Jean logs out of her computer, buttons her lime green peacoat, and heads out of the office. Helen wishes her a good evening, her face the picture of innocence.

Peter stops Jean on her way to the lift, squeezing her shoulder. 'I'm glad to see you're taking our talk about work-life balance on board,' he says. And Jean grits her teeth in what she hopes will pass for a smile.

By the time she gets to Strata, Frank's waiting outside. Tall, white, unexceptional. Grizzled hair down to his shoulders, blowing on red hands. His eyes light up as he catches sight of her. 'Jean! You look even better than you did in the picture.'

'Thank you.' Jean says, submitting to a kiss on the cheek. 'Shall we go inside? I reserved a table.'

Frank leads the way, holding the door open for her. And right away the heat wraps around Jean like a duvet.

Happy hour is a popular choice, the hubbub of chatter drowning out that eternal electronic thump disguised as music. Of the few empty tables, it's easy to guess which is hers – right in the centre, close to the bar, with a panoramic view of the venue. Just as Jean had requested.

If Frank is curious about why she didn't ask for a booth or at least a table far from the crush of the bar, he doesn't show it. Instead, he holds out Jean's chair and asks what she'd like to drink.

The moment he leaves, Jean scans the bar, eyes searching. Her heart leaps, a fish out of water, as she catches sight of Ava. Her head tilts back as she laughs – today the curls are piled on top of her head, held in place with a burgundy scarf, exposing the slender column of her neck.

Sat beside her is a plump white girl with a heart-shaped face, framed by a sleek dark bob. And her eyes are glued to Ava. She tips forward, laughing. Rests a familiar hand on Ava's shoulder. And it's still sitting there when Frank returns, blocking Jean's view.

He sets her martini down on the table and holds out his pilsner.

'Thanks.' Jean clinks her glass against his bottle, and swigs her drink. It's not dirty – Frank forgot the olive juice – but the gin still does the job.

'Blimey.' Frank nods to her glass, already half empty. 'You must be thirsty.'

Jean laughs as if he's said something witty. 'Long day at the office,' she says, lips curving upwards. 'So, Frank. Tell me about yourself.'

And it works like a charm. Frank waxes lyrical about his paintings, his technique, his upcoming showing at a gallery in Shoreditch. Jean nods and makes sounds of approval in all the right places. But her gaze slides under Frank's ear, to where Ava's arm wraps ever so casually around her companion's shoulders.

Either they're still laughing at the same joke or something else has amused them. Perhaps Ava's regaling her date with stories of past conquests; the middle-aged woman who'd asked to be railed then ran away.

Jean's chest constricts at the thought. The dull roar of chatter, the relentless heat, it's all too much.

'You okay?' Frank's hand covers her own, slick with sweat.

Jean pulls away. Her eyes lock with Ava's. She pushes her chair back. 'Would you excuse me for a minute?'

Without waiting for an answer, Jean pushes through the throng, not looking at Ava's table as she passes.

The bathroom is mercifully empty. As Jean runs cold water over her hands, the door swings open.

'Jean.' In the mirror her eyes are full of concern. 'Are you alright?'

'Fine.' And now Ava's here, it's true. Jean breathes in the stale air; steadies herself as she grabs a paper towel. 'Actually, I hoped I'd bump into you.'

Still Ava lingers by the door. Not going. But not coming any closer either. 'Oh?'

'Yes.' Jean turns, dropping her towel into the bin, looking Ava in the eye. 'I shouldn't have left that night. I'm sorry.'

Ava's silent for a long moment. She tilts her head, considering, a lone curl brushing her cheek. 'Is that all you wanted to say?'

Jean presses both hands to her stomach to still their shaking. But she doesn't look away. 'No.'

The admission's short, but it costs her, and Ava sees it. She steps closer; near enough to see Jean tremble. Leans in close enough to kiss her. But Ava just smiles. Says: 'How quickly can you get rid of him?'

—

After Jean's disappearance it's not difficult convincing Frank that she's ill. An allusion to hot flushes and night sweats is all it takes to deter his attempts at rescheduling. It's high time the change of life gave Jean something in return, she thinks. Her cheeks warm with a different kind of heat as Jean slips out onto the street, striding along Islington's broad pavements, unable to believe her own daring.

She lingers by the tube station, opening her phone to scan Alexander's update on Leonides. But it might as well be written in Greek – Jean reads through the same paragraph three times, taking nothing in. She gives up then, scrolling emails, though the cold makes her fingers clumsy.

Jean shifts from foot to foot on her heels, scanning the steady flow of commuters streaming into the station. Her signature red soles lend Jean an extra four inches of height, and a sharp feminine edge that says *don't fuck with me*.

Perhaps Ava means to stand her up. Repay the slight of being walked out on that first night. It's exactly what Jean would have done, once upon a time. And she can't help but admire the calculated savagery, even as disappointment cuts through her with the glacial sharpness of the January wind. But just as Jean opens the Uber app, a flash of burgundy catches her eye.

Ava jogs towards her pink-cheeked, aided by the practicality of those combat boots. And Jean's heart swells. 'You certainly took your time,' is all she says.

'Sorry. I felt guilty ditching Zara – she's nice.'

'Then why didn't you stay with her?' The words carry an acid sting Jean hadn't fully intended.

But Ava only smiles, and once again Jean has the sense of being utterly transparent. 'Because,' Ava says, 'there are far more interesting things than nice. Now let's go back to mine – if we're quick we can get the tube straight through to East Ham.'

'I don't mind ordering us an Uber.'

But Ava shakes her head. And though she keeps a straight face, there's a wicked gleam in her eye. 'This way's faster.'

Jean's pulse quickens. Who is she to argue with such logic? She follows Ava down into the station, tapping her card against the barrier and passing through. It's been years since Jean was forced to rely on the tube – she'd fallen in love with the plush comfort of DDH's private car service upon making senior associate, and taken them as her due by the time she'd ascended to legal director.

But the underground isn't as bad as she'd expected. While the air still reeks of metal, grease, and unsavoury heat, the warmth is welcome. Mercifully, the tsunami of rush hour has ebbed to a steady trickle. Ava whisks her into a near empty carriage, the nearest commuter half a coach away. And while Jean hates the thought of being crushed up against a stranger, she doesn't mind the press of Ava's leg against her own. Though her face is a mask of composure, Ava's knee jigs up and down, restless.

It's this rare display of nerves that gives Jean the courage to speak. She leans in close to Ava, though there's nobody to overhear above the train's dull roar. It is essential that Jean make this one thing clear: 'I'm not a lesbian. Or bisexual. Or whatever else you're calling it these days.'

Ava nods, placid. 'Okay.'

The lack of resistance catches Jean off guard. She'd expected to be presented with evidence to the contrary and have Ava, the all-knowing lesbian, pass judgement. To be met with a smirk at the very least. 'What do you mean, *okay*?'

'Exactly that. It's not my place to define your sexuality.'

'Oh.'

A frown wrinkles Ava's brow. 'You seem disappointed. Do you... want me to tell you that you're a le—'

'No!' Jean clears her throat, looking around. But there's nobody except her and Ava; their reflections bent towards one another in the window's dark mirror. 'No. I just wanted to make sure we're on the same page. That you understand I'm straight. I don't have relationships with women. And I can't offer you anything beyond a casual, discreet... arrangement.'

Ava's lips brush against Jean's ear, sending a shiver through her. 'You mean you want to be fuck buddies? Cool. You could have just led with that.'

'So that... arrangement...' Ava's lips twitch, and Jean would find it maddening if she weren't currently anticipating how good they'll feel clamped around her nipple. 'It works for you, too?'

Ava nods. 'It might not be success the way you'd define it, but I have big work goals this year. And that doesn't leave room for dating. But a girl still has needs.'

Curiosity snags Jean's attention – perhaps Ava is not without ambition after all. But asking about these plans, cherished above romance, would fly in the face of *casual* and *discreet*. And it would be madness for Jean to break her own rules so soon after making them. So, instead she says: 'Deal.' Holds out a hand for Ava to shake.

A current jolts through her fingertips as their palms brush together. And ever so subtly, Ava's thumb caresses her knuckles. In that moment Jean knows beyond a shadow of doubt that she won't be the one to end their arrangement.

Anticipation pulses between her thighs as Ava says this is their stop; guides Jean up and out into the streets. The night air can't touch Jean as she strides towards that now familiar high-rise. Ava marches along beside her, urgency feeding Jean's own. Fortunately, the boys have found somewhere warmer to spend their Wednesday night – they make it into the lift without interruption. Jean doesn't even mind the piss scent this time, knowing it's a small price to pay for the pleasures that await her.

Chapter Five

They're barely through the door before Ava's lips crash against hers and they're peeling off each other's coats. Jean knots her fingers in Ava's curls, pulling her closer. And they stumble towards the bedroom, bumping into the couch.

Then Ava's pulling away, eyes bright with mischief. 'Wait right here,' she says.

Ordinarily Jean would bristle at such a command, but the words flip something low in her belly. She remains in place as Ava retreats into the bedroom, heart hammering at the unmistakable opening of a plastic crate.

Sure enough, when Ava reappears, she's fitted in the harness. And Jean marvels at her body, lean and yet round in all the right places. She goes to kick off her shoes, pull off her dress, but Ava shakes her head.

'Oh no. I want you exactly like this.' Ava circles behind Jean, the dildo pressing into her back while Ava licks at her ear, nuzzles into her neck. 'You put this outfit on just for me, didn't you? You were thinking of me when you got dressed up; how it would feel when I stripped you.'

'Yes.' Just like in the bathroom, Jean can't get over it, how vulnerable that one word makes her.

Ava hums in pleasure at the admission, vibrations passing from her mouth to Jean's throat. But she doesn't push any further, always mindful of Jean's limits. 'Good. Then I should show you some appreciation.'

Jean loses all coherent thought as Ava reaches into the scoop of her neckline and catches her nipple, rolling and teasing until Jean slackens against her.

Then Ava's kissing the hollow of her throat, whispering: 'More?'

Jean can only nod. She bends, pliant, as Ava guides her hands to rest on the back of the couch. She'd never let Henry fuck her like this. Nor any of the unremarkable men that followed. But – while Ava would certainly stop if she asked – Jean's powerless to resist the temptation of giving herself over to it. Her want sharpens to an ache as Ava rucks the dress up around her thighs; tugs Jean's tights and underwear down just far enough.

Then Ava's hand slips between her legs, testing. But Jean's more than ready for her, thighs slippery. Her breath hitches as Ava's fingers skate over her sex. Jean had wondered if it was a fluke the first time, the intensity of her body's response to Ava. Or maybe the product of pent-up frustration after years of unsatisfying one-night stands. Dr Byrne had said it could take time for her desire to resurface, and Jean had been too ashamed to admit never feeling the passion she described for any man – before or after. But here and now, bent over Ava's couch, every atom of Jean longing for her, she's forced to admit there's an irresistible magnetism between them.

Ava takes her, slowly at first, breath ragged as Jean's while she eases inside. Inch by glorious inch. She's still for several moments – stroking Jean's back, her hair – until Jean has time to adjust to the dildo's girth at this angle. There's no room for such gentleness in the realm of casual, yet it's what enables Jean to let go, to tilt back and meet Ava's hips.

Even when Ava begins to move, she rocks gently. Jean bites her lip to keep from crying out as the length of it fills her, again and again. But there's no holding back when Ava reaches between them, circling Jean's clit in perfect time with each stroke.

White hot pleasure burns through the last of Jean's modesty, and she's breathing 'fuck' and 'please' and 'harder' in a frantic voice she doesn't recognise. And Ava, it turns out, is excellent at following instructions. She picks up the pace, driving into Jean until her legs tremble. And every thrust brings such an exquisite pleasure that Jean can't bring herself to care about the slick sound of Ava driving into her sex, or the unmistakable scent of her own arousal.

There's only Ava slamming into some sweet spot Jean had never guessed at possessing; Ava's deft fingers catching at Jean until she breaks apart. The force of Jean's orgasm leaves her limp as a ragdoll. Only Ava's strength keeps her upright. But Ava doesn't stop, though she slows. She eases back, sliding just the tip in and out until another uncontrollable shudder runs through Jean, gentler this time, but almost unbearable this close to the last.

Jean reaches back, words beyond her, and Ava seems to understand. Ever so careful, she withdraws the dildo, dropping a kiss against the nape of Jean's neck. Together they slide down onto the floor, flushed and sweaty, slumped against the back of the sofa.

'Fuck,' Ava says, still panting. 'That was amazing.'

Her limbs have the uncoordinated twitch of orgasm, though Jean had been unaware of her coming, too lost in the intensity of her own pleasure. And an earlier question surfaces in her mind, though Jean's too dazed to phrase it elegantly. She gestures towards the dildo, glistening in the glow of the fairy lights. 'How does that... work for you?'

Ava gives a breathless laugh. 'You know, an orgasm's mostly about what happens in the brain. And using this is like catnip to me. Also...' She pauses to unbuckle herself, wriggling free. 'The way the base sits against me really hits the spot.'

Jean shifts, pulling her ruined tights and underwear free. 'So, I don't have to worry about being a selfish lover.'

'No. I'm good.'

'I'm glad.' Jean hesitates. Considers Ava's body. The expanse of tanned skin, glowing with exertion. 'But would you mind? If I touched you?'

Ava shakes her head. 'No. I'm not stone.'

Jean reaches out then, laughing. 'Of course not. You're so warm.' She shifts closer, skimming fingertips along the outer contour of Ava's ankle to her thigh. 'And soft in all the right places.'

Ava laughs again, properly this time. 'I meant stone butch. There are some lesbians who only like to fuck their partners, but not be touched in return.'

'Oh.' Jean's hand stills on the swell of Ava's waist, uncertain. There are so many things she doesn't know. If Ava's not stone and enjoys being touched, no doubt she can find a woman capable of doing it more skilfully than Jean. It had been naïve to think she could successfully explore the secret dips and curves of another woman.

'You don't have to do that. Not if you don't want to.'

'I do want to.' Jean sits up, freshly conscious of the slickness between her legs. Her dress will be coated in it, the nature and location of the stain making its origins unmistakable to the dry cleaner. But, drinking in the sight of Ava's body, Jean finds it impossible to care. 'I wanted to touch you last time as well. It's just…'

'What?' Ava tucks a strand of hair behind Jean's ear to better look at her.

'You made it so good for me, and I'm not sure how well I'll manage to return the favour.' It's ridiculous, carrying on like a nervous virgin halfway into her fifties.

Ava shrugs. 'That's not a big deal. We all have to start somewhere. Believe it or not, I wasn't always this good. And I'm not expecting you to be some kind of vagina virtuoso.'

Jean laughs in spite of herself. Shifts so that they're sitting closer. 'Okay. But how do I… Any advice?'

Ava's smile widens, devilish. 'What feels good when you touch yourself?'

Jean's cheeks burn. She can't meet Ava's gaze. But she does have an answer. She takes her time, stroking Ava's cheeks, her throat, her arms, all so smooth. Jean doesn't miss it, the scratch of stubble or the thick pelt of body hair.

Careful not to catch Ava's curls, Jean pulls the t-shirt up over her head, eager for more of that peachy soft skin. And realises Ava isn't wearing a bra. Jean's gaze flits to her lap, the ceiling, her cast off shoes. Until Ava smirks, says: 'I know you want to look. You can even touch.'

Jean doesn't need telling twice. Her fingertips trail the dip of Ava's clavicle, the hollow of her sternum still slick with sweat, the perfect swell of Ava's breasts. They're smaller, perkier than her own. They fit comfortably in Jean's hands, a pleasant weight. And beneath Jean's palm is the hammering of a heart through the thin wall of her chest, the stiffening of both nipples into tight little buds. They're darker than Jean had expected, a pretty nut-brown shade. And – before Jean can overthink it – she lowers her head.

Ava stills as Jean sucks at her nipple, gasping as Jean's tongue flicks the tip. And knowing firsthand the silvery pleasure she's inflicting brings an unexpected satisfaction to the act. With a free hand she reaches for the bud's neglected twin, plucking and suckling 'til Ava's arching against her.

Jean pulls away to survey her handiwork, Ava flushed and panting, her mouth a moue of disappointment. But as Jean's hand trails down her belly, her expression morphs to surprise – then delight as Jean reaches her goal. Jean cups Ava's mound, short curls bristling against her palm. She feels as much as sees the sharp intake of breath when she makes contact. And Ava parts to the touch, already slick from their earlier coupling.

Jean traces her labia, astonished by the molten heat of Ava. Instantly her fingers are coated in desire – and the silken texture is surprisingly pleasant. She probes deeper, seeking more of it. Feels the subtle clench of Ava's walls as she sucks in a breath.

'Gentler,' she says. 'Y-you have to build up to that.'

And Jean does as she's bid, pulling back and using all that slickness to circle the nub of Ava's clit. Soft and slow – just the way Jean herself would like it. Only when Ava's rocking against her murmuring incoherent praise does Jean slide a finger back inside. This position is hell on her knees, but she could no more pull her hand free now than cut it off. All around her, hot and pulsing, is Ava. She's literally inside Ava. No wonder men get drunk off the sexual power play of penetration, the animal part of her thinks – it's an incredible feeling. An almost unbearable intimacy.

Jean has known power in her life – at a young age she learned that, with the right combination of words, she could engineer all manner of outcomes. At university her razor-sharp wit and the grit of determination allowed her to pull ahead, graduate into a job with a top firm. Then she went further still, climbing over every obstacle and rival to reach the very top floor of DDH. A single step from managing partner, absolute control so close she can taste it.

But Jean's never known power quite like this. Never revelled in the pulse jumping at the base of her lover's throat, the eyes so dark with desire that pupil is indistinguishable from iris. Every shiver and gasp running through Ava can be traced back to the tips of her fingers. In turn Ava's urgency, her need, transfers itself to Jean.

'More,' Ava breathes. 'I need more.'

Jean slips another digit inside, Ava's walls tight around her. She is rewarded with a low noise of pleasure – and Jean can actually feel the vibrations of it in her fingers. Fresh slickness coats her own thighs, but there's no room in Jean's mind for anything save Ava's lust.

Then Ava covers Jean's hand with her own, pressing it firm against her sex. With every stroke the heel of Jean's hand rubs against her clit. And this pressure must be exactly what Ava's craving, because she clenches tight around Jean's fingers, shuddering hard. And pride warms Jean as the orgasm ripples through her. Just as Ava had done, Jean keeps going until her trembling stills. And Ava pushes Jean's hand away.

The air is cool on her fingers, pruned a little and coated in Ava's wetness. Jean wipes the excess off on her dress, which is surely beyond salvaging. Better to order another than no longer be able to meet her dry cleaner's eyes.

'Congratulations, Jean,' Ava says when she's recovered herself. 'You've passed Introduction to Fingering with flying colours. A natural.'

'Ah... thank you,' Jean says. Even now she knows there are people who'd say what she and Ava have done to one another is anything but natural. Yet Jean can't bring herself to regret touching Ava, nor being touched by her. And what Jean gets up to in the privacy of her fuck buddy's home is nobody else's concern.

'There's a sink over there, if you want.'

Grateful, Jean clambers to her feet and pads through to the kitchenette. She washes her hands thoroughly. And as she dries Ava takes her place at the sink. She's watching Jean strangely, amusement quirking her lips.

'What?'

Ava looks her up and down as she rinses. 'You're so small without your heels on. It's adorable.'

For a moment Jean can only stare, incredulous. She's been called plenty of things over the years. *Imposing*, is how the junior associates describe her. *Code Red* when she's out of earshot – and Jean rather likes it, the panic she inspires in her underlings. But *adorable* has never entered into it. 'I am *not* small. You're just abnormally tall.'

Ava smirks as she pours a glass of water. 'Both of those things can be true at once.'

'I'm five foot four. That's average height.'

'Maybe on tiptoe.'

'Fuck you,' Jean says, wishing not for the first time that she could stretch her height as easily as the truth. It's been a long time since anyone caught her in a lie, or had the courage to call her out on one.

'You already did.' Ava waggles her eyebrows. 'But I'm game for round two if you are?'

Jean hesitates. She'd been planning on covering up with her coat and catching an Uber home. If Jean stays, she'll need to be up at four to get home in time to shower before work. Sleeping over isn't exactly casual. But then, Ava's not suggesting sleep. And fucking is, by definition, what fuck buddies do.

'Alright,' she says. And right away Ava's smile grows. 'But you're fucking me in bed this time – I want an orgasm and decent back support.'

Chapter Six

After that it's straightforward enough with Ava. They both get what they want from the arrangement: sexual satisfaction, no strings attached. In the interests of casualness, Jean only ever texts to ask whether she might drop by that night in the afternoons, as if the thought came to her spontaneously.

But there is a pattern to their meetings, one of her own design: never more than three nights a week, and never two nights consecutively. Jean clings on to these unspoken rules – she will not let this strange new passion burn through everything she has fought so hard to build, nor let it distract her from claiming the firm.

Jean needs boundaries. Because Ava has woken appetites that Jean never suspected herself of possessing. She'd never understood the fuss about sex as a teenager; had accepted it as the price of a relationship in her twenties. *A cold fish*, Jean's first real boyfriend at Oxford had branded her. And privately she'd suspected Ian was right. But now Jean can't stop thinking about it. Ava's deft fingers, that wicked tongue, the silicone shaft that fills her so completely.

Of course she would never enter their appointments in any diary, analogue or digital, but her days fall into the category of *Ava* or *No Ava*. The Ava days pass in a frenzy of anticipation, Jean counting down the hours until her next orgasm. And on the post-Ava days, Jean is newly aware of her body, the previously unguessed at capacity for pleasure in every muscle and sinew.

Flashes of their nights together come to her at the most awkward moments. When Grant mentions his latest lover, a tantalising detail proffered to pull Jean through her push-ups, she can't help but recall how – mere hours before – she'd been on her hands and knees in entirely different circumstances. When she catches notes of cedar in a client's aftershave, Jean pictures the unguarded ecstasy that flickers across Ava's face as she climaxes.

The most inconvenient memories surface in her dealings with the Henshall negotiations. Jean has inadvertently created a Pavlovian response within herself. Whenever she has a meeting with George Henshall, she arranges another with Ava for that night – a reward of sorts. A way of venting her frustrations that has zero professional repercussions.

There is nothing gentle about those nights. Jean rides Ava like fury, tugging on her curls, yanking her close enough to kiss. In retaliation Ava catches Jean's skin between her teeth, biting hard enough to bruise – always below the neckline, never anywhere another person will see, but a branding, nonetheless. And it sends her over the edge every time.

Jean fingers the latest love bite as George Henshall rants, under the guise of adjusting her blazer, wakening a delicious ache beneath her clavicle. Intercedes as the buyer, Katherine, bristles. With all it had taken to get them into the same room together, sitting at this table, Jean cannot let this meeting go south. Katherine already cancelled once, all but sending George into apoplectic fit as he got the message loud and clear: Katherine

Parker-Kato's time is more precious than his, and Parkato International has more urgent concerns than taking over one little microchip company.

And now, as Katherine glances at her phone tight-lipped and confers with her counsel, Jean has the distinct impression she's getting ready to walk again.

She turns to face Jean, sleek black bob swinging. 'There are other factories that fit my needs, and with much less hassle.'

'Not in this ballpark.' Though her heart hammers, Jean matches Katherine's tone of cool disinterest. 'And not in this region. That's why you're here: you want the factories in Vietnam because they're by the coast, meaning you can ship larger products by sea and keep your distribution costs to a minimum, maximising profit.'

Katherine's carefully plucked eyebrows climb. But she's quick to recover herself. 'At least someone here has done their homework. You're right about my motives, but wrong if you believe this is my only option.' The smile she directs towards Henshall is as bright and devoid of warmth as midwinter sunlight. 'I'd recommend bearing that in mind as you consider this next offer, which will be my last.'

Her counsel slides a piece of paper across the table, which Hugo lifts for Henshall to examine. Judging by the silent working of his jaw, he's less than impressed. Before Henshall can kick off, Jean nods in acknowledgement. 'We'll take that into consideration.'

'Good.' Katherine rises, tugging invisible creases from her Balenciaga blazer. 'I'll expect your answer by the time I get back from Kyoto.'

Katherine sweeps from the room, her entourage scurrying in her wake. And Henshall recovers his voice. 'I am fucking sick of that woman and her puffed-up pride.'

'George,' says Lana, his long-suffering PA.

'No!' He thumps the table, and Jean tenses. 'I'll say my piece. I am sick to the back teeth of dealing with that slant-eyed dyke.'

Hugo's jaw drops – Jean's certain he's heard worse on the journey from private school to his private members' club, in rooms filled with other men just as white and wealthy, but this is the first time he'll have heard slurs in a professional setting.

'That's just as well,' Jean says, gathering her papers. 'Because this will all be over inside a fortnight. I'll leave you to think things over.'

She strides from the boardroom, Hugo close behind. Knows deep in her heart that Marianne would have done more than be curt with Henshall. Even back in their junior associate days, she'd had the courage to speak up; to cite policy and enact procedure in the face of wrongdoing. As always, Jean finds herself falling short against Mari's memory. But Jean hasn't made it this far by pushing back against men's bullshit directly. The top job will be hers, and where is Marianne now?

When they're alone in the lift, Hugo clears his throat. 'Anything else I can do for you today, Ms Howard?'

'No. Go and bring Alexander and his team up to speed, then you can go home.' He won't – Jean recognises the hunger in his eyes, the way Hugo is at his sharpest on the days when his path intersects with hers. But at least she offered.

Their illustrious founder, Will Decker, never would have gone home when there was still work to be done.

And it's the work ethic he'd nurtured in her that keeps Jean at her desk until at least nine. Not every Ava Night, but those following on from them. She's too close to let up now. And the Leonides case requires close management – few of the junior associates have yet to work with an international client operating on this scale, but then few men have built empires on a par with that of Andreas Leonides. Jean pores over his portfolio, the history of his business; the legend of his self-made success, going from a paper-round age twelve to buying the foundering local news outlet age twenty and bringing it into the modern era.

From there Leonides had developed an unshakeable instinct for which businesses were salvageable, and which ought to be stripped for parts, buying and selling his way into the Forbes 500. Jean admires his ingenuity, knowing firsthand the struggle of inventing oneself from thin air, no money or social standing to fall back on. It's engrossing work. But tonight is an Ava Night, and Jean will do better for coming back refreshed in the morning.

She logs out of her computer, packs her things, and leaves her office with Helen. No doubt she has her suspicions, but Helen's smart enough to know when to stay silent – a quality Jean prizes in an assistant.

Of course, Peter catches her on the way out. 'Jean! There's something different about you, but I can't put my finger on it. Whatever it is, keep doing what you're doing.'

'Thank you,' Jean says, straight-faced. 'I've taken up badminton. It's an excellent way to destress in the evenings. In fact, I'm on my way to meet my partner now. So, unless there's anything urgent...'

Helen's looking resolutely skywards, as if the overhead lighting has become suddenly fascinating. But Peter buys it.

'See!' He nudges her. Peter has known Jean long enough – first as her boss and then, since Will's retirement, the closest thing he has to an equal – to get away with it. 'You thought work-life balance was nonsense. But now look at you. Glowing, isn't she Helen?'

'Absolutely.' Helen's face is the picture of innocence. 'Maybe I should take up a new sport.'

'You see, Jean? Leading by example.' He clasps her shoulder as they step out into the lobby. 'Actually, that's what I wanted to talk to you about. Could you excuse us please, Helen?'

Jean swallows, mouth suddenly dry, as Helen disappears through the revolving doors. She has been waiting for Peter to bring up the matter of succession, not wishing to force his hand. And then, like an actress at the Academy Awards, she will settle on an expression of gracious surprise as a response.

'I would like you to represent DDH at the London Legal Network Conference. Be the face of the firm.' Peter's eyes twinkle. 'And try to have some fun while you're there. What do you say?'

'Really?' Her smile at least is entirely unfeigned. 'If you think it's best, I'd be glad to step in.'

They bid each other goodnight, and Jean mulls it over in the car. It's not how she would have chosen to soft launch her leadership of DDH. Whereas icebreakers and reverse mentoring are exactly the kind of blue-sky crap Peter thrives on, there's a higher chance of Jean having fun during a root canal.

Yet for all his faults Peter has changed the culture of DDH for the better. Standards have tightened considerably since he took the helm. On the first day of her internship the junior associate charged with watching over Jean had asked whether her carpet matched her drapes, and from there it had been open season – she'd taken a vicious pleasure in leapfrogging Angus to associate, more still in laying him off when she was promoted to management. But there was no Marianne to share her victory with, and that hollowed out the joy. The life that should have been theirs was Jean's alone.

Chapter Seven

Ava buzzes her in, and Jean gets the lift to the ninth floor. The door's on the latch, so Jean lets herself in and locks it behind her. Ava's working at the sunny little table, typing hell for leather.

'Just give me a minute,' she says without looking up. 'And I'll be right with you.'

Jean says nothing, fully aware of how irritating it is to be pulled out of a task prematurely. If she'd known Ava was busy, she'd have stopped to pick up a sandwich at Waitrose. Still, it can't be helped – Jean doesn't want to encourage communication beyond the strictly necessary.

She takes off her coat and shoes, gravitating towards Ava's bookshelf. There are well-thumbed novels by Malorie Blackman, Bernardine Evaristo, Jackie Kay, Zadie Smith. The memoir Anita Hill published after giving testimony against Clarence Thomas – Jean pushes it back onto the shelf, and instead examines a framed photograph.

It's a professional shot, Ava clad in a flame-red bridesmaid dress, and Jean can't help but smile at the everpresent boots peeping out from beneath its hem. The bride stands beside Ava, every bit as tall and slender. She's got the same plump lips, high cheekbones, and broad button nose. The same warm brown eyes and playful smile. But her skin is significantly darker than Ava's, contrasting beautifully with the white of her gown. And her hair has been straightened smooth.

'That's Aaliyah. My sister.'

Jean startles, almost dropping the frame. She hadn't heard the door open, and Ava moves softly in socked feet.

'She's beautiful. And very like you. Are you...' The first half of the question slips out before Jean can think of a prudent way to finish it. There is no tactful way to bring up the disparity in pigmentation, but they're otherwise identical.

'Biracial?' Ava takes the photo, setting it back down on the shelf. 'Yeah.'

'That's not – I wondered, but I didn't feel entitled to your life story.' The silence stretches between them, and Jean's sure of having made a blunder. 'That isn't what I was going to ask, though.'

'No?'

'No. Are you twins?'

Ava's smile is instantaneous, softer and sweeter than any Jean has yet witnessed. 'Yeah, we are. Aaliyah was born six minutes before me, and she's been bossing me around ever since. I guess you could say the printer ran out of ink.' She cracks up at the look on Jean's face. 'You're allowed to laugh.'

And Jean does, half in relief at having bridged this sticky moment between them. Then Ava's pulling her close, kissing her deep and slow. Jean flicks the light off without breaking away, her body sparking to life as Ava's hands wander.

But as Jean hits the mattress, her stomach gurgles. And the warmth in her cheeks has far more to do with shame than desire.

Ava pulls back. 'Are you hungry?'

'Yes.' Jean kneels, presses a kiss to the corner of her mouth. 'For you.'

'God, you're sexy.' Ava pushes Jean back against the mattress. Kisses and nips a trail down Jean's throat. Ever so careful, she undoes Jean's blouse, a button at a time, nuzzling the newly exposed skin and sending Jean into a frenzy.

And Ava's right above her stomach when it rumbles again – an unmistakable growl. For the longest moment of Jean's life, they're perfectly still. Then Ava's rolling over, switching on the bedside lamp. And the moment's gone. 'Sorry,' Jean says.

'Don't be – everyone needs to eat. Matter of fact, I'm getting pretty peckish.'

'Then we'd better get on with it. The sooner we both come, the sooner we can have dinner.' Only as the words leave her mouth does it occur to Jean they might be construed as an invitation. 'Separately. After I leave.'

Ava looks at her, incredulous. 'What, fuck buddies can't eat together?'

'It makes things messy. I'd rather keep the nature of our arrangement' – Ava snorts, but Jean ignores her – 'clearly defined.'

'Then why didn't you eat earlier? You're obviously starving.'

Jean sighs. 'After work my driver dropped me home. And then I got an Uber straight here. When precisely would I have had time to eat?'

To her amazement, Ava simply laughs. 'Girl, you're hangry. Wait here and I'll get us food that will blow your mind.'

She's up off the bed before Jean can protest, throwing on a coat and grabbing her purse. Then the door closes behind her – and for the first time Jean finds herself alone in Ava's home. It's an unexpected intimacy. Part of her wants to rifle through the crate beneath Ava's bed; find out what other toys she owns.

But it's the photographs that really call to her. Jean rolls out of bed with much less grace than Ava had managed, scanning the other pictures displayed around the flat. There's an official graduation photo of a baby-faced Ava in cap and gown, grinning at the camera. She's flanked on either side by her parents – a beaming Black woman startlingly like her daughters, and a scholarly looking white man with a greying beard and owlish glasses.

There are other shots, more recent, of Ava dancing with a group of women Jean doesn't recognise – the cropped haircuts, masculine clothes, and proximity between two of the dancers lead her to suspect the nightclub's a gay venue. A faded polaroid of a tiny, beaming Ava being held aloft by a Black man – more a boy, really, despite his height – who looks up at her with infinite tenderness. He doesn't, she notices, appear in any recent shots. Jean's favourite is a slightly blurry print from a beach she doesn't recognise. Ava with her arms wrapped around two young children with her same golden skin and loose curls, all three of them laughing.

There's so much love in these photos that Jean finds it unbearable. She retreats to the kitchenette. And though she has no idea where Ava's things are kept, it's small enough that there's a short process of elimination. Jean finds two matching plates, cutlery, even paper napkins, and lays them all out on the sunny yellow table, complete with placemats. An old habit comes to her, and she can't resist folding the napkins into swans. Ava's laptop and paperwork she moves to the other end, careful to keep the documents in order.

The sheet on top catches Jean's eye, with a logo she doesn't recognise – Lady Justice, eyes blindfolded, scales held aloft. The figure on one side has dark skin, the figure opposite pale, and both are equally weighted. In bold lettering it reads *Colourblind Justice Caucus*. The writing beneath looks like the draft of a governing document, with notes scrawled in the margins, words underlined, and others crossed out. If the big work goals Ava mentioned amount to setting up a charity, no wonder she doesn't have time for a girlfriend.

Then the key turns in the lock. Jean remembers herself – that she has no business reading any of this, no interest in Ava's career – and drops the document, scooting into the kitchen to fetch glasses as Ava steps inside, carrying a brown paper bag stamped with *Iri's Peri Peri*. Her eyes go wide as she takes in the table. 'Oh my days, this looks fancy!' A frown creases her brow. 'It's just chicken and chips, I hope you don't mind. I'd thought since you had wings at Strata, you'd like it, but—'

'It's perfect,' Jean says, sitting down and helping Ava unload the piping hot Styrofoam containers. As Jean catches the scent of spices and vinegar, her stomach gives a yearning clench. 'Really. But you didn't have to get me dinner. At least let me pay you back.'

Ava shakes her head, curls bouncing. 'No need. Iri gives me a special discount.'

'Oh.' Jean pauses with a drumstick halfway to her mouth as a thought occurs to her. Neither she nor Ava had stipulated an exclusivity clause – there's no reason, she reminds herself, that Ava shouldn't have other lovers. 'Are you and she…?'

Ava cracks up, almost spitting out her Sprite. 'No!' she says when the coughing fit passes. 'Iri's the straightest woman you'll ever meet. But when she wanted to open a second shop, there was a problem with planning permission, so I helped out.'

'I see.' Jean bites into her chicken with relish, ignoring Ava's amused expression as she devours the perfectly spiced meat.

'Don't worry, Jellybean. I'm not giving you the community strap.'

It's Jean's turn to choke then. She's never heard that expression before but has no trouble discerning its meaning. Her eyes water, the pepper and paprika catching in her throat. Ava pours Sprite into her glass and Jean gulps at it, thankful – but not enough to let the nickname slide. '*Jellybean?*'

'You know.' Ava tips more chips onto both their plates. 'Tiny Jean. Jellybean.'

Jean's eyes narrow into the glare that makes even seasoned associates sweat.

But Ava simply shrugs. 'I thought it was cute. You know, most women would take that as a compliment. Sweet, delicious, fun to eat...'

'I'm not most women.'

'No,' Ava says. 'You're one of a kind.'

Jean's cheeks radiate heat, and she hopes Ava will simply chalk it up to her coughing fit or the spiciness of their chicken. Her brain reaches, haphazardly, for any topic that will steer them towards safer territory. 'So, your sister—' Inwardly, Jean curses menopause brain. Family is hardly a more casual topic. 'Is she a lawyer too?'

If Ava's perplexed by this shift in conversation, she doesn't show it. 'Doctor. A cardiothoracic surgeon. Which is just as well.'

'Why?'

'You know that Gina Yashere joke about Nigerian kids only getting four career choices?' Ava ticks them off on her fingers. 'Doctor, lawyer, engineer, or disappointment. And we never could have gone into the same field – too competitive.'

'Well, your parents must be equally proud.'

'Not quite. Dad's the typical white hippy *I-don't-care-so-long-as-you're-happy* type.' Beneath the mocking, there's unmistakable fondness in her voice. 'But Mum would have preferred me to go commercial. She doesn't get why anybody would spend six years studying just to end up making struggle money at the Afro-Caribbean Women's Rights Centre.'

Privately Jean understands those concerns. But it's not her place to voice them. 'What does that involve?'

'A mix of things. Giving women legal information, advice, representation... More often than not, they wouldn't be able to afford it otherwise. We mainly support survivors of domestic violence and sanctuary-seeking women.' Ava dips a chip in ketchup, not looking at Jean. 'It can be difficult. But fulfilling.'

Jean knows herself to be lacking in the selflessness such a career requires. The daily drudgery of a job without prestige or personal assistants, overworked and undercompensated for it, with no clear path to professional advancement... Yet the stakes are high with every client, the consequences of failure cataclysmic. This work must feed Ava's mind as well as her spirit. 'It sounds like you make an incredible difference in your clients' lives. Your mother must be proud.'

'Yeah.' A shrug. 'But she's still pissed off that I'm not going to give her grandchildren. Aaliyah's got me permanently beat on the domestic front – a husband and two beautiful kids.'

The question slips out before Jean has time to measure her words – something of Ava's spontaneity is clearly catching. And she's wondered, from time to time, whether Ava's ardent desire for an older woman might not be connected to some sort of mother wound. 'Does she mind, that you're…?'

'A lesbian?' Ava rolls her eyes. 'Saying it isn't going to make you one, Jean. But no, Mum's cool. She, Dad, and Aaliyah marched at Pride with me the year I came out. Mum's even set up a community group in her church, encouraging parents to support their gay kids.'

Jean blinks. It's not that she'd assumed homophobia was specific to Black families; rather, it hadn't occurred to her that acceptance might be so straightforward for anyone. Especially not with the church involved. She tears into another drumstick – though Jean's rapidly approaching full, the tender meat is irresistible.

'What about you?' Ava tilts her head, curious. 'Any family?'

Even now, the question catches Jean off guard. She delays by popping another chip into her mouth, and takes her time chewing. 'I have a sister. Bridget. Nine years older than me.'

'And are you close?'

'No.' It would have pained their parents, Jean is certain, had they lived. But then if they had survived, Bridget wouldn't have felt so trapped, being mother and father to a little sister when she was still in need of both herself. 'We don't have much in common.'

Ava's still looking at her. And Jean realises that she has offered altogether too little in exchange for the confidences placed in her. 'Bridget's a housewife in Devon. President of her local WI Chapter. Very Jam and Jerusalem.'

'That never appealed to you?'

'No.' Jean hesitates. 'My ambition, more than anything, killed my marriage. I always put work first. Truth be told, an arrangement like this suits me far better. No expectations, no obligations, just...'

'Occasional fried chicken and regular orgasms?'

'Precisely.' Jean pushes her empty plate away. 'But you've only delivered on one front so far. Now I want the other.'

And Ava doesn't disappoint.

Chapter Eight

Thus far Jean has done her best to avoid Friday nights. It's easy enough – often Ava has plans with friends. Plus, Fridays are Jean's favourite time at the office; a hangover from her days as a junior associate, when the men left together in packs, bound for bars and strip clubs. Then the space became hers – and Marianne's. Peter had noticed their dedication, and through him, so had Will. And though Marianne's long gone, Jean still revels in the quiet of the office.

But when Ava texts asking whether Jean would like to find out how many times she can come in the space of a full night, Jean can't deny that she's curious. Curious enough to head home at the same time as Helen, dig a babydoll negligée from her underwear drawer, and head over to Ava's.

Jean expects her to pounce the moment she steps out of the bathroom clad in sheer green lace and silk. And yet, though Ava's eyes go gratifyingly wide, jaw slack as she takes in Jean's curves, she exhibits punishing restraint. Ignoring Jean's mounting pleas, Ava kisses and caresses Jean's body, inch by square inch. Forehead, nose, cheeks, ears, throat, shoulders. Under Jean's arms, the tender insides of her elbows, the hollows of her wrists. On she goes, until Jean's entire body is alight with it. Never in

Jean's life has she been so turned on, a pulse drumming a fierce tattoo between her legs.

It takes her a moment to realise Ava intends to kiss her there too, and the thought triggers a less pleasant squirming in the pit of her belly. She reaches down to halt Ava. And though perplexed, she is respectful of Jean's wishes, crawling up the bed to kiss her mouth instead. And Jean melts against her.

Only when Jean's thighs are slippery with want does Ava reach between them. But even then, Ava draws it out, stroking slow and steady. And when Jean tries to buck against her, to rub herself to climax, Ava pulls away. Jean actually whimpers then.

Ava climbs up the bed, takes Jean's chin between her thumb and forefinger. Looks her dead in the eye. 'You don't get to rush this. Understand?'

Jean nods.

And Ava kisses her. 'Good. I'm going to make it worth your while.'

She does, too. Slipping the dildo inside Jean and rocking – by turns slow and gentle, frantic and urgent – until they're both trembling too much to move. Jean slumps into Ava's arms. Though she's unbearably hot and sticky with all manner of substances, she nestles in close. And Ava smooths the hair from her forehead. Strokes Jean's back until she dozes off.

And when Jean wakes again in the small hours, aching but wanting all over again, Ava reaches between her legs. Strums ever so gently until one climax is indistinguishable from the next, every atom of Jean's body blissed out.

'Nine times by my count,' Ava whispers.

Jean's too breathless to laugh. Too boneless to move. But she drops a kiss against the curve of Ava's shoulder.

Even if her legs could carry her, Jean wouldn't get up. And she knows, in a distant sort of way, that she'll worry about that later – but right now she gives herself over to it fully, the simple pleasure of being held. It's not like with Henry, where Jean shied away from affection lest he take it as an invitation for more. And not just because Jean will gladly let Ava take her as many times as she pleases. But because here, snuggled tight in this bed, Jean feels... safe.

—

Jean's late to brunch. Naomi, Cora, and Imogen are all settled into the booth with cocktails when she arrives straight from Ava's place. There's no hope for her hair, which somehow manages to be both flat and frizzy without a proper blow dry – she'd brushed it back into a chignon in the cab. Yet even with messy hair, minimal make-up, and too little sleep, Jean knows she looks good. Her skin has a glow to it that no facialist can replicate, and her eyes are bright in spite of a solid week spent squinting at a screen.

Ordinarily, being anything under fifteen minutes early sours Jean's mood. But nothing so petty can touch the marrow-deep contentment left over from her night with Ava. She lets the waiter take her peacoat and makes a beeline for their usual table, striding through the mirrored hallway and wondering whether there's ordinarily such a sway to her hips as she walks or if she's simply more aware of her body than usual.

'Jean!' Naomi pats the empty space beside her, rings glittering in the light. She's had her sandy hair cut short, a shattered pixie that suits the angular lines of her face. 'Good of you to finally join us.'

'Sorry.' Jean takes a seat, tucking her skirt beneath herself. 'I got held up. Something unavoidable.'

She'd been certain Ava had wrung every possible drop of pleasure from her body the night before. Yet Jean was powerless to resist Ava in the morning, fingers drawn inexorably to the constellation of freckles on her shoulders exposed by pale sunlight.

'By whom?' Imogen gestures to the waiter for another margarita, flashing her most charming smile – the one which, in the early days of their careers, made Jean think of the flower mantis. Pretty enough to lure in her prey; placid enough that, combined with her honey blonde locks, men and women alike underestimated the sharpness of Imogen's mind.

'What makes you think I was with someone?' Though Jean's tone is casual, she lets the barest hint of a smile grace her lips.

The table erupts with innuendo and speculation. Having known each other long before becoming titans in the legal world, all four women relish the rare opportunity to cut loose without fear of being judged. It's why – despite four constantly busy schedules overseen by PAs – these brunch dates are still going strong after thirty years. The waiter sets her glass down, and Jean prolongs their agony by taking a deep drink. Only with these three does Jean swap her usual martini for tequila, lime, and salted rims. A sweet regression to her student days.

'Let's review the evidence, shall we?' Ever the barrister, Cora pauses for dramatic effect, ticking each point off on manicured fingers. 'You arrive late, but your hair's still damp. You needed to shower but didn't have the time to do your hair – or perhaps your mystery companion doesn't own a hairdryer. Which indicates that he's male.'

'Conjecture,' Jean says.

But Cora continues as if she hadn't spoken. 'And that blouse is hopelessly creased; either you crammed it into an overnight bag, or your companion couldn't keep his hands off you. Have I missed anything?'

Cora's right on both counts about the blouse. Right about the shower. Right about everything except the sex of her mystery lover. Even with all her swagger, her curious scent, the ease with which she tops Jean, nobody could ever mistake Ava for a man.

Imogen eyes Jean, thoughtful. 'She's moving like a cat that's slept in a patch of sunlight. It had to be good.'

'It really was.' Jean licks the salt and lime from her lips, exquisitely tart.

Cora and Naomi share a glance.

'Did you...' Imogen leans in close, enveloping Jean in a floral cloud of Oscar de la Renta. And though her signature scent is more sophisticated now than it was at Cambridge, Ginny still has the same gentle tact that first drew Jean to her. 'Did you get there last night? All the way?'

'Of course,' Jean says, not meeting Imogen's eyes. She's the only one who knows there's no *of course* about it.

Naomi leans forward, setting the teardrop pearls at her ears swinging. 'How many times? Twice?'

The margarita stops halfway to Imogen's mouth. 'Three times?'

Jean can't help herself; she laughs. 'You'll never guess. It's almost too good to be true.'

Cora's dark eyebrows draw together, giving her a hawkish look. 'More times than I could count on one hand?'

Imogen gasps, and Naomi appears gratifyingly scandalised.

Not once, since the early days of her marriage to Henry, has any aspect of Jean's personal life been the subject of envy. And so she enjoys being able to say: 'Nine times in a single night. And again this morning.'

'Holy shit!'

If Jean keeps going at this rate, even for a few months, she'll more than make up for the dry years; all those times she'd faked orgasm just to bring about a natural conclusion.

'Well, I'm delighted for you,' Cora says. 'Henry's a darling, but let's face it: he wasn't exactly ringing your bells. And it's about time someone did.'

Naomi frowns, stunned. 'But so many times... Is that scientifically possible?'

'I can assure you,' Jean says, 'it is. With the right person.'

'And you still came to brunch?' Imogen shakes her head. 'We'd have understood you giving this month a miss.'

'Oh, no. This is a strictly... practical arrangement.' Even when she's absent, Jean pictures Ava scoffing at the word. 'I don't want to send mixed signals.'

'Are you insane? This man is a keeper.' Naomi speaks so earnestly she doesn't notice the flicker of discomfort that passes over Jean's face. 'I'd be ironing shirts and serving roast dinner on Sundays.'

'No, no.' Cora shakes her head. 'Any sudden move towards domestic life gives them the fear. Samuel only proposed because he thought it was his idea.'

'Oh, please.' Imogen rolls her eyes. 'He's head over heels in love with you.'

'Both things can be true at once,' Cora says.

'Never mind romance, ladies. If it's casual, is he open to other… arrangements?' Naomi raises her eyebrow. 'This semester's barely begun, and splitting my time between here and New York is already punishing. I could use a little stress relief.'

'No!' Jean colours at their knowing expressions, forces herself to speak calmly. 'No. We're both too busy to have anyone else.'

'That doesn't sound entirely practical to me,' Cora says.

It's a relief when the waiter interrupts, asking if they're ready to order. Jean scans the menu, selecting avocado on toast with smoked salmon. But even after the waiter leaves to action their requests, the others remain undistracted.

'So, do we know who he is?' Naomi eyes her with open curiosity. 'This mystery man?'

A ripple of discomfort warps the surface of Jean's satisfied calm. But then she never said that Ava was male; simply let them fill in the blanks and assume.

Cora frowns, considering. 'Is it Ciarán Donnelly from Bedford Row? I thought there was something between you at that mixer.'

'No.' Jean had turned down Ciarán's advances, repulsed by the thought of his stubbly cheek against her skin, and promptly forgot him.

'Don't be ridiculous,' Imogen says. 'Jean can do much better. Besides, snoring is the only way Ciarán's keeping a woman up all night.'

Jean joins in their laughter, half scandalised. Imogen's moments of savagery are all the more enjoyable for their rarity.

'Then who is he?'

'Nobody you know,' Jean says.

The waiter sets their plates down along with a fresh round of margaritas, and attention is diverted – at least for now. Jean digs into hers with relish, savouring the creaminess of the avocado, the freshness of her salmon. It's one of those rare meals that's both delicious and Grant-approved. Yet she doesn't object when Imogen cuts off a generous square of Biscoff French toast and slides it onto her plate – 'to keep your strength up.'

'Good point.' Naomi waves her fork, a piece of bacon speared on the end. 'Do we know anybody with that kind of stamina?'

'Hmm. High energy and strictly casual. Is he younger?' Cora's eyes glint. She's never satisfied until she's wrangled out every last detail. And Jean must offer up this truth to keep her from another less convenient detail.

'Quite a bit.'

'In his forties?'

'Lower.' Jean almost manages to keep the smugness from her voice, but not quite.

'In his *thirties*?' Cora's voice is a scandalised whisper, but her expression is delighted.

'Thirty-six.'

Naomi lifts her margarita, says: 'Here's to you, Mrs Robinson.'

They clink their glasses, toasting Jean. And she can't help but savour this moment. She's spent decades listening to the others brag about their various conquests, and had little enough worth sharing in return.

Chapter Nine

In the end Henshall has no choice but to sign the deal. Jean knew he would from the moment of that obscene outburst at the boardroom table, a final impotent raging against the inevitable. He arrives early, grey with defeat, making a crass joke about catching the last chopper out of Saigon. And it's a relief to have Alexander escort him upstairs.

Jean herself waits in the lobby for Katherine Parker-Kato, who is precisely on time. And impeccably suited as always, despite the long-haul flight. It suits her — Katherine's tailoring emphasises her willowy build to great effect as she strides towards the lift, and her make-up free skin is perfectly smooth.

Yet Jean can't imagine the courage it must take, leaning into butch presentation in a professional environment. Katherine is supremely comfortable in her own skin — that boundless confidence is part of her charm, what makes her such an effective leader and persuasive negotiator. There's no way to ask — not a client, and certainly not in her place of work — but Jean would dearly love to know whether Katherine is ever anxious about stepping out into the world without the safety net of conventional femininity.

Katherine notices her staring, eyes meeting Jean's in the lift's mirror. 'See something you like?'

Heat infuses her cheeks with a rosy blush, and for the millionth time Jean curses her Irish colouring. 'Your suit.' Jean clears her throat. 'Galliano, isn't it?'

One corner of Katherine's mouth lifts in a sardonic smile. 'It is. Good eye.'

Then the doors open and the strange moment between them is broken. Katherine is all business as she enters the boardroom, and Jean pushes that foolish line of enquiry deep down in her imagination. It's a relief to sink into the familiar monotony of clauses and signatures, gently nudging George across the finish line.

Afterwards, though substantially richer and free from the burdens of a mismanaged company, he exits with ill grace, not so much as a thank you for the firm or a handshake for Katherine, which is likely for the best. An ego so fragile couldn't handle such a bruising grip, and Katherine isn't the type to hold back for the sake of male pride. Though she is magnanimous in victory, thanking the team before Jean escorts her back downstairs.

As the lift descends, she catches Jean's eye in the mirror once more. 'I'd like the opportunity to work with you again.'

Jean smiles, sure-footed on familiar terrain. 'The firm would be delighted to represent your interests.'

'That's not what I meant, Jean. There's a place for you on my team, if you fancy switching sides.' Katherine's eyes twinkle with mischief, though her expression otherwise remains serious. 'I'll work you hard and the hours will be long, but I guarantee you it'll never be dull.'

'Why me?'

'If you can talk that cantankerous old git into compliance, you can do anything.'

Jean allows herself a chuckle. 'True.'

'You don't have to decide right away.' The doors open and Katherine steps out into the gleaming lobby. 'The offer stands – for you I'm willing to wait.'

—

At Ava's suggestion Jean takes the District Line directly through to East Ham, sweating even with her portable fan on the highest setting. And though Jean had fantasised about how they might spend those bonus minutes and seconds, her feet ache with every step as she approaches Ava's block of flats. She kicks off her Louboutins the moment she crosses the threshold, ignoring the softening of expression that typically accompanies words like *tiny* and *adorable*, dumping her bag by the door.

Ava's eyes narrow as she takes in the racket poking from Jean's tote. 'What's that?'

'Badminton.' Jean approaches, leaning in to kiss her. But Ava's not so easily distracted.

'Yeah, I can see that. And you brought it here because...?'

Jean's sigh stretches into an uncontrollable yawn. There's no reason for Ava to know anything about her life at DDH – personal details, one and the same with professional in Jean's case, are off the table as far as *casual* is concerned. Yet she's watching Jean with a troubling curiosity. 'Our managing partner noticed that I seem—' Jean shakes her head. She is *not* different. This arrangement changes nothing of consequence. 'That I've been leaving the office earlier on occasion. And I needed an alibi of sorts.'

'You told him you play badminton?' Ava presses her lips tight together.

'As opposed to what?' Jean rolls her eyes, flopping down onto the couch. If they're going to have this conversation, she might as well get comfortable. Though of course her fan, the last line of defence against hot flushes, chooses this moment to crap out. *'Let's circle back to that merger tomorrow – I'm off to get my back blown out by my lesbian… sex acquaintance and her strap-on.* I don't think so.'

Ava's silent for a long moment – and when at last she speaks, Jean gets the impression her initial question has been weighed up and discarded. 'So, you went out and bought a racket?'

'No! My PA did.' Helen asked all manner of questions about Jean's specifications and preferences until, at last, Jean offered an extra day's leave. And Helen returned precisely forty minutes later with the racket and receipt, silk press immaculate despite the rain.

'Well, la-di-da Ms Executive Level Business.' Ava retrieves a tower fan from the cupboard and angles it towards Jean before joining her on the couch, lifting Jean's feet onto her lap. She's just about to pull away, conscious of how they must smell after a day crammed into tights and heels, when Ava's thumb presses into the curve of her arch.

Pleasure radiates from this point of pressure, so sudden and unexpected that Jean can't stifle a moan. Emboldened, Ava grips her foot properly, kneading the ache from Jean's flesh until she lies slack against the cushions. Those hands and their knack for bringing her bliss… Combined with a steady flow of cool air, it's nothing short of heaven.

Jean opens her eyes when Ava stops, unwilling to put her disappointment into words.

'I have an idea.' Ava speaks hurriedly, not quite meeting Jean's gaze. 'And before you freak out, there's no conflict with the terms of our arrangement. You keep yawning, and I'm shattered after work, so maybe we could put on facemasks and drink wine. I'll get some lotion and give your feet a proper massage. Are you in?'

It sounds wonderful – which is what fills Jean with misgivings. She's supposed to be keeping things simple. And what possible interest could Ava have in her beyond the physical? 'That doesn't sound like sex acquaintance behaviour, unless – this isn't some kind of fetish thing?'

'Yeah, actually it is,' Ava says, deadpan. 'But not mine. I figured we could sell pictures of your feet on OnlyFans and spend the proceeds on a filthy weekend away.'

Jean rolls her eyes. The more time they spend together, the less Ava's joking is restricted to post-coital moments. 'That's ridiculous.'

Now Ava's dark eyes watch her, intent. 'Which part?'

'Well – why my feet? Why not yours?'

'Because they're dainty and French manicured.' She strokes Jean's toes. 'Or is it *French pedicured*? Either way, you're standing on a gold mine.'

Jean laughs in spite of herself. And ten minutes later she finds herself in one of Ava's oversized t-shirts, tighter around her own bust, face mask on and glass in hand. None of Ava's bottoms would fit her, so Jean simply luxuriates in her pants – it's cooler anyway. Ava herself wears boxers and a camisole, hair tucked into a deep red silk bonnet. She opens a tub of cream scented with minty eucalyptus and aloe vera, and it's pure ecstasy when Ava works the cool salve into Jean's soles.

And Jean's mind drifts as Ava massages each foot in turn, lavishing attention on heel, arch, ball. The space between each toe.

Ava had been joking about the feet pics – though Jean's less certain about the filthy weekend. It's been years since she had to think twice about booking a trip, though she rarely takes her days of annual leave – they've been piling up like the interest on her portfolio. Longer still since she had to scrimp and save for anything. But Ava must, if her tiny flat and eclectic mix of second-hand furniture are anything to go by.

The flat is decorated to Ava's tastes, but it doesn't reflect the sharp edge of her ambition; the drive it takes to build an organisation from the ground up, adding countless hours onto a working day already comparable with Jean's own, or Katherine Parker-Kato's. Not for the first time, it occurs to Jean that these women from disparate parts of her life are similar – ambitious biracial lesbians sharing an unconventional relationship with gender.

The daughter of an English financier and a Japanese engineer, Katherine kept her mother's name too and leaned into her multiracial status to make the most of connections on both sides of the globe. She built an international tech conglomerate, becoming a millionaire by twenty-two and featuring on Forbes 30 Under 30. Now Katherine herself and the company are worth billions – the knowledge of which had only stoked that egotistical gammon Henshall's resentment.

While Ava's features are more ambiguous, the surname Harris standard British, she's obviously made a similar choice. Her books, her art, her very career – all of it speak of a strong tie to Ava's Black heritage.

Sensing Jean's gaze, she looks up. 'Everything to madam's satisfaction?'

Jean flexes her toes, pleasure resonating in the muscles. 'Oh yes.'

'You look like you're having deep thoughts.'

'Probably nothing you'd consider profound.' Perhaps Ava will think her gauche or clumsy. But then she's never yet made Jean feel foolish for the multitude of things she doesn't yet know. And there's an intimacy to this beyond sex, sitting top to toe on the sofa dressed purely for comfort. 'Ava, can I ask you something?'

'Sure.' She brings Jean's foot to rest on her thigh, rubbing the excess cream into her own elbows.

'It's not exactly sex-acquaintance territory.'

Ava's lips twitch. 'Now I'm intrigued.'

'You have big career plans. But you work in a field that's... heavily weighted against you.'

Ava gives a non-committal hum, expression indecipherable behind the mask. If she sees where this is going, she doesn't seem inclined to help Jean get there. But it's too late for tactical retreat.

'I know what the law is. I joined a firm in the nineties, when women were constantly being reduced to objects and told how empowering it was. And that sexism bled through into office culture.' An old image slips into her mind; Will's liver-spotted hand on Marianne's jacket, the Harvey Nichols suit she'd been thrilled to nab on sale, a gesture that might be construed as paternal protectiveness – until that hand slipped down to cup the swell of her backside. Jean blinks the memory away, speaking before Ava can. 'I know what inequality is like. But I don't understand, when opting out might be possible, why a person would choose to keep fighting on that front. Aren't you ever tempted to go incognito instead of pinning your colours to the mast by working for an explicitly Black organisation? Or work in an area of law that's less... emotionally demanding.'

The top of Ava's mask shifts, and Jean's certain her brows are knitting together. She's silent for so long that Jean's sure of having made a terrible faux pas. But then she speaks, with a pensive note Jean hasn't yet heard. 'You're right,' Ava says. 'That's definitely not fuck buddy territory.'

Ordinarily it's Ava eroding that particular boundary, with her takeaways and foot massages, the not-quite-joke about a weekend away. And in a perverse sort of way, her current reticence only whets Jean's curiosity. But it is a personal question; the most personal she has yet asked. 'If you don't want to tell me, I understand. It's not remotely close to being any of my business. I only wondered…'

'Why?'

'Why, what?'

'Did you wonder?' Mischief twinkles in Ava's eyes, and relief soars in Jean. 'I didn't get the impression you thought about me at all beyond sex.'

Jean walked into that one. But it's impossible to feel regret, mellowed by cool wine and dexterous fingers. 'I… DDH had dealings with a woman who reminds me of you. Negotiations concluded today, very much in her favour. She offered me a job.'

'And will you take it?'

'No. It would involve lots of long-haul flights, and I'd never leave London.' Jean considers. 'But I think she was flirting with me.'

Ava shrugs, the strap of her camisole falling down a bare shoulder. 'That could be fun. A forbidden relationship with your hot lesbian boss.'

The wine curdles in Jean's mouth, souring as she swallows. 'I don't mix business with pleasure.'

There's a hint of Code Red fury behind her abruptness, and Jean almost regrets it enough to apologise – there's no way that Ava could know; it was all so far before her time, and they move in completely different circles. But – to her amazement – Ava smiles, uncharacteristically shy. 'That's cool. I don't fancy sharing you.'

Jean scoffs. 'As if I have time for more than one sex acquaintance. Besides, keeping the numbers down minimises risk.' A familiar thought occurs to her – and there will never be a better time to ask. 'But what about you? We never made our arrangement exclusive and, if not with Iri, I'd assumed—'

She has said far too much. Even with the TV's murmur, the silence is thicker than the lotion Ava lavished on her feet.

But Ava smiles, triumphant. 'Jellybean! You *do* think about me.'

'I never said I didn't.' Jean huffs a sigh. 'You're not bad, as sex acquaintances go.'

'Neither are you.' Ava squeezes her foot. 'Though none of mine ever called me a *sex acquaintance*. It sounds so official. I might have to add it to my CV. Put you down as a reference.'

Jean pulls her foot free, throwing the cushion at Ava. But she's laughing too hard to launch it with any real force. 'You don't get to complain about me calling you *sex acquaintance* while you insist on using that bloody nickname,' she says, setting Ava off again.

Breathless and pink-cheeked, Ava says: 'Then I guess I won't complain, Jellybean.'

Jean's yawn swallows her protest whole. And as Ava shepherds her through to the bedroom, she can't bring herself to object. Pressed together at the tiny basin, she and Ava wash the sticky remainder of the masks from their faces.

Their reflections make an unlikely pair in the mirror, Ava eternally tanned and glowing in a way that has little to do with the mask's properties; Jean pale and unmistakably lined under the relentless light of the LED bulb. But then Ava ducks to kiss her temple – and all Jean can see is her own smile, a look of unguarded pleasure.

The feeling lasts until Jean realises that she's forgotten a toothbrush. But Ava opens the cabinet as she brushes, revealing at least a dozen packets stacked on the lower shelf. 'Pick whichever colour you want.'

It takes Jean a moment to make out her words, distorted by minty foam. She looks from the stack to Ava. 'You just have those lying about? What, do you buy them in bulk for all your women?'

'I may have.' Ava spits in the sink. 'Before I became a sex acquaintance.'

Jean selects a green toothbrush, turning to search for the bin as she tears off the packaging. Her smile is like the sun – too bright to do more than glance at.

They climb into bed together, Ava under the cover, Jean with an arm and leg atop the duvet. Ava rolls over to face Jean in the shadow. And Jean tries to rally – sex is not an unrealistic expectation after that foot rub, and it is the foundation of their arrangement. But Ava simply drapes an arm over her, stroking Jean's back until the last of the day's tension melts away.

Jean's all but asleep when Ava speaks. And though her voice is soft, barely more than a breath against Jean's hair, it pulls her right back into the land of wakefulness.

'Hiding never occurred to me,' she says. 'It would have killed my mum if I'd rejected her heritage, the culture she gave us. And it would have killed something in me too.'

Jean says nothing; just nestles into the hollow of Ava's neck and listens.

'My sister's name is Aaliyah, but everyone else knows her as Leah. That started when we went to uni – she didn't want anybody writing her off as ghetto. She's Leah at work too, anywhere professional.'

Though it's dark, Jean can picture the particular frown that creases Ava's brow when she's weighing up words with care.

'And I'm not judging Al for any of it – her being darker than me has made her life so much more difficult. As a doctor she needs to hold authority with her colleagues and be taken seriously by her patients. The other year a woman refused to be treated by Al because she didn't want a Black doctor's hands inside her.'

'Jesus,' Jean says. It hadn't occurred to her that anyone would be willing to die for their racism.

'Yeah... When I came out, Al joked it was because I wanted to beat her in the Oppression Olympics.' Ava's breath is warm against Jean's hair. 'I used to wish it was the other way round. That I had her name, her hair, her colouring. Right up until Aaliyah confessed the same thing. That she just wanted an easier life. We've always been close but, when we were younger, there was a kind of tension between us. Aaliyah resented it when people treated me better than her, and I hated that people would recognise her Blackness while they questioned mine.'

'It can be so complicated with sisters.'

'You never really talk about yours.'

'No, it's...' Jean trails off, uncertain how to voice it delicately. And Ava stays silent, continuing to stroke her back while Jean deliberates. 'I'm very conscious of what she'd think about me doing this. With you. Or any woman.'

'You don't think she'd be alright with it?'

'Understatement of the century. Bridget was horrified when I got divorced.' Jean toys with the strap of Ava's camisole. 'The church was a big comfort to her, after our parents died and she got saddled with me. And Bridget buys into Catholic teachings completely.'

'I'm sorry,' Ava says, heartfelt. 'Really.'

'Don't be. It's not as if Bridget's ever going to find out, or anybody else for that matter.'

After that Ava falls silent, though something about her stillness tells Jean she isn't sleeping. But she carries on caressing Jean's back, slow and soft, until dreams claim her.

Chapter Ten

Helen meets her outside the hotel, Jean's redeye and her own latte in a cardboard cupholder; surviving conferences requires an ungodly quantity of caffeine. She hands Jean her pass on a ruby lanyard – Helen's own, in the sunny yellow of the assistant rank, is already looped around her neck. Such efficiency, unprompted, is the reason she's lasted close to five years as Jean's assistant. While Jean will certainly write a glowing reference when the time comes, she dreads having to train a replacement.

They pass the queue together in the lobby, a sea of navy, black, and grey. The forest green of Jean's suit sets her apart – at the start of her career she'd decided on a statement colour, bold yet tasteful, the perfect contrast to her hair. And she has never looked back.

Elizabeth Granger from Pearson Taylor catches her elbow, and they air kiss.

'Jean Howard – fancy seeing you here! I'm surprised Peter's missing this; ordinarily he's the life and soul of the party.' She flashes Jean a knowing smile. 'Unless he's thinking of succession?'

Jean shakes her head, demure. 'Peter was unavoidably detained on urgent business. He sends his apologies. In the meantime, you're stuck with me.'

'Then perhaps we'll see him next year?' Elizabeth's grey eyes sparkle with mischief as she toys with her own crimson lanyard. 'Either way, let's do lunch soon. My assistant's floating around somewhere.'

'On it.' Helen turns on her heel, making a beeline for the cluster of young women in yellow lanyards.

Jean bids Elizabeth goodbye, a spring in her step as she approaches the cloakroom. There's only one woman ahead of her, in a slate grey suit. And as Jean draws closer, she catches the unmistakable scent of cedar mingled with jasmine. Her stomach flips, upending the quiet satisfaction brought on by Elizabeth's speculation. And the caffeine chooses this exact moment to hit Jean's bloodstream, sending her heart off at a gallop.

Surely not. But the woman is tall enough to be Ava, towering above Jean even in ballet flats. Her hair's combed into a rigid bun, not a curl in sight, but it's the same shade of glossy chestnut. The woman has not only Ava's voice but her politeness as she thanks the teenager attending the cloakroom.

Jean stands frozen in place as she turns. Ava's eyes pop wide as they lock with Jean's. But she's quick to recover, that familiar grin never far away. 'Morning,' Ava says, and saunters away.

For a moment Jean can only watch her. When Ava had mentioned an important work event, the last place Jean's mind went was this, a waste of time better devoted to the Leonides expansion. But here she is in corporate cosplay.

Then the spotty girl behind the desk prompts her: 'Can I take your coat, ma'am?'

And though sweat prickles beneath Jean's arms, averting this crisis is infinitely more important than shedding an extra layer. The face masks, the fried food, all of it was a colossal error in judgement. An erosion of the middle ground separating Jean's real life from a passion that cannot, *must* not, live outside the four walls of that cosy little flat. She strides after Ava, catching up just as Helen rounds the corner.

Hearing the rapid click of Jean's heels against polished marble, Ava turns. And Jean grasps her wrist – tight enough to still the trembling in her own fingers.

Luckily for her, Ava's too surprised to resist as Jean pulls them both into… the utility closet, away from prying eyes. Jean closes the door behind them. Trays with cleaning sprays, bleach, and jay cloths line metal shelves against each wall. Above the scent of antiseptic lemon, damp permeates the air, which Jean traces back to a mop propped upright in a bucket. Between the storage units and an industrial-sized carpet cleaner, there's little standing room. They're pressed together like pilchards in a tin.

Ava's close enough to kiss – though, as her bewilderment morphs into anger, Jean doubts it would be welcome. Not that she has any intention of trying, with representatives from every major firm and chambers in the building. Which raises the question of how and why Ava's charity has a delegate here.

'Jean, what the fuck?' Ava pulls her arm free, gesturing around the dingy cupboard.

'I could ask the same thing,' Jean hisses. 'What the hell are you doing here?'

Ava tugs on her blue lanyard, thrusting the nametag beneath Jean's nose: *Ava Harris, ACWRC / Colourblind Justice Caucus*. Save for the colour it's almost identical to the one around Jean's own neck, printed with the LLN logo.

'I'm here for the London Legal Network conference. Or I was until a madwoman dragged me into a fucking closet.'

'But why? You told me you weren't into – and here I quote – *soulless corporate shit.*'

Ava pinches her brow, as if holding a headache at bay. 'Because my old supervisor got me a place. He thought it would be a good idea for my...'

'Your what?' Sweat prickles beneath Jean's arms, panic bubbling over into hot flush territory.

'I don't owe you an explanation. I'm not here for you, Jean,' Ava scoffs. 'What, did you think I'd hacked your diary and gone full Glenn Close?'

'No.' Jean folds both arms tight around herself. 'I just – I panicked, okay?'

'Yeah, I got that from being dragged into a cupboard against my will. Which, by the way, isn't exactly super *discreet.*' Ava looks at her for a long moment, and Jean's still reaching for an adequate response when she relents, full lips twitching. 'You've put us in the closet, get it?'

Unfortunately, Jean does – but having lost the high ground, she's in no position to bitch about a crack regarding her sexuality. And besides, Ava's humour works out in her favour. 'I'm sorry; I'm being completely crazy.' Jean covers her face as a terrible thought occurs – after all, she's jeopardised her dignity and sex arrangement by acting unhinged. 'Oh god. *I'm* Glenn Close, aren't I?'

Ava's hand rests against her back. 'Yeah. But mostly you're *Damages* Glenn Close, not *Fatal Attraction* Glenn Close. And Patty Hewes was hot.'

'Never seen it.' Perhaps if Jean keeps her face covered long enough, the floor will simply open up and swallow her whole.

'Well,' Ava says, 'we could stream *Damages* sometime. If you'll watch all five seasons with me, maybe we can forget about this.'

Night after night curled up on Ava's sofa… For the first time in Jean's life, she isn't sorry about having no leverage. 'Alright. But how do we get out of here?'

Footsteps and voices echo through the corridor. And Jean's panic rises on the tide of chatter.

'I don't know. You were the one who got us into this mess.' Ava sighs. 'Maybe we could wait until the opening session's started and sneak out.'

An urgent knock sounds on the door. And Jean pulls away, tipping the mop in her haste.

'Ms Howard?' Helen's voice is laced with concern. 'I've got the shirt you requested. There's an M&S across the street. And I'm so sorry about the coffee, it won't happen again.'

'Holy shit,' Ava says. 'Your assistant's a genius.'

Then she slips out of the closet. And Helen takes her place, green carrier bag in hand. 'Give me your coat, your blazer, and your shirt.'

Jean does as she's told, handing over her coat then turning round to preserve her modesty. 'Helen, I can explain. It—'

'Put this on.' The blouse Helen sourced is similar in style and cut to the one she was wearing, but crisp cotton instead of silk, and white rather than champagne coloured. It's of Jean's usual size and aesthetic, yet noticeably different to the one she'd arrived in. As an executive assistant, Helen has made a point of learning all about Jean's preferences – but now Helen knows, or at least has reason to suspect, more than Jean ever intended to reveal.

'This isn't what it looks like. It's not what you're thinking.'

As Jean buttons the new blouse, Helen produces a bottle of iced coffee. And – holding Jean's discarded top over the bucket – she splashes dark liquid over the silk. Helen speaks as she examines her handiwork. 'I'd assumed you wanted to talk to her about badminton. You know, I'm partial to an odd game myself.'

Jean's hand slips, and she fumbles the pearly button. 'Y-you are?'

'Sometimes.' Helen scrubs the top until the stain sinks in. 'It's not the only sport I'm into, but I don't judge anyone who plays.'

'I see.' Jean takes her blazer back, watching Helen drop the sodden blouse into the M&S bag.

'Good. Then we don't need to discuss this again, Ms Howard.' Helen produces a tiny pair of scissors from her handbag and snips the label free, complete with the tag's stem.

'Thank you, Helen,' Jean says, meaning it.

'You're welcome.' Helen leads the way out into the corridor, now deserted. 'The opening talk just started – we should be able to slip in at the back. Then you're due in the Wren Room for the Knowledge Exchange workshop – Mr Dennings personally added it to your agenda, but the rest of the day is yours. I'll drop off your coat after this talk, then head to the Hadid Room with the other assistants.'

Jean accepts the proffered itinerary as they climb the stairs. 'That all sounds great.' Having come this close to disaster, even Peter's mandatory fun doesn't seem so terrible.

–

The harder Jean tries to avoid Ava, the more frequently their paths cross. First the closet debacle. Which meant

Ava was scarcely earlier than Jean to the keynote. She's sat two rows in front, head bent over a notebook, oblivious to Jean's gaze as she takes fervent notes. The talk's not bad – an international human rights lawyer enthusing about infinite possibilities contained within the legal framework. Her stories are compelling, sprinkled with celebrity titbits from her high-profile cases.

And Jean remembers that earnestness, how it had fuelled her years of study like liquid hydrogen in a rocket. But – like all her peers – Jean had quickly jettisoned optimism; ironically, holding on to hope had a way of manifesting the worst possible outcomes as a junior associate. Cool pragmatism has served her well over the years. Jean wouldn't have made it over the first hurdle, never mind this last jump, with that millstone dragging her down. Yet the speaker's sincerity needles at Jean until she's forced to look away.

There's no harm in letting Ava hold her attention while she's oblivious to it. Ava, who has held on to that optimism with both hands, even though it limits her potential. Ava, who is determined to use the law for good rather than material gain. And perhaps that's part of her appeal: the path not taken. There's no other reason for Jean to be aware of her every movement as Ava stands to applaud; gathers notepad and pen; fishes the schedule from her bag.

Jean makes a beeline for the exit, swift enough that there's no possibility of Ava catching up with her in the corridor. Her earrings swing with every stride, pearls bumping into the column of Jean's neck. A spot Ava never misses in their foreplay – and Jean has taken Coco Chanel's advice of dabbing perfume there, where she expects to be kissed. She'd applied it this morning without thinking.

But no. Today's not about passion. At least, not the personal kind. Jean is here to put her best foot forward; to represent the firm. *Her* firm. The sooner she can shake off the strangeness of her morning, the better.

A voice calls her name, low and melodious, unmistakably male. Jean halts, turning to watch Robert Blake approach. With his snowy hair and beard, that ever-expanding belly, Rob's appearance puts Jean in mind of Father Christmas. And Rob certainly plays up to the image, turning on the paternal charm. But there's a canniness to him, a knack for extracting more information than you'd ever intended on revealing, that Jean greatly admires.

She leans in to accept a whiskery kiss on the cheek. 'Rob! It's good to see you.'

With seventy fading in the rearview mirror, Jean had wondered whether the university might finally oust him – but Robert has never mentioned retirement in her hearing, and Jean suspects he'll be teaching until he drops. He's lost nothing of his usual Machiavellian sparkle. 'You're just the woman I was hoping to run into. Tell me, is Peter here?'

'He's with a client, but I'll tell him you said hello.'

Rob's eyebrows climb. 'Very interesting, given Peter once told me this event was an annual highlight. But it does mean you're even better suited to my purposes.'

'That sounds ominous.' They step closer to the wall, still amid the steady flow of delegates.

'Not at all. And it works out rather nicely for DDH on the corporate social responsibility front.'

'Now I'm really worried,' Jean says, not entirely joking. But then, in the not-so-distant future she'll have absolute control over what to delegate.

'Don't be – in fact, I suspect you'll enjoy this challenge. She's like you, Jean; never opting for the path of least resistance. There she is!'

He waves. If Jean was remotely superstitious, she'd suspect the universe to be having a laugh at her expense. But there's nothing fated about this meeting with Ava – it's only the product of an old man's machinations.

Ava's smile speaks of unguarded pleasure as she takes in Robert – but then she catches sight of Jean and her expression freezes. Behind Rob's back Jean widens her eyes, nodding almost imperceptibly towards him.

Ava approaches, not looking at her. 'Robert! Thanks so much for having me here toda—'

He waves her words away. 'Don't thank me yet.' Then Rob steps aside, ushering Jean closer to Ava.

And for a wild moment her eyes dart around, searching for any possible way out of this. She recognises Imogen in the surge of bodies and instantly dismisses the idea – bringing the most perceptive of her friends and her sex-acquaintance together would be a disaster.

So, Jean has no choice but to stand and smile as Rob speaks. 'Meet an old friend of mine: Jean Howard. She's a partner at Decker Dennings and Howard.'

Sensing Robert's gaze on her, Jean holds out a hand. Doesn't betray so much as a flicker as that familiar tingle travels from Ava's fingertips through the barrier of Jean's skin. 'Pleased to meet you,' she says, unable to apply her usual pressure.

Ava too is gentle, thumb brushing Jean's knuckles in a subtle caress as she pulls away. Robert carries on with the introductions, and Jean scarcely hears over the thunder of her own pulse.

'This is Ava Harris,' he says. 'She was one of my most promising students, fully living up to that potential by setting up her own non-profit for an urgent cause – but Ava can explain it all much better than I do.'

'That sounds wonderful, Rob. But I'm due in the Wren Room – unless we hurry, we'll be late for our next sessions. It'll have to wait.'

'Actually, Ava's heading there too.' Rob beams, not like Father Christmas at all, but someone just handed the biggest present under the tree. 'I hoped you might take her under your wing, Jean – few rival your corporate law expertise, and your connections couldn't hurt either.'

Christ on a bike. Which is more unethical: to mentor the woman she's fucking, or withhold assistance like some penalty for their sexual relationship? It's not a dilemma Jean could have foreseen. And her mind's still reeling from their encounter in the closet, too dazed to puzzle it out. Ava won't meet her eye, but Rob's still watching Jean, expectantly. 'Let's talk it over on the way to our session.'

'Splendid!' Rob claps his hands together. 'My work here is done – I'm off to brush up on property law. Until later, ladies.'

He travels in the opposite direction, effortlessly parting the dwindling crowd. And Jean speeds off in the direction of the Knowledge Exchange session. But Ava doesn't fall into step beside her. When Jean looks back, she's exactly where Robert left her, all earlier certainty gone.

'Are you coming?'

Ava jogs after her, still not looking at Jean when she catches up. 'Sorry, I had no idea you were the person Robert wanted me to meet.'

Jean shrugs. After her earlier slip towards Glenn Closean tendencies, she's keeping it mellow. Collegiate, even. 'There's no way either of us could have known.'

They're silent for a long moment, passing a cluster of panicked junior associates arguing over the map. Ava stops to help them puzzle it out, but is seemingly just as confused. Huffing a sigh, Jean pulls the sheet from her hands and points them in the right direction.

They make it to the Wren Room with moments to spare. Bernard Crane's facilitating, one of Henry's old colleagues from his stint at Maddox Waring. And he'd been kind to Jean, back when she was still performing the role of Wife, asking interested questions about her own career; even intervening when Greg Waring asked pointed questions about when she and Henry planned to start a family. Of course, it did nothing to bridge those long silences on the journey home, nor to stop Henry walking round looking like a kicked dog after the inevitable argument – but Jean appreciated his solidarity all the same.

Jean's pleasure at seeing him is sincere, if undermined by Bernard's arrangement of the room: all around, chairs have been set in distinct pairs. The intimacy of one-on-one teambuilding exercises is excruciating to Jean. Ava weaves between them, heading for the board where the delegates are clustered.

And Jean asks Bernard how he's enjoying life at the top of Maddox Waring. Henry never shared his ambition, nor Jean's – yet, since it was Henry who brought them together, the conversation inevitably turns towards him.

They make plans for dinner and a proper catch up, Ava lingering all the while, watching for a gap in their conversation. With a grin, Bernard turns to face the other delegates.

'Welcome, everyone, and thank you all for coming! I'm Bernard and today I'll be taking you through some team-building exercises designed with two goals in mind. The first is to have colleagues across all stages of their careers engaging with one another – a Knowledge Exchange.'

He catches Jean's eye then, as if reading her mind, and the corners of her lips twitch upwards.

'And the second is to strengthen our communication skills. In law, being able to connect with people, reading them and responding appropriately, is at the heart of what we do.' Bernard gestures towards the chairs. 'We'll be working in pairs today. If you haven't already, check the board to see who you've been allocated. You have precisely three minutes to find them and take a seat.'

Jean's on her way to look at the list when Ava blocks her path, hands in shallow suit pockets. She's ill at ease in this environment – and Jean doubts her presence is the only problem. Ava looks nothing like herself in sedate grey, the life combed out of her curls. And Jean wonders whether this might be her fault, if Ava took her comments about appearances and fitting in to heart. But there's no time to ask, even if they were free to speak.

Then Ava opens her mouth, and every coherent thought is obliterated. 'I'm your partner.'

The pit of Jean's stomach goes into freefall. 'Wh... what?'

'For the exercise.' Ava speaks as if it were the most obvious thing in the world, and Jean feels a fool for imagining any other possibility. 'We're next to each other in the alphabet.'

'No. We're not.' Desperate, Jean gestures to a passing judge. 'Amelia Hawthorne's here – that comes between Harris and Howard.'

'Yeah, but she's senior track.' Ava points to her own lanyard. 'Like you, she's destined to mingle with us blue peasants.'

Colleagues across all stages of their careers engaging with one another. Jean nods. 'Right.'

In the time they've been talking all the nearby seats have gone, but Ava darts off to claim a pair in the corner. Jean follows, grateful that they're at least out of the way. Tugs her skirt into place as she sits.

'Great!' Bernard looks thrilled as he takes in the room, every duo seated. 'This bodes extremely well for what's to come next. We're going to play a classic game: two truths and a lie.'

Excitement dances in Ava's eyes. And Jean can remember playing it years ago with Naomi, Cora, and Imogen, splitting a bottle of tequila between them. Their workload had been too intense to cut loose often – but when they did, they'd made it count. She reaches for fact and fiction as Bernard outlines the rules, mindful of Ava's unending curiosity.

'You first,' Jean says.

'Alright. Two truths and a lie coming right up.' Ava leans forward, elbows balanced on her knees, regaining something of her usual swagger as she speaks. 'My middle name is Taiye. If I hadn't gone into law, I'd have been an actress. And my first crush was Jessica Rabbit.'

Jean's Irish colouring betrays her as she flushes scarlet. And Ava's smirk confirms the truth about Jessica Rabbit: apparently curvy redheads are her type.

Jean weighs up the remainder of her words carefully. Ava mentioned her mother passing on Nigerian culture, whispering the words into Jean's hair – perhaps Taiye is part of that. But an actress? That seems unlikely. Ava's too passionate about her advocacy work.

'Jessica Rabbit and Taiye are true. Being an actress was the lie.'

'Ha!' Ava slaps her thigh, delighted. 'Wrong. Taiye is Aaliyah's middle name – *first born of twins*. Mine's Kehinde. *Second born*. I win!'

'Not necessarily,' Jean says. 'I haven't had my turn yet. You only win if you guess correctly, otherwise we're tied.'

'Alright. Your turn, Ms Corporate.'

Ava's eyes never leave Jean's. And she can't resist drawing the moment out, revelling in the attention. 'I hope you're ready, because I'm not going easy on you. My middle name's Euphemia. I was blonde for a brief, regrettable period in the Nineties. And I can play all four of Vivaldi's seasons on piano.'

'Hmmm.' Ava frowns. 'Euphemia's some Victorian shit – but then truth is stranger than fiction. Or you could be trying to Uno Reverso me after I got you with Taiye. We'll come back to that one later.'

'One minute left!' Jean starts at Bernard's voice. From that first night, it had felt as if she and Ava were the only two people in the world – and Jean assumed it was because they spent all their time together cocooned in Ava's flat. But even in a room full of people, Ava is enchanting. It's impossible to resist their chemistry. The thought is a disquieting one.

'Better hurry up,' Jean says, with more bite than she'd intended.

'Alright, alright.' Ava's frown deepens. 'Piano's exactly the kind of hobby a girl like you would have, and I can totally see you being into classical. But you were born to be a redhead – I mean, your entire wardrobe's green. I can't see you being dumb enough to mess with that.'

'Final answer?'

'Final answer.'

Jean's smile unfurls, the victory sweet. 'I was blonde from April to October in 1994.'

'Noooo!'

'Too stubborn to admit it was a mistake right away – there are no surviving photos.' A small mercy. 'But it was worth it to see the look on your face.'

Whatever Ava's about to say is lost as Bernard pulls the group's focus back into the room. 'Great job, everyone – I hope you learned something new about your partner. Next up you're each going to share one item from your bucket list. One thing you want to do before you die. Five minutes on the clock, starting... now!'

'I want to make managing partner.' Jean speaks without hesitation, voice low and urgent, for Ava's ears only. It's the truest thing she has to offer, that desire is the engine pulling her forward.

But Ava simply scoffs. 'Yeah, no shit. That doesn't count.'

Jean blinks. It hadn't occurred to her that Ava would want more. What more is there to want? 'Bernard didn't say we couldn't pick career goals.'

'He didn't have to – it was implied!'

Those puppy dog eyes don't work on Jean. 'Every good lawyer knows the devil's in the details.'

'That's a fucking cop-out and you know it.'

Justice Hawthorne shoots Ava a filthy look – until Jean peers at her with a single eyebrow raised.

Ava watches this silent exchange, amused. 'I said what I said.'

'And so did I.'

Ava looks at her for a long moment, a challenge in those eyes. But Jean stares right back until Ava concedes. 'Fine,' she says, in a way that suggests it's anything but. 'I want to visit Nevis.'

'In the Caribbean?' Ava has never mentioned having family out that way. But that doesn't rule out the possibility.

'Yes.'

'Why?'

'Oh no.' Ava holds up a hand. 'Bernard never said we had to answer more questions.'

Jean opens her mouth, but isn't fool enough to step into the trap Ava has set out in front of her. She won't beg and she won't attempt to cross this boundary. Because Ava's curiosity about Nevis has no bearing on their arrangement. 'Fine.'

For a long moment they're silent. Jean tunes into the conversations around them, overhears Ken Samson's longing to make a perfect soufflé. The earnest young woman opposite him wants to sleep under the stars – perhaps if she'd offered up a similar trite cliché, Ava wouldn't now be contemplating Jean like she's a jigsaw puzzle waiting to be solved. Henry looked at her that way too, until he decided Jean had a piece missing and gave up.

It's a relief when Bernard claps his hands and Ava's focus shifts towards him.

'Alright,' he says. 'Now that you've got to know one another, it's time for our third and main task. An exercise in legal thinking.'

'Thank god,' Amelia says, drawing laughter.

But Bernard takes it in his stride, reflecting the group's smiles. He outlines the hypothetical case – a stockbroker pocketing clients' money above and beyond his company's stipulated rates of commission – and charges them with mounting a prosecution strategy. Jean pulls her chair closer to Ava's, near enough that their knees brush and their hushed whispers will not be overheard.

Chapter Eleven

Once again, the world melts away. Only this time she and Ava are united by shared purpose, working together to analyse the scenario and assemble their response. Ava's mind moves in different directions to Jean's – she has a solicitor's doggedness, and an eye for opportunity. Whereas Jean built her career talking round recalcitrant clients and superiors, planting her own ideas in the minds of others, Ava's unswervingly direct. Yet instead of clashing, their styles complement one another perfectly. Not since her nights with Marianne, when the office became their domain, has Jean worked so seamlessly with an ally.

Anticipation builds in the pit of Jean's stomach as Bernard goes round the teams, allowing them to present their strategy to the group. It hadn't occurred to her that she'd end up caring so deeply about a moot of all things, standard fare back during her studies – but the thrill of outlining their plan is undeniable. She lets Ava take the lead; the whole point of this exercise is enabling growth in the blue tier. And a curious second-hand pride glows warm and unfamiliar in her chest as Ava hits her stride in outlining their rationale, methodology, and plan of action. Even Justice Hawthorne looks impressed by the time she's finished.

And Jean's not in the least bit surprised when Bernard declares them the winners, although Ava's jaw drops.

She actually squeals when Bernard hands over the envelope with their prize: 'Tickets for a musical about some of the greatest legal minds that ever lived.'

Jean doesn't get the reference – musical theatre has never been her scene. She'd devoured *Wolf Hall*, even gone to see the play with Imogen, but heard nothing of a musical about Cromwell, More, or any great Tudor statesmen. She casts her mind further back, doubting Cicero's chances of appearing in the West End.

But Ava seems to understand, grinning so wide her cheeks dimple. Bernard shakes her hand as Ava babbles her thanks, and suggests dinner with Jean the following Wednesday. By the time she adds it to her diary, Ava's excitement seems to have abated. She's quiet as they make their way to the next session, subdued until Jean suggests they have lunch together.

Though her dark eyes flash with excitement, Ava watches her for a long moment before responding. 'Are you sure?'

'Positive. Rob asked me to hear out your proposal, and I'll honour that commitment.' The message could not be clearer: *strictly business, nothing more.*

Ava nods, tucking a rogue curl back into its pin. 'That would be great. I *think* I'm on the right track, but I've never done anything like this before, and it would be useful to get your perspective.'

They find a quiet corner in the Scott room, Helen delivering the requested wraps for lunch and disappearing before Jean can invite her to stay. After all, there is nothing currently passing between her and Ava that could not be witnessed. Jean eats her crispy duck wrap while Ava talks, halting at first, growing surer as Jean's attention does not waver. Though she'd picked up the gist of it from papers spread across Ava's table, it's another thing entirely, seeing Ava lit up with purpose; being entrusted with these plans, dearer to Ava than even the possibility of finding love.

Ava scarcely stops to take a bite as she explains the purpose of the Colourblind Justice Caucus, an organisation designed to provide affordable legal representation to underserved and overpoliced communities. Her aim of securing support from wealthier backers, and having firms donate time as well as money. Between grants, savings, and the backing of a Black British rapper, Ava has scraped together enough to make a fledgling start. But the first year will be crucial.

'When do you plan on launching?' Jean opens her calendar app, ready to mark the date.

'The beginning of October,' Ava says between bites – most of their lunch hour has melted away. 'That way we get Black History Month buzz.'

'Smart.' Jean updates her calendar accordingly, performing a quick mental calculation. 'A tight schedule with your current job, though.'

'I'm leaving in July – that gives me two months of full time preparation. And a holiday.' Ava grins. 'At least in theory.'

Jean's mind flits to Ava's not-quite joke of a weekend away together, but she banishes the thought instantly – that way lies madness. She recommends a list of barristers and firms likely to be sympathetic to Ava's cause, along with companies and former clients in desperate need of good press. All the while Ava takes notes in her rapidly filling notebook.

'I think it's brilliant,' Jean says, when Ava's eyes are safely fixed on the page. 'What you're doing.'

Ava's hand stills then, a pretty blush colouring her cheeks. 'You do?'

'Absolutely.'

'Phew.' Ava relaxes back into her seat. 'I wasn't sure what you'd make of it.'

'Why not?' It's Jean's turn to be uncertain – is it because she's a white woman? Has she said or done anything that might cause Ava to believe her resistant to racial justice, or blind to structural inequalities? But the question had slipped out from between her lips before Jean had realised she might not want to hear the answer.

Ava half-shrugs. 'It's not going to be profitable. Aside from paying employees a fair salary, everything will go into the organisation. And there's a chance we're going to end up in the red if my funding applications for the next couple of years fall through.'

'I'd be glad to help you with them,' Jean says, meaning it. It's only when Ava remains silent that the full implication hits her: she's imagining a future, a year or more from now, when the two of them are still in contact. Jean gulps at her ice water.

—

After the conference, preparation for onboarding Hephaestia takes up the bulk of Jean's days. Peter has her take point on this too, and Jean will not stumble during this first real test of her leadership. Still, unable to resist the excitement of DDH landing a whale like Leonides, he checks in often. So, it's no surprise when Peter steps into her office one rainy afternoon, sushi and sparkling water in hand. But he doesn't suggest lunch.

'Helen,' he says, 'would you mind giving us the room?'

In one smooth motion Helen gathers her bag and rises, slipping out. She leaves Jean alone with Peter – and the growing certainty that something is wrong. Drastically so. 'What is it? Did Leonides back out?'

'No, no. Nothing like that.' Peter stands by the window gazing out over London, rocking from his heel to toe. Before him the Thames stretches flat and grey towards the horizon, mirroring the dull sky above. 'All those years we spent dreaming of the view from the top floor, and how often do we stop to appreciate it?'

Jean rises. 'Peter. Tell me.'

He takes another moment to steel himself. Only then does Peter turn and look her in the eye, coming close enough to speak in a low, gentle voice. 'I just got off the phone with Lilian Decker. Will died last night. And I wanted to speak with you before telling the office.'

Jean leans against her desk, glass cool and slippery beneath her palms. When she'd first joined the firm, freshly minted as Decker & Dennings, Will had presided over them all. To a junior associate he'd seemed as remote and powerful as the inhabitants of Mount Olympus. Though their paths had rarely crossed to begin with, his smallest decisions had shaped the entirety of Jean's days – and often her nights as Jean strived to prove herself, sacrificing sleep for advancement. It was impossible to imagine the firm without him, or the world, which had seemed one and the same.

Peter touches her elbow, interrupting Jean's thoughts. 'Are you alright?'

'Fine.' Jean straightens. Wipes both hands against her skirt and watches both misting prints fade from the tabletop, as if they never were. 'How did it happen?'

'A massive stroke. Will was gone by the time the ambulance arrived.'

'I see.' Once she'd fantasised about this moment, manifesting it with the intensity of a child yearning for Christmas. But the reality is... surreal. Another hollow victory without Marianne. 'Any word on the funeral?'

'Saturday next at the RAC Club.' He squeezes Jean's shoulder. 'I told Lilian that I'd be there to represent the firm. And Emily's organising a wreath. Don't worry about any of this, alright?'

'I think that we should both be there, all things considered.'

Peter's eyes pop, round as his sushi rolls. And though he's quick to recover, it's obvious he didn't anticipate the conversation moving in this direction. After all, he'd spent years arranging things so that Jean's meetings with clients, conferences, courses, and rare days of annual leave all coincided with shareholder meetings to save her from any potential overlap with Will – a silent piece of tact that Jean simultaneously resented and appreciated. Even after Peter's months of wining and dining the board had come to fruition and they'd forced Will out, there had been no way to pry him from his seat.

Will had flat out refused to sell his shares, not even for triple their asking price, unwilling to relinquish this last hold on the company he'd built from the ground up. And Jean had almost admired his tenacity. Would have, if it wasn't for the fact that the mere sight of Will had her breaking out in a cold sweat; regressing into that compliant junior associate and losing every inch of ground she'd gained in all the years between. Jean despised her own weakness, and hated Peter for seeing it even as she'd loved him for that unspoken kindness.

It's there in his eyes as he looks at her now, uncertain. 'That's not necessary, Jean. Don't feel obliged.'

'It sends the right message.' Still, doubt lingers around Peter's mouth. Jean looks him dead in the eye. 'I want to be there.'

'Oh.' Understanding dawns. 'Oh! That's, ah, understandable given the circumstances.'

'Yes. Now if that's all you came to discuss, I'd better get back into this.'

But Jean doesn't start working when Peter leaves; not right away. She fishes her personal phone from the desk drawer. Writes: *Tonight?*

Ava messages back at 13.02 p.m., gratifyingly close to the start of her lunch break. *Sure.*

And though Jean has every intention of losing herself in passion, washing her thoughts away on a tide of dopamine and endorphins, Ava too senses that something is off. For the first time Jean laments that she is nothing like a man, able to fuck first and ask questions later. The more urgent Jean's advances, the more she pulls away. Until at last, Ava breaks their kiss, smoothing Jean's hair back from her cheeks.

'Is everything alright?'

Jean catches sight of herself in the mirror and scrubs the remaining lipstick from her mouth. 'Of course. Why wouldn't it be?'

'I don't know.' Ava bites her swollen lip, and that uncertainty softens something in Jean. 'You seem on edge. Not yourself.'

Jean's skirt strains as she straddles Ava. 'Well, maybe you can think of a way to help me relax.'

Ava rests an automatic hand against Jean's back, the other stroking her thigh. But there's nothing sexual in her touch. No attempt to advance upwards, inwards. And though her face is mere inches from Jean's breasts, she looks at them without seeing. 'This is what I'm talking about. You're taking the lead, which would ordinarily be hot, but you're not even a little bit turned on. Don't argue,' she says when Jean opens her mouth. 'I know your body well enough to tell the difference.'

The fight melts out of Jean as she sighs, sitting on Ava's lap so they're eye to eye. 'My old boss, Will Decker. He died yesterday.'

'Oh my god.' Ava's arms lock tight around Jean, pulling her close. And Jean buries her face in the thicket of hair, breathing in cedar and the subtle macadamia scent of Ava's curl cream. 'I'm so sorry. That must have been a terrible shock.'

'Not really. Old men have strokes every day.'

There's surprise in the tightening of Ava's shoulders, so brief that Jean could almost have imagined it. 'Well. I think you're in need of a self-care night. We could curl up on the sofa and watch mindless television. Iri's shut on Mondays, but I could get us a munchy box from the kebab shop. What do you say?'

It's not an unappealing thought. And Jean can't find it in herself to resist. They spend an evening bingeing *Damages* – Jean is entranced by the connection between Patty and Ellen – and greasy carbohydrates, then curl up in Ava's bed.

'You know,' Ava says. 'We don't have to fuck every time. If you want to just… hang out or whatever, we can do that too.'

The words stay with Jean long after Ava falls asleep, following her through the week. They're a pleasant distraction from the dread and anticipation warring in the cavity of Jean's chest every time the funeral comes to mind.

—

Bogdan slows as they approach a crowd of mourners, and Jean scans every face, searching out familiar angular features. But so many mourners have their backs to her, clustered together in conversation or filtering into the church. Jean's heart constricts as she catches sight of a chestnut bob tucked back over neat little ears. But there's no guarantee Marianne still wears the same cut. And her hair might not even be the same colour — so many brunettes their age transition to blonde as the greys take hold.

Peter covers her wrist, and Jean tears her gaze away from the crowd. 'Did you hear what I said?'

'No, I—' Jean shakes her head. 'Sorry.'

'That's alright. Just let me do the talking.' Peter squeezes her hand. 'And we should stick together.'

Jean nods her assent. Then Peter lets go and they step out into the cool March drizzle, the quiet intimacy broken. But — true to his word — Peter doesn't leave Jean's side. With a steadying hand on Jean's back, he guides her through groups of mourners. Jean shakes hands and exchanges dutiful pleasantries, but it's Peter who steers each conversation, just as he steers them on an inexorable path towards the church.

And all the while Jean glances through the crowd. Mari was always the braver of them — she'd have the courage to appear like Maleficent at the christening. But Marianne was never the villain, and they're here to celebrate death instead of life.

Inside, Jean gravitates towards an empty pew near the back, where she'll have an unimpeded view of all those who enter and exit the church. But Violet Grundy waves to Peter, and there's a gap like a broken tooth in the thick of the mourners. She's claimed the first pew behind the empty rows reserved for family – and if anyone has the right, it's Violet. She'd lived and breathed DDH, presiding over Peter's diary with the same officious pride as if serving a premier or diplomat.

Violet embraces Peter, giving a tight smile as he kisses her powdery cheek. She'd always favoured the young men. As Will's eyes and ears in the old open-plan office, Violet's observations often led to feedback so forcefully delivered it would travel through Will's closed door. Yet she'd also dispense comfort, hard butter candies, and a sprinkling of sage advice – just enough encouragement that the fellow in question wouldn't give up.

None of these kindnesses were ever afforded to Jean or Marianne. The era of Girl Power had entirely passed Violet by. With hindsight Jean understands her resentment, watching younger women claim education, opportunity, and advancement she herself was denied. But at the time it had stung worse than any comment from her male colleagues.

Little about Violet has changed in the twenty-something years since their paths last crossed. Her hair's still blow-dried into the same bouffant. Her mouth is overlined with that eternal peach lipstick, a minor miracle it hasn't been discontinued. And her lips wear a familiar downward twist as she takes in Jean.

'So, you're here.' Violet sniffs. 'I'd wondered whether the Other One might join us. Always was a troublemaker. No sign of her yet.'

Jean's smile freezes. *The Other One*. The nickname she and Mari had shared, as the only female junior associates in the office. '*Fetch the girl,*' a senior associate might say. Followed by: '*Not her, I meant the other one.*' It had also been a jibe about her closeness with Marianne, the way they'd been joined at the hip. But how else was it supposed to be when the men closed ranks against them?

'It's a pleasure to see you again, Violet. I hope you've been keeping well?'

'Mm,' says Violet, then continues as if Jean hadn't spoken. 'Wouldn't put it past her to intrude. No sense of decency whatsoever.'

A retort sits razor-sharp on the tip of Jean's tongue: the hypocrisy of Violet, proverbial mistress at a funeral, to talk of decency while she sits behind the dead man's grieving widow. Jean bites down hard enough that her mouth is awash with copper and salt.

Peter intervenes, giving a subtle nod towards the door. 'The Deckers are here.'

Jean turns in time to see Lilian being escorted down the aisle by William Junior, frail yet dignified. Behind them comes the daughter – she can still picture the photographs that had sat atop Will's desk in pride of place. His daughter astride a horse, beaming as she held a trophy aloft. Father and daughter arm in arm, dressed in formalwear at William Junior's wedding. Daddy's little girl. It had reassured Jean in the beginning, that she and Mari were only a couple of years younger than Diana. Impossible to forget: a horse-mad girl named for a huntress. She and Mari had joked about that piece of nominative determinism.

But whereas the goddess remained a virgin, Diana and her brother both married; both continued the Decker family line. There are shades of Will in the sombre procession. A grandson with that lantern jaw. A granddaughter's tearstained face partially shielded from view by a thick curtain of jet-black hair. A little girl, too young to understand what's happening, peering round the church with curious grey eyes. Even after the family shuffle into the pews, the child stares over her mother's shoulder. There's none of Will's calculation in her expression, nor that knowing gloating look. But still Jean glances away, picking up the order of service.

The minister lavishes praise on Will as a lawyer and a businessman, as a husband and father. And the unspoken eulogy sits blazing in Jean's throat. But there would be no point burning Will's reputation to the ground, or damaging herself in the process – not now he is altogether powerless to block Jean from taking his company and making it entirely her own. Marianne would have done it, public self-destruction to claim a pyrrhic victory, but Jean is playing a longer game.

Peter takes her hand then. Only when Jean looks down does she realise the order of service is crumpled into an accordion in her right fist. She smooths it out on her lap, ignoring Violet's scandalised glare.

Chapter Twelve

The interment is long, the wake longer. After her third cup of tea Jean retreats to the bathroom. Takes her time reapplying powder and lipstick, longer for the tremor in her hand to still. Unwilling to give herself the Joker's smile, Jean caps the lipstick and twists the hot tap all the way round, letting it run from tepid to scalding. Only when steam rises from the sink does Jean allow herself to withdraw her reddening hands from the water.

She tucks them into her sleeves and exits the women's room, refreshed. Until Lilian rounds the corner, giving a tremulous smile as she catches Jean's eye.

'Jean! I don't feel glad of much at the moment, but it's good to see you today.' She clasps Jean's shoulders and pulls her in for an embrace, bird-boned beneath her black Chanel suit. 'You know, I'd always hoped for the opportunity to thank you for the way you stood by William during that dreadful business with Marianne.'

'Oh.' Jean clears her throat, dry despite the endless tea. 'No thanks necessary.'

'All the same. William appreciated it, and so do I.' Lilian takes her hand and squeezes the tender flesh, oblivious to Jean's discomfort. If anything, she appears moved when Jean's eyes water. 'Oh dear, the last thing I wanted was to set you off. But you should know that William remembered you fondly. And if you're ever in Epsom, I'd be delighted to meet for lunch or coffee.'

'I'll keep that in mind. Thank you, Lilian.'

And though it's Lilian who kisses her cheek, Jean knows herself to be the Judas.

—

It's dark by the time Jean arrives home. She fixes herself a drink that's gin as much as tonic, savouring the burn in her throat as she climbs the stairs. In the bedroom she kicks off her shoes and pads through to the bathroom. It's the size of Ava's entire open plan living and kitchen area, tiled in Italian marble with underfloor heating.

The shower's spacious enough for three grown men, not that Jean has ever felt inclined to try it – since Henry walked out, she's never sought a serious replacement for the His end of the His-and-Hers basins. Instead, her own toiletries and cosmetics have taken over the entire counter. Yet while the bathroom was designed with every possible material comfort in mind, its walls have never echoed with laugher or sighs.

Still, there's a pleasure here that Ava's spartan bathroom is incapable of delivering. Jean sets her glass down on the tub's rim; twists the plug mechanism and turns on the hot tap. As the water gushes into the bath, she pours in a generous dash of oil, eucalyptus and lavender, fresh and cleansing.

Jean peels off her blazer, unbuttons her blouse, unzips her dress. Sets her jewellery down on the dark marble counter. She rolls off her tights and kicks them onto the heap of forgotten clothes. In her underwear Jean perches on the edge of the tub, drinking and trailing her fingers through whorls of steam as it fills. Only when it can take no more without spilling over does Jean turn off the tap, the metal slick with condensation.

The thick blanket of silence is precious after all the words crammed into her day. Jean shimmies out of her underwear, tugs her bra free, and knocks back the rest of her drink. With the back of her hand she scrubs away the drip trailing down her chin. Then, not giving herself time to balk, Jean steps into the bath. One foot then the other, before her brain has time to register the heat.

Sweat beads on her forehead. Inch by inch she lowers herself into the tub, and there's no room in her head for anything save the burn licking up her calves, her knees, her thighs. Teeth grind, bone against bone, as she crouches; dipping buttocks, belly, the swell of her breast. Every second, Jean reminds herself, is a victory. Not only proof of her own steel-plated will, but a reclaiming of her body.

She stays in for a full half hour, scrubbing every inch of skin until she's pink as a newborn. The water's perfectly pleasant by the time Jean pulls the plug. Only now does she allow her body any tenderness, patting herself dry with a fluffy bath towel and smoothing cool aloe vera moisturiser into her skin.

Jean dons satin pyjamas, every movement a caress as the material whispers against her skin. In bed, cocooned in the goose-down duvet, she gives her emails and messages a customary check. After all, crisis may strike at any moment. But there's nothing that can't wait until morning. Then, with the same anticipatory buzz of reaching into her bedside drawer, Jean unlocks her personal phone.

There are two messages from Ava.

> **9:08:**
> Thinking of you today. Hope the service goes well x

> **21:57:**
> Want to come over tomorrow? I'll be home from six p.m. 😊

Jean's heart kicks against her ribcage. The timestamp is less than ten minutes ago. It takes two tries for her thumb to hit the phone icon beside Ava's name. An eternity yawns between that moment and the first ring. And it occurs to Jean that Ava might not pick up – either because she doesn't hear the phone, or doesn't want to spend the remainder of her Saturday night talking about a funeral of all things. Then Jean's name will show up red on her call log, irrefutable proof of this moment of weakness.

But Ava picks up on the third ring. 'Hey Jellybean, how are you doing?'

'I'd be better if you stopped calling me that infernal nickname.' Yet even as she says it Jean relaxes against the pillows and cushions, putting Ava on speaker and balancing the phone on her knees.

'Oh, please. You love it.' A beat. 'But really, are you alright?'

'Fine.' The fact she's calling at all contradicts that claim. 'But the funeral… the church was full, but it felt empty. I'd expected…'

'That's understandable,' Ava says, not understanding at all. 'It's still a recent loss. Give yourself time to grieve and process.'

There is no way Jean can explain to sunny, straightforward Ava that she does not mourn Will Decker. Not without exposing the shadowy, twisted aspects of herself. 'I'd rather not talk about it. Tell me about your day?'

Ava's silent for several seconds. And without being able to see her face, it's impossible to gauge her reaction. Jean's on the cusp of apologising and hanging up when she speaks. 'It was quiet. But good. I went to the gym then met an old client for lunch – she moved into a flat with her girlfriend and their kids. I'll miss that part of the AWCRC, seeing women flourish. But afterwards I spent the day working on CJC stuff, and it's all coming together.'

'What stuff? Did you choose an assistant yet?'

'Yeah, Beth's perfect. It's finding office space that's a struggle.' Ava's sigh crackles through the speakers. 'The estate agent doesn't give a shit – it's small potatoes to him, and I guess I should be grateful he squeezed me in on a Saturday, but nothing he'd found fit my brief *and* budget.'

'If the estate agent is failing to meet your expectations, use another. Try Chanter Pryce. Insist on Judith. Tell her I sent you.'

The click of a keyboard. And a subtle intake of breath. 'Jean, I appreciate the thought… But this is miles beyond what I can afford, and they'd never be interested.'

'They will. Judith owes me a favour.' Several, for the miracle she'd performed keeping Martin Chanter out of trouble with the FCA. 'Look, I'll write an email introducing you in the morning.'

'Alright. That would be great.' Still, Ava sounds uncertain. 'I know Robert asked, but you really don't have to keep helping me.'

'I know. But I want to.' And it's true: all of Ava's needs are straightforward, even if she doesn't see it. So easily within Jean's reach. There's nothing difficult about connecting and directing – it's a delicious novelty, pulling strings for someone utterly unmotivated by greed.

'Well, thanks all the same.'

'No problem.' Jean sinks down into the mattress, setting her phone on the pillow.

'So... Are we still on for Friday?'

Mind fogged, it takes Jean a moment to puzzle out what she's getting at. The *Hamilton* tickets. 'Yes, but I still don't understand why you're so excited. It's just a musical. What can there possibly be that you didn't pick up the first five times?'

'You'll see,' Ava says, a smile warming her voice.

Privately, Jean doubts it. But she's not about to rain on Ava's parade. Sooner or later life will knock that capacity for joy from her, and Jean won't hasten the process.

'Hey, I had a thought—'

'Congratulations.'

'Fuck you very much,' Ava says, but she's laughing.

'What was this thought?'

'I don't even want to tell you now.'

Jean smiles to herself. 'Yes, you do.'

'You're right.' There's a rustling that suggests movement, and Jean pictures Ava pacing across the breadth of her tiny living room. 'We're both coming from work, and it goes on until after ten, so maybe we should get food first. Together. There are good pre-theatre deals.'

Jean blinks. In any other scenario, Ava might be asking her out on a date.

'I thought it'd be... practical.'

'I see.' Jean reaches for the only safe part of this proposition, playing for time. 'What do you mean, it goes on until after ten? I thought the performance started at seven-thirty.'

'*Hamilton* lasts two hours and fifty minutes, including the interval.'

'What could possibly justify a three-hour musical?'

'You'll see,' Ava repeats, a smile in her voice. 'And you'll appreciate it even more if you're not hangry.'

Henry had deployed these little tricks with the goal of coaxing Jean out of the office, getting her to understand that there was more to life than the next promotion. And that silent implication of *I know better*, the way he'd carried on believing that Jean would change if he only persisted, only stoked the flames of her resentment. Made her say *no* more often than she should have, and find satisfaction in the refusal.

But there's nothing passive aggressive about Ava's tactics. Only a hope that shines all the brighter for going unspoken. And it's not like there will ever be another scenario allowing for anything that resembles a date. The thought hooks something behind Jean's ribs and tugs until she can't help but say: 'Alright. Dinner it is.'

'Cool. I'll text you the details.' Ava's voice is casual, steady. But Jean hears the skip in her step, socked feet thumping against the linoleum.

It's not a video call, so Jean doesn't even try to stop herself smiling as she bids Ava goodnight. Barely a minute later, her phone pings with another notification: confirmation of the restaurant booking. Ava has given her no time to back out.

Chapter Thirteen

Jean's not alone in spending her days in a state of suspense. A week from now, Andreas Leonides and his entourage will be among them. When she arrives on Monday, the office carries an unmistakable scent of fresh paint, so thick Jean can taste it – applied just in time for the odour to fade. But not quickly enough for Jean – it lingers in her sinuses until her head throbs. There's no time to retreat from her monitors, never mind sleep it off. Jean chugs ibuprofen and paracetamol, sending Helen to every shop in a half-mile radius to stock up her personal desk pharmacy.

Even Peter locks in, turning a blind eye towards the hungrier junior associates pulling all-nighters with 'gym bags' containing fresh outfits, travel toothbrushes and endless caffeine supplies. It's a trick Jean well remembers, though it had been easier in her youth, with only she and Marianne likely to use the women's bathroom.

Hugo leaves at the same time Jean does, or pretends to – as her car passes by, she spots him doubling back to the office. It's as if he's hoping the regular sight of his face will imprint itself on Jean's mind. Rebecca corners Jean as she steps into the lift with Helen, launching into a spiel of self-promotion before there's time for a single sip of coffee. Jean doesn't even have to say anything; she simply skewers Rebecca with a look, puncturing that manic momentum until the girl's words trickle away to nothing.

Then there's modesty to a fault; ironically, the most capable candidate has the least to say for herself. Though fully deserving, the junior associate Jean chooses to assist her on the deal doesn't even try to put herself forward. But when she does speak up in her quiet Edinburgh burr, every word is worth listening to. Rhona's competence, her ability to set ego aside and focus on the bigger picture, are exactly what's needed. Jean dispatches Helen to buy two meal deals from the cafeteria – a prawn mayonnaise sandwich and a mediterranean vegetable wrap – and bring them back with Rhona.

A knock on the door. 'You wanted to see me, Ms Howard?'

Rhona's Mary Janes, pinafore ensemble, and headband remind Jean of her old school uniform. And Rhona carries herself like an errant schoolgirl summoned by the headmistress, one hand clutching the opposite elbow. It's not difficult to imagine how Edward steamrollered her into handing everything over.

Jean flashes her a smile. 'Rhona. Sit down. I seem to recall you having done environmental studies as part of your undergraduate degree – you knew renewable energy would appeal to Andreas Leonides. Didn't you?'

Rhona's face lights up as she outlines how renewables can detoxify not only the environment, but the Hephaestia brand. Leonides is taking heavy hits in both the court of law and public opinion, facing a Group Litigation Order over multiple oil spills and fierce backlash from Greenpeace to Gaia's Children – though Rhona is smart enough to avoid giving away her personal opinion on the matter, sticking only to strategy and solutions.

In this brief flash of confidence, Jean glimpses the lawyer Rhona will become. She gestures to the sandwiches perched on the corner of her desk. 'Let's talk about your involvement with the Leonides portfolio over lunch. Pass me the wrap, would you?'

Rhona does as she is bid, expression freezing as she takes in the remaining sandwich.

'You like prawn mayonnaise, right? It's a classic.'

Rhona nods, jaw set as if she's facing the gallows. 'Seafood's my favourite.'

Jean's gaze roams heavenward. If there is a God up there, she will need all the strength he can spare to reshape this one. 'If you plan on lying to me – which I don't recommend – at least make it convincing.'

'I'm not—'

'Rhona, put down the sandwich. You're vegan for Christ's sake.'

Obedient, she drops the packet.

'By the time I'm done, you won't hesitate to speak your mind. You have good instincts and valuable insights – but they're no use to you or the firm if you're too afraid to share them.'

Rhona blinks, uncertain. 'Thank you, Ms Howard.'

'I want you on my team for Hephaestia. You'll accompany me to meetings, take notes, present your findings – whatever else I require.' As she speaks Rhona nods, eager. 'You'll see firsthand how Mr Dennings and I operate, learn about the inner workings of this firm, and gain invaluable experience with an international client. Play your cards right and this will be a big step towards promotion.'

That familiar hunger gleams in Rhona's eyes – all the confirmation Jean needs that it's the right decision. Decent tailoring and a precision haircut will make a new woman of Rhona, but those are discoveries she'll make for herself. For now, it's enough that she leaves Jean's office walking taller.

—

April showers are torrential, yet Ava's waiting for her outside the restaurant, cheeks pink in the chill night air. Her face lights up as she catches sight of Jean amidst the sea of tourists and commuters. Yet Ava exercises restraint, not attempting so much as a hug or chaste kiss in greeting. Though she's gallant as ever, holding the restaurant door open for Jean and pulling her chair back.

Inside they each shed a layer, Ava shrugging off her mac to reveal a bold burgundy suit and crisp white shirt unbuttoned far enough to cause a glitch in Jean's mind. Ava's curls, artfully tousled, have the look of a Regency rake – and her smirk when she catches Jean looking only adds to the impression.

But Ava's smugness proves short-lived as Jean drapes the pea coat over the back of her chair. Her green wrap dress shows Jean's bust and legs to their best advantage while providing generous cover of her middle – the perfect choice for a dinner… meeting. Its silken material glows subtle as a priceless emerald in the restaurant's warm light, and Ava is entranced. She hinges her jaw while Jean sits down, stammering out a compliment.

The restaurant's an excellent choice, a tastefully decorated bistro promising a taste of Paris. A waitress brings the pre-theatre menus and a carafe of red wine, which she pours into their glasses before retreating.

Ava holds her wineglass aloft. 'To knowledge exchange.' If the half-smile she wears is anything to go by, Bernard's workshop is the last thing on Ava's mind. 'Long may it continue.'

'To knowledge exchange,' Jean echoes, clinking their glasses together, though she won't speculate about its duration. 'How are things with you? How's the CJC going?'

Ava's smile grows sheepish. 'Fine, but I don't expect you to keep asking – you've already done so much.'

'I wouldn't ask if I wasn't interested. I've known people who set up charities, but never one that...' Never one that wasn't ultimately about ego or whitewashing corporate greed. The more time she spends with Ava, the further Jean travels from caution. 'Never one with so much potential to achieve material, tangible good. Besides, it makes a nice change from mergers and acquisitions.'

'Alright then.' Ava toys with a dog-eared corner of the menu. 'But only if you promise to stop me when I bore you.'

Jean gives a most unladylike snort. 'False displays of modesty are what bore me. You're taking a risk to do something courageous and unconventional – own it.'

'It's not false. Or modesty.'

'Then what?'

'I'm not used to talking about it, is all. My colleagues agree in principle that it's needed. But we're under-resourced and understaffed, which means they feel like I'm jumping ship when I leave. And my family...' Ava swirls the wine in her glass, peering into its depths. And Jean imagines what ACWRC could achieve with even half DDH's quarterly earnings. 'Racism in the criminal justice system, it's a difficult subject for them. It's how we lost my uncle, Ephraim.'

Oh. It explains so much about Ava's sense of purpose. 'I'm so sorry,' Jean says, meaning it. She remembers firsthand hating how people would either pry for details she couldn't bear to give, or wallpaper over her sorrow with cheerful prattle, and instead leaves space for Ava to elaborate or shift subject.

'So, you see why I can't talk about the CJC with them?'

Jean doesn't know whether to feel disappointed or relieved by the lack of disclosure. But she's certain of being able to provide a sounding board for Ava's ideas.

'Then tell me. You need to get used to talking about this. Work out your core message and how to shape it into a narrative.' Jean sips her wine – a full-bodied Rioja that washes the tension from her shoulders – and presses her advantage. 'You might as well do this with an interested third party who understands the mechanics of what you're trying to achieve. Besides, I'm genuinely curious.'

A teasing edge sharpens Ava's smile. 'That's not very… sex acquaintance-like behaviour.'

'Then maybe we don't have to be sex acquaintances.' Jean puts her glass down and presses both hands against her knees, concealing their tremor. 'We could be two people out for a meal together, enjoying each other's company. Just for tonight.'

Ava's brow furrows. And Jean doesn't rush her, recognising that need to deliberate before speaking, though with every passing second she feels more foolish. There are plenty of people in Ava's life, many more closely matched to her in age and background than Jean. But then, if Ava wanted, she could be sitting here right now with any one of them.

'Like… friends?' Ava speaks gingerly, as if testing the word out. And it doesn't spook Jean. If anything, it warms her more than the wine.

'Friends,' Jean confirms. 'For tonight.'

Ava doesn't push any further. She launches into an update, curls vibrating with excitement as she reveals that *the* Kelani Griffith has agreed to sit on her board. 'I mean, she revolutionised the way discrimination law is understood, not just in the UK but across the world. Kelani was part of the reason I decided to study law in the first place. I still can't believe she said yes.'

'I can.' While she's amassed an international following, Kelani has remained true to the principles that propelled her into the spotlight. No doubt she sees a kindred spirit in Ava.

'It's all coming together.' Ava shakes her head, as if astounded by her own success. 'And Judith found the perfect space in Brixton – between the grant and what I have saved, we'll just about make it work.'

The waitress returns then, and they scan the forgotten menus. Jean orders the salmon fillet, Ava the butternut squash. And it's easy losing herself in good food and better conversation. Ava's excitement is infectious as she goes over her plans for the next six months. Jean interjects with the odd pointer, relaxes into laughter, and basks in the simple pleasure of being the person Ava shares her hopes and dreams with.

But Ava doesn't dominate the conversation. She asks perceptive questions about Jean's work, and DDH. Though Jean is scrupulous in avoiding names, and Ava makes no attempts to probe beyond the veil of confidentiality, it's easy enough to convey the urgency of the office and the scope of opportunity ahead.

None of it sparks the same fervent excitement that Ava had demonstrated over the CJC, but then Jean has been at it for decades longer, and novelty always lends its own unique thrill. Representing the interests of Hephaestia, taking point as Peter contemplates retirement, it's not so much a new goal as the final stretch in a marathon Jean had mapped out for herself years ago. The high of satisfaction will surely come when Jean crosses the finish line and secures the ultimate promotion, presiding over the firm for the rest of her life – unlike Peter, she has no intention of retiring.

Still, Ava listens closely. And Jean doesn't shy away from the mundanity of her world outside DDH, certain it will deter feelings neither of them can afford. But Ava is delighted by the revelation of Jean's sessions with Grant.

'Oh my god, your personal trainer's a gym twink!' Ava drops her fork, laughing too much to eat without serious risk of choking. 'That's priceless.'

'What on earth is a twink?'

This question only sets off a fresh wave of giggles. 'A young gay guy, on the camp end of the spectrum. I just find it pretty funny.'

It's all going well, until she mentions dinner with Bernard; the pleasure of catching up with an old friend. The laughter between them is snuffed out in an instant, Ava's face a blank mask.

'You remember him, don't you? From the Knowledge Exchange workshop.'

'I do.'

There's a curtness to the response that Jean can't make head nor tail of. 'I thought you liked him. Bernard was the one who organised the tickets as a prize.'

'He seems like a really great guy.' Ava drives her spoon down hard enough to shatter the crust of her crème brûlée.

'Then why are you acting like you wish you could drive that spoon into his skull?'

Ava takes a breath, gaze fixed upon her napkin. In a quiet voice she says: 'I don't think you want to do this here.'

But Jean is out of patience. In the final months of her marriage, she'd endured enough of this unspoken discord to last a lifetime. She scans the surrounding tables – there's not a single face she recognises, and all the other diners are intent on their own candlelit meals. Still Jean doesn't understand it, how quickly the air in their own little bubble has shifted. 'No – we're doing this here and now.' Jean leans forward, pushing her pistachio ice cream aside. 'Tell me what's going on with you rather than subjecting me to passive aggression.'

'You really want to know?'

'That's what I said, isn't it?'

'What you say and what you do aren't always…' Ava shakes her head, curls bouncing around her collar. 'Fine, but you don't get to act pressed when I tell you.'

'How can I know what my reaction will be until you've said your piece?'

Ava simply stares, unyielding.

'Alright. Whatever it is, I'll give you a fair hearing.'

Ava nods slowly, pressing her lips together. In the background Edith Piaf warbles about unlikely dreams. 'I saw how Bernard looked at you. He was thrilled when you asked him out for dinner.'

Incredulous laughter spills from Jean's mouth. That Ava should be jealous of Bernard… It's clear she doesn't see the funny side, though, looking anywhere except at Jean. 'But I wasn't asking him out; not in the way you're suggesting.'

'Maybe not.' Ava stares at the tea light as if it contains the secrets of the universe. Twin reflections glimmer bright in her eyes. 'But you could have been. And he'd get to be more than a sex acquaintance.'

'I don't—' Jean lowers her voice, slides a surreptitious hand across the table until her fingertips brush Ava's. She looks up at the contact, meeting Jean's eyes. 'I don't want more than an acquaintance.'

Ava swallows. Continues as if Jean hadn't spoken. 'He'd get more than one night like this.'

Jean shakes her head, her voice low and urgent. 'Bernard wouldn't even get one night like this. Because I have no intention of going home with him. He's a good man, but he's not... not my preferred acquaintance material.'

And Ava's unable to resist the baited hook. 'You're coming home with me?'

'I'd been planning to, before you went all *Fatal Attraction*.' But there's no sting to her words, softened by the memory of Ava's understanding when – in a fit of blind panic – she had parted ways with logic and gone a little Alex Forrest herself. 'Still will, if you want. Perhaps we both have a little Glenn Close in us.'

'Maybe.' Ava's thumb skims Jean's knuckles, and every last atom in her body becomes freshly aware of the woman sitting opposite.

But then the waitress arrives to take their empty plates and Jean pulls away, lifting her wineglass to drain the dregs.

Chapter Fourteen

Ava leaves her resentment in the restaurant, and the last of the strangeness between them melts away as they approach the theatre. Ava insists on taking pictures before the glowing marquee, a grinning selfie, and a shot with Jean. 'For Robert, obviously,' Ava says when she hesitates. 'It should be enough to get him off your back about helping me out.' And though Jean has her doubts about Ava's motives, she edges into the frame.

Inside the stately old theatre, they join the press of people queuing. Ava flashes their tickets, and the usher points them upstairs. Jean follows her up the red carpeted staircase and through the snaking corridor, down the short flight bisecting the curved rows of seating. It's easy enough to find their places: front row in the circle, with a perfect view of the stage below. Jean's unable to resist making an enquiry, 'How do you feel about Bernard now?'

'A true prince among men,' Ava says. 'I'll name my firstborn cat after him.'

Jean laughs, her knees pressing against the swell of Ava's thigh as they let a trio of teenage girls past. 'No doubt he'll be honoured. But I thought the cat thing was a stereotype.'

'Not even a little bit.' Ava leans in close to be heard over the cacophony of voices, lips grazing the lobe of Jean's ear. 'Lesbians love pu—'

'That's low-hanging fruit,' Jean retorts, ignoring the irrepressible tingle between her thighs.

'Well… if I can't impress you with my wordplay, how about my snack provision skills?' Ava rifles in her rucksack. 'I brought us a Twix each. And jellybeans. For Jellybean.'

Jean's heart flutters as she accepts the bag, like she's some blushing seventeen-year-old out on her first real date. 'There's no possible way you can eat sweets after a two-course meal.'

'Bet,' is all Ava says.

Then the lights dim, and an expectant hush falls over the crowd. Ava sits up straight, watching avidly as the curtain rises, and her anticipation is catching. The music is fun, the lyrics whip smart. But it's the story that really gets to Jean. A self-made orphan with a thirst to prove himself; a lawyer with the ingenuity to use his profession as a ladder and climb.

Every so often Jean catches Ava staring not at the cast, despite the extraordinary magnetism of their performances, but at her. She's drinking in Jean's reactions as surely as the musical itself. And every time, Jean returns her smile before turning back to the stage, self-conscious as she senses Ava's gaze upon her.

The truth of it is that Jean had expected Ava's interest to ebb over time, once the thrill of introducing a novice to lesbian desires wore off. To be replaced by a string of nubile new conquests who never sweated through her sheets. Yet here Ava is, taking Jean's hand under a blanket of shadows. Giving Jean a cutesy nickname and bringing her snacks – which, Jean must admit, are incredibly moreish. And all through their candlelit dinner she'd looked upon Jean with more hunger than at the delicious spread before them.

In any other scenario, this evening would make a perfect date. Ava must be thinking along the same lines, with her talk of *Bernard* and *other nights*. And Jean accepts that it's her own fault for muddying the waters with talk of friendship. Yet, it occurs to her, every previous erosion of the boundaries between them has been Ava's handiwork.

Jean's first thought is a threat: *If you tell anyone that I cried over a musical, then so help me God...* But then the lights come up and Ava's face is shining with tears too. Jean's mascara is unsalvageable – waterproof was false advertising. Ever practical, Ava reaches into her rucksack and produces a pack of wet wipes, which Jean gratefully accepts. 'I may not have been a Scout,' Ava quips, 'but I do always try to be prepared.' And just like that her tears are no longer a source of shame.

It's easy between them, so easy, on the tube ride from Covent Garden to East Ham. Jean grows animated swapping details about which lyrics they'd enjoyed, which scenes had moved them. On her phone Ava displays a picture of the year she'd gone as Alexander Hamilton to Heaven's Halloween party, complete with pencilled-on facial hair and a straightened ponytail in the style of Lin-Manuel Miranda. It's utterly ridiculous, yet there's something undeniably dashing about Ava in costume.

'Let me get this straight,' Jean says. 'You wore this to a gay venue. Where you were hoping to attract other women?'

Ava's grin takes on a gloating quality. 'There was no "hoping" about it. Drag kings are always popular, and Alexander's reliable with the ladies.'

The tube rocks them, roaring through a dark tunnel. 'I don't know how to respond to that.'

'So, we won't be doing Hamilton roleplay any time soon. Good to know.'

On the way back to Ava's, walking through the cool night air, Jean's jaw aches with the effort of stifling yawn after yawn.

Ava makes a pot of coffee on her little stove – Jean should insist on decaf this late, but there's no resisting that rich aroma. As Ava brews the grounds, Jean can't help searching out the details of Hamilton's life. Later, when her brain isn't sluggish with sleep, Jean will track down verifiable resources. But – for now – she settles for Wikipedia, squinting at the tiny print.

Born out of wedlock in Charlestown, Nevis, Hamilton was orphaned as a child... And the truth behind Ava's bucket list slides into focus. 'You want to go to Nevis because he was born there! Of course.'

Ava returns with two mugs of coffee and a plate of sugared amaretto biscuits balanced on a tray. 'Nice detective work, Jellybean.'

Jean folds both legs underneath herself, making room for Ava to sit, and accepts the proffered coffee. 'You really admire him.'

It's not a question.

Ava nods. 'As a lawyer, anyway. He didn't treat the women in his life particularly well. But Hamilton was brilliant too. The way he used the law as a tool to reshape the world, to build... That inspires me.'

'No wonder you want to make a pilgrimage.'

'One day.' Ava ducks her head as she drinks. 'It would mean a lot to me.'

A companionable silence settles between them, broken only by the faint pulse of music from a neighbouring flat. Jean sips from the steaming cup until its contents revive her.

In a few hours the sun will climb high enough to wash over the estate, glittering bright in every column of windows. It'll melt the dew from the grass, and burn through the tender shoots of friendship growing between her and Ava. If Jean is to make any kind of confession, now is the time. 'I'm sorry I shot you down over the bucket list question in Bernard's workshop. I wasn't trying to give you nothing. And I'm sorry it came across that way.'

Ava neither accepts nor declines the apology, but she rests a reassuring hand against the curve of Jean's knee as she thinks, touch warm through sheer tights. 'Then what was it?'

'I didn't know what I wanted.' Jean lifts a biscuit from the plate, more for something to do with her hands than from any real hunger. 'It's been so long since I've thought to want anything outside of my career goals. They've defined everything – had to, for me to reach this point. But now I'm about to get everything I hoped for, and I wonder...'

'What?' Ava's voice is gentle, her expression free from judgement. There's only the same intent curiosity that Jean still hasn't grown used to sparking.

'I wonder what will be left to want for after this next promotion.' Only when the words hang in the air between them does it occur to Jean, just how much she has exposed here. 'God, that's depressing. Forget I said anything – I drank too much at dinner.'

But Ava only shakes her head. 'It's natural to feel that way. It's how the rat race is designed. We make getting to the next big thing our priority – a degree, a pay rise, a promotion, a new job – and that urgency doesn't leave much room for reflection. But it's good to start asking yourself those questions.'

'It is?' Nothing about the gaping, empty pit that's opened up beneath her feels good. Success is like walking a tightrope: the balancing act only works if you don't look down.

'Definitely.' Ava pops a biscuit into her mouth and chews, spraying crumbs over herself in her excitement. 'Hey, that's what we'll do! Before we go to sleep, we'll brainstorm bucket list ideas.'

The sweetness of it forms an ache behind Jean's breastbone. 'Ava, it's after midnight—'

'But still night. You said friendship for one night only – as far as I'm concerned, that counts until morning.' Still Ava watches her, and the magnetic lure of those big brown eyes pulls Jean back in.

'You're such a lawyer.' Jean reaches out to tuck a stray curl behind her ear, hair she will never grow tired of knotting her fingers in, at once silken and springy.

'Guilty as charged.' Ava covers Jean's hand with her own, holding it in place against her cheek. 'But I think that's why you like me, or at least part of it.'

'Mm.' Jean neither confirms nor denies, but she's had the same thought herself about the ease between them. She brushes the downy skin of Ava's cheek with her thumb.

Ava closes her eyes, leaning into the touch. Her breath is warm against the inside of Jean's wrist. 'Let's start off simple. Are there any new places you want to visit?'

In the earlier years of Jean's marriage, Henry had taken great pleasure in planning trips to all the obvious destinations. Paris, Venice, Rome... everywhere that the world was meant for two. And as she'd climbed the ranks at DDH there came skiing trips in the Swiss Alps, weeks spent sunning herself and swimming through the tropical blue ocean by Peter's home in the Bahamas. If the marriage had lasted, no doubt Henry would have suggested a sunny second home of their own. But after the divorce there was no longer any need to maintain the pretence of caring about time off.

'Not the southwest,' Jean says, conscious that Ava is watching her. 'Not Devon. Beyond that... I don't know.'

'If you don't want to go southwest, you could go northeast.' At last Ava breaks away, retrieving her phone from the table and scanning a map of Britain. 'What about... Edinburgh?'

Jean sets her empty cup and saucer down. 'Why there?'

'Why not?' Ava shrugs. 'The whole point of a bucket list is to experience new things. It doesn't have to be that deep. Mine includes going to the USA for a stack of IHOP pancakes.'

The castle, Arthur's Seat, craggy beaches... It's not a bad thought. 'Alright. My bucket list now has one item.'

'That's one hundred per cent more than it had this time yesterday.' Ava drops a kiss on Jean's forehead. 'Well done.'

Jean rests her cheek against the curve of Ava's shoulder, warm and full and close to contentment. Her eyelids are heavy, even with the caffeine coursing through her body, but she blinks them open. She can't waste these stolen moments on sleep.

'Can I confess something potentially embarrassing?'

The words rouse Jean. She lifts her head, intrigued. 'More or less embarrassing than dressing up as a Founding Father?'

'Eh...' Ava's shrug turns into a stretch, mouth twisting as she swallows back a yawn. And her arm drapes around Jean's shoulder. 'Depends on where you're sitting, I suppose.'

'Oh, don't be a tease. Tell me.'

Beside her, there's an unnatural stillness to Ava's body, like she's forgotten how to breathe. 'I just – I wish this night didn't have to end.'

Jean's eyes prickle. And she curses that stupid heartfelt fucking musical for bringing her emotions so close to the surface, blinking away her tears. 'Me too.'

Though Ava's face is blurred, she hears the sharp intake of breath. 'Yeah?'

All Jean can do is nod. She clears her throat, forcing down a swallow of the coffee. 'Yes. It's been a long time since I've done anything like this with anyone. And I had a really good time with you, Ava.'

The cushions shift, then Ava's crawling along the sofa to cup Jean's cheek, thumb catching the edge of her cheekbone. 'But don't you see? We could keep having good times together, just like tonight.'

Jean twists away, taking in their silhouettes reflected in the television's flat blank screen. 'No. Ava, I was clear from the beginning. A romantic relationship with another woman doesn't fit into my life. That's not the person I am, not really. And I can't change it now, not when I'm so close to having everything.'

'I'm not talking about romance. And you don't have to change anything.' Ava kneels on the cushion, imploring. 'We keep hooking up. But we also hang out socially. Maybe we could go to the theatre again, or a wine bar now and then. Or – if we're too busy – you could bring your laptop round and we could just work together.'

There aren't enough coffee grounds in the City of London to keep her exhaustion at bay. 'Ava—'

'No, seriously. Think about it like an upgrade; a way of making things more… efficient. Our social and sexual needs taken care of in the same relationship – two for the price of one.'

It's all but impossible making friends outside of the law – the nine to five crowd don't understand why anyone would choose the kind of job where a phone call could whisk you away at a moment's notice to firefight on multiple fronts, never mind why anyone would relish it. And those who harbour similar professional ambitions are often just as busy. Henry hadn't understood – the scale of his goals waning as the years passed by – and he'd nursed a grudge over every dinner cancelled, every holiday interrupted.

But Ava's not the type to get pissy if Jean's plans change at the last minute. If anything, with a fledgling charity to nurture, she's just as liable to request a rain check at short notice. And Jean can't deny it calls to her, the possibility of more nights like this; the image of them working separately yet side by side. 'I suppose that might be viable.'

'Yeah! I mean, the term fuck buddies *does* indicate a friendship dimension to the relationship.'

'You're not wrong.' Jean nods as the idea takes root. 'Friends with benefits, people do call it that.'

And what harm can there be in Jean having her pistachio ice cream and eating her jellybeans too?

Chapter Fifteen

Andreas Leonides is smaller than photographs suggested, barrel chested with stubby legs. There was a time when Jean would have worn her most diminutive court shoes to this first meeting – and every other. But that time has passed. She steps forward in suede green Louboutins, heels clicking against marble, offering the first hand Leonides shakes upon striding across the atrium.

His grip is a vice, and Jean returns the pressure until bone shifts beneath the pads of her fingers.

'Mr Leonides, it's a pleasure to welcome you. I speak for the whole of DDH when I say that we're thrilled to have you.'

'Andreas, please.' Even after releasing Jean's hand, Leonides fixes her with those steely blue eyes. 'And may I call you Jean?'

It's not a question, not really. So, Jean nods, exposing an appropriate flash of teeth.

'Andreas, then.' Peter doesn't so much as flinch as Leonides grasps him by the hand. And there, glinting in his eyes, is the sharp edge of ambition. Jean thought it lost to years spent winnowing down his handicap. But it was simply lying in wait; an old friend she hadn't been aware of missing.

Upstairs they settle in the biggest conference room, the firm on one side of the oval table, Leonides and his entourage from Hephaestia on the other. Pastries and green bottles of San Pellegrino mark out the no man's land in between. As the team presents, Jean takes stock of the Hephaestia team. She recognises their people from the briefing documents, from headshots posted on the company website, from press conferences and shaky footage of the shareholder meeting.

Ekaterina Nowicki sits at Leonides' right hand as Hephaestia's head of communications — though she remains largely silent throughout, her dark eyes glitter like polished onyx as she takes in every last detail. Three times she bows her head, a curtain of dark hair obscuring her mouth as she whispers into Leonides' ear. And three times he angles his body to listen, turning away from whomever else might be speaking at that moment.

Conversely, Hephaestia's general counsel is a vocal participant in the meeting. Layton Wexler — a good old boy dripping with Southern charm, missing only the lariat and pistol at his hip to complete the image of a cowboy — interjects often, seemingly whenever the mood takes him. But Wexler's drawl and folksy witticisms are nothing more than a smokescreen for that reptilian mind.

Though she spends little time on the front lines these days, Jean can see what it would be like to go up against him in court, the one-two punch of showboating and sharp wit. An inexperienced lawyer might be lured in by the music of Wexler's voice, dancing to his tune before they realised — Jean makes a mental note to keep a close eye on the junior associates.

Then Rhona rises, replacing Andrew before the projector's glow. And though Rhona's expression is mild, Jean gets the distinct impression she's enjoying herself as she asks Hugo to change the slide — competition to wash away the nerves, sure as a shot of bourbon. Jean will find a way to make this last-minute personnel change up to him, but there's so much more at stake than the ego of a single junior associate.

Rhona warms to her topic, enthusiasm matching knowledge. Even the jocular doubts of Wexler, whose family wealth sprung from Texan oil fields, aren't enough to throw her off the scent. Nowicki murmurs something, and Leonides nods approval.

Jean flashes the junior associate a rare smile as she fields questions. Though nobody could accuse Rhona's suit of being stylish, it is at least well-tailored. And with her hair pinned back in a bun, Rhona has every appearance of a woman growing to be comfortable in her own skin. In this way Jean will grow the firm, beyond what Will Decker ever imagined possible.

—

Ava's proposal of working together proves a godsend; those companionable hours are her only incentive to leave the office. Ava's energy grants her a second wind. With the months dwindling away to weeks before Ava leaves ACWRC for good, she's tying up loose ends while laying the groundwork for her future, as well as running herself ragged with overtime to compensate for her guilt over leaving. In spare moments, Jean can't resist helping – redrafting an email to sound more authoritative, providing introductions with firms likely to donate time and resources, and the less quantifiable task of holding faith when Ava is plagued by doubt.

There are nights when they lose themselves in each other, and just as many when they curl up together, exhausted. As those nights together stack up, Jean can't resist the tug of responsibility, a compulsion to keep Ava from subsisting on Twixes and Monster Energy drinks. During a late-night call with Peter, Jean fries them up a mushroom omelette – simple yet filling, and far less fattening than Iri's fare. Ava wolfs it down so eagerly that Jean takes to cooking for them, always adding a third portion to the fridge in the hope Ava will consume at least one vegetable in the time they're apart. It works, too – even the Tupperware filled with spinach and garlic sits gleaming on the draining board by her next visit.

On weekends Ava insists they get up and out, strolling around Plashet Park or meandering through East Ham Nature Reserve, savouring the churchyard quiet of St Mary Magdalene. To her surprise, Jean adores the latter – an unlikely reprieve from London's relentless urgency. She takes a morbid pleasure in finding the graves of those lost aboard the Titanic. And though the headstones are weathered, the church crumbling, new life is relentless even in the face of decay. Tiny chiffchaffs flit from branch to branch among the plush green leaves. Bluebells carpet the ground and perfume the air.

The reprieve from texts and calls, emails and Slack channels, is golden. There is no particular need for Jean to be anything other than present in this soft intimacy; a closeness that binds them even without hand-holding or kisses. Though there are moments when Jean catches herself slipping; wishing for the possessive warmth of Ava's palm against her back, but in public Ava's restraint is meticulous.

And yet, in private moments, the solidifying friendship between them enables Ava to grow bold. 'Can I ask you something?'

Jean looks up from her document, taking off her reading glasses to scrub tired eyes. 'Evidently: you just did.'

But Ava doesn't meet snark with snark – and her pensive expression alerts Jean to the fact that something bigger is coming. Sure enough: 'No, I meant... something personal.'

Wary, Jean saves her progress, though she doesn't close the laptop – work may yet prove a welcome refuge. 'Such as?'

'We've done a lot of stuff, right?'

'You'll have to be more specific.'

'Things you hadn't tried before.' Ava licks her lips. 'But things you enjoy.'

Every act a revelation, Jean thinks. *No use denying it.* 'Go on.'

'But we're also... friends. So, can I ask you something? With my friend hat on?'

'You could have asked me several somethings by now.'

Again, the barb merely glances off Ava. She clicks her pen open and closed against the tabletop. 'There's something I've been wondering about. Specifically, why you never want me going down on you.'

Heat scalds Jean's cheeks, though when she presses her fingertips against the blush Jean's skin remains smooth, unblistered. 'That's not a friend question.'

Ava shrugs, the strap of her camisole slipping down a smooth bare shoulder. 'Sure it is. Women talk about sex with their friends. Classic female bonding ritual.'

'Well, yes.' Jean clicks open a new window, but doesn't add anything to the Google Doc. 'Platonic friends. Not the female friends they're also having sex with.'

Ava's brows climb. 'Oh, so you're an expert in sapphic friendships now?'

A look is all it takes to blunt that mocking edge. Whatever else has shifted underneath the surface, at least Jean has that to fall back on.

'Okay, okay. But you can ask for things. You know that, right?'

The concern knitting her brows together is genuine, yet Jean can't help but laugh. 'I never have to, not with you. This is complicated for me, in so many ways, but – in that regard – you make it very simple.'

'If you don't want to, I'll respect that. Of course I will.' Ava picks at the laminated corner of a placemat. 'But this is a first for me too. I've never been with a woman that didn't want...'

'Well, you could always find another sex acquaintance if you feel something's missing.'

'That's not what I'm saying,' Ava says, voice deliberately even. 'And I think you know that.'

'Yes. I do.'

A beat.

'Look, don't take it personally. I never enjoyed that.' Jean's gaze remains fixed on the blinking cursor. She doesn't want to see pity or any of its cousins peering at her from soulful brown eyes. 'Why do you care so much, anyway? It's not like you get anything out of it.'

Ava's head whips round so quickly that her hair is shaken free from the confines of an elastic, springing wild around her shoulders. A whole myriad of expressions flit across her face, faster than Jean can make sense of them. Finally, her lips curve. 'You're kidding, right?'

'No? You don't have to feel obliged.'

'Obli—' Ava covers her face with both hands, tilting forward so a thick curtain of curls covers her face. Several seconds pass before she composes herself, and Jean wishes the ground would open up and swallow her whole – a feeling that only escalates as Ava continues to speak. 'Jean. You're talking about it like an obligatory side of Brussels sprouts. But I see it like chocolate chip brownies. Fresh hot puff-puff. Coconut ice cream.'

Personally, Jean would rather faceplant into a bowl of *escargot*. But each to their own. She smiles, in spite of herself, bemused. 'A king-sized Twix bar?'

'Now you're getting it!' Ava slaps the table. 'Not literally. I'm not trying to pressure you. In fact, forget I said anything at all.'

They each retreat into their own work until it's time for sleep, Jean reading over Rhona's query about how to approach Wexler in the conversation about renewables. And they are scrupulously polite while getting ready for bed.

Ava makes a final adjustment to her scarf, reaches for the lamp, and blankets them in darkness. There is nothing sexual about their embrace. But Jean can't forget those earlier words. In fact, as Ava nuzzles into her side, it's all she can think about. How the mouth pressed against the hollow of her neck might feel pressed instead to the hollow between her thighs.

Jean doesn't get much in the way of sleep that night, hyperaware of the blankets brushing against her skin, the warmth of Ava's body beside her. In the morning, she rises before Ava wakes, yawning her way through a session with Grant. But he senses her mood and avoids any speculation about Jean's nocturnal activities. She is, after all, first among his executive clients. And Jean throws herself into the workout, determined to burn off all surplus energy.

Even so, the thought plagues her. Between meetings, in the car to and from work, Jean's mind wanders. Ava's fingers pluck the sweetest notes of pleasure from Jean's body; with the strap she has every nerve singing an ecstatic symphony. What, then, might her tongue do? Ava's mouth at her breast has worked such wonders that Jean's come from her suckling alone – the first time Jean thought it a fluke, the second a miracle. One by one, Ava has unearthed her body's secrets – capabilities and a carnality that Jean had assumed lost beneath an ocean of Catholic shame.

And though Jean shuns Ava every evening that week, ignoring the invitations, it's herself she punishes. Her underlings put Jean's sharpness down to Leonides – mixed in among the genuine requests are tests of DDH's mettle. Moral dilemmas intended to uncover how much they're willing to ignore. Even with the ink drying on the contract, Leonides remains cautious – paranoid, even. But that refusal to settle into anything resembling trust has kept him going all these years, the difference between an average man and a juggernaut.

Simple longing comes as a relief, by comparison. Though Jean despises the weakness of her own flesh. A menopausal woman horny as a teenager, and with that same lack of regard for consequences. Even her dreams are no safe harbour. Ava's tongue delving inside her cunt. Ava's tongue suckling until she begs for mercy. Ordinarily dreams trickle away like sand as she tries to hold on to them, but this image imprints itself on her mind. And each time it surfaces, Jean must cross her legs.

After a final meeting with Wexler about Gaia's Children, Jean has Bogdan drop her at the tube station. She offers him nothing by way of excuse or explanation, only her thanks, and gets the underground straight through to East Ham. All the way a dull pulse echoes between Jean's legs, keeping time with every rattle and clack of the train.

Chapter Sixteen

Ava opens the door, clad in a raincoat and subtle bronze lipstick. Her hair's in a bun – not scraped back like at conference, but pinned proud on top of her head, loose curls framing her face. She looks beautiful. And she looks like someone about to leave for a night out.

'Jean,' she says. 'I wasn't expecting you.'

'Sorry. I should've realised you'd have plans – it's Friday night. I just... I wanted to talk to you.' Jean backs away, pressing the button to summon the lift. 'Never mind. It can wait.'

'Come in for a bit. I don't need to leave right now.'

Even mashing the button doesn't bring the blasted lift. 'No, no. It was nothing important.'

Ava steps out into the hallway, covering Jean's hand with her own. 'Come in.'

Inside, Jean lingers by the door, toying with an opal on her ring as she speaks. 'I've been thinking. About what you asked me.'

Ava's expression remains carefully blank, but her breath stutters – silence, then a sweet little gasp. The exact same sound she makes whenever Jean catches a nipple between her teeth. 'Yeah?'

'Yes.' Jean shifts her weight from foot to foot, the friction offering a moment's relief to the ache between her thighs. 'Actually, I can't stop thinking about it. Day or night. I keep trying to imagine what it would feel like.'

'Fuck,' Ava breathes. Her eyes close, and the knowledge that Ava's picturing it — savouring the thought of her sex — has slick heat pooling silken smooth between Jean's thighs.

'Precisely. It's been torture.'

Ava licks her lips. And when she opens her eyes, there's resolve in the set of her jaw. 'Hang on. Just let me text Lin and Petra to cancel. Then you're all mine.'

A pulse jump starts in Jean's clit, relentless. Yet her conscience prickles. 'If you've made plans, you should keep them. We can do this another night.'

Ava scoffs. 'Don't be such a tease — you can't just show up talking about how you've been dreaming of me eating you out then act like it's no big deal.'

'It's not the only thing that matters.' The words ring hollow even to Jean's ears.

'But it is a particular fantasy of mine.' Ava's thumbs fly across the screen, and there's the whoosh of an outgoing message.

And Jean knows that she should feel guilty. That she's crossing all kinds of lines, and there's nothing remotely casual about her behaviour. But the tension melts from her shoulders in an instant. Ava has chosen her; this untameable thing between them. 'You're staying, then?'

'I'm staying.' Fondness softens the sharp edge of lust in Ava's eyes. 'Listen, if a hot woman showed up on their doorstep begging to get eaten out, I'd want Lin and Petra to live their best lives too — they're in an open relationship.'

Jean bristles. 'I did not beg.'

'Not yet.' Ava steps closer, into Jean's space. So close that Jean must look up to meet her gaze. 'But you will.'

Lust rolls over in the pit of Jean's belly. 'Prove it.'

Ava's eyes darken, pupil melting into iris. She pulls the combs free from Jean's hair and tangles both hands in, pulling just hard enough that Jean tilts her head up for a kiss.

They end up on the bed, limbs knotted like vines. And Jean rocks against the sharp point of Ava's hip, craving friction. Her bliss proves short-lived: Ava wriggles away, pinning both wrists above Jean's head.

She cups Jean's sex with her free hand, surely able to feel the heat of it even through tights and silk. But the touch is fleeting. Even when Jean whimpers, Ava doesn't return the pressure. Instead, she descends, rolling Jean's tights down, inch by inch, pausing to kiss every last square centimetre of newly exposed flesh. Her lips find the hollow behind Jean's knee, a startling intimacy. Her fingertips trace a vein down Jean's calf, ghostly pale beside the bronze of Ava's skin.

Then Ava works her way up the other leg, eyes meeting Jean's as she plants a trail of kisses up the swell of her inner thigh. Jean shifts so that her legs tip open – a not-so-subtle hint – and Ava's smile becomes wicked. She plants a kiss square against Jean's cunt through the thin scrap of satin, already hopelessly ruined, contoured to her folds by desire.

The sight of it, or maybe the scent, drives Ava into a frenzy. She nuzzles Jean's sex, the fleeting pressure of it stealing a gasp from Jean's throat.

'Fuck,' Ava says, in a dazed voice. 'You're so wet.'

Jean inches her thighs together, swallowing back disappointment. It's not as if she's in a hurry to bury her face in another woman's slippery want, so why should she expect the same in return? 'Sorry. You're right.' She sits up, glad the fairy lights are dim enough to conceal the worst of her flush. 'I'm all sticky – it'd be too messy.'

But Ava only smiles, resting a hand on Jean's bare knee. 'Oh Jean, that's the point. You're delicious and I want a proper taste.'

Jean's pulse quickens, the throb of it rattling in her very teeth. 'It's not something that's ever done much for me – and you should know that I've never come that way.'

Even in the early days of her marriage to Henry, it had felt like being lapped at with the finesse of a dog drinking from its water bowl. By tacit agreement they'd removed cunnilingus from their sexual repertoire, and Jean has turned it down from all her one-night stands since.

But Ava's undeterred. 'That sounds like a challenge.' Though for all her confidence she stays put, tracing Jean's rib with her fingertips. 'Do you really not want me to?'

'It hasn't worked for me before, and I don't want you to be disappointed if you can't get me there.' Jean flops back against the pillows. 'Don't feel obliged to keep going – you can stop when you're bored.'

'I don't think that's going to be a problem,' Ava says, with the rigid expression of someone trying not to laugh. But a crease appears between her brows. 'You sure you're up for this? Sweet as you taste, I'm not going to do anything if you don't want it.'

Jean laughs, reaching down to stroke Ava's mop of curls. 'I trust you. And, well – I'm curious.'

Jean's thighs relax, sinking into the mattress. And Ava's breath comes sharp and urgent as she draws close, though her touch is gentle now.

She puts an arm beneath Jean's thigh, bringing it to rest pillowed against her shoulder. Places her other hand on the swell of Jean's lower belly. And Jean winces at the direct contact with a problem area she was unable to shift even in her early twenties – FUPA, as Grant calls it, claiming even Beyoncé struggled wit— *FUCK.*

The glide of Ava's tongue obliterates all coherent thought. Jean's hips arc from the mattress of their own volition. Only the arm locked round her waist keeps Jean from bloodying her nose.

Ava pulls back, breath hot against Jean's thighs. Her shiny lips stretch into a smile. 'You alright, Jellybean?'

'Y-yes.' A shuddering breath. Her body's taut as a bowstring. 'Don't stop.'

A huff of laughter blows through her pubic hair. Then Ava bows her head. Her mouth is on her, tongue circling, probing, always teasing.

Ava sucks Jean's clit into her mouth. And Jean's brain short circuits. The tip of Ava's tongue catches that tender pearl again and again, flicking until she writhes. Only when her lungs begin to burn does it occur to Jean that mewling sound is coming from her own mouth. She scarcely has time to draw in a shaky breath before Ava's fingers play at her entrance, pushing Jean to the very precipice.

Then Ava thrusts inside, fingers curling against Jean's front wall. And there's no controlling the tremor that runs through her body, no escaping that tongue. Ava holds fast as Jean bucks against her, lashing Jean's clit through the storm of her climax, holding her on a knife edge between pleasure and pain.

Jean's too weak to push her away as the orgasm ebbs. But Ava, better versed in Jean's pleasure than any other, draws back. She presses one final kiss against the inside of Jean's thigh and climbs up the bed.

The lower half of her face is coated in Jean's desire — even her nose shines with it. And even after Ava wipes it off with a tissue, her eyes remain wild; intoxicated. Yet Ava's gentle as she folds Jean into her arms, stroking her hair until Jean stills.

'You alright?'

Though her muscles feel limp as cooked spaghetti, Jean manages to nod. She rests a hand against Ava's collarbone, trusting the gesture to say what words cannot.

'Go to sleep. I've got you.'

'What about…?' Jean trails a limp hand down Ava's belly. But before she can reach her destination Ava takes it, presses a kiss to the back of Jean's knuckles, and brings their linked fingers to rest outside the duvet.

'It's been a big night for you. And I loved every second of it.' The brush of lips against her temple. 'Rest now.'

And Jean does.

—

In the morning Ava takes great pleasure — almost as much as Jean — in a repeat performance. She kisses a trail from Jean's lips, down her collarbone and throat. Months have passed, and the wonder she finds in Jean's breasts shows no sign of dulling. Fervent lips lock around her nipple, Ava's tongue lashing the bud into a stiff peak.

Only when Jean knots her fingers in those silken brown curls and pushes Ava's head down does she move on. Ava covers Jean's cunt with her mouth, tongue darting inside until Jean's trembling grows uncontrollable. Then Ava hums as her tongue finds purchase on Jean's clit, and that vibration as she suckles sends Jean tipping headfirst over the edge.

Ava doesn't relent there. With Jean's sex at eye-level, she skates her fingers through the slippery folds.

'Show me yours,' Jean says, and for a moment she fears that vein might burst. But Ava shimmies out of her pyjama shorts and gets on all fours, a knee planted either side of the cinch in Jean's waist. Then she bends over, raising those pert cheeks to the ceiling, and her centre opens to Jean.

With dawn's gilded light pouring through the window, it's the best view Jean's ever had of another woman's sex. And not even Ava's stroking can distract her from this prize. Of all the words that could spring to mind, *pretty* is the last one Jean expects. Something of a vulva's look and texture reminds her unavoidably of molluscs, slimy invertebrates curled in a shell. Yet Ava's pussy is tantalising, her labia neat and even. And Jean's hand rises of its own volition to chase the secret flash of pink at her core.

Ava's thighs tremble as Jean's fingers delve and curl, diving to catch a pearl. And the glisten of her sex, the briney sharpness of her perfume, only urges Jean on. It would be easy to hook both arms around Ava's unresisting waist and pull her down close enough to taste. Panic paralyses Jean, a great wall of it rising in her chest; an impenetrable barrier to the orgasm Ava's stroking offers.

Yet Ava herself bucks against Jean's fingers, cunt clenching. A gasping cry tears from her throat, and she slumps to the side, boneless. But even then, Ava continues her quest, intent on Jean's pleasure. With a leg draped across Jean's chest, head pillowed on Jean's thigh, she pushes two fingers inside slow and easy, applying firm pressure.

With her tongue she laps at Jean's clit, the tip just glancing – tender from her last orgasm, it's all Jean can take.

Each time she withdraws there's an obscene slicking pop. But Jean's too far gone to care – though dawn's light has faded, it's as if she's absorbed the gold of sunrise through her skin where it licks at her insides, bathing them in pure delight. It fills Jean until there's no room for breath, no room for anything except the exquisite glide of Ava's fingers.

A spasmodic post-coital twitch runs though Jean as Ava's tongue makes a final swipe. And then, looking Jean dead in the eye, she licks her fingers clean. 'I can't get enough of the way you taste. It drives me fucking crazy.'

Jean huffs a laugh, sweat cooling in the valley between her breasts. It's been a long time since her body inspired such ardent confessions. 'I think you were already a little crazy to begin with.'

Rolling onto her side, Ava drags the duvet with her as she shuffles up the bed, draping it over them both. 'If that's true, I don't want to be sane.'

It's not long until Ava dozes, thigh draped across Jean's. But even under that welcome weight Jean can't join her in the land of nod.

Though Jean feigns sleep, her mind won't rest. While her limbs are heavy with the golden resonance of orgasm, there is no stilling those thoughts. A persistent fear burrows into her brain: what a cruel joke that Jean should only discover what had been missing now.

Ava smooths the hair back from Jean's brow and rolls out of bed, footsteps receding. A minute later comes the shower's dull hiss, the gurgling of pipes, while Jean contemplates the countless nights wasted. Years stacked one on top of the other. Decades, even.

All this time she could have been glorying in her body's capacity for pleasure. Not openly – there's no way Jean would have ascended so far in a straitlaced field while shouldering the double burden of being a woman *and* some manner of gay. Whenever June ends, every one of their corporate clients lose the rainbow lanyards and Pride-themed merch until next year, when making noise about inclusivity becomes advantageous again. But there could have been other arrangements, discreet and rewarding.

There had been moments with Mari, heads bowed together in laughter, those blue eyes sparkling with mirth, when Jean had imagined daring to close the gap; to press a kiss against her open lips. But Jean had been a sleep-deprived junior associate; on those long nights she'd also thought she'd heard, more than once, her parents' voices in the neighbouring office. Neither line of enquiry had felt worth pursuing – impossible yearnings better set aside.

Jean sits up, seizing her phone from the bedside table to deal with the inevitable messages. Rhona's a solid worker, bright and consistent, but her constant need for affirmation grates at Jean's nerves – it's a slow weaning process. She types:

> Again, good work. Though you don't need to run every detail by me outside our 1-2-1s. You have the skills to work independently: use them.

Seconds later, her phone pings with a response.

> Thank you, Ms Howard.

Ava returns then, a dressing gown wrapped around her body and a towel turbaned around her hair. 'Morning, sleepyhead.' Ava drops a kiss on her forehead. 'You okay?'

'I'm not made of spun glass. You don't have to keep asking me that.'

'I know.' The mattress shifts as Ava plops down beside her, dressing gown peeking open to offer a tantalising glimpse of thigh. 'But new experiences can bring stuff up. And I wanted to check in.'

'I'm fine.' Jean meets those worried eyes. 'Really.'

Ava's brow remains creased, a clear indication she doesn't wholly buy it. But — to Jean's relief — she doesn't press further. 'Alright. How about I cook breakfast while you shower. You've earned it.'

Jean doesn't quite follow the logic in that, given Ava did most of the work for both their orgasms. But she's too grateful to argue, stumbling into the shower on Bambi legs. She borrows Ava's shower gel, the steam scented with clean cedar. But even as Jean scrubs herself a fresh wave of lust hits.

She dresses quickly in a blouse and skirt creased from having spent the night in her bag. And Ava greets her with scrambled eggs, spinach and toast. They eat together at the table bathed in bright spring sunlight, upbeat Eighties pop playing on Ava's Bluetooth speaker. The music of Jean's youth. And Jean feels something of that old recklessness as she snakes her ankle round Ava's — the past has gone, taking Jean's juvenescence with it. *But there is now*, Jean thinks. *And to hell with casual behaviour.*

For her boldness she's rewarded with a kiss. And another. Ava's hands sinking into her hair, still loose and damp from the shower. Ava shifting to the seat beside hers, lean body curling around Jean's.

And Jean's fingers search out the feel of her skin, freshly moisturised with shea butter. She reaches beneath Ava's flannel shirt, the t-shirt underneath, and caresses a stomach that – for all she seems to live on Twix bars and takeaways – remains perfectly flat. Savours the sharp intake of breath as she reaches up to the hem of Ava's plain cotton bralette.

Then comes the unmistakable click of keys in the lock. They turn as one to watch the door swing open. A little girl with golden curls and light-up trainers bounces into the living room, closely followed by a woman who looks so like Ava that Jean's mind malfunctions.

'Evie, wash your hands please.' Aaliyah's top lip even has that same cupid's bow. 'You've touched every possible handle and button on the way here.'

The girl sighs, and Jean slides her hand free, giving Ava's shirt what she hopes is a surreptitious tug back in place.

'Okay, Mummy.' The child disappears into the bathroom.

Aaliyah's eyebrow, waxed into a perfect arch, climbs. 'Morning, baby sister.'

'There are six minutes between us,' Ava says, exasperated. 'Not nearly enough for you to be calling me that. Like you crammed so much life experience into three hundred and sixty seconds.'

'Well, it gave me enough of a head start that I've got myself and both kids fed, washed, and dressed; dropped Theo at rugby; and brought Evie here for a day with her favourite aunty.' Aaliyah's wry smile is the mirror image of her sister's. 'All in the time it's taken you to roll out of bed.'

Though Jean keeps her face carefully neutral, there's no doubt Aaliyah would have sussed them out, even if she hadn't caught Jean red-handed. She's just as sharp as her sister. But Ava doesn't seem to mind their meeting, giving a languid shrug in response to Aaliyah's inuendo. And this is what decides Jean's plan of action.

'Jean Howard.' She holds out a hand. 'Pleased to meet you. Ava mentioned she's a twin, and I've been curious about you.'

'Leah Clark. And I'm pretty curious too – most women my sister brings home disappear when the sun comes up, like vampires. But here you are.' Leah's gaze flits towards the empty plates and matching mugs, expression inscrutable as she takes in the undeniable air of domesticity. Then she takes Jean's hand, grip firm. 'Pleased to meet you.'

Something unreadable passes across Ava's face as she watches them shake, and Jean's still puzzling it out when Evie races back into the room then, the stars on her trainers glowing bright with every step. She collides with her mother's legs, hiding behind Aaliyah's skinny jeans.

'Morning, Peanut.' Though hoarse, there's an undeniable warmth to Ava's voice.

But the child glances at Jean through wary brown eyes.

'Hello there,' Jean says, immediately regretting her formality. She's always been terrible with children, had never known what to say to her nephews or niece until they reached the other side of puberty. Bridget had accused her of talking to them like little adults without ever explaining a viable alternative.

Like dogs, children have an uncanny gift for sniffing out discomfort. Evie continues to squint up at Jean. 'Why are you here?'

'*Evelyn.*' Her mother's whisper is sharp as a whip crack. 'What have I told you about minding your manners?'

But the child is undeterred. 'That I had to say please and thank you.' She looks back to Jean. 'What are you doing here, *please*?'

Ava's too busy giggling to be of any help.

Leah rolls her eyes heavenward. 'That is *so* not what I meant.'

'It's alright.' An ache blossoms in the apples of Jean's cheeks with the effort of trying to smile naturally. 'Ah... I'm a friend of your aunt's. I came over this morning to see if she wanted to spend some time together.'

'But Aunty Ava's taking me to the petting zoo today. They have lots of bunnies.'

'I— I did not know that.'

'Next time you should message first to check she isn't busy.'

'I'll bear that in mind.' Jean stands, checking her phone, although there are no new notifications. Not even from Rhona. How the junior associates would laugh to see Code Red getting demolished by a pre-schooler. 'Now I should probably—'

'But since you're here, you can come with us.' The girl nods, imperious as Caesar. And the window of time in which Jean could have reasonably extricated herself from whatever the hell this is slams shut. 'Just this one time. So you don't miss the bunnies.'

'That's very big of you, Peanut,' Ava says.

But her sarcasm passes over the curly little head. 'I know.'

'Well.' Aaliyah claps her hands together. 'I'll leave you three to your adventures. See you at five!'

Panic claws at Jean's chest as the mother kisses Evie and turns, closing the door behind her with dreadful finality. The implication being that she – Jean Howard – is now partially responsible for this child.

But neither aunt nor niece seems fazed by Aaliyah's departure. Evie chatters quite happily on the journey, first by foot and then by tube. On Ava's other side, as her lover asks serious questions about starting Rainbows, Jean can't help but wonder how she wound up here. How they went from red hot passion to rabbits.

And yet it's fascinating, this glimpse into Ava's life. She throws herself into the role of aunt with vigour, teasing and threading them both into the conversation until Evie grows used to Jean. Such outings are clearly regular events – Evie takes Ava's hand automatically as they step from the tube out into the busy station, and again each time they approach a road to cross.

In the queue for the petting zoo, where Ava matter-of-factly points out it's cheaper to get a family pass and insists on paying, Jean takes a chance with Evie. 'So,' she says, as they wait by the entrance. 'Why does Ava call you Peanut?'

'She says I looked like a peanut when I was born.' Her tiny nose wrinkles. 'But Mummy showed me photos and I was very cute.'

Still is, though Jean knows better than to voice such thoughts. 'You know, she calls me Jellybean.'

Evie giggles, exposing pearly white milk teeth. 'That's silly.'

'I think so too,' Jean says. 'But I don't mind. Not really.'

After that, she and Evie become allies of sorts. When Ava's arms grow tired, she lets Jean lift her up to continue patting the llamas, and all her hours with Grant pay off – though Evie is tiny, the child is solid, far heavier than Jean would have guessed. In return Evie allows Jean to stroke the velvety ears of the bunny sprawled across her lap – Jean pretends not to notice Ava photographing this moment. Evie even tips some of the feed from her paper packet onto Jean's hand as well as Ava's, so that all three of them can feed the chickens.

In the guinea pig enclosure, they watch as a staff member carries a sack laden with vegetables into the rodents' pen. The moment the boy steps through the gate, the fluffy creatures emit a chorus of high-pitched squeaks, swarming him so intently that Jean considers it a minor miracle none are crushed under his heavy work boots.

'Look at them go,' Jean says. 'Like ambulance chasers after a car crash.'

Ava laughs as the boy tips lettuce leaves, kale, and carrot out for the horde of furry menaces. 'That's the only thing I'd hate more than corporate – no offence.'

'None taken,' Jean says, surprised to find that she means it.

Evie tugs on Ava's sleeve. 'What's corporate?'

'It's the kind of law that Jean practises. To do with big, big companies.'

Evie looks up at Jean with fresh curiosity. 'Are you a lawyer like Aunty Ava?'

'You're right that I'm a lawyer.' Jean crouches to look Evie in the eye. 'But not quite like your aunt. I work with a firm, which is a group of lawyers that work together as a team. Like the guinea pigs surrounding that boy so he'll feed them faster.'

Evie considers. 'Do you put bad guys in jail?'

'Not often.' Jean's smile grows rueful; how to explain the ins and outs of her days in a way that won't dent a small child's faith in right and wrong? 'I make sure companies don't get in trouble, or I help them get bigger.'

'That's boring,' Evie says, watching two guinea pigs squabble over a carrot top.

'Peanut,' Ava chides.

But Jean only laughs. 'It can be dull. But tell me, what would you like to be when you grow up?'

'That's easy. I'm going to be prime minister.' The curly head tilts. 'Or a famous scientist. I haven't decided yet.'

They part ways at the train station, Ava shifting as if she means to hug Jean goodbye, only to freeze. And Jean is glad of her restraint, or should be – it's ridiculous to get wistful when they'll see one another again in two or three days. There's no telling when she'll see Evie again, though. So, Jean shakes the small hand, barely wide enough to span her own palm, and tells the girl it was a pleasure to meet her.

Chapter Seventeen

Hugo breezes into her office on a tide of Boucheron and braggadocio. He straddles the chair before Jean's desk and launches into an explanation of the meeting with Wexler's underlings; how they'd spent the session dotting the i's and crossing the t's – a concession here, a demand there. The whole time Nowicki had sat in the corner, silent and impassive – unsettling because neither he nor Rhona had been able to discern her purpose.

'I mean, it's not like she's a lawyer.' Hugo scoffs, not bothering to hide his disdain. 'Surely it would've made more sense for Wexler himself to be there.'

It's a valuable piece of the puzzle, even if Jean can't yet tell where it fits. Nowicki's purpose had nothing to do with the law – but what else might Leonides want from her? 'This is all very well, Hugo, but where's Rhona?'

A glint of annoyance flashes through his careful mask. 'She decided to delegate – said it would be alright if I briefed you instead.'

'And what's she doing that's so much more important?'

His mouth twists into a sneer. 'Mr Leonides called at the end of the meeting, and Ms Nowicki asked her to join them for dinner to discuss renewables, since he was *so excited about Rhona's vision*.'

Hugo might be incapable of seeing beyond his own jealousy, but Jean is not. The hairs on the back of her neck prickle. She leans forward. 'Where?'

Hugo blinks, taken aback. 'I— I don't know. It's not like I was invited.'

'Think!' Jean thumps the desk so hard her palm stings, the silver band on her finger chipping glass.

Hugo jolts upright. 'The Shard. They were going to The Shard. But there are seven different bars and restaurants in there, and I don't—'

'Come with me.' Jean snatches her phone from the desk and rises, retrieving her handbag.

The idiot boy gapes at Jean as if she's the one who's lost her mind. 'But I'm supposed to meet Alexander for—'

'Sod Alexander. You join me now and make this right or you find another firm – the choice is yours.' Jean strides from the room, not waiting to see whether Hugo follows, messaging her driver as she approaches the lift. Peter, of course, is long gone. There's no time to see who else could help – no time at all.

Hugo squeezes between the closing doors, quiff collapsing onto his forehead. 'Ms Howard, if I've done anything—'

Jean holds up a hand for silence, phone pressed to her ear with the other. The lift plunges towards the ground as the call rings out, going to voicemail. *'You've reached Rhona Baird. Sorry I'm not able to take your call ri—'*

'Fuck!' The walls are closing in on Jean, and Hugo's eyeing her with naked panic and confusion.

But just as the question forms on his lips the doors slide open and Jean runs across the lobby, flying past a baffled Helen and the paper bag containing her dinner, out onto the street. Hugo follows hot on her heels, all but colliding with Jean as she wrenches the car door open.

She ignores Hugo's apologies and slides across the leather seat. He's barely closed the door when Bogdan pulls out to join the stream of traffic. 'The Shard, Ms Howard?'

'Yes.' Sweat prickles under Jean's arms. 'Fast as you can, please.'

Still panting, Jean tries Rhona's number again, heart hammering against her ribs as the call goes to voicemail.

'Rhona, it's Jean. Please call me back as soon as you get this message.'

For good measure she types it out as a text. Bogdan swings round a corner, and as Jean sways towards Hugo it occurs to her that she hasn't fastened her seatbelt. She clips the buckle in place.

Hugo clears his throat. He's watching Jean warily, that eternal confidence withered away to nothing. But the junior associate can wait.

Jean tries to text Helen too, but her sweaty fingers keep slipping across the screen to produce garbled nonsense. The sooner there's a paper trail, the better. She settles on a voice note instead: 'Send an urgent message from my office to Leonides' PA, his secretary, and Ekaterina Nowicki directly as well as her team: *Please send Rhona Baird home immediately. Her mother's ill, and she needs to be on the next available flight to Edinburgh.* And let me know the second there's a response.'

Still nothing from Rhona; not even a tick to confirm the message has been read.

Next, she dials Peter. But his phone doesn't even ring. And it takes all of Jean's self-control not to leave a message about how he can ram his work-life balance up his arse.

Instead, with a bite of frost in her words, Jean says: 'Peter, we might have a situation on our hands. I'm on my way there now, and I'll update you as soon as I can. But text me the moment you get this – we need to be on our guard.'

Then Jean drops the useless phone onto her lap and meets Bogdan's eyes in the mirror. 'Can't you go any faster?'

'I'm sorry, Ms Howard. It's the tail end of rush hour.' Sure enough, they're stopping and starting, stopping and starting, locked in a growing tailback.

Jean closes her eyes, rests her head against the window. Perhaps if she doesn't peer at the road, willing the light to stay green and the traffic to melt away, it will go quicker.

'I didn't know Rhona's mother was sick.' There's contrition in Hugo's voice, a pleading note, as if Jean alone has the power to grant him absolution. 'If I had, I wouldn't ha—'

'Wake up, Hugo. There's nothing wrong with Mrs Baird.'

'What? But you got Helen to contact his team.'

Jean's eyes snap open. 'Why do you think I did that?'

'Because you need to talk to Rhona. You're giving her an iron-clad excuse to leave.' Hugo's brows draw together. 'But why? If Leonides likes her plan so much, he might offer her a job. What's it to you if he poaches her, though?'

'You really think Andreas Leonides – a billionaire with whole teams devoted to this stuff – is in the habit of personally offering jobs to first year associates? No.' Acid scorn burns through every word. 'Why do you think he's *really* taking Rhona to dinner?'

'I don't understand.' But he's starting to – Jean sees it in the shiftiness of his gaze.

'Remember that speech in your interview? Big words about how *excited* you'd be to seize any learning opportunity I saw fit to provide you with.' Jean glances down at her phone. Nothing, still. 'Well, tonight's your chance. A lesson you won't forget.'

Hugo's wise enough to stay quiet then. And finally, the car's inching across the other side of London Bridge. The moment Bogdan pulls over, Jean unclips her seatbelt. Hugo leaps out of the car, holding the door open for Jean, and together they hurtle towards the pyramid glowing crimson in the sun's dying light.

They pass through the revolving doors into the atrium, a futuristic fusion of glass and marble. Shoulders back, Jean approaches the front desk, Hugo lingering by her shoulder. 'Hello. My name is Jean Howard, and my firm represents one of your guests, Mr Leonides. I need to speak with him as a matter of urgency. Apparently, Mr Leonides is currently eating in one of your restaurants. Please could you tell me which one?'

The girl behind the desk flashes an apologetic smile. 'I'm sorry, Ms Howard. But company policy dictates that we can't give out information about any guests.'

'I'll take the odd floors, and you can take the even,' Hugo says. 'I'll call you if I find them.'

But Jean holds a finger up for him to wait.

'Mr Leonides runs a company worth billions. He could buy and sell this building.' Jean steps closer, staring pointedly at the name badge pinned to the receptionist's neat cerulean lapel. 'What do you think he'll do to you, Gemma, when he finds out that you delayed him from dealing with an emergency?'

Gemma gulps, casting an appealing gaze to her colleague – but the girl catches Jean's eye and disappears into the back office. Gemma picks up the phone. Punches in a number and speaks, voice low, into the receiver. Then she looks up at Jean. 'Mr Leonides was in Aqua having dinner with a guest. But they've gone now.'

A guest – singular. Jean sways, clutching at the counter. 'Then tell me which room he's staying in.'

'I can't.' Gemma's voice is tiny, pleading. 'I'll lose my job.'

Jean opens her mouth, no amount of self-hatred keeping her from asking how Gemma expects to keep her job after Mr Leonides brings the colossal weight of his empire down upon a mere receptionist. But her phone rings as the tirade begins to take shape, vibrating in Jean's hand as she lifts it to look at the name: *Rhona Baird*.

Jean staggers away from the reception desk, phone soldered to her cheek. 'Rhona!' Her voice echoes through the lobby, drawing stares. 'Rhona, thank God you're okay. Where are you?'

'Miss Howard?' Her voice is scarcely more than a whisper, breaths coming hard and fast through the speaker.

'Yes! Now tell me your location and we'll come and find you. Hugo and I are in The Shard now.'

'You are?' A jagged intake of breath. 'I missed our one-to-one. I'm s-so sorry, Ms Howard, I… I should have let you know myse—'

'Never mind that now. Are you in one of the hotel rooms?'

A series of thumps carry through the line, so loud the phone slips from between her fingers – only Hugo's quick reflexes keep it from falling to crack against the marble. He lifts it back to Jean's ear, stepping close enough that they can both hear.

'Yes. I'm in his bathroom,' Rhona whispers, voice pulled taut. 'I've locked myself in. I went for dinner with Mr Leonides and M-Ms Nowicki. But then she got a call. And she left.'

Jean swallows. She'd read an article once, about the importance of using a person's name in a hostage situation – a psychological trick to discourage the kidnapper from evolving into a killer. But perhaps it works with victims too. 'Where did he take you, Rhona? Is he there now?'

'K-kind of.' A male voice undercuts Rhona's words – far enough away that Jean can't make out specific words. But at the wheedling tone, Jean's stomach churns. 'He keeps trying to m-make me come out.'

'Stay exactly where you are, Rhona. Just let us know the room number, and do not come out until I tell you to.'

'It's room six hundred and fi-fi—' Rhona's voice is so thick with tears that Jean can't make her out. Her look of alarm haunts Hugo's features. 'Six five zero. An executive suite.'

'Okay. Stay on the line, Rhona.'

Hugo sprints towards the lift, hammering the up button while Jean races after him. The doors draw open as Jean approaches, disgorging a pair of giggling young women whose tequila-laced perfume suggests they've made liberal use of the bar. Jean pushes past. 'Hello? Are you still there, Rhona?'

A sniff. 'Yes.'

Hugo presses the button for the sixth floor and – ignoring the grey-haired couple waving as they shamble over – the button to slide the doors closed.

'Good.' Jean's stomach swoops as they glide upwards. *One...* 'That's very good, Rhona. Now what can you tell me about where you grew up?'

'Ms Howard?'

Two...

'Edinburgh, Rhona. Tell me something I don't know.'

Three...

'There are beaches. Everyone loves Portobello, but Cramond's my favourite.'

Four...

'Why Cramond, Rhona?'

Five...

'It's beautiful. My parents have a little beach house there.' A muffled sob. 'I want my mum.'

The words are a lance through Jean's heart.

Six... The doors glide open. Hugo grabs her free wrist and pulls Jean along the corridor, so quickly that she scarcely has time to read the sign differentiating between ordinary rooms on the left and the executive suite to the right. His legs are longer, and as the former captain of his rugby team he sets a breakneck pace, but Jean spends the last of her breath on maintaining the flow of conversation. 'We're nearly there, Rhona. We're on the sixth floor.'

As they approach, Jean slows, giving Hugo no choice but to follow suit. Leonides is much more likely to open the door if he believes she is alone, not a threat. *How little he knows...*

'Hide,' Jean hisses, waving at the jutting pilasters framing the wall on either side of the door. Obedient, Hugo ducks behind the wooden panelling to the right. The second he's in place, Jean raises a shaking hand and raps against the door. 'Mr Leonides?'

Muffled footsteps brush against carpet. 'Can you not read? The sign says *Do Not Disturb*. Fuck off!'

'Mr Leonides, it's Jean Howard. I understand my associate is there with you now, that the two of you had a meeting.'

The door swings open to reveal Leonides in a white terrycloth robe, his paunch creating a deep enough V that Jean glimpses more than she ever wanted to of his scrubby black chest hair. His ordinarily sanguine smile is interrupted by a wince – a cut splits his lip, oozing fresh blood as Leonides speaks. 'What of it?' He shrugs. 'I liked her ideas, and wanted to hear more.'

'We've been trying to get hold of Rhona as a matter of urgency.' A quick glance over his shoulder offers no sign of the girl, nor any obvious doors along the narrow corridor.

A single eyebrow climbs, thick as a caterpillar. 'And why might that be?'

No accusations. Only the established facts, even if they are of Jean's own making. 'Her mother's sick – as our communications with your team will show.'

'And what, you're sending the little girl home to her parents? It makes sense.' An expansive shrug. 'After all, you sent a child to do a woman's job.'

Jean swallows back bile. 'Rhona Baird is a thoroughly competent junior associate; she has the potential to go far. Surely you agree, Andreas? Why else would a man with all your concerns spend an entire evening on Rhona's proposals?'

His eye twitches, a subtle tell. 'Out of the goodness of my heart.'

'In that case you'll have no trouble with me taking Rhona. Where is she?'

'You believe I know this how, precisely?' It's a lawyer's answer, parrying question for question. In another life Leonides would have made a sharp solicitor, shielding fraudsters and rapists from the consequences of their own actions. In this one it's unlikely he'll ever see the inside of a courtroom.

'Because there are two glasses on that table behind you.' Though the bottle has been righted, a crimson stain's splattered across the carpet; it could be a murder scene.

Leonides half turns to crane over his shoulder, and Jean darts forward. But he bars her way with an arm across the door frame. Jean bounces back, stumbling in her heels, and his lips twitch. She will not make it past his stocky frame by force – and Leonides knows it too, the smile reaching his eyes.

Hugo stares as Jean rights herself, poised like a hare in the moment before flight, a question in his eyes. But Jean gives the subtlest shake of her head. *Not yet.* With diplomacy she might still be able to get them out of this relatively unscathed – Rhona and Hugo, client relations, the firm. But if she is careless…

'You're wasting your time here, Ms Howard. I recommend that you leave.'

'Not going to happen. I have Rhona on the line right now; she's in your bathroom.' Jean bares her teeth. 'Perhaps dinner didn't agree with her.'

A Gallic shrug. 'The young are frail in constitution.'

'All the more reason to get her home.' Jean puts her iPhone on speaker. 'Rhona, the car's waiting downstairs – would you like to come with me?'

Leonides straightens, brows knitting together as he takes in the device. 'What exactly are you accusing me of?'

'I haven't accused you of anything, Mr Leonides.'

'Come on now, Jean. You're a sensible woman – pragmatic. Are you really going to throw away your firm's biggest client on the say-so of a jumpy little girl?'

Jean's eyebrows climb. 'I haven't mentioned anything about terminating our contract with Hephaestia.'

'We both know you're the power behind the throne. You're at the office every night long after Peter's gone home.' His voice is oily, wheedling. 'Why not let me turn in for the night. And then tomorrow we can sit down together, discuss a personal retainer. There's no need for hostility.'

Jean bites back a sigh. 'You're right – we can end this amicably. But you and I both know Rhona's in there. So why not let m—'

He grabs Jean's wrist in a vice grip without warning, tight enough that a whimper escapes her lips. They're far enough away from the other hotel rooms that nobody would hear her scream. Their eyes lock and Leonides licks his lips, as if savouring the taste of her fear.

Jean stills. She'd read about trauma responses in the years after it all happened, when Henry had suggested therapy as a solution to the panic that remained with her long after Will left the firm. Fight or flight are the big ones, seized upon by evolutionary biologists, fawn and freeze the poor cousins. She'd despised her own weakness, locked in place like a fieldmouse before an adder – and dedicated herself to changing.

But all those courses on confidence, elocution, leadership – every rung of the ladder she has climbed over the years – dissipate into nothing as Leonides tightens his grip. Deep down, Jean's the same now as she was then;

the knowledge pains her more deeply than any wound this man is capable of inflicting.

But Hugo doesn't fawn or freeze. And though he flies, it's entirely in the aid of fight. He darts around the corner and, seizing upon Leonides' shock, launches himself at the billionaire's thickset waist. Leonides holds her wrist tighter still, yanking as Hugo tackles him to the ground. A cry rips from Jean's throat, the pain blinding her as something delicate ruptures between bone and sinew.

'Ms Howard.' While Leonides is still winded, Hugo rolls him over, both arms pinned behind his back, a knee fixing him in place. 'JEAN! Get Rhona. *Now.*'

Jolted into action, Jean hurries past the two men sprawled on the floor. With her left hand she knocks on the bathroom door.

'You think you can *attack* me? That you will get away with it?' Leonides spits with all the venom of a cobra, red-faced under Hugo's muscular bulk. 'I have *destroyed* people for less.'

'Rhona, it's me. It's Jean.' Sweat beads on Jean's forehead; she lifts the phone to her mouth, praying Rhona hears her above the litany of threats and curses and feet thumping against the floor. 'Open the door and we'll leave together. You can do it. I'm right here.'

The lock clicks and Rhona tumbles into her arms, red-faced and clinging to her torn blouse. A tide of acid bile rises in Jean's throat as her wrist is wedged tight between their bodies. Jean pulls away, keeping her good arm wrapped around Rhona's shoulder, propelling the girl past her captor.

Leonides is puce with the effort of squeezing words past the weight of Hugo's knee. 'I will burn your fucking firm to the ground, do you hear me? And you can kiss any chance of a career goodbye, you worthless little cocktease.'

'Almost there, Rhona.' Jean guides her out into the hallway.

'I'll call the police the second you release me. You really think they'll just let you get away with this?' Even with both arms pinned behind his back, he wears the grin of a man with the upper hand. 'Andreas Leonides has friends in high places.'

Rhona pales, her breath coming in shallow rapid wheezes. Jean looks from her to Hugo; she can't jettison one to save the other. *Why couldn't Peter have answered his fucking phone?*

'I'll stay with him.' Jean's gaze darts around. 'Tie his hands with the belt from that robe and I'll stay.'

'Respectfully, Ms Howard, I have a better idea.' Hugo grunts with effort as he rolls Leonides over. 'Time to put our heads together and find a solution.'

Hugo raises his head and brings it down hard, and Jean winces at the clash of bone against bone. Leonides sags on the floor, unresponsive as Hugo checks him over – only the slow rise and fall of his chest indicate that he's anything other than a corpse.

'Hugo, what did you do?' Rhona's breath comes in panting sobs. 'You'll go to jail and it's all my fault. Oh *God.* I'm so sorry.'

Hugo clambers to his feet and dusts himself down, seemingly unhurt despite the welt forming on his forehead. 'Leonides isn't the only one with friends in high places. My sister's in the Home Office – and she's godmother to the foreign secretary's son. Now let's go.'

Hugo closes the door behind him and, demonstrating more tact than Jean had ever imagined him capable of, leaves Jean to help Rhona. The lift is waiting when they reach it, Hugo blocking the door sensors with his body, one foot on solid ground and the other inside.

As they descend, Jean shrugs off her jacket, purple spots blooming across her vision as a sleeve snags her wounded wrist. With her good hand Jean drapes the blazer over Rhona's shoulders, tucking it to shield the rip in her blouse as the doors open. She and Hugo steer Rhona through the lobby, one on either side like sentries.

And relief soars in Jean's chest as she spies the car; Bogdan, still waiting. Hugo opens the door, and Jean helps ease a sniffling Rhona inside. The girl tries to pull Jean in after her, relinquishing her grip only when Jean promises to return soon.

The second she lets go, Jean staggers round to the back of the car. With her good hand balanced against the boot Jean vomits into the gutter, ignoring the jeers of pedestrians.

Hugo's eyes dart between the sweat pooling above her upper lip; the way Jean cradles her wrist against her chest. 'You're hurt! London Bridge Hospital's not far – Bogdan can drop you off on the way to Rhona's.'

'My wrist isn't broken; I can still move it. I'll get it taken care of after I've seen Rhona home,' Jean says. And though it's not a lie, her conscience prickles. But there's another more pressing matter: Peter needs to know. 'Hugo, I'm sure I don't have to tell you the importance of keeping all this confidential. Not just for Rhona, but for the firm and your future with us.'

'You don't have to threaten me, Ms Howard. I know I've been a prat to Rhona – I was jealous that you chose her for Leonides. But...' Hugo shakes his head, as if attempting to dislodge the memory. 'I won't say anything about it. Unless she wants me to testify, of course.'

Jean blinks, taken aback. Even knowing the likely repercussions for himself, for DDH, he would risk it all to do right by Rhona. His rival. Which is more than Jean ever did for her dearest friend. The realisation is a hefty blow to the gut, sure as if Hugo had tackled her too.

'Anyway, I'll get the tube to Rosalind's – she's overdue some brotherly love.' He gives a tight smile and turns to go, carried on a tide of pedestrians.

'Wait!'

He turns. And though the animal part of Jean's brain is screaming that they shouldn't linger, she cannot leave without making this final point: 'You're a good man, Hugo. Thank you.'

Chapter Eighteen

With Rhona safe, damage limitation becomes Jean's primary concern. While Bogdan drives them to the junior associate's flat, she speaks to Henry for the first time in fifteen years and gets him to send Rhona's cousin home from Lawson and Pierce. Meanwhile Helen books both Bairds on the first flight to Edinburgh. The sooner they're in Scotland, the better. Isla's waiting when Bogdan pulls up, her face white with worry – to her Jean dispenses clear instructions for getting photographic evidence, to Rhona a final hug and a promise that her place with DDH remains secure. Over Jean's dead body will Rhona's career become a casualty of Leonides.

Bogdan wants to take her straight to hospital, and Jean is sharper than she intends, turning Peter's address into a command. But without Rhona to comfort, without the rush of adrenaline, there's nothing to distract Jean from the ache pulsing through her wrist with every heartbeat; every jolt of the car. And still Peter doesn't answer his fucking phone. Jean's own gives a low battery warning as they curve round the driveway, but her fury could charge it ten times over. She bids Bogdan a curt goodnight, planning to double his annual bonus by way of apology, and rings the doorbell.

Peter's wife opens the door. Caroline's smile caves in as she registers Jean grim-faced on her doorstep. And Jean doesn't take it personally: her being there is a terrible omen. And after decades of work coming first, Caroline Dennings has been enjoying the return of her husband – theatre dates, trips to the Bahamas, Peter home in time for dinner. The house is fragrant with onion and garlic, and the sound of laughter spills from the house, though Caroline doesn't step aside to allow Jean entry to the porch – not right away. Even though time has proven that Jean has never had the slightest design on Peter, an edge of competition sharpens Caroline's approach to her. Real Wife vs. Work Wife.

'I take it you're here for Peter?' The subtext in her words could not be clearer: here to take him away from his wife, his friends, this charmed circle of domesticity.

'Yes.' There's no point beating around the bush. 'I'm sorry to intrude, Caroline, but it's a crisis.'

Something of the evening's strain must show on her face, or perhaps it's the wrist bent stiffly against her chest, because Caroline's expression softens. She steps back. 'Come in. There's fresh coffee, or gin if you'd prefer something stronger.'

'Is that Jonty?' Peter's voice echoes as Jean enters the hallway. 'What time do you call this, you old – Jean. What's wrong?'

He looks so utterly at ease with the world, loose-limbs and flushed cheeks from the quality vintage no doubt being served with dinner.

'What's *wrong*?' Jean marches across the hallway, jabbing an accusatory finger into his chest. 'What's *wrong*? You would know the answer to that question if you'd answered your phone, Peter. Why the hell didn't you pick up?'

Peter's brows draw together. 'Sorry, I turned my mobile off. But did you try the landline?'

'Of course I tried the fucking landline. I'm not an idiot or Gen Z; I know what a housephone is, Peter. Do *you*?'

Caroline bristles, back straight. The laughter has died away in the lounge, replaced by a hushed silence. 'He deserves a life, Jean. We both do.'

She sees it; the moment understanding dawns in Peter's eyes, Caroline's culpability becoming clear. But it does nothing to mitigate the fury coursing through her veins. She rounds on Caroline. 'You unplugged the phone. Didn't you?'

Caroline folds her arms. Hatred twists her face into a sneer. 'And what if I did? I'm sick of the firm coming first. Before our marriage, before our children. You were always married to the job, so it might have escaped your notice, Jean. But some of us actually enjoy having our husbands around.'

The words are a slap across the cheek. Jean's still reeling when Peter steps between them, more swiftly than the United Nations ever intervened. 'Darling, please could you excuse us? Our guests are waiting, and I need to speak with Jean.'

'I've spent the last thirty-nine years excusing you.' Caroline slams the door behind her, leaving them alone in the hallway.

Peter sighs, running a hand through greying hair. Between the clash with Caroline and the knowledge of impending disaster, he's lost that air of easy contentment. 'How bad is it?'

'Black Wednesday meets the Hindenburg. On a par with the Will situation.'

Peter's eyebrows twitch before he can school his face, and Jean understands the shock – she can count on one hand the number of times they've spoken about 'the Will situation', and it was never she who chose to resurrect that particular ghost.

'Let's go through to the den.' Peter leads the way, past the kitchen and downstairs bathroom, flipping on the lamps to bathe the room in warm light. It's less opulent than the lounge, but far more comfortable. Peter takes his usual armchair, and Jean the squashy sofa opposite. 'Tell me everything,' he says. 'From the very start.'

And so Jean does, from Hugo arriving in her office alone from the Hephaestia meeting to reassuring Rhona on the drive home. She does her best to keep it factual, falling into the same dispassionate tone with which she'd itemise a list of evidence early in her career. But no amount of blinking can keep her eyes from spilling over as she recounts the night's horrors. Peter gets up to bring her a box of tissues. And though the urgency of the situation hovers over them like a cloud, he makes no attempt to rush her, simply squeezing Jean's shoulder until she's ready to keep going.

The second Jean mentions her wrist, swollen and impossibly tender, he races off to fetch an ice pack and a first-aid kit. Jean dry swallows four ibuprofen, gagging on the sugary taste. And only her most dire warnings about what Leonides will do if he finds them unprepared keeps Peter from calling an ambulance then and there. Peter settles only when Jean asks him to take photos, her uninjured wrist held up for contrast.

He disappears again before they delve into damage-limitation strategy, bidding goodnight to his guests and – Jean suspects – disclosing pertinent details to his wife. Sure enough, Peter returns with a laden tray recognisable as Caroline's handiwork: diagonal cut sandwiches made with the evening's gammon joint, spread with homemade chutney. A fresh pot of coffee. A plate of lemon biscuits.

Only then does it occur to Jean she missed dinner. She devours her sandwich, lining her stomach for a fresh round of painkillers, as they outline every possible scenario. Leonides could press charges for Hugo's assault and go public, attempting to take control of the narrative. Rhona could choose to press charges against their client. Rhona could agree to sign an NDA, becoming wealthy in her own right overnight. Or she could go to Leonides' enemies in the press – the *Guardian* or the *New Statesman*. There's also the scorched earth scenario: Leonides makes a very public exit, bad-mouthing the firm and taking an infinite supply of billable hours to a rival. If DDH stays silent, the firm looks weak, but if they comment publicly on a former client, unprofessional enough to alienate prospective business.

But Jean can't think about that right now, the fight to keep her victory from turning to ash. Her mind is too full of the ache, that gaping white bathrobe, Rhona sobbing like a child in her arms.

'I'm not going to lean on her,' Jean says. 'Whatever Rhona chooses.'

'And I wouldn't ask you to.'

Dawn's creeping over the horizon by the time they finish, the sky shifting from black to blue like an old bruise. All that remains is for Jean to confess her own guilt. 'This is my fault, Peter. I told her to work more independently; that she had to stop running every little decision by me if she was ever going to stand on her own two feet.'

'It really isn't. You handled that situation admirably, and met our duty of care to Rhona.' Peter rubs his knuckles against his eyelids. 'In retrospect it was so obviously a set up – to have Nowicki there so that Rhona would feel safe, then conveniently disappear when it was time for Leonides to sink his claws in. But it certainly wouldn't have occurred to me to charge across London and rescue her in time.'

'I don't think you're giving yourself enough credit.'

'You're very kind, Jean. But you are selling yourself short.' Peter leans forward, earnest now. 'You did something extraordinary in going to Rhona. You protected her, even though it couldn't have been easy.'

Jean has to look away, then. 'Perhaps it was time I made amends.'

'You can't keep blaming yourself for that.'

'Of course I can,' Jean says, her voice a hoarse whisper.

—

Though generous, DDH's healthcare package doesn't cover emergency medicine – so there's nothing for it but to have Bogdan drop her at hospital on the way back from Peter's. He offers to wait, but Jean's eaten into enough of his weekend, even with overtime. There's little to do except look at her phone as the minutes tick by – Urgent Care, it turns out, is something of a misnomer.

She texts Rhona, typing out and erasing multiple drafts of a message until striking the right balance of professional tact and personal support, all the slower for her left hand's clumsiness. They message back and forth until Rhona has a plan of action for telling her parents – even while drowning in her own sorrows, the junior associate remains unfailingly kind.

> I hope you have someone in your corner too, Ms Howard.

And Jean knows precisely who to call. In that moment it's so obvious, so simple.

Ava picks up on the third ring, and Jean's eyes prickle at the warmth of her greeting. 'Hey, Jellybean! What's new?'

'Nothing good.' Jean's throat thickens, her eyes blurring. Everyone else is too wrapped up in their own drama to care, but she feels utterly ridiculous, tearing up like a character in a soap opera. 'There was an… accident. I'm alright except for my wrist – they're going to x-ray it.'

She's still trying to puzzle out an acceptable way of asking to set aside the terms of their arrangement for a day when Ava speaks: 'Where are you?'

Jean names the hospital, slumping back against her seat, teeth gritted against the pain. She breathes deep and slow, in and out, imagining each one as the wall of a square – Dr Byrne's old exercise for moments of overwhelm. Then Ava's there, faster than Jean could have imagined possible, jogging into the waiting room. Their eyes lock across the rows of chairs, and Jean's heart seems to levitate, lighter than it's been since the moment Hugo walked into her office.

Ava rounds the rows of seats and crouches before Jean, openly drinking in every detail. 'Hey! What happened to your wrist? Are you okay?'

'Don't worry; I told you, it's nothing serious.' For just a moment, Jean lets herself rest a hand on Ava's shoulder. But an unbearable longing fills her ribcage. And Jean pulls away before she forgets herself.

Ava reaches up to touch her own shoulder; the place where, moments before, Jean's fingers had sat. She closes her eyes, and for the briefest of moments Jean sees her own sorrow echoed on Ava's face. Her hair's combed back into a ponytail, her face, bare arms, and t-shirt all speckled with indigo paint – only then does Jean remember that she'd planned to help her sister decorate the Clark family's new home this weekend.

'I'm sorry,' Jean says, for the interruption and much more besides. 'You were busy – I shouldn't have called.'

'Don't be silly, Jean! You're hurt – of course I came.' She takes the neighbouring seat, undeterred.

'I'm fine – really. I don't even think it's broken.' Gingerly, Jean lifts her arm for Ava's inspection.

'Jesus. That looks sore.' Ava sucks in a breath as she takes in the swelling, the unmistakable bracelet of fingerprints bruised mauve. 'How did it happen?'

Jean breathes in air stale with sickness, disinfectant, and canteen food. 'That I can't tell you.'

Ava's tone changes, shifting into something Jean's never heard before; something utterly at odds with her usual warmth: fury. 'Who hurt you?'

'I can't talk about any of it until we figure out how to proceed.'

'What's there to figure out?' But Ava's eyes narrow, and a second later she answers her own question. 'Did a *client* put his hands on you? Fucking hell, Jean!'

'*Keep your voice down,*' Jean hisses. 'We're dealing with it – I promise. But I can't go running my mouth, and neither can you.'

Ava folds her arms. 'Then why did you ask me to come, if it's so hush hush?'

'Because until now you've shown a reasonable aptitude for discretion.' Her wrist throbs, a dull hot ache. 'And because I like having you around. This has been the shittiest twenty-four hours in a long, long time. And I thought that if I saw you...'

'Yeah?' Though Ava's voice is soft, her eyes shine with brilliant intensity.

'I thought that—'

'Jean Howard?' A nurse peers around the waiting room, and Jean stands.

Ava's smile grows wry. 'Saved by the bell.'

—

The doctor – an enthusiastic young woman – diagnoses a moderate sprain. Leonides tore the ligaments in a desperate bid to keep himself from falling, though that's not an explanation Jean can give. At her caginess the doctor grows alert, alternating between care instructions and oh-so casually delivered questions about Jean's personal life. Whether she's in a relationship. Whether anything like this has ever happened before.

'It happened at work, not home.' Jean sighs. 'I was with a client.'

The doctor's eyebrows climb. 'Oh!'

'I'm a lawyer...'

'Oh.' Her shoulders sink down from the vicinity of her ears, the thread of tension cut. With clever children parents talk as if doctor or lawyer were interchangeable career paths – the underlying belief being it doesn't matter which is chosen, because both lead to success. But the doctor's poker face, or lack thereof, gives a lie to this parental fantasy.

'Yes, and I'll need a copy of my medical records for my firm.'

Armed with a splint, prescription painkillers and a print-out of her care instructions, Jean returns to Ava.

They're in the process of booking an Uber, heads bowed over Jean's phone in the lobby, when a familiar voice rings out. Two of them to be precise, both calling her name. In an instant, dread covers Jean like cold sweat.

She turns to face her two oldest friends, plastering a smile on her face. If Jean can be open and easy, they'll suspect nothing, chalking any strangeness up to recent trauma. But Cora and Ginny both have built careers on their ability to scent unease and follow it all the way to hidden truth. And they have known Jean longer than anyone.

'Jean! We were about to text, but there you are.' Ever so careful, Imogen hugs Jean's uninjured side. 'Peter called to say there'd been a situation, and that you could use a hand getting home and settled.'

Jean raises a single eyebrow. 'More like he sent you to keep me from going back to the office.'

'That too.' Cora smiles, unrepentant. 'Naomi's still in New York, though she sends her love. I was going to say you'd have to make do with just the two of us... but who's this?'

She's eyeing Ava with avid curiosity, gaze lingering on the spatters of paint. But Ava simply tucks her hands in the pockets of her dungarees, that oasis of easy confidence evaporating faster than water under the Saharan sun.

'This is Ava Harris. As a matter of fact, I'd hoped to introduce you – though under different circumstances.' Ava perks up then, stepping closer, all the encouragement Jean needs. 'She's a lawyer too, with the Afro-Caribbean Women's Rights Centre. But Ava's currently setting up a charity with the goal of connecting overpoliced communities with first rate representation – which is where you two come in... Ava, meet Cora Klein, a barrister with Garden Court Chambers. And you know Imogen from the conference – she represents the interests of an international bank.'

'I'd tell you which one, but I'd have to kill you.' Ginny winks. 'I'm only kidding – it's Deutsche Bank.'

Jean risks a glance at Ava then, keen to see what she makes of these introductions. Between them Cora and Ginny have the skills and resources she's so urgently trying to funnel into the CJC. But Ava's smile takes on a fixed quality as she shakes their hands, and she won't meet Jean's eye.

'Why don't you come back to Jean's with us, and we can talk about it?' Imogen touches Ava's elbow, keen to reassure. 'No sense putting off to tomorrow what can be accomplished today. Besides, I'm curious – there isn't always much altruism in our profession.'

Ava tucks a flyaway curl back into her ponytail. 'I, ah, don't want to intrude. Not when Jean's tired and in pain.'

'But how could you be intruding if Jean asked you to come here?' Cora's brows knit together. 'Before her oldest friends.'

Then all eyes are on her – Cora and Imogen curious, Ava searching for a cue. And Jean knows she needs to say something, anything, because suspicion grows with every passing second. But she freezes, mouth gaping, icy panic washing every word from her mind.

Ava clears her throat, and the awful spell is broken. 'Actually, I was visiting my sister for lunch – she's a surgeon here. And I bumped into Jean on my way out.'

Relief balloons in Jean's chest, instant and pure. Until the realisation that this lie hastens Ava's departure punctures her calm; their quiet afternoon together dissipating into nothing. She speaks without thinking: 'You're still welcome to come with us.'

'Ah, well I—' This time it's Ava who freezes.

And this time Jean understands her awkwardness: never before has she witnessed Ava lie. On top of that, not once in the months they've been... *involved* has Ava visited her home. And she's never complained about it, nor any of the measures Jean has taken to compartmentalise her life. She'd assumed that Ava would be glad of it too — the control that comes with keeping things on your own territory. But her photos and music, her books and her art, all these things provided Jean with a window into Ava's life, a sense of her everyday context. And Jean has offered only a blank wall in return.

'You wouldn't be intruding.' Jean tries to say more with her eyes, but still Ava won't meet them. 'Not at all.'

'There — it's settled.' Cora chivvies them out into the afternoon, where even London's polluted air tastes fresh after the hospital. 'Besides, we could use an extra pair of hands to whip up freezable dinners for Jean.'

-

It's the last thing Jean would have chosen, to have her secret lover and two of her oldest friends who are capable of seeing right through her, all in the same place. Yet she can't bring herself to regret Ava's quiet presence — and not only because the tramadol has buoyed her up above anxiety's reach.

Ava's practical, decanting both ice trays into sandwich bags and refilling them with water so that Jean will have a ready supply to treat the sprain. And though Ava's eyes are bright with curiosity as she takes in Jean's home, she exercises that iron self-restraint and refrains from handling Jean's photographs and mementos. Briefly, she fingers the fridge magnet depicting gondolas in Venice. And Jean remembers details of her honeymoon she hasn't shared with anyone; how, even as a new bride, sleeping with Henry had been something she tolerated – like brushing her teeth before bed or filing taxes on time.

Ava minces garlic, chops onions and peppers and assorted meats, an uncomplaining sous chef for Imogen. Even now, Jean can't help but admire the strength and sureness of her hands. Before Ava, she'd been blind to that subtle eroticism, and so much more.

From her perch by the island, Jean encourages Ava to share her vision with Imogen and Cora, and it's a pleasure simply to listen. The painkillers have well and truly hit her bloodstream, leaving Jean mellow as if she'd had wine with lunch. Best to say little when she's like this. It's easy enough smiling whenever one of them looks at her, to ward off fears that she's dwelling on the previous day – though Jean can see Ava doesn't entirely buy it, from her furtive stares. That perceptiveness, her knack for reading Jean, extends well beyond the bedroom.

Despite Ava's doubts, she joins with Imogen and Cora in plying Jean with tea and light chatter; in this bright kitchen, surrounded by women who care about her, the horrors of yesterday begin to recede. It's as close to okay as Jean can possibly hope for. Until Cora speaks.

'So,' she says, dropping bay leaves into the fragrant stew and stirring. 'Ava. Do you happen to know any young men?'

Dread runs a chill finger from the back of Jean's neck to the base of her spine. She sits up straight. 'Don't, Cora. You'll make her uncomfortable.'

Cora's head tilts, avian. 'Am I making you uncomfortable, Ava?'

'No... I have a nephew. Theodore. He's seven now, and already beating me at chess.' A shrug. 'Beyond that, not my area of expertise.'

'It wasn't a nephew I had in mind.'

'Cora,' Jean begins, mouth suddenly dry.

Ginny steps between her and Ava, lifting a spoon for Cora to taste. 'What do you think? It needs something else – more salt or red wine?'

'Both.' Cora turns to face the stove, sprinkling Himalayan rock salt over the beef and stirring in a generous dash of cabernet sauvignon. And though it's obvious she's just building up to something, Jean's mind is a blank – she can think of nothing to stop it from happening. Sure enough, moments later: 'You don't happen to know a fellow called Aiden, do you?'

Ava's head rears back, surprise scrunching her features. 'No... Should I?'

'You mean Jean hasn't told you?' Cora tips in the butter beans. 'I thought she'd be bragging about it to everyone.'

'Cora, that's enough.' This time her voice is sharp enough to cut through the conversation.

'Oh, lighten up Euphemia. When you're having so much more fun than me, it's only right that I should get to tease you a little.' Cora's smile is wolfish as she refills her wine glass.

'I'm not having much fun at the moment.' It's true: sweat prickles against Jean's back, pinches beneath her arms.

Ginny's eyes flit between them like it's a tennis match, missing nothing.

'Perhaps not now. But you still have your boy toy.' She sidles up to Ava, confidential. 'Jean's been dangling him over our heads for months. This lad she's been seeing, in his thirties.'

Jean sees it, the moment understanding breaks across Ava's face – the flicker of hurt before her expression goes blank. 'Ava, it's not—'

'That's great, Jean. Good for you.' Ava's lips give a spasmodic twitch. 'The stew's nearly finished, and the lasagne's in the oven – I'd better get going.'

'You really don't have to,' Jean says, pain jolting through her wrist as she hops down from the stool.

But Ava tugs the apron over her head, not stopping even when its loop gets caught in her hair, just yanking herself free.

'Yeah, I do.' Ava steps around her, pocketing her phone and shouldering her tote. 'I'm supposed to be watching my niblings this evening. Leah and Simon never get enough time to themselves – both surgeons with two kids under ten.'

Only Jean herself knows that Ava came straight from Aaliyah's to the hospital, yet her words are clearly stamped with the hallmark of a lie, too much information freely given – any lawyer knows as much. Ginny's watching Ava with concern. 'At least let me drive you. I could—'

'No!' Ava forces a smile. 'You've both been very kind, and I'm glad you're taking care of Jean, but the underground's faster. Bye.'

Jean's still searching for the perfect combination of words to make Ava understand without giving herself away when the door bangs shut. And Ava is gone, leaving only a faint trace of her cedar scent, but even that's soon lost to the kitchen's steam.

'Blimey.' Cora fills the sink with soapy water. 'I hadn't realised Aiden would be such a sore subject. I'd just assumed that because they're round about the same age, they might know one another.'

Though Cora has come dizzyingly close to the truth, still she remains blind to it. And Jean ought to be relieved – it is, after all, the best-case scenario. But all she feels is weariness. 'I'm going to lie down,' she says, putting the ice Ava made into a sandwich bag and holding a handle with her teeth to tie it shut.

She pads out of the kitchen, every step a throb in her wrist.

'You're like a bull in a china shop,' Ginny hisses, just audible above the extractor fan.

Cora makes a noise of disgust, not bothering to lower her voice, words following Jean up the stairs: 'Yes, yes. But I want to know what happened there. Did Jean steal that girl's boyfriend? Is that why she's helping Ava out, to ease a guilty conscience?'

Jean doesn't stick around long enough to hear the response, closing the bedroom door behind her. She fumbles her phone in the one-handed attempt to unlock it, calling Ava on speed dial, heart in her throat as it rings.

And rings.

Ava could be on the underground, Jean reasons.

And rings.

Perhaps she's put her headphones on, walking through the city centre. There is always music in Ava's flat; it's like water or air to her.

And cuts out.

Or maybe she's plain angry. It's a theory that bears out when Jean wakes that evening, dry-mouthed and aching. She dials Ava again. But the call goes straight to voicemail.

Twice more Jean tries before giving up – she can take a hint. Though Jean does leave a text:

> I'm sorry. Can we talk?

> That depends. Sorry about what you did, or sorry you got caught?

Caught, as in red-handed. Caught, as if Jean has committed some type of crime.

> I couldn't have been clearer about my situation. And I'm sorry today was difficult, but my friends can never know.

> There's a difference between not telling your friends about me and making up a male lover. If you can't see that, there's no point taking this conversation further.

Jean's thumb jabs the screen, typing and deleting. *That's totally out of...* No. *You're blowing this whole thing...* Too confrontational. In the end, she settles on:

> It's not that big a deal. Nothing has changed.

She waits, face lit by the screen's pale glow. But the three bouncing dots do not appear, though Ava has read the message.

Chapter Nineteen

After that Ava doesn't take Jean's calls. And when Jean texts suggesting that they meet up, she's met with monosyllabic refusals.

There's nothing easily refuted; with a mere fortnight left at ACWRC, Ava's no doubt swamped, too conscientious by far to leave anything half-finished. But no matter how busy Ava was in the past, she'd always had time for Jean – even on the nights they'd sat working side by side, absorbed in their own tasks, Ava's care had been palpable in the endless cups of tea and kisses dropped atop her head. All of that is gone now, hidden behind a wall of impenetrable silence.

From that dreadful moment of premonition before Cora resurrected her phantom lover, Aiden, Jean had known Ava would take it badly. But she couldn't leave any room for doubt to creep in. Couldn't risk being outed by ambiguity. And if Ava can't see that, she's not as open-minded as she evidently believes.

Jean will not beg for scraps of her time or attention. She won't plead. Won't make herself contemptible. But a soft, secret part of her buried deep inside Jean's chest wants to – that's the scary thing. Knowing how easy it would be to surrender. Every day without contact, the prospect grows sweeter.

It's almost a relief, throwing herself into damage control. All-consuming work that requires laser focus and a pristine attention to detail. Long days spent in the war room, snatching only a few scant hours of sleep at night when the painkillers kick in.

And yet, in spite of the sleep deprivation, Jean is buzzing. Adrenaline fizzes through her veins like sugar – she wonders if this is how Thatcher or Napoleon felt, their power feeding itself in a perfect circuit. Every decision she makes has far-reaching consequences, and always it is necessary to think twelve moves ahead. How Wexler might parry, what could be gained, what risks being lost as a result, and on and on and on.

First Wexler makes noises about pressing charges against Hugo. Sends a photo of Leonides looking into the camera with baleful eyes, forehead bruised and lip bloodied; a side-on shot highlighting the goose-egg swelling.

DDH retaliates with the shot Jean had taken of Rhona, face blotchy with tears, blouse torn open. The bruising and scratching beneath. And Jean's purpled wrist, swollen to twice its usual size.

Despite the cloud hanging over his career, Hugo remains calm, never doubting his sister's influence. And

Rosalind delivers. A permit Leonides was relying on is denied, an acquisition for Hephaestia falls through due to rigid interpretation of an arcane by-law. The kind of paperless backroom deals that Hephaestia will never be able to prove, though they'll know as well as Jean does that strings have been pulled for the Earl of Wiltshire's great-nephew.

Every night Jean falls into bed, exhausted in mind, body, spirit. There's no room for dreams, no room for longing. Yet in the daylight hours it's Ava Jean wants to share her triumphs with, or find respite with in gentle silence when Hephaestia grows obstreperous. There's no more *Andreas! Call me Andreas*. Only *Mr Leonides* or *my client* in Wexler's hand.

Helen reminds Jean to do physio every few hours, standing over her desk with the briskness of Nurse Ratched until she complies. For her painkillers Jean requires no prompting, desperate for that piercing ache to recede into a low throb. In those molasses-slow minutes between Jean and her next dose, she has never been so grateful for DDH's air conditioning system.

Still, there are ways of keeping herself busy. Jean continues as Rhona's point of contact. She explains the decision to end their contract with Hephaestia, an offensive strategy that works to delegitimise whatever claims Leonides might make about the firm – though not Alexander's shock and fury over losing those bountiful billable hours. She outlines Wexler's response, offering quiet acceptance and sizeable payouts on the condition that Rhona, Hugo, and she herself all sign NDAs. She summarises the internal legal department's view of the matter: the best possible outcome for DDH, with no public fallout for the firm or private litigation of individual employees.

'So, you think I should sign?' A muffled tapping echoes through the line – even without video, Jean can picture Rhona clicking her pen against the desk.

'That's not what I said,' Jean says, without sting, pacing her office in stockinged feet (tights had turned peeing into a logistical nightmare for her wrist). 'Rhona, I told you. Nobody will pressure you either way. You have a place here no matter what you decide.'

Rhona's silent for a long time then, only the steady rise of seconds on her screen assuring Jean the call continues. Outside her window London glitters brighter than the galaxy above. And though Jean knows the Thames to be filthy, there's no denying its beauty, shifting and sparkling beneath a starless sky.

'Ms Howard?'

'Yes?'

'I appreciate how kind you're being. But you don't have to treat me like a wee kid.' The crackle of a sigh. 'I know it'll be bad for the firm if I say no. I can't stop thinking about that.'

'Then Peter and I will both go home, since you're doing our job for us.' Rhona doesn't laugh, and Jean doesn't expect her to; humour is thin on the ground this far into a fourteen-hour day. 'But really. What would be bad for you, and what would be good for you?'

'Tha—'

'No, no. Don't tell me – not right away.' Jean rests her forehead against the windowpane, breath fogging its glass. 'Take time to think. Talk over your options with Isla.'

There was a time when she'd have resented the pastoral care, wiping tears and assuaging fears; being 'mummy' while men got on with the business of law. Yet she feels real kinship with the junior associate. Their calls and messages are a trail of breadcrumbs, making sure Rhona can find her way back to the office when she is ready. Jean would sooner accept a dinner date with that lecher Leonides before approving Rhona's resignation. Her career cannot be allowed to go the same way as Mari's – and it's a much sweeter penance than ten Our Fathers.

Each day, regardless of whether they've spoken, Rhona sends her a picture from her walks along Cramond. And for the first time, Edinburgh's lure seems truly worthy of a bucket list. Jean has never supposed herself to be any kind of romantic, but she can't help wondering what it might be like to walk barefoot along the shore with Ava by her side, the North Sea washing over their feet.

–

The weeks pass, summer taking firm hold of London. Rooftop bars open, pale sunbathers lie sprawled across towels in parks, and tourists swarm the streets. It's always a relief, sinking into the leather upholstery of Bogdan's Jaguar, cool air a caress against her skin. And yet – even knowing how miserable the underground would be, pressed against strangers sweating through their commute, Jean misses having a reason to brave it.

When Bogdan drops her off at home, instead of heading indoors, Jean opens the gate to the residential garden. The air is fragrant with lilies, and the path is lined with the bedding plants the neighbours have been meticulous about maintaining since retirement, petals just beginning to close as the sun retreats behind their row of houses.

Ava, always keen to make sure Jean got outdoors enough, would appreciate this little oasis; the quiet broken only by the bees buzzing past, heavy with pollen. And yet, Jean suspects, she would oppose this garden being reserved for the privileged few.

Jean sinks onto the bench, kicking off her heels to curl her toes in the warm grass – suspiciously verdant amid another hosepipe ban. And, before she can second-guess herself, Jean dials Ava's number. Grips the bench's wooden arm so tightly paint flakes off beneath her fingers as it rings.

'Hello?'

Jean startles, heart working overtime as hope and fear do battle inside her chest. There's still a hint of a laugh in Ava's voice, as if she's just broken off a joyful conversation.

'Ava. Thank you for picking up. I— I'm sorry.'

'Yeah.' A sigh. 'You said that before.'

'And I'll say it again. As many times as you need to hear it.'

'Jean…' So much weariness tied to her name.

'Just listen. Words aren't the only thing I wanted to offer.' Jean's stomach knots tight. If Ava turns her down there will be no saving face, no coming back from the humiliation. 'I wondered whether you'd like to come over to my house this weekend. For dinner.'

Ava says nothing, though Jean could swear her breath hitches.

'We've spent so much time at yours, and I'd like to return that hospitality. Show you a little bit of my world.' Jean catches her lower lip between her teeth, tugging a strip of dry skin free, but the sharp sting of it does nothing to distract from the ache behind her ribs. 'If you're still interested in seeing it. In seeing me.'

An engine rumbles – if Ava's on the bus, she'll be en route to Aaliyah's straight from work. 'Okay. Does Saturday work? I'm taking my niblings to the cinema at three, but I could come round after?'

'Yes!' Jean has to push the word out past the blockage in her throat, and it comes out more forcefully than she intends. 'That would be – yes. Saturday is perfect.'

'Cool. I'll drop the kids off at Al's on the way. Say half six?'

'I can't promise haute cuisine – I'm still wearing this stupid splint half the time. But there'll be good wine.' Jean's lips curve upwards – if Ava is to forgive her, this will seal the deal. 'And I think you'll enjoy dessert.'

'Jean Euphemia Howard. Are you propositioning me?'

'No!' Jean's face burns, though the sun has dipped beneath the roof – she has very deliberately not tried to seduce Ava into forgiveness. 'There really is dessert. Get your mind out of the gutter!'

Laughter bubbles through the line, pouring over Jean like champagne.

Chapter Twenty

Ava arrives at precisely six-thirty. She wears a tank top and a check shirt long enough to skim the hem of her cutoffs – the sight of so much bronzed bare skin on display has Jean seriously questioning her decision to leave sex out of the forgiveness campaign.

One of those legs turns inwards, leaving Ava pigeon-toed as she lingers on the doorstep. 'I brought Pinot Grigio.' She holds the bottle aloft. 'It's supposed to be good in summer.'

She's nervous too. Elation soars in Jean, bright and powerful as a firework. Ava wouldn't be nervous if she were indifferent, uncaring about this evening's outcome. Jean takes the bottle, sweating softly against her palm. 'Perfect – I'll put it in the fridge.'

Without Cora and Imogen, freed from the necessary cage of secrecy, Ava is easier tonight. She explores the space, taking in Jean's photos and curios; the various awards lining her shelves. But it's not any of the glass trophies Ava goes for – she lifts a silver frame tarnished with age down from the shelf, peering intently at the photo.

'My parents,' Jean says, coming to stand beside her. They're younger even than Ava in that shot, beaming newlyweds on their honeymoon.

'I can tell. You have your dad's hair and colouring, but your face is the image of your mother's.'

Jean takes the picture. As a child she'd longed for her mother's looks – she'd seemed as glamorous as Jane Birkin, even in mended clothes. But beauty had burned brighter in her sister, with just a smidge left over for Jean herself. 'People have been telling me that my entire life, but I never see it.'

'I do.' The air between them grows charged, thick and heavy as the moment before lightning strikes.

Jean pulls away, though every part of her yearns to tilt her face up towards Ava's. 'I'd better check on dinner; it should be ready now.'

'Let me help?'

In the kitchen she passes Ava a pair of oven gloves and stirs the sauce bubbling gently on the hob. Ava lifts out the salmon then the roasting tray of vegetables, setting them down on broad marble chopping boards.

Sure enough, the salmon is baked to perfection when Jean prises open the tinfoil, steam scented bright with citrus. She cuts off two generous slices, retrieving her pot from the stove to drizzle them with lemon *beurre blanc*. Finally, as Ava tips the vegetables into a tureen matching their dinner plates, Jean garnishes each portion with fresh cut lemon and dill. 'Voilà! Dinner is served.'

Between them they carry the dishes through, Ava darting back into the kitchen before Jean can. 'I'm pretty sure this counts as haute cuisine,' Ava says, setting down the tureen of potatoes.

They sit on opposite sides of the table, and Jean shakes her head. 'There's nothing to it – you just season the fish and vegetables, then throw them in the oven. Even the sauce only takes fifteen minutes.'

Pink and sizzling, the salmon is perfection, melting beneath the gentle pressure of their forks. 'If I were you, and I could cook like this, I'd eat salmon every single day.'

'It never seemed worth cooking an entire fish for one. This was my fallback meal whenever Henry and I had friends over.' Jean could curse herself – dwelling on past lovers is the ultimate date faux pas.

But Ava's eyes are alight with curiosity. 'He's your ex-husband, right?'

'Yes. He's Lawson and Pierce's legal director now. We were together for just over a decade.' Jean sighs. 'There were so many times when I thought Henry and I were better as friends than as lovers, especially after we got married. But past a certain point there's no rowing back.'

Ava's laughter is low and musical. 'Been there. A major peril of the lesbian scene: the dating pool and friend pool are one and the same.'

'I never thought about that. In the straight world it's assumed that friendship is a step on the way to something else between a man and woman.' In retrospect it had been obvious Henry wanted her from the beginning, but Jean was blindsided by his declaration – until realising just how far it might work to her own advantage. Henry's ring was a shield to ward off male advances, and incontrovertible proof that she – Jean Howard – was the *right* kind of woman. 'But he was decent, safe. And I wanted…'

Jean breaks off, on the cusp of revealing far more than she'd intended. Barely halfway through her first glass, it's not the wine loosening her tongue, but Ava.

Sensing Jean's unease, she moves the conversation along. 'What's he like? Henry, I mean.'

'Thoughtful. Slow to anger and quick to forgive. Always ready to laugh. In another life, I think the two of you would get on like a house on fire.'

Ava stops chewing then, frozen still, and the absurdity of Jean's words hangs in the air between them. Jean sets her fork down, massaging the ache blossoming behind her forehead. 'I'm sorry – I don't know why I keep saying these things.'

Ava's hand finds Jean's on the table, whisper-soft against her injured wrist. 'Don't be. I like it, hearing about your life. When you stop worrying about what other people think and open up.'

Jean has no notion what to say to that, never mind what it makes her feel; there's simply nothing to compare it to. Slow enough to keep from jostling her wrist, she laces her fingers through Ava's, savouring the skim of thumb against knuckles.

Afterwards, Ava insists on carrying their plates back through to the kitchen. And Jean retrieves dessert from the fridge, setting the glass platter down on the counter.

Ava rinses their plates and loads them into the dishwasher, eyes popping as she takes in the pièce de résistance. 'Oh my god, this looks amazing. What is it?'

'An edible Twix arrangement.' Jean points to each item in turn. 'There's salted caramel Twix cheesecake, Twix cupcakes, and fruit covered in Twix chocolate.'

Ava bounces with excitement then, curls shifting with their own gravity. She wraps both arms around Jean, careful not to crush her injured wrist, and plants a firm kiss against the swell of Jean's cheek.

Ava doesn't pull away then. And Jean holds still, scarcely daring to breathe. She just drinks it all in. The swell of Ava's hip beneath her hand; the sliver of warm skin in the gap peeking between Ava's denim shorts and soft cotton top. The quickening rise and fall of her ribs pressed flush against Jean's breasts. The heady aroma of Ava's cologne, and beneath it an even more intoxicating scent – the natural perfume of Ava's sun-warmed skin.

Perhaps if she stays like this, Ava will continue to cradle her. Time will freeze, the two of them fused together.

But no. Ava's fingertips caress Jean's back, from the nape of her neck to the dip of her spine. Even this ghost of a touch is enough to set Jean trembling, which she'd have assumed would be permission enough.

Yet Ava, always exquisitely careful with her, pulls back just far enough for Jean to glimpse pupils blown dark and wide as the disc of a sunflower. 'I'd like to kiss you.'

Breathless laughter catches in Jean's throat. 'I think I'll go crazy if you don't. And there's no need to keep asking me every time.'

What they have needs no grand declarations. She's been all Ava's since that first night, when, even as a stranger, she'd set every nerve in Jean's body alight.

'I don't *have* to. But I like to.' Ava presses a kiss against Jean's temple. 'It's been a while. Besides, something's going on with you. Ever since your wrist.'

'It is,' Jean allows, rubbing the flannel lapel of Ava's shirt. 'But I feel good with you. Safe.'

Jean's embarrassment proves short-lived as Ava ducks down to kiss her, chaste until Jean sucks at that full lower lip. Then Ava's pulling her close, Jean balanced on tiptoe, kissing her breathless.

'You know,' Ava says, lips warm against Jean's hair. 'I wouldn't mind a break before dessert.'

Jean's heart pounds against the drum of Ava's skin, such a fierce tattoo that she must surely feel the vibrations. 'Oh?'

'Yeah.' Her hands slide round Jean's body, coming to rest on either side of her hips. 'I was thinking maybe you could show me around upstairs?'

'I could do that.' Jean holds out her good hand. Leads the way.

Then they're in Jean's bedroom. In bringing her here, having Ava and being had by her here in the bed where Jean sleeps every night, she's relinquished all possibility of ever being able to exorcise Ava's ghost. Even after she leaves tomorrow, and later for good, the memory of her will linger in the dip of the mattress, in the empty space in Jean's bed.

'You alright?' Ava's hand finds Jean's cheek, jolting her out of the future. Back into the present where Ava is flesh and blood and filled with animal craving.

'I'm feeling good.' Jean loops her arms around Ava's shoulders. 'About to be feeling better still.'

But Ava doesn't lean down to kiss her. She keeps on watching Jean through eyes darkened by lust that she doesn't act upon. 'You sure? We don't have to do anything. Things will be good between us either way.'

Tenderness tightens to an ache in Jean's throat. 'I really want this. I really want you. So much that it scares me.'

Ava wears a peculiar expression, frowning and smiling at once. 'I'll never give you a reason to be afraid of me, Jean. I promise.'

And just like that Jean's face becomes a contradiction too, tears brimming even as she laughs. 'I know that. I've known it since the first night we met. It's just…'

'What?' Ava smooths the hair back from Jean's face. There's no place to hide, but she doesn't need one.

'My life... my past. It can be complicated.'

'Then let me give you something simple now.'

Ava moves slowly, giving Jean every chance to stop her. But instead, Jean melts into her arms, tilting her face up for a languid kiss. Lets Ava steer her to the bed. When the backs of Ava's thighs knock against the frame she sits down on the mattress, and Jean steps into the space between her legs.

One after the other Ava slides the straps of her sundress down Jean's shoulders, and they fall into the dips of her elbows. The dress pools around Jeans hips, and Ava plants a trail of kisses above the curve of her bra, the silken brush of her curls sending a shudder through Jean.

Every sinew comes alive as Ava's lips lock around Jean's nipple, and she sucks the bud into her mouth, tongue darting over the tip until Jean's mewling, back arched. Her grip on Ava's shoulders loosens, and only a steadying hand against Jean's back keeps her knees from buckling completely. Yearning hollows the pit of Jean's belly. She wriggles out of her sundress. Straddles Ava's thigh, rocking against bone and muscle, only the damp strip of silk separating them.

Their lips meet and Jean slides her tongue into Ava's mouth, searching, hungry for more. Ava must share her appetite. She lifts Jean off her leg and onto the top end of the mattress – even in her passion, she's careful not to jostle Jean's wrist. And while Jean has never been one of those women who fantasises about being dainty and pliant in her lover's arms, there's no denying that Ava's strength is hot.

Ava shucks off her shirt and cutoffs, climbing onto the bed in her tank top and boyshorts alone. The second she's close enough Jean pulls her down, sandwiched between that lithe body and the mattress.

Their eyes meet – it could be a second, or an eternity – and Jean reaches up to tuck the curtain of curls behind Ava's ear. Ava rolls, pulling Jean with her so that they both lie on their side, and Jean rests her injured wrist safe against the subtle curve of her hip. But as Ava's hands rove, the ache of it recedes. There's only the whisper of skin against skin, and the tantalising possibility of more.

Between the tangle of legs Ava cups Jean's sex, tracing its contours through the silk. 'I'm afraid I've ruined your good underwear.'

'That's half the fun of wearing silk.' Jean smirks, rolling her hips. 'Though I never knew it 'til now.'

Ava bites her lip, eyes dark as midnight. 'You're a dangerous woman, Jean Howard.'

Then her fingers hook around the hem of Jean's panties, pulling them free so that she lies naked as the day she was born. Ava covers Jean with her own body, an arm wrapped tight around her shoulders. The other circles Jean's areola until her breath is ragged, plucking and rolling the nipple between her fingers. It's sweet torture. And when Jean can take it no more, she grips Ava's hand, sliding it down her belly until Ava cups the cropped curls of her mound.

She parts to the touch, Ava's caress velvet smooth. And it occurs to Jean that any residual shame she felt over her wetness has vanished, burned away by the heat of Ava's desire. Ava revels in it, sliding about Jean's entrance until she aches for more.

'Don't tease me.' Jean bites her lip as Ava's fingers probe and withdraw. 'Please?'

'Shhh.' Ava pulls her close, pressing a kiss to Jean's parted lips. 'I've got you, Jellybean.'

Jean opens her mouth to object to the nickname, but it's at that moment Ava's fingertips make contact with her clit, one pressed on either side. And that gentle kneading is enough to drive all conscious thought from Jean's mind. Just when it grows unbearable, Ava pulls away, dipping two fingers in and out of her entrance until Jean's bones are liquid and she's moaning without a care that her neighbours might hear through the wall.

Those throaty cries only egg Ava on. Her heel of her hand finds Jean's clit, sure and relentless. Even as Jean bucks against her Ava maintains that excruciating rhythm, holding Jean on the precipice until she's dizzy and breathless.

'God, you feel so good. Every single time.' Ava kisses her neck, her jaw, the fleshy lobe of Jean's ear. 'Your cunt drives me wild. The way you smell, the way you taste. That slick little noise when I fuck you. It's everything.'

Even if Jean could think of a response to that, words are utterly beyond her. But Ava takes mercy, curling her fingers to press against Jean's front wall. It's an exquisite fullness, heightened by the steady pressure building against her clit – up and down, just the way Jean likes it. A sweet agony.

'That's it,' Ava whispers. 'Let go. I've got you.'

Then she's coming hard, this riptide of an orgasm slamming into her. Tucked safe in the crook of Ava's neck, Jean shudders and twitches, the tension ebbing from her limbs, pleasure flowing in its wake. All the while Ava strokes her back until she stills.

But before Jean can get her breath back, the hand between her legs stirs. The faintest stroking. Jean hums at this gentle post-coital pleasure. Ava leans down to kiss the tip of her nose, her mouth. She matches the glide of her fingers to the rhythm of their tongues. Languid and heady as spiced wine. And Jean finds herself on the cusp of another orgasm, one she hadn't even been aware of chasing.

Ava swallows her surprised gasp – no matter how many times they do it, Jean finds fresh wonder in her body's aptitude.

'Good?'

Jean laughs. Surely the limpness of her body is answer enough. 'What, do you want a performance review?'

'Just making sure you're satisfied.'

'I am.' Jean rolls onto her front. 'But you're not. Come here and let me feel you.'

'Your wish is my command.'

Jean pulls the top over Ava's head, eager as a schoolboy to explore what's underneath. But at the strain on her wrist she gasps, sharper than the sounds she'd made in pleasure.

'I could try with my left hand,' Jean says, doubtful. 'But it's not very co-ordinated. Or I could use my tongue.'

Ava's teeth sink into her swollen bottom lip. But she shakes her head, crushed curls bobbing. 'Maybe another time, if you want to. But for now, I have another idea.'

Disappointment drops into the pit of Jean's stomach, a stone sinking to the bottom of a pool. But there's relief too, its brightness unmistakable. 'What do you have in mind?'

'Sit back against the headboard.' Jean complies, angling a pillow to sit vertical behind her back. And Ava pulls off her boyshorts, rising to plant a knee either side of Jean's leg.

Ava reaches down to part the lips of her sex, spreading herself wide as she sinks onto Jean's thigh. The hot slide of her sends Jean into a frenzy. Her fingers bite into Ava's hips, rocking her until the whites of her eyes show. Her breasts are irresistible as she rocks, and Jean seizes a nipple between her teeth.

In retaliation Ava's hand snakes between their thighs, rubbing flush against Jean's sex. A cry rips from Jean's throat as Ava's fingertips catches her clit, achingly tender. Then they're coming together, falling to lie slumped against the pillows.

'Fuck,' Ava breathes, the shallow rise and fall of her chest. 'That was intense.'

'Was it good for you?' Jean twists against her, their bodies slippery with sweat. 'I mean, four orgasms and you did the work for all of them.'

Ava smirks. 'Because taking a beautiful woman to bed is such a *terrible* hardship. Woe is me!'

Beautiful. Ava has repeated it often enough. But with no barriers between them, the word pierces Jean. 'You'll tell me, though? If you think I'm being selfish.'

'There's nothing selfish about giving me exactly what I want.' Ava's fingers, still buried inside Jean, curve enough to unspool the argument in her throat. 'I'll never get tired of doing this; of making you come.'

'You might,' Jean gasps. She rests a hand on Ava's arm, and at once her fingers ease their way free.

'And the sun might stop shining.' Ava gathers Jean into her arms, tugging the sheet up to cover their cooling bodies. 'The moon might fall from the sky. The stars might all go dim.'

Out of every possible combination of words in the English language, not one exists that is both adequate and safe. But Ava doesn't seem to expect a response. Her breathing slows, as does the hand caressing Jean's back.

All the same, Ava has shared some vital part of herself; exposed her jugular to sharp teeth and claws. Jean can't pay her back in poetry or professions. But there is one truth to share. The certainty that's sat within Jean all these weeks is clawing at her throat, persistent as an itch.

'Ava?' Jean kicks off the sheets, sweat pooling in the hollows of her knees and elbows.

'Mm?'

'I'm going to tell you something.'

Ava rolls onto her side to look at Jean, scrubbing sleep from her eye.

'And it doesn't – it can't – change anything. But you ought to know.' Jean's stomach churns, the ease of her orgasm drained quite away. 'I don't think I'm straight.'

Ava's silent for a long moment, brows drawn together. 'Thank you,' she says at last. 'For telling me.'

'You don't seem surprised.'

She reaches down between Jean's legs, her fingers slipping through the residual slickness. 'This.' Ava eases her fingers into Jean's mouth, and she licks them clean, tongue swirling. 'Is a dead giveaway.'

'No, but I mean – beyond the obvious. There's a difference between sexual tourism and a real basis of attraction.' Jean addresses the freckles on Ava's shoulder. 'Or at least a lot of lesbians on the internet seem to think so.'

Ava snorts, breath ruffling Jean's hair. 'The fact you went online and researched this is Peak Jean.'

'Fuck you, don't laugh at me.' But the giggles are catching, as they so often are with Ava.

'I'm not laughing at you. But you've got to admit you're relentlessly Type A.'

'I have to admit nothing.'

'Seriously, though. I don't think straight people spend much time or energy interrogating the possibility that they might not be.' Ava adjusts the blanket, tucking it over Jean's shoulder. 'That said, there are some pretty standard tells.'

'Such as?'

'When Gillian Anderson comes on the television, do you ever think about how hot she is?'

Jean huffs a sigh. 'Hasn't everyone felt that way since the mid-nineties?'

'Good point. Next question: in your personal life are you particularly drawn to women?'

Jean has more acquaintances on file than shares in her ISAs. But with close friends she's always gone for quality over quantity – Naomi, Cora, and Imogen had been enough to fill her heart. Until this unquantifiable thing with Ava, tilting from fuck buddies (Jean still despises that term) to friends that also fuck. Actual friends, with trust and gentleness and laughter. Peter's really the only man in her life now, and even that's partly down to him being the only one who knows where the bodies are buried, having picked up a shovel and helped her dig each grave.

'Yes.'

Ava nods, tone casual as if she's asking Jean about the weather. 'And have you ever had particularly intense friendships with women?'

She's thought of Marianne less since that first fateful meeting with Ava. But she's never far away, too much a part of Jean to ever be truly exiled. Both scholarship girls, both ambitious women determined to make it in a man's world, they'd shared an instinctive understanding.

Though Jean had been thrilled about being taken on as a junior associate, the thought of working united with Mari towards a shared goal had invigorated her at least as much as its accomplishment.

And Jean had cherished the little moments. The easy intimacy of sharing a cigarette – Bridget's dire warnings of cancer had been enough to put Jean off ever becoming a serious smoker, yet she'd been unable to resist putting her lips to the ghost of Mari's lipstick. Those nights when they'd stayed up until the small hours plotting, drunk on cheap Merlot and their own glittering potential. Those glorious seven months when they'd shared a poky one-bedroom flat, trading the bed and the sofa every other week. Jean had always put off changing the sheets, blaming work for her slovenly habits, when really – a truth glimpsed only from the corner of her eye – she'd savoured breathing in Mari's melon shampoo while drifting off to sleep.

Ava's out for the count now – her patient silence has shifted into slow, even breaths, a little sigh on every exhale. Yet even after Ava's face slackens, she holds on tight to Jean. Pillowed in the hollow between her breasts, Jean hears every beat of Ava's heart pulsing against her cheek. Through the membrane of skin, she whispers her confession to that tireless muscle: 'Yes.'

Chapter Twenty-One

Over breakfast – the edible Twix arrangement for Ava, and poached egg on toast for Jean – she chances an invitation to the Women in Law luncheon. It's an excellent opportunity for Ava to network before her launch, but – knowing Ava is unlikely to accept on those terms – Jean sells her presence as a friendly non-DDH face to help ease Rhona back in. Even shielded by the cloak of a fresh NDA, Rhona is anxious about returning to the legal world.

When the day comes, Ava is good as her word – warm enough to set Rhona at her ease, but formal enough that the junior associate never clocks the dynamic between them as a point of interest. They register together, picking up purple tote bags loaded with Moleskine notebooks, artisan soap, aromatherapy candles. Ava swaps with Rhona to give her the vegan dark chocolate, instantly winning a friend.

Then it's time to split up, Jean gravitating towards a session on women in leadership. The blurb describes nothing Jean hasn't already digested via assorted books, courses, and podcasts. But Elizabeth Granger waves Jean over and they sit together in the corner of the back row, Elizabeth's head bent towards Jean's ear as she enquires about upcoming vacancies in upper management at DDH; whether they intend to recruit internally, or from further afield. And though Jean's non-committal in her response, a bland reminder that keeping a CV up to date never hurts, they both leave the session satisfied. Elizabeth wouldn't be unpleasant to work with; she knows when to push and when to step back into the shadows. An essential quality in a deputy, and one found far more readily in middle-aged women than their male counterparts.

Lunch is held in an exquisite old music hall, chandeliers bathing the room in light the colour of champagne. Pillars lining the back wall hold up the circular balcony above, should the space be used as a theatre or lecture hall. The dancefloor is covered in fleur-de-lis carpeting, muffling the growing chorus of voices.

Two dozen circular tables are spread evenly around the hall. Ava and Rhona are deep in conversation in their allotted seats at table eight, right in the heart of the action, with a space in the middle Jean takes to be hers. They don't notice her approach, Rhona laughing until she's pink-cheeked and breathless. Jean lingers to watch them, lifting a flute of prosecco from a passing waiter's tray. 'I'll swap places with one of you, if you want to continue.'

'Oh no, Ms Howard. That really isn't necessary. Ava was just telling me about her mother's church.'

'Oh?'

'Yeah.' Ava chuckles. 'Her pastor had a harder time accepting me being a lawyer than a lesbian. Kept on quoting Isaiah: *No one calls for justice; no one pleads a case with integrity. They rely on empty arguments, they utter lies; they conceive trouble and give birth to evil.*'

The bubbles catch in Jean's throat, and she coughs, waving off her companions' concern through watering eyes. Whatever denomination of the church Mrs Harris belongs to, she doubts very much it's Catholic – Father Fulton preached eternal damnation so often that Jean could practically smell the brimstone, and her own burning hair. She'd stopped going to Mass upon moving to Oxford, stopped believing long before, yet the portrait of hell that he'd painted remains vivid in Jean's imagination even now.

'He changed his tune when a member of the congregation tried to make an insurance claim against the church.' Ava grins. 'First and only time I've ever used the Act of God defence.'

Rhona dissolves into fits of giggles once more, and Jean musters a weak smile. Though the junior associate knows Ava's sexuality, she doesn't seem to guess about Jean's own. All the same, this conversation needs careful management. 'So, tell me. Have either of you met anyone interesting today?'

Rhona sobers a little, though as the hall fills, she chatters happily about her various encounters. An old chum from her all-girls' school now working as a junior associate for Lawson and Pierce; a guest lecturer from her university days.

'I caught up with someone too – an old colleague of sorts.' Ava's face lights up with a sudden epiphany. 'Actually, Jean, she reminds me a little of you. The confidence, the immaculate wardrobe – she just radiates competence. Which makes sense, because she said you used to work together.'

Jean ignores the foie gras being set down before her. 'What's her name?'

'Kate Brennan. She's a prosecutor now, with Minerva.' Ava thanks the waitress, lifting her cutlery. 'I got to know her through AWCRC; she's taken on some of our bigger cases. In court she's absolutely terrifying – a total Valkyrie. But the rest of the time she's fun.'

Jean frowns. Before menopause her memory never drew absolute blanks – but then having once sat in on the same meeting or course might easily have been embellished, reworked into a collegiate relationship. 'The name doesn't ring a bell – is she married?'

'Yeah, to Liza Devlin from Women's Justice League.' Ava flashes Rhona a quick grin. 'The women's sector can be pretty incestuous.'

So, Brennan was always her surname. 'Doesn't ring any bells. Sorry.'

Ava frowns. 'She was talking like she knew you really well.'

'People can be like that with Ms Howard.' Rhona raises her fork but does not eat, red pepper and chickpea pâté speared on its tines. 'Maybe Kate thought you could get her access, so she played up the connection.'

'Now, Rhona,' Jean says. But inwardly she smiles, thinks: *Rhona Baird, I will make a shark of you yet*. A sweet, unthreatening exterior to hide the cunning, just like Imogen.

'Oh shit.' Ava's brows knit together. 'I didn't even think of that. Kate said she was hoping to speak with you.'

'Don't worry about it.' Jean allows herself a wry smile. 'I'm sure I'll cope.'

Looking back on it, Jean's certain these are the words that damned her, sealing the deal on this cosmic jinx.

After the plates have been cleared away, in the lull between dessert and coffee, delegates hop tables to network. Ava takes Rhona to meet her colleague Amari while Jean swaps pleasantries with Amelia Hawthorne, a surface-level conversation, yet intent enough to ward off unwanted interruption. When Jean's companions reappear, Amelia turns back to her own table. And it's just as well because Jean's face freezes in a rictus smile as she catches sight of the third woman.

The chestnut bob has long since grown out, hair spilling down past her shoulders. Yet instead of dyeing it she's let every strand pale to natural silver. It frames her angular face just so, giving the impression of an elf queen plucked straight from a Tolkien novel, flowing robes replaced by a sharp charcoal suit. Those eyes have lost none of their old intensity, vivid as the sky on a midsummer afternoon. Yet they hold none of the old warmth as they take in Jean gaping up at her.

'Hello Jean.' Her voice is the same too, those smooth polished vowels they'd practised with one another until it became habit.

Ava steps forward, a new wariness in her expression. 'This is—'

'Marianne.'

'It's Kate now.' She sits down in Rhona's empty seat. 'Kate Brennan.'

'Your mother's maiden name.' The reason Jean has never been able to find her on Facebook, nor dig up recent Google results.

'I needed a fresh start after what Will did to me.' She reaches across the table, twirling the stem of Jean's wine glass between her fingers. 'And you.'

Jean's heart stutters. A twitch starts beneath her eye and, even when Jean presses her hand to the skin, it carries on with the spasmodic pulsing.

'I – I'll leave you two to catch up.' Rhona rises, the scrape of her chair drawing Amelia's interest. She's gone before Jean can think how to manage this moment being witnessed by a subordinate; gone before it even occurs to Jean that management is needed.

'Give us a minute,' Marianne says to Ava.

But she rests a hand on the back of Jean's chair. 'I don't think that's such a good idea.'

'Go on,' Jean says. There isn't a single word Marianne's likely to speak that will improve Ava's opinion of her. Soon she will realise that Jean isn't kind at all; not when it really counts.

Still Ava hesitates, a thousand unspoken questions shining in her eyes.

'Please,' Jean whispers. The edge of her pinkie finger brushes almost imperceptibly against the side of Ava's hand, delicate as a butterfly's wing. Yet Jean sees it, the moment her touch nudges Ava into acceptance; Marianne's knowing smirk as she retreats.

'Mm.' Mari swigs the wine, leaving an orange lipstick kiss on the glass. 'I always wondered whether you'd get there. The selfish part of me hoped you'd be just as isolated and unsure as I was, when I had to start from scratch. But this is better – I'm going to enjoy pulling the wool from Ava's eyes. She's so… principled.'

The room swims, all the surrounding chatter impossibly far-away – or perhaps her peers, scenting trouble, have fallen silent to better hear her humiliation. Jean tries to take a steadying breath, but it's as if every last drop of air has been sucked from the hall's domed ceiling.

'I'm sorry,' Jean says, the world narrowing to her and Marianne. She's close enough that Jean could reach out and touch her, feel the warmth bleeding through that severe jacket. She's on the far side of an impossible gulf stretching out between them, all that love and warmth and loyalty lost to the chasm below. 'If I could take it all back, if I could return to that moment… I'd make entirely different choices.'

Marianne drains the glass, lips turned down though the vintage is sweet. 'You actually believe that, don't you? It's this comforting lie that you've wrapped around yourself all these years. Same old Jean – whatever version of events best suits your interests becomes the truth.'

'It's not a lie. Every single day for the last twenty-five years I've regretted betraying you.' Jean's eyes burn with unshed tears, but she doesn't look away from Marianne, doesn't break the tenuous thread of connection between them. 'Losing your friendship hurt more than anything.'

Henry had known it too; having held Jean together through her grief over Marianne, it was obvious that Jean didn't feel the same devastation when he too began pulling away. A friendship cherished far more than a marriage.

Marianne's eyes glitter hard and bright as diamonds. 'Then why stab me in the back?'

'I was scared!' The cups and saucers jump as Jean slaps the table. 'Terrified out of my mind over losing everything I'd worked for – my career, my reputation, any prospect of advancement.'

'So you took all that from *me* instead?' Marianne's smile grows bitter. 'Made me into the liar. The attention seeker. The whore. Pleading temporary insanity doesn't get you out of this one, Jean.'

'Will did that. To both of us. But he's dead now.' Marianne's fury dims, replaced by dull shock. And Jean leans forward in her seat, pleading, heedless of the stares she's attracting. 'Peter's retiring this autumn. Then the firm will be mine. *Ours*. I'll fast-track you to where you should have been: senior partner. And it'll be just like we imagined when we were young.'

'You still dream about that?' Mari's bright malice fades. She stands, looking at Jean for a long moment, considering. And hope flutters in Jean's chest, a white flag on the battlefield.

Jean rises, unable to keep the note of pleading from her voice. 'You don't have to decide right away.' She swallows, ignoring the eyes swarming over her like ants. If she can just make this right with Mari, they can run damage control. *Together.* Come back to this very lunch next year with an empowering session on DDH's all-female management. The year after that, a rebrand: swap Will's name for Marianne's – or Kate's. Whatever she prefers. 'Take your time, think about it.'

'I don't have to.' Mari steps closer, close enough that her breath grazes Jean's cheek. 'I'd rather be flayed alive and have my flesh covered in salt than ever work with you again.'

Jean sinks against the table, legs slack. And Marianne presses her advantage, not a trace of mercy to be found in her face.

'I always wondered about you, Jean. Did you enjoy getting on your knees for him, or was it the price you paid to get ahead?' Her words are a fist to the gut, stealing Jean's breath. But even if she could speak Marianne leaves no room for interruption. 'Either way, it hasn't worked out too badly. *Managing partner after your big promotion.* Nobody left to blow on your climb to the top.'

A sharp intake of breath – not her own, but the crowd's. Jean's vision swims, a sea of shocked faces blurring together, the chandelier overhead breaking into a kaleidoscope of crystal and light. And Ava materialises by her side as the first tears fall.

'What the fuck, Kate? None of what you're saying is fair. And you've done enough work with trauma to know that.' Though Jean has never heard her speak so harshly, Ava's hand is gentle resting against Jean's back, subtle and steadying.

Marianne's gaze flits between them. And her lip curls. '*Fair?* I feel a responsibility to tell you who Jean Howard really is, Ava.'

'I know exactly who Jean is,' Ava says, her chin at a defiant tilt. 'You're the one that I misjudged.'

Ava, who always thinks the best of people. Ava, who would likely have made entirely different choices – better choices – had she been in Jean's shoes. Jean stands, rooted to the spot as her life implodes.

'Then you'll know that our old boss, William Decker, abused his power over us. And when I reported him for sexual misconduct, Decker and Dennings, as it was then, opened an investigation.' Marianne makes no effort to keep her voice down, and her words ripple through the hall, killing any pretence of conversation across the room. 'And when they interviewed her, your *friend* here lied. Said Decker was innocent of all wrongdoing, and she couldn't imagine him going after any female subordinate.'

Humiliation scorches Jean's cheeks. Her voice can't squeeze past the ache in her throat. And Jean remembers a different kind of pain; the ache after Will had jammed his turgid pink slug between her teeth until she'd gagged. Ava too is silent, and it's a relief that her beautiful face is so blurred Jean can't make out her expression.

'Jean Howard is a liar who would throw anyone and anything under the bus to get ahead. She kept her mouth shut when I needed help, but was all too happy opening it when Will Decker ha—'

'*Enough!*' Ava's voice ricochets against the walls, stripped of all warmth and gentleness.

Jean doesn't know whether that fury is directed at Marianne or herself. She doesn't stick around to find out. The shock of Ava's voice jolts her back into motion. And the same self-preservation Marianne had condemned her for carries Jean from the hall on shaking legs.

Steps jerky, she teeters into the corridor. But a group of delegates is clustered at the other end, queuing to get into the bar. And there's no stemming these tears, the dam of Jean's self-control crumbling against the pressure behind her eyes. Before they can take notice of her, Jean pushes through another door.

Inside is a single toilet, one sink, a lone dryer positioned low down. The disabled loo. It's wrong for her to take up this space, yet Jean can no more cross the threshold again than she could crawl across hot coals. She slides down the wall to sit on the filthy floor.

'Jean?' A knock on the door. 'Jean, it's Ava.'

Jean closes her eyes. As revenge goes, it's nothing short of perfection – Marianne poisoning her relationship with the only woman Jean has craved since.

'I know you're there. Please let me in.'

It will be worse if Ava makes a scene in the hall. Better that she come inside and denounce Jean to her face. Jean reaches up to unlock the door, pulling both knees to her chest as it swings open.

But there's no condemnation hardening Ava's features. She kneels before Jean without a thought for her suit. 'Hey. Look at me. Let's take some deep breaths together, okay?'

Only then does Jean realise that ragged wheezing sound is coming from her chest. She gives a jerky nod.

Breathes in. And out. In. And out. When she's calmed enough to speak, she says: 'I think I'm having a heart attack.'

'No.' Ava grips her hand. 'It's a panic attack. You'll be alright soon — I promise.'

'A panic attack?' Jean knots her fingers in her hair, pulling it free from the careful chignon. 'That's stupid — those aren't real.'

'Yeah? Then you won't have any problem naming five things you can see.'

Ava's still giving her that look, like she's a baby bird with a broken wing. Jean casts her eyes around the dingy bathroom. 'There's the sink. Mirror. Paper towel dispenser. Bin. And the baby changing table.'

'Good job.' Ava rests a hand atop Jean's knee, squeezing. 'Now give me four things you can feel.'

'Sweat — this blouse is plastered to my back, my hair's sticking to my forehead.' When Jean leaves this bathroom, it won't be with her head held high — rather, as a smeary, sticky mess. Her breath hitches painfully tight. Anyone who looks at her will see the ugly truth of Marianne's words. 'Oh God.'

'You're fine,' Ava says. 'Look at me, Jean. Three more things. You've got this.'

'My shoe's chafing at the ankle — I think there's a blister.' Ava nods encouragingly, but Jean's mind is like a hummingbird, flitting from thought to thought too quickly to zero in on any one sensation. Until Ava squeezes her knee again. 'Your hand; it's warm. And, uh, the tiles are cold through my tights.'

Damp too, though the thought of mystery bathroom liquid seeping into her clothes doesn't bother Jean — Marianne has stretched her mind to stress capacity. Wild laughter gushes from Jean, snot bubbling from her nose. Ava simply fishes a tissue from her pocket and wipes Jean's face. It is without doubt their least erotic exchange of bodily fluids to date – there can be no coming back from this, assuming anything remains to come back to.

'You're doing so well. Tell me three things you can hear.'

'Your voice.' Jean wants to comment on how it never seems to stop with the stupid questions; yet they are the bridge carrying her from one unbearable second to the next. 'The tap dripping. And the hand dryer next door.'

'Wonderful,' Ava says, as if she'd recited pi to the thirty-seventh decimal place. 'Now name two things you can smell.'

'Really?'

'Just go with it.'

Jean does as she's bid. 'Cheap lemon cleaning products. And that scent you wear. With the cedar and jasmine – and something else that I can never place.'

Ava's smile is at once ordinary and breathtaking. 'It's patchouli. Last but not least, is there anything you can taste?'

'The mints they put out after dessert – there's peppermint, but also an ungodly amount of sugar.' Jean rolls her eyes. 'Satisfied?'

'Yeah.' Ava rocks back onto her heels. 'Okay, now you're a bit more settled I'll get our things.'

'What about Rhona?' A quarter of a century spent cultivating the respect of her peers, a healthy degree of fear from her underlings, flushed down the toilet in a single afternoon. Rhona will never look up to Jean again, let alone trust her – the ache of it is piercing.

'Rhona's fine. A little shaken, but Amari's going to hang out with her for the rest of the sessions and evening drinks.' Ava plants a kiss on her forehead. 'You hang tight here and then we can go.'

The tightness in her chest – the panic attack – flares back into life as Ava rises. 'It would be more expedient for you, for the CJC, to cut ties with me. Publicly, at the very least. You don't need my mess staining your reputation.'

Ava sinks back down, cupping Jean's tear-slicked cheek. 'Not going to happen, Jellybean. Not in a thousand years.'

'You should think about it,' Jean says to her retreating back. There are worse parting gifts to bestow than pragmatism.

Chapter Twenty-Two

Ava refuses to leave Jean, bundling her into the taxi then reciting Jean's home address as she buckles both their seatbelts. As Jean stares in disbelief, she looks up. 'Don't worry. I haven't gone Full Glenn. But I called your office, and they put me through to Helen. I told her. So that your firm can get their crisis management people on it.'

Helen. She'll learn all about Jean's sordid history at DDH soon enough. The whole office will. Nothing travels faster than gossip in the legal community. She and Peter had known about Amelia Hawthorne's drink driving and resultant stint in rehab before she'd even reached the clinic.

And now – despite all Jean has done to keep her life clean and uncomplicated – her own dirty laundry is being aired in front of her colleagues and peers. And her sex-acquaintance-turned-friend. Marianne couldn't have exacted a more perfect revenge.

Jean slumps against the door, peering out at fuzzy cars and buildings, rain pattering against the windows. Her eyes drift closed, though it's impossible to sleep with the driver swerving between lanes and cursing cyclists. But there's comfort in the pretence – no need to make conversation, nor reckon with any of the questions Ava has left unspoken.

She reaches for her bag when the sway and curve of the streets grows familiar. But Ava covers her hand. Says: 'It's okay. I've got the Uber covered.'

Weariness bone-deep, Jean doesn't have the energy to argue – though she makes a mental note to repay Ava's kindness tenfold as she emerges out onto the pavement. Jean opens the gate; has it halfway closed when she realises that Ava's following her. 'You're coming in with me?'

'Of course.' Yet Ava lingers on the street, uncertain, as the rain continues to pelt them. 'I don't think you should be alone right now. But we can call someone – Imogen, or Cora, or Peter – if you'd be more comfortable with them.'

Jean doesn't move despite the deluge. 'Why are you being so nice to me?'

Ava looks at her with an intensity that makes Jean's shoulder blades prickle. 'Because you deserve it. You've had a terrible shock.' Ava steps closer, gaze never wavering. 'And because I – I care about you, Jean. So much.'

'But it—' Jean's voice splinters. She clears her throat, tries again. 'It was all true, Ava. What Marianne said. Every lousy fucking word.'

'She's hurting. And so are you.' Ava reaches out to tuck a loose strand of hair back beneath Jean's hood, and she shivers as those fingers brush against her ear. 'Now let's get inside, where it's dry.'

With clumsy fingers Jean fishes the keys from her bag. And though her trousers are surely soaked through, Ava says nothing to rush Jean.

They step inside, Ava disappearing into the kitchen. And Jean sinks down onto the stairs, limbs leaden. She's dimly aware of the kettle boiling; the only sound other than a clock ticking. The house is quiet in a way that Ava's little flat, with its steady hum of ambient sound, never is. Until now Jean has never considered the moneyed hush of Kensington to be hollow. Lifeless.

Then Ava reappears with two steaming, mismatched mugs. She hands one over and squeezes in to perch beside Jean on the stair. They're pressed together from shoulder to elbow, hip to knee. Ava's closeness is a balm, warming her surely as the mug cupped in her hands. She watches, expectant, until Jean sips the tea.

It's so aggressively sweet that Jean can picture a cavity forming and growing with every mouthful. Yet she carries on drinking, too tired to protest. All the while Ava strokes her back. And Jean's heart is slower, her hands steadier, by the time she finishes.

'That's good,' Ava says. 'Is there anything else you want? I could make dinner, we could watch a film, or you could rest if you're tired.'

Jean considers. She's not hungry. There won't be enough room for her to begin sifting through the rubble Marianne left with Ava at her side. Yet, alone in bed, there will be nothing at all to distract her from that wreckage. Her fingers lock around the empty mug, and its fading warmth gives Jean an idea. 'A bath,' she says. 'I'd like to take a bath.'

'Okay. Whatever you need.'

Jean leads the way upstairs, and it's as if she's wading through treacle. Every step saps at a strength she doesn't have. When they reach the bedroom Ava guides her to sit on the ottoman, and it's a relief to simply let her take charge.

Ava whistles, taking in the bathroom. 'I still can't get over this place. It's like something out of *Ideal Home*.'

And Jean stays silent, unwilling to admit drawing inspiration from their articles; the relief of being told what she ought to like and the simplicity of being able to procure it. She twists to rest her head against the doorframe, watching as Ava sets both taps running and inspects her shelves of toiletries. In the end she settles on Ambre Vanillé, shaped like a humble pot of honey. With a child's delight Ava takes the wooden dipper and drizzles it into the bath. Then Ava grows self-conscious as she catches Jean looking, rinsing off the dipper and returning the set to its place in the line-up of toiletries.

'I'll take the mugs back to the kitchen, if you want to get ready.' Ava drops a kiss on the crown of Jean's head as she passes.

The moment her footsteps recede Jean enters the bathroom, inhaling tangerine and rich brown sugar as she turns off the cold tap. She takes off both shoes and peels off her clothes, down to her blouse and pants by the time Ava returns, taking off her own blazer as she steps into the steaming bathroom.

'Look at those bubbles! I know that brand's bougie enough to cost the same as my weekly shop, but that's some quality foam density.' Though her tone is light, the concern remains in Ava's eyes, unmistakable as her gaze meets Jean's.

'You aren't asking me about it.'

Ava's brow furrows. 'I figured if you wanted to tell me about it, you would. And you're welcome to share. But I'm not going to pry; that wouldn't be fair.'

Even now she holds on to those binaries. Fair and unfair. Right and wrong. Just and unjust. Jean faces the wall, unbuttoning her blouse.

'Do you want me to give you some space? I ca—FUCK!' There's a splash, and Jean whips round in time to see Ava yank her elbow from the water. 'Sorry, I thought I'd put enough cold in.'

She reaches for the cold tap, and it's as if Jean herself is doused in icy water. 'No! I'm sure it's fine.'

'Don't be silly, it's boiling.' Ava reaches for the tap.

'I don't mind.' Jean shuts the cold back off. And her attempt at light-hearted lands like a bowling ball between them, smashing through Ava's confusion.

'Fine.' Ava nods, the speed of her compliance rousing Jean's suspicions. 'Make it as hot as you want. But I'm getting in too.'

'No way.' Jean would as soon dunk a newborn in the searing heat. She blocks Ava's path, perching on the tub's rim and stretching across it.

'Watch me.' Ava yanks the shirt over her head, not bothering to undo the buttons. The top trio ping free, clattering against the tile, but Ava ignores them. She wriggles out of her damp trousers and kicks them into a heap with the abandoned shirt.

Ava advances in a mismatched bralette and boyshorts, hair frizzing into a nimbus in the steam. And Jean's heart leaps, desperate and flailing, at the sight of all that warm tan skin exposed.

'You're being...'

'What, Jean?' Ava's eyes shine, overbright and zealous. 'What am I being?'

Jean winces. *Crazy* hangs in the air between them, reverberating louder than if it had echoed against the tiles.

Ava doesn't back down. 'Either we both burn, or neither of us do.'

It's the perfect stalemate. Wordless, Jean concedes defeat, twisting the cold tap. Before her the foam multiplies, iridescent bubbles connected by a web of suds. And Ava shifts to stand behind her, an arm looped around Jean's shoulders.

She ducks to bury her face in Jean's hair, breathing deep. And though her voice is quiet, the words are firm. 'You don't deserve to suffer. Whatever Kate says.'

'You don't know the first thing about what I deserve.'

'Alright, then.' Ava's thumb finds Jean's cheek, brushing away tears even as more take their place. 'Try me.'

The water is a warm caress against her skin. And though Jean yearns for more, a heat that obliterates every thought and feeling, its absence is undisputable proof of Ava's care. Cocooned in such tenderness, the tension ebbs from Jean's body... and with it her resistance.

'I was twenty-five years old when the firm hired me. I read law at Oxford and graduated with a first. But for any of this to make sense I'd have to go back to the beginning.'

'I've got time.' Ava settles down on the bathmat beside the bath, still clad in underwear. 'I've got all the time in the world for you.'

So Jean explains in fits and starts; how she and Bridget lost their parents the summer Bridget had turned eighteen. Saddled with a clingy eight-year-old sister and a whole host of adult responsibilities, Bridget gave up her place studying fashion and textiles to work in Woolworths. Even then Jean had felt guilty in ways she couldn't explain. Bridget's only comfort had been the church, where sacrifice and self-denial were venerated as the one true path to salvation. And though Jean doesn't believe, doesn't keep to the church's teaching, she still feels it lying dormant inside herself.

Jean describes how the Almighty's authority had lent weight to the moral judgements of a teenager, and her own fixation with rules had emerged from the constant struggle of puzzling out what might please God the Father – or Bridget the sister. How Bridget had pinned all her hopes on Jean, pushing her to study hard and apply to Balliol College, then resenting her still more for living the life she herself could not.

'Oxford was an education on two fronts. I studied through my lessons and reading. But I also paid attention to what people wore, how they spoke, how they carried themselves. And through borrowing here and there I become someone else, someone more than just an orphaned outsider.' Jean sniffs. 'That makes me sound like Tom Ripley. But it worked. You actually believed I grew up having piano lessons. And the firm – Decker and Dennings as it was then – hired me right after graduation.'

'Not Ripley – it isn't like you killed anyone.'

'Only Marianne's career. But I'm getting ahead of myself.'

Ava dips Jean's sponge in the water and slathers it with her Chanel bodywash, soaping Jean's arms and back as she talks.

'Marianne had the same goal. We were the only women taken on as interns. The first day we met she saw right through me, and I saw right through her. We agreed then and there that the energy we'd spend fighting one another would be better spent on getting ahead. If we couldn't join the old boys' network, we'd make our own.'

Henry had tried to excavate the truth many a time, but Jean always clammed up at his probing. Ava cups water in her hands to dampen Jean's hair and massages shampoo into the roots, letting Jean take her time. And so, with words she tries to capture Mari's magnetism, her warmth. The rare and unexpected gift of being understood. Waking up in their little flat for the first time only to discover herself wrapped in the sense of belonging that Jean had been so sure died with her parents, potent as Christmas morning. But Ava's face remains carefully neutral, and Jean is certain the ugliness of Kate's words over lunch have eclipsed the beauty of Marianne in her eyes. And Jean doesn't know how else to show it, this yearning she's spent half a lifetime concealing. 'Sorry. I'm not explaining this very well at all.'

'You're doing fine.' Ever so careful not to get suds in her eyes, Ava rinses Jean's hair. Massages conditioner evenly through her tresses. 'I've got you.'

Ava's persistent certainty that none of Jean's ghosts have the power to drive her away grows unbearable. Jean lies back, sliding under the water to rinse off her hair. It's tempting to linger beneath the surface, every sound muted, but Ava's still on high alert since their standoff over the taps.

So, Jean clasps the rim of the tub and pulls herself upright, water dripping down her shoulders. There can be no further delay. In short, halting sentences she tells Ava the rest. How Peter, senior associate at the time, had listened to their ideas and rewarded them with opportunity instead of stealing credit. He had praised them to Will.

Bitterness twists Jean's lips. 'At first I was so absurdly grateful that Will Decker noticed me. Saw me the way I wanted to be seen. He built that company from the ground up. All of it – and all of us – lived and died by his say so. He had the final word on all promotions. And if you left the firm, a good reference from Will could get you past Saint Peter himself. But if you were in his bad books, you'd be lucky to end up writing wills in Skegness.

'With Will in our corner, there was no way for management to keep freezing us out. I got promoted to associate first. And he called me into his office the evening before I was due to start, for a briefing. We were sitting on the couch in his office. And he leaned in to kiss me.'

Ava's expression doesn't betray so much as a flicker of shock – Jean's sordid little workplace #MeToo tale must seem like small potatoes after years spent absorbing the suffering of her clients. And this certainty gives Jean the strength to continue.

'He'd touched me before. A kiss on the cheek, a hand on my knee – small things I'd have looked crazy challenging. But I never saw that kiss coming. And I was too shocked to move.' Even now Jean can feel it; the graze of stubble against her cheek, that tongue pushing into her mouth, slimy and boneless as the liver Bridget used to fry. 'Until he unbuttoned his trousers, pulled down his fly. And I... knelt. You're probably wondering why I didn't fight or run or scream.'

'I wasn't thinking any of those things.' Ava brushes back the curtain of cooling hair surrounding Jean's face and wraps it in a towel. 'Actually, I was thinking that Will Decker sounds like a textbook abuser. He knew how isolated you were with your colleagues, and what it would cost you to say no. And he used all of that to coerce you.'

'You sound like the therapist I saw.'

'She sounds like a smart woman,' Ava counters.

'She is.' Jean breathes deep, the steam easing her congestion. 'I know you've wondered, why I never questioned not feeling anything with men. Dr Byrne said that after Will it was perfectly normal – but I couldn't tell her that I didn't feel anything, not before and not after learning to live with it. That's why I stopped seeing her, in the end.'

Ava's quiet for a long moment, though her hand never leaves Jean's shoulder, thumb resting in the dip of Jean's clavicle. 'Did she help you?' The sound Jean makes lives on the border between laughter and sobbing. 'As much as I could be helped. You see, I thought that at least if Will was doing it to me, he wouldn't bother Marianne. But then I found her crying in the stationery cupboard, the knees of her tights ripped, and I knew in an instant.'

The rest of it comes pouring out, a tide Jean couldn't stem even if she'd wanted to. Marianne had been sure that if the two of them came forward, Will would be made to pay. She'd lodged a complaint with HR, giving both their names even though Jean had begged her not to. And Jean had denied everything thrice – in writing, sitting across the table from HR, to an ashen-faced Peter – weak as the disgraced disciple.

Marianne had quit, utterly discredited. And Will had carried on finding moments to fondle Jean with impunity. 'It was only when I brought Henry along to the Christmas party that it completely stopped. I liked Henry. He was smart, funny, and no matter how busy he was, he always had time to give me advice.' Jean sniffs. 'I brought him along as a way of saying thank you. He read more into it, and I tried to let him down gently. But then a month passed without Will trying to get me alone, and another. When I realised that Will would respect another man's claim, I agreed to become Henry's girlfriend.'

'Ah, Jean.'

'NO! Don't you look at me that way, like you're sorry for what happened. I was mercenary with Henry and Marianne. That is who I am. So why the hell aren't you blaming me?'

'Because.' Ava tilts Jean's chin up to look at her. 'It's not your fault.'

That absolute certainty leaves her dazed. Jean is silent while Ava drains the tub. Silent while Ava rubs her dry with the fluffiest bath towel. Silent while Ava makes a valiant stab at her usual skincare routine, massaging lotion ordinarily reserved for Jean's face into her body. Silent even while Ava dresses her in soft flannel pyjamas – a gift from Bridget stuffed in the bottom of her drawer, utterly at odds with Jean's wardrobe and the curated elegance of her home.

Only when Ava's tucking her into bed like a child, pulling down the blinds to block out the lightning, does Jean recover her voice. 'You're still here.'

Ava's smile is tired but genuine. 'Of course.'

There's no *of course* about it. Her continued presence is nothing short of a miracle, so vast that none of Jean's words come close to capturing it.

Unperturbed by her silence, Ava tucks the duvet around Jean's legs. 'I'll stay with you all night. It's up to you where I go. I can take the chair or the guest room if you need some space – and it's totally fine if you do.'

Throughout the whole of this nightmare, only Ava's presence has brought with it any measure of peace. Jean pushes back the cover and pats the space beside her. 'I like having you near.'

Ava digs into her overnight bag, the one intended for her family home, changing in record time into a camisole and boxers. She tucks her hair into a silk bonnet and climbs into bed, gathering Jean close. Jean rests her forehead against Ava's sternum, burrowing into her side. Rain patters against the windowpanes, a sound which – at any other time – would be soothing.

'They'll all be talking about it. About me.'

'It won't necessarily be bad.'

Jean snorts. 'Spare me.'

'I'm serious.' Ava shifts so that they're eye to eye. 'Look, Kate didn't do herself any favours going at you like that. For a lawyer in her field to be publicly victim-blaming someone? At a conference that exists to challenge institutional sexism. No. I can't speak for the more corporate end of the spectrum, but it's not going to play well with the VAWG teams, and we made up at least half the delegates.'

Thunder splits the sky open, lightning spilling through the cracks to fill the room with flickering light, enough to illuminate Ava's face.

'Marianne would have known that too; the risk she was taking with her colleagues.' *And she'd done it anyway, so furious that even a pyrrhic victory felt better than outright loss.*

'Don't think about that now. Forget her and all the rest of them.'

'I should tell Peter. I have to call him—'

'In the morning. You can barely keep your eyes open. Hell, you're shaking. Come here.' Ava pulls her close, warming Jean with her body.

Chapter Twenty-Three

When Jean wakes in the morning, Ava's face is slack, her breathing even. Slowly she extricates herself from the protective circle of those arms, careful not to jostle the mattress. She pads from the room, retrieving the phone from her handbag. Jean scrolls through the endless list of notifications. Calls from Naomi, Imogen, Cora. Messages of comfort and condemnation both, from virtual strangers. A text from Rhona declaring not only her continued respect, but an offer to stay at her parents' beach house in Edinburgh. And – of course – an email from Peter asking to talk at her earliest convenience.

The screen darkens then, in power-saving mode. And Jean retreats to her office, closing the door behind her. She plugs the phone in and dials Peter's number. He answers on the first ring.

'Jean. Rhona told me what happened – are you alright?'

In spite of everything, he sounds relieved to hear from her. Jean squeezes her eyes shut. 'I'll resign. For the good of the firm.'

'Not accepted.' Peter doesn't take even a single second to consider the possibility; to weigh up DDH's options. 'I want you as my successor. And if that's not enough, think about the optics. A woman losing her job over a sexual misconduct scandal? One of the victims? Terrible. Enough to confirm all the worst rumours about DDH.'

'Fuck the optics, Peter. I don't deserve to stay, never mind take over the firm. Not after what I did to Marianne.' Sweat prickles under Jean's arms, pooling beneath her breasts – opening the windows offers no respite, summer blazing in the storm's wake. She drinks in the soupy air with tight gulps.

'I told you, Jean – you can't keep blaming yourself for that. It isn't healthy.' The shuffle of footsteps: Jean can picture him pacing. 'Will was the truly guilty one. And think about it: if you quit, he wins. Don't let that old bastard's ghost cheat you out of everything you've spent the last two decades working for.'

'But I—' A crack runs through Jean's voice. She pushes the sweaty hair back from her forehead. 'I don't know how I come back from this. I don't even know what to think, what to feel.'

'Then take some time off – that's not a suggestion, by the way. You've got enough leave accrued that you could take the rest of this summer if you need it. A holiday will be just the ticket.' He sounds so certain. 'I'd offer you Mandalay, but Caroline's niece is honeymooning out there.'

'I screw up and you're rewarding me with a holiday? What's next – we give Andrew a bonus next time there's a discrepancy with his expenses?'

'You didn't fuck up, Jean. You didn't start slinging mud back or escalate the conflict.' Peter's breath echoes down the line. 'Consensus is that Marianne's in the wrong here. There was a big stink on social media, and Minerva put out a statement about victim-blaming not aligning with their founding principles – no names mentioned, but the timing makes it obvious why.'

Jean's heart pounds as if it means to smash through the wall of her chest and make a bid for freedom. She slumps against the wall. '*Jesus.* I can't let Marianne lose a second career because of me.'

'You may not have a choice. But I can reach out to Minerva on your behalf and say as much.'

'Please do.' Jean swallows, voice thick. 'Right away.'

'And you'll take that holiday?'

It's not the decision a managing partner should make; but Marianne will never be a managing partner or anything close to one, because of her. And Jean can't let her lose a second career. 'Anything. Just do it.'

'Alright.' Peter sounds almost as weary as she feels. 'Take care of yourself, Jean.'

—

She finds Ava in the kitchen, still in her pyjamas, flipping a misshapen pancake on the stove.

'You didn't have to make me breakfast.'

'Who says it's for you? I always get pancakes on my birthday. Aaliyah's are way better, but we'll have to make do.'

Guilt knots Jean's stomach tight. She'd forgotten Ava's party plans, the reason for her overnight bag, after everything with Marianne. 'Oh, Ava, I'm sorry. I've messed up your birthday from the start. Did Aaliyah mind you not coming over last night?'

'She knows it was an emergency.' Ava turns to pour a tablespoon of fresh batter onto the skillet. And Jean doesn't have the energy to call her on the evasion.

'Let me take over.' Jean side-steps Ava, lowering the heat and prying the scorched pancake loose. It's almost impressive, the way it manages to be simultaneously burnt and undercooked.

'Why, because you're such a domestic goddess?'

Jean spoons butter into the pan, tilting it left and right so the bubbling liquid covers the pan. A decent birthday breakfast is the least she can do. 'I grew up Catholic – Pancake Tuesday is our culture.'

And it's a relief, throwing herself into the familiar task. Serving Ava perfectly fluffy birthday pancakes, drizzled in lemon and sugar. They share a plate, Ava feeding Jean mouthfuls when she picks at it.

'I'll wash up,' Ava says when they're done. 'But first I need to call Aaliyah, tell everyone to go ahead without me.'

'You can't miss your own birthday party, Ava. Especially not when it's your farewell party too.' Jean cups her cheek, waits until Ava meets her gaze. 'I'll be fine. I promise.'

'Jean, I'm not leaving you.' Her eyes are serious. 'No way, no how.'

A solution presents itself, dazzling in its simplicity. And what does being careful matter now that her reputation lies in tatters? 'Then take me with you.'

At last Jean will be able to satisfy her curiosity about Ava's parents; her old colleagues from ACWRC; the friends Ava has mentioned in passing over all their nights together. But Ava's quiet for so long that doubt begins to gnaw at Jean's gut. Perhaps the secrecy of their arrangement had suited Ava too – after all, how would she go about introducing a white woman eighteen years her senior?

'Never mi—'

'Are you su—'

They both break off, and Jean flushes. 'You go first.'

Ava nods, though the words are slow to come, heavy with deliberation. 'Are you sure that's something you'd feel comfortable with?' Her hands come to rest against Jean's shoulders. 'Don't get me wrong, I'd be over the moon. But you've always been so adamant about keeping things on the downlow.'

'And where did all that caution get me? At this point, gay rumours would be the very least of my problems.' But the words do nothing to dispel the cloud gathered on Ava's brow. Jean sighs. 'I have to admit that I've been curious about your life; the people in it.'

The palest blush graces Ava's cheeks. 'Yeah?'

'Oh yes.' Jean steps closer, leaning against Ava. 'If it's at your parents' house, does this mean I get to see your childhood bedroom?'

'Only if you promise not to laugh at my old posters.'

'Scout's honour,' Jean says, and finally Ava cracks a smile.

Getting ready doesn't take long. Ava rocks a pale peach linen suit, curls piled into a bun atop her head. Her usual boots have been replaced by Birkenstock sandals. She spritzes herself in scent – and if Ava hadn't tucked the bottle into her bag afterwards, Jean might have been tempted to mist the spare pillow with it. But surely a trace will linger.

Though Ava teases her about femme stereotypes, Jean doesn't take much longer than she does. In this heat, there's little point in anything more than minimal make-up – sweating through it is an inevitability. So, Jean sticks to the basics, going for a pillar box red lip. She picks out a chartreuse sundress, simple save for the deep V in the bodice held together by a bow over the bust, and a pair of tan wedge sandals.

Ava's mouth hangs open as she takes in the ensemble, gaze pogoing between Jean's breasts and her eyes.

'Is it too much?' Jean lingers at the top of the stairs. 'I can change if you'd prefer something more formal.'

'You're perfect.'

—

Less so by the time they arrive, wilting from the underground's furnace-like heat. Yet there's a bounce in Ava's step as she leads Jean down the driveway of an Edwardian semi-detached house with a hodgepodge of flowers blooming from bright ceramic pots. Ava unlocks the door with a key fished from her own pocket, gesturing for Jean to go in ahead of her.

She steps into the corridor of a house just as bright as the front garden, with statement walls in loud primary colours and a riot of funky prints covering its furnishings. A colossal vase filled with fresh blooms emerges through a doorway, Leah's face obscured behind it.

'Ava! Perfect timing. We've just finished tidying and vacuuming.' Her peach bodycon dress displays every curve to its best advantage, and Jean has the discomfiting realisation that the body beneath is likely a mirror of its twin. Perhaps Aaliyah even has the same constellation of freckles on her back.

'Happy birthday to you too, sis.' Ava closes the door behind her. And Jean stands rooted to the spot, feeling like an intruder as she spectates yet with nowhere else to go while Leah blocks the corridor. 'Look, I would have been here last night if I could. But yesterday was all kinds of messed up.'

'Mmhmm.'

Ava steps close to her sister, taking the gargantuan crystal vase. And though her voice is low, intended only for Aaliyah's ears, Jean hears every word: 'She needed me.'

Leah's lip curls. 'I'll bet she did.'

'Al, please. I'm not fucking around. Be nice today.'

A long look passes between the twins, a conversation conducted entirely without words, and Aaliyah's the first to turn away. 'Jean, if you want to help with the sides and the salads, we could use another pair of hands in the kitchen. Ava, you're on marquee duty.'

She even manages a tight smile, which Jean returns. 'Happy to assist.'

'Good,' Aaliyah says. 'Mum will make a big fuss about how guests don't help in her house, but if you ever want to be more than that you'll need to roll up your sleeves.'

Jean takes in the leopard print lampshades, the bold Rothko prints, looking anywhere except at either Harris sister. 'I've never been afraid of hard work.'

Ava leads the way through the dining room, elbowing her sister as she passes to set the vase down in the middle of the table runner. They follow a catchy beat all the way to the kitchen, where three women are preparing food.

A pretty, plump dark-skinned woman Jean recognises from many of Ava's photos stirs a pot – her mother. Another woman with the same pert nose slathers chicken in rich dark sauce, gold bangles jingling as she works – though Jean doesn't recognise any individual herbs, the scent of it floods her mouth. At the opposite end of the kitchen, seated alone at the table, a striking South Asian woman chops carrots into sticks. Thick black hair threaded heavily with grey tumbles down to her waist. All three of them beam as they catch sight of Ava.

'If it isn't our other birthday girl!'

'Ava!' Her mother abandons the stove, flinging an arm around her second born and reaching out for her first. 'It's good to have my babies together.'

Aaliyah embraces her without hesitation, a smile softening the edge of her words. 'You know we're thirty-seven now, Mum. I'm not sure you can still call us babies with middle age breathing down our necks.'

Jean lingers in the doorway as Mrs Harris gives her girls a final squeeze before pulling away, waving a dismissive hand. 'When Theodore and Evelyn are grown with little ones of their own, those two will still be your babies. You'll see.'

'I can't wait to find out. They're driving me mad. Dad's been sneaking them sweets since we got here.' Aaliyah adds fresh stock to the pot of jollof rice, stirring gently.

'You say that now, but you'll change your mind when they go off to university. And so what if your father dotes on the little ones?' Mrs Harris waves a wooden spoon at her eldest. 'No point in having grandchildren if you can't spoil them.'

Aaliyah raises a single sleek brow. 'Is this the same woman who wouldn't let us eat dessert unless we finished every single vegetable? Including broccoli?'

'Let it go, Al. Mum would have the local Conservatives round for tea before she sides against Dad. You know what they're like.' Mrs Harris opens her mouth as if to argue, but Ava clears her throat then, ushering Jean into the kitchen. And though Jean struggles not to fidget under the weight of those curious stares, it's a relief that even amidst all this love Ava has not forgotten about her. 'I'd like you all to meet a friend of mine, Jean Howard. She's a lawyer too; we started hanging out at a conference. You'll like her, Mum; Jean's exactly the type of lawyer you wish I was.'

'I'm very pleased to meet you, Mrs Harris.' Jean holds out a hand for Ava's mother to shake, wondering whether she stressed the professional side of their relationship for Jean's sake or her own. Then again, no matter how supportive a mother might be, no parent likes to think of their children picking up stray conquests in bars. 'I see a lot of you in your daughter; both of them, in fact.'

But she ignores Jean's hand, manoeuvring round the island to pull her in for a hug. And though it's unexpected, Jean finds herself relaxing into the straightforward warmth of this embrace. 'So, you are a woman of business! Please call me Chibundo. We don't stand on ceremony here – my husband's a passionate communist, so I'd suggest calling him Alasdair too.'

'Chibundo, then.' Jean's smile comes easily. 'Though I don't think your husband will be so approving about my line of work.'

'Oh, you'll be fine – just quote the classics at him.' Ava takes her arm, guiding Jean towards the others, introducing her to both aunts; Chibundo's sister, Patience, and Laila Singh, whose name Jean recognises as a trustee from CJC paperwork. Laila's wariness falls away as they work together preparing food, chatting about the project. And Jean's panic is minimal when Ava is called away to assist her father with the marquee.

Ava's fingertips brush the bare curve of Jean's shoulder as she passes, raising a trail of tiny hairs in their wake. And though Jean schools her face, Laila sees it, gaze flitting between Jean and Ava's retreating back. But she passes no comment, simply shows Jean where the pesto and pinenuts are, as if there is nothing at all out of the ordinary.

It's a comfort to throw herself into the simple rhythms of chopping and stirring. Here in this kitchen, in the company of women who have never met Marianne or heard of DDH, Jean's professional worries are a world away.

Chibundo and Patience take great delight in having a fresh audience for stories about Ava's youth. And through these women's reminiscences, she gleans valuable insights into Ava's life, her history, and the people who made her. It's no hardship listening to their tales.

Chapter Twenty-Four

With food to lay out, and banners and streamers to hang, there's no time for Jean to stop and question what she's doing there. Beneath the shade of the marquee, she feeds Ava a string of fairy lights to weave through the metal frame. Leah's husband, Simon, returns with the two children, both of whom race across the lawn to greet their aunt. She swings them into the air one by one, plastering each face with kisses. Theo is more interested in turning cartwheels across the grass than meeting Jean, which she doesn't take personally. But Evie sticks out a hand, expression serious. 'Good to see you, Jean.'

Ava turns to hide her smile as Jean takes those tiny fingers in her own. 'You too, Evelyn. I'm glad you're here, because we could use some help putting these lights in the bushes.' Jean releases Evie's grip to hold up a string of bulbs. 'We especially need someone who knows how to make it look pretty. Think you're up to the job?'

Evie nods, taking great delight in festooning hedges and bushes with the glimmering LEDs. And when Aaliyah calls her offspring inside to change into party clothes, a task wisely left until the last minute, she and Ava redistribute the lights more evenly.

'You're great with her,' Ava says, draping a row of lights over the hedge's top row.

Jean stares at her. 'I shook a small child's hand. Again. Like she's a forty-year-old woman working in HR. Which you laughed at both times, I might add.'

'Evidently she liked it – I think there might be a repeat whenever she sees you.' Ava dusts off her hands. 'Not that I expect it'll happen often. Anyway, how are you doing? If any of this gets too much, we can go. Just say the word.'

She'd do it, too. Walk away from her own party. Colleagues, friends, family... 'Don't worry about me. Your family have all been wonderful.'

'Cool.' Ava peers round the garden, but they're alone save for the myriad of lights; the rich perfume of roses; sparrows chirping in the branches above. She presses a chaste kiss to the corner of Jean's mouth, raising it into a smile. 'I'm glad you hit it off.'

Jean's on the cusp of returning that kiss with interest when footsteps approach. Together they turn to face the newcomer: a man in owlish glasses and a white shirt patterned with blue palm fronds. Alasdair Harris stands comfortably at six feet, even with the academic slouch hunching his shoulders. And he beams at the sight of his daughter.

Ava embraces her father, and he kisses the top of her curly head – and Jean realises that it was from him Ava inherited not only her height, but that easy affectionate manner. When he releases Ava, those keen blue eyes light on Jean, curious now. 'Hello there,' Alasdair says, still with a broad Glaswegian accent even after all his years teaching at LSE. 'Who's this you've brought along?'

Ava runs a hand through her curls, looking between them, and Jean stands a little straighter. 'Dad, this is Jean Howard. She's a friend of mine. A good friend. And a lawyer too – she's been a lifesaver getting CJC off the ground. And this is my dad, Alasdair.'

'Pleased to meet you, sir.' Jean holds out a hand, which she lets fall before he can take it. 'Oh *God*. I'm sorry! Your wife mentioned your politics, and here I am calling you sir. Alasdair. And before we go any further, I think you should know that it's corporate law that I work in. Just to get that speedbump out of the way.'

Jesus. Ava's staring at her as if she's sprouted another head. And no fucking wonder. Not since her gauche and stumbling days as an intern, overawed by every person – every actual lawyer that she met – has Jean crashed and burned this badly. But then entire decades have passed since Jean's been the one scrabbling to impress.

Alasdair's beard twitches, and Jean gets the distinct impression he's trying not to laugh. 'Yes, well, nobody's perfect. Lucky for you, the firing squad took a day off in honour of our celebration.' He takes Jean's limp hand, gives it a brief and gentle squeeze. 'You're very welcome here, Jean – it's not every day that my daughter introduces me to a female companion.'

'Oh! No. That's not what's happening here.' Ava colours a magnificent shade of scarlet under her father's scrutiny. 'I mean, I did introduce you to Jean. And she is female. Obviously, she's a woman in that dress. But I'm not, *we're* not—'

'My mistake,' Alasdair says, though his eyes sparkle with mischief. 'Either way, I'd better fire up the barbecue. I'll see you later, Ava. Comrade Howard.'

Alasdair retreats across the garden, hands behind his back, whistling – unless Jean is very much mistaken – the former USSR's national anthem.

'Sorry about that,' Ava says, still not looking at her. 'Dad enjoys teasing people, but I think he liked you.'

'No, I'm the one who should be sorry.' Jean itches as the conversation replays itself in her mind. 'I'm a complete and utter fucking mess right now. Why the bloody hell did I have to go and call him sir? That's going to haunt me.'

'No, the best bit was when you outed yourself as a fully paid-up member of the bourgeoisie.' Ava cackles at the pained look on her face. 'On the bright side, Simon's never managed to make him crack a smile in twelve years. You did it in under two minutes.'

And Jean can't help but laugh at the absurdity of it. Ava slumps against her, helpless with the giggles. Of course, Alasdair looks up from tipping coals into the barbecue then, drawn by the sound of their laughter. He raises his fist in a classic communist salute.

'He didn't seem to mind,' Jean says, when she gets her breath back.

'What, that you're helping millionaires turn into billionaires?'

'No. Well yes, there's that. But your father didn't seem opposed to it. The idea that you and I might be…'

'I told you, he's the least judgemental person you'll ever meet.' Ava shrugs. 'It's not a big deal.'

'I can't speak for my parents, but there's no way that my sister would be so relaxed about it.'

Ava must read something of those memories on her face. She steps closer to Jean, brow creased with concern. But Aaliyah steps out onto the patio, smoothing invisible creases from the peach dress that is – Jean realises – a perfect match for her twin's suit.

'Come on – the guests are starting to arrive.' She looks between Jean and Ava. 'And I'm not greeting them on my own. Bring Jean if you must.'

'She's nervous,' Ava whispers, her hand coming to rest in the small of Jean's back.

We have that in common, is what Jean wants to say. But Ava will worry about her – enough to keep her from smiling and hugging and shaking hands – and Aaliyah will resent her for it. So, Jean rallies. Together they join Aaliyah on the terrace.

She meets Grandpa James, helped by cousins Ella and Faith. Stands by as Ava's former manager, a majestic dark-skinned woman named Zora, wraps her in a long hug. And catches her eyes overspilling when two former clients introduce Ava to their newborn son.

Then more cousins arrive, and Jean accepts that she's never going to remember every name; just smiles every time Ava says, 'And this is Jean,' offering no further explanation.

And when guests begin to pour in earnest through the doors, Jean stands out less than she might have expected. The Harris-Emmanuel family, their colleagues and friends, are London at its most multi-cultural – though Jean has claimed the city as her home for close to thirty years, the higher she has ascended in the world of corporate law, the less her day-to-day life has reflected this plurality.

At a joint thirty-seventh birthday party, Jean had expected to be conspicuously older than most of the twins' guests. But she's surprised on that score too. Along with the senior generations of the family, there are the registrars and consultants from Aaliyah's place of work. Some of Ava's colleagues look to be around state pension age – yet when Jean speaks to these women, they give no signs of slowing down, animated by the same pure passion that drives Ava.

Though Jean recognises Amari as the sweet-faced hijabi who'd taken Rhona under her wing, and is quite certain the entire ACWRC is aware of her plight, it's not at all awkward with them. But then every one of these women chooses to sit with trauma every single day. There is nothing about Marianne's fury, nor even her and Jean's story, that has the power to shock.

Amari's friendly, yet doesn't treat Jean as if she's liable to break at any moment, perfectly natural while explaining that she and Rhona have decided to stay in touch after hitting it off. They've even made plans to attend a mixer for young lawyers in the autumn. And Jean's delight is platinum-pure: definitive proof that Rhona intends to keep on going.

Robert's there too, in a tan linen suit, dabbing at his forehead with a pocket square. If he's surprised to see Jean in the Harris family's back garden, he gives no sign of it. Jean brings him to shelter under the marquee's shade, fetching them both a sweating cup of crisp white wine.

Rob too knows about everything that happened with Marianne and the resultant scandal – Jean can tell by the way he watches her when he thinks she isn't looking. But he doesn't broach the subject directly, instead reminiscing about Ava as a student; his pride in teaching her how to channel the same zeal that carried her through countless marches and protests into her coursework.

Ava appears, wrapping both arms around Robert. And when they're done catching up, she whisks Jean away with her to safer ground; to people who have never heard of Jean, of Marianne Walker and Kate Brennan, or even

DDH. Among them are women Ava knows from the gay scene – though some of them lean towards stereotypically butch presentation, there are women in gauzy dresses and flowing skirts too.

It's not their look that tips Jean off, nor even Ava herself, so much as the way these women carry themselves. An indefinable quality Jean cannot put her finger on – what her junior associates might refer to as 'the vibes.' And though Ava has the presence of mind not to touch Jean, or tilt towards her when she speaks, every one of these women wears the same knowing smile.

Then it's time for the toasts, Ava's father clinks a fork against his wine glass and the hum of chatter falls away. Ava pauses the music on her phone. Alasdair praises his daughters' intelligence, hard work and good hearts. 'Any father would be proud to have one such a daughter,' he says, eyes bright. 'And I consider myself extraordinarily blessed to have two.'

Both the Harris twins hug their father, Ava fishing a tissue from her pocket to dab at her eyes. And in that moment Jean aches to go to her. To stroke Ava's back, to clasp her wrist; the little everyday touches that say *I'm right here with you*. But she stays in place, catching Robert's eye across the crowd.

Aaliyah, who maintains her composure, goes first, thanking everyone for coming and talking about how good it is to have all their people together in one place. 'We're here to celebrate our birthday, but more than that we're here to celebrate my baby sister as she closes one chapter in her life and begins another.' She swallows. 'Ava, I don't say it nearly enough, but I'm proud of you. You have the talent and the drive to do anything at all in this world, and every time you choose to make it a better place.'

Ava's a goner after that, with streaming eyes and shaking shoulders. When able to speak, she thanks her former colleagues for all they've taught her as a lawyer and a human. Her family for their love and support. Robert for continuing to nurture her well beyond graduation. Then Ava's eyes lock with hers, the rest of the world melting away as she speaks. 'And Jean – you're the busiest person I've ever met, yet you've still helped out every time I've asked, and even more times when I haven't.'

A warmth that has little to do with the sun overhead spreads from Jean's chest out to every atom of her being, thawing the chill that had taken hold during Marianne's accusations. Theo's the last to get up and speak. He climbs up onto a chair and shouts: 'Grandpa would like me to tell you it's time for dinner!'

Chapter Twenty-Five

Evie finds them in the queue for the food, now clad in a frilly blue sundress the colour of the sky above, and tugs on the belt loop of Ava's trousers.

'Hey, Peanut!' Ava strokes the child's hair, styled in elaborate Dutch braids.

Evie doesn't say anything, looking up at the crowd of unfamiliar grown-ups, though they greet the child warmly. She gestures until Ava bends down to listen, and pushes Ava's curls aside to whisper in her ear.

'Of course you can sit with me for dinner,' Ava says. 'What kind of birthday would it be if I didn't get to hang out with the world's best niece?'

But Evie pulls her close again, and Jean hides a smile.

'I don't think Jean will mind at all.'

'I definitely don't – not after you showed me the bunnies. In fact, I'd be delighted.'

Still the child doesn't look convinced.

'Can I tell you a secret, Evelyn?' She nods, and Jean crouches down to look her in the eye. 'I get nervous meeting new people too. Especially in crowds.'

The child looks at her through wary eyes, as if expecting a trick. Whispers: 'Don't believe you.'

'Why not?'

'Because you're a grown-up. And you don't *look* nervous.'

'Ah, but that's the secret part: if you act like you're confident for long enough, your brain forgets that you're pretending.' Jean's smile grows rueful. 'The bigger you get, the more you'll realise that adults fake it until we make it.'

'But Mummy says make believe is for kids.'

'This is a different kind of pretending.' They continue the conversation all through the meandering queue for the food table. And Jean's heart fills with the sweetest ache as the girl takes her hand, though she knows better than to express even a flicker of amazement. Ava's watching, though, with the most tender smile.

The barbecue is delicious, meat grilled to perfection. Evie sits wedged between Jean and Ava at the picnic table, chattering happily. And while this night is an anomaly, an accident brought about by extraordinary circumstances, it's also the happiest that Jean can remember being.

—

On her way out of the bathroom, Jean bumps into Aaliyah in the corridor. She tilts her head towards a door, and Jean follows her into what can only be Alasdair's home office, closing the door behind them. The room is lit only by streetlight pouring in from the bay windows, and on the other side of the house the party music and chatter dulls to a low murmur. There are books on every possible surface, stacked double on Alasdair's groaning shelves; a desk with a laptop, a World's Best Dad mug filled with pens and highlighters, assorted titles open face down on the table.

Aaliyah's back is to Jean as she straightens the piles on her father's desk, slotting bookmarks to save each place and stacking the tomes. 'I don't know what kind of magic you've worked on Evie. But when I tucked her in, you were all she talked about. Well, you and the cake.'

'Oh.' Jean looks down at the hand Evie had taken automatically, as if there wasn't a single reason in the world she shouldn't trust this particular grown-up. 'She's a sweet girl.'

Aaliyah turns at last, lips quirked. 'Not usually. Most people can't get more than two words out of her.'

'I find that hard to believe. My sister always said I was terrible with kids.'

'I don't think so. You talk to her with respect, and you listen like you're taking her seriously. I've tried to raise her to know her own worth, but little girls don't get enough of that, especially the brown ones.' Aaliyah shakes her head, as if dispelling unwanted thoughts. 'Anyway, my daughter would be delighted to see more of you, if you ever fancied stopping round for dinner. Or coming along with Ava when she visits.'

A beat. From this distance, Jean can just make out a catchy refrain from the *Hamilton* soundtrack – without her sister there to contest song choice, Ava is making the most of her freedom.

'I think it would make my sister happy too.'

Jean swallows. 'Aaliyah, I don't know what exactly Ava has told you about our... situation, but—'

Aaliyah cuts her off with a laugh. And though the register is familiar, it's entirely devoid of her sister's warmth. 'She didn't have to tell me anything. All our lives we've always known precisely what the other was thinking. Plus, it's written all over her face. Every single time she looks at you.'

Fondness, yes, but not what Aaliyah is suggesting. 'We're not actuall—'

'No, I'm talking now. And you're listening.' Aaliyah steps closer, her face in shadow. Her scent's unlike

Ava's too, a sophisticated floral number from Yves Saint Laurent. 'My sister can be very... gallant. For a lesbian feminist in the twenty-first century, she has these old-fashioned ideals about chivalry. Ava is ridiculously kind and generous, and she would do anything for the people she... the people she cares about.'

Aaliyah pauses here, and Jean nods. She absolutely recognises Ava from the portrait her sister paints.

'Most women Ava's dated have taken advantage of that, in one way or another. Which has led to her getting hurt. That's why Ava decided not to get... entangled with anyone while she's setting up the CJC. It's too important for her to risk getting distracted, or so she said.' Aaliyah tilts her head, as if looking at Jean for the first time. 'But then my sister met you. And all that resolve went out the window.'

'I wasn't looking for anything beyond the transitory when I met Ava,' Jean offers. 'And while we've reached a more lasting... arrangement, we're friends more than anything else.'

Even without a light source to illuminate her features, Jean can tell she's not impressed. Aaliyah folds her arms. 'If you want to be with Ava properly, great. You two would have my full support. But don't leave her hanging in some in-between place. Don't mess with her feelings just because she puts yours first. Don't treat my sister like she exists just to add spice to an otherwise straight life.' Aaliyah's voice drops to an angry hiss. 'And don't you *dare* let her fall for you if you've got no intention of loving her back. Are we clear?'

Jean can only nod. The truth of it fixes her in place like venom. Aaliyah passes her by, and a moment later the door falls shut behind her. As soon as she's alone, Jean slumps into the leather office chair, cool against the backs of her knees. There she sits, as if by staying perfectly still she need not move into a future shaped by Aaliyah's words.

Until her phone beeps, startling Jean out of her reverie. She'd set it to silent after calling Peter, forgetting that she'd altered the parameters of Do Not Disturb to allow Rhona's messages through anytime, day or night. Sure enough, *Rhona Baird* lights up the screen. They haven't spoken since Jean fled yesterday and, while she's clearly getting on with Amari, it's entirely possible the junior associate feels abandoned.

So, Jean takes a deep breath. And another. And opens the message.

> Hi Ms Howard,
> I hope you don't mind me getting in touch. I just wanted to thank you again for taking me along yesterday. Mr Decker said that you were taking annual leave – and while I'm sure you've got better places to be, I wanted to remind you that the offer of my parents' beach house by Cramond still stands. They're heading for the States to visit my brother, so it'll be free all summer. You're welcome any time, and you can bring a friend too – there's a guest room. I'll text you the code for the key safe.
> Either way, have a good break.
> With the greatest of respect,
> Rhona

The screen blurs. Jean drops the phone on the desk and covers her face. She'd assumed that Amari's politeness continued in part because Rhona had refrained from bad-mouthing her, suspecting unerring professionalism to be the prime motive. But the sincerity in Rhona's message goes beyond anything Jean had allowed herself to hope for.

The door creaks open, and Jean scrubs the back of her hand across both cheeks. But not fast enough to keep Ava from seeing her tears.

'Hey.' She kneels before Jean, peering up at her through concerned eyes. 'Laila said she saw you and Aaliyah go in here together – did she say something to upset you?'

Jean shakes her head. 'No, no. Nothing like that. She wanted to thank me for how I was with Evie.'

Ava's mouth twists. 'Then why are you sat here crying in the dark? If you tell me what else Aaliyah said, we can go now, and I'll talk to her later.'

She'd do it, too; risk the other half of her heart to make things right for Jean. Aaliyah's words echo in her ears, ringing with truth. *Don't mess with her feelings just because she puts yours first.*

'It wasn't Aaliyah, and it's not sad crying.' Jean passes Ava her phone. 'Look at this.'

'Oh. Jean, that's so lovely.' Ava's teeth are pearlescent in the phone's pale glow. 'She really cares about you. And I'm glad about that – but we can go if you need to, if it's too much.'

'Don't be silly.' Jean rises, pulling Ava to her feet, reverting to being the one who has to look up. She leans against Ava, revelling in her height, her solidity. 'This is your party. And you should get to experience every single bit of it.'

'Well… if you're sure?'

Jean nods her encouragement.

'There is one thing I'd like to do.'

'What's that?' The Harris family seems healthy enough that she doubts Ava's going to ask if they can fuck in her father's office, but the possibility makes Jean wary.

So, it's a relief when Ava says, uncharacteristically shy: 'I want to dance. With you. If that's okay.'

'I don't dance.' Jean breaks away, using her pocket mirror to check for any obvious signs of crying, but keeping the make-up minimal had worked out in her favour on that score. 'Though let's go back, and you can.'

Ava obliges, leading the way from Alasdair's office, though she doesn't relent. 'Sure you do. Everyone dances.'

'But I'm terrible. I have two left feet.' The music grows louder as they pass through the kitchen, where a cousin canoodles with her girlfriend.

'So? Nobody's watching.' They step out onto the terrace, gazing at the crowd of people united by two things: a fondness for *Funky Town* and the Harris twins. 'They're all just going for it.'

'If I start dancing, I'm going to prove every possible stereotype about rhythm and the Caucasian race.'

Laughter cracks Ava's serious expression, but still she doesn't relent. 'So does my dad, but he's still having the time of his life.' It's true – though his relationship with the beat is tenuous, Alasdair Harris throws himself into the music with wholehearted glee. 'You know what your problem is? You think way too much. Dancing isn't about what you should do, or what other people think. It's about just feeling it. Forgetting everything else and savouring the moment.'

'I'm good at precisely none of those things.'

Ava just laughs. She links her fingers with Jean's, swaying their hands back and forth in time with the movement of her hips. 'See? This isn't so bad. The world's not ending.'

'No. It isn't. But there are plenty of pretty girls who want to dance with you.' Jean tilts her head infinitesimally. 'I think Zara's been waiting half the night for you to ask her.'

'She's going to be waiting a whole lot longer. I like Zara, but I don't give a fuck about dancing with her or anyone else, except for you. And I'm the birthday girl – or one of them. For the next hour and forty-two minutes, it's illegal for you to say no to me.' Ava sighs. 'Never mind. You can always say no. We don't need to do anything if you're totally hating this.'

Even when she's trying to get her own way, Ava remains incapable of pressuring Jean. In every aspect of their relationship, active consent has remained an absolute. Standing there in the garden, breathing in barbecue smoke and rosemary, it occurs to her that this is why Ava has proven so adept at scaling her walls – with her, Jean's safe enough not to need them.

'I never said I hated it. I'm just completely out of my comfort zone.' The tune ends, replaced by sultry seventies rock courtesy of Alasdair Harris. Jean hops down onto the grass, pulling Ava towards the throng of bodies. 'But that's been true since the very first moment I met you. And it hasn't been a bad thing.'

'No?' At the edge of the crowd Ava spins her, Jean's dress flaring round her knees.

'No.' Jean reaches up to drape her arms around Ava's shoulders, stepping closer. They sway together, kind of silly and kind of not, Ava keeping her more or less in time. And Jean gives herself over to the buzz of the good wine, better music, perfect company.

A thought occurs to her, ensconced safely in Ava's arms. And it's still there hours later, when they're wedged together in Ava's childhood bed, the ceiling spinning gently.

'Ava?'

'Hrrrr.'

'Ava.' Jean shakes a bare shoulder, almost toppling her from the single mattress.

On instinct Ava reaches for the wooden bedframe, righting herself. And the shock of it is enough to sober her, at least a little. 'S'up?'

'I'm going to Edinburgh.'

It takes a moment for the words to fully register but, when they do, Ava beams at her. 'Yeah?'

'Yes.'

'That's amazing.' Ava kisses Jean's throat. 'I'm happy for you.'

'Thank you.' Jean clears her throat, peering up at the swimming glow-in-the-dark stars. 'But I was hoping you'd do more than be happy. I was hoping you'd come too.'

Ava stills beside her, not even daring to breathe.

'Will you?' Jean's voice is small in the dark – perhaps she has misjudged. Perhaps the filthy weekend was only ever meant to be a joke, an impossibi—

'Of course.' Ava burrows into Jean's side, head pillowed against her breast. 'I'd go anywhere with you, Jean Howard.'

Jean strokes Ava's hair until her breathing evens. Keeps going until the sky begins to lighten and at last her own heart settles.

Chapter Twenty-Six

It's easier than Jean could have imagined. She'd wondered whether Ava might have been too drunk, too sleepy, to hold onto their plan; if it would melt away with the stars come morning. But at precisely nine forty-five a.m. Ava meets her at King's Cross station and, mindful of Jean's wrist, insists on wheeling both their cases along the platform. Together they board, Ava stowing away their luggage while Jean locates two seats opposite one another.

As the bustle of London fades away, replaced by open fields and meandering rivers, Ava's ankle nestles against Jean's beneath the table. She doesn't look up from her weighty Hamilton biography while playing footsy, but the corners of her lips curve gently upwards in a way that Jean is certain has little to do with the U.S. Constitution's fiercest advocate. And though whirlwind trips with lesbian lovers are a world apart from the reality of her life, and her name is doubtless being fed through the rumour mill at this very second, Jean can't help but bask in the simple pleasure of their adventure.

The further north they get, the less London and all its problems matter. And by the time they reach Edinburgh, Jean feels like another person entirely. After all, as far as the people milling round Waverley Station are concerned, she could be anyone. An MI5 agent or a call centre rep. It doesn't matter to them how Jean spends her days or nights.

She and Ava bundle into the back of a black cab, peering out of the windows as they glide through an unfamiliar city. With its quaint cobbled streets and ancient castles, Edinburgh could almost be another world.

The Baird family's beach house is just as Rhona had described – a timeless whitewashed bungalow overlooking the bluest sea Jean has yet seen. She pays the driver and hops down onto the sand-strewn pavement, forgetting everything as she takes in the sea's miraculous aquamarine, the little island's verdant greens, pale wisps of cloud floating across an open blue sky. Even the breeze, warm against Jean's cheeks, tastes of salt.

'Look at this, Ava!' She turns to face her companion, struggling to find words adequate for Scotland's majesty. 'Have you ever seen anything more beautiful?'

Yet, despite the marvels before her, Ava's gaze remains fixed on Jean. A little breathless, she says: 'Never. Not once in all my life.'

Jean ducks her head, warmth blossoming across her scalp. 'Don't look at me like that – we still need to go grocery shopping.' Though there's nobody around, Jean still lowers her voice, enough that Ava must come closer to hear. 'And we'll never make it to the beach today if you get me in bed.'

Ava simply laughs, towing both their cases towards the house. 'It is beyond adorable that you even make an agenda on holiday.'

'You think?' Jean frowns as she enters the lockbox combination from Rhona. It had driven Henry to distraction towards the end, the way she could never simply go with the flow.

Ava trails a fingertip down her spine, and Jean almost drops the silver key. 'I know.'

The door swings open. Inside the house is simple, yet tastefully decorated, with a classic nautical theme. The walls are painted in whites and delicate shades of blue, with shells and sea glass glued around the driftwood mirror above the fireplace. 'This is so lovely.'

Ava closes the door behind them, her arms sliding round Jean's waist. 'It really is.'

'I'm going to unpack our things and change into something more outdoorsy.' Jean holds up a hand, warding off any attempts to follow. 'You go and make sure the freezer's switched on – if there's no ice tray, we can get one in town. And write down foods you want from the shop, so we don't forget anything.'

Ava salutes, eyes bright with mirth. 'Yes ma'am.'

The master bedroom has a queen-sized bed, a wardrobe, and a dresser, wood all painted white in textured chalk paint to give a rustic effect – though the Baird family, with their second home, are anything but. Jean unpacks methodically, hanging up crease-able items with care and stowing the rest of their things in drawers.

In Ava's case, stowed beneath her raincoat, there's a bag Jean assumes contains her bonnets or scarves for sleeping. But then her fingers close around something long and firm and cylindrical, the dimensions of which she is intimately acquainted with – Jean drops it back into the case, uncertain about the etiquette of strap-on storage as a guest in someone else's home.

She changes into a sage green camisole and matching loose linen trousers, her white cover-up Jean's only concession to the summer sun. As she touches up her lipstick in the mirror, Ava's voice filters through the house: 'I don't think we need to go food shopping.'

'How come?' Jean rolls her eyes at her own reflection. 'Is this because you want fish and chips for dinner? We are not living on Twix bars and takeaway during this trip.'

'Come and see.'

Jean pads through the living room in her sandals, and into the kitchen. Ava stands before the open fridge, stocked with deli meats and wedges of artisanal cheese, olives and chocolates, fresh fruits and vegetables. There are even two generous steaks wrapped tight in plastic. The cupboards hold seeded loaves, crisps, crackers for the cheese. Enough food for a small army. On the counter there's a magnum of champagne with an envelope balanced against it, which Jean prises open.

> Ms Howard,
> Though we can never hope to repay the care you've taken of our daughter, we hope you enjoy this token of our appreciation.
> Yours sincerely,
> Thomas and Sandra Baird

At Jean's thunderstruck expression, Ava reads the card over her shoulder. 'Fucking hell. Did you save Rhona's life?'

'Nothing that dramatic.' Jean sticks the champagne inside and closes the fridge. 'They're just kind people.'

Ava stares at her, clearly not convinced.

'You know.' Jean steps closer, fingering the button of Ava's shirt. 'If we're not going to the shop anymore, that opens a slot in our schedule. Any ideas on how to fill it?'

Ava's breath hitches. 'I... might have some ideas.' Her fingers close round Jean's before they can wander. 'But if you're not able to talk about it, or you don't want to, I'm not going to push. You don't need to use sex to distract me.'

Jean stills, fingers sandwiched between Ava's hand and her heart.

'In fact, while we're talking about it, we don't have to do anything like that if you don't feel in the mood. I get that what happened with Kate brought up difficult things for you. And I'd never assume…'

Jean stands on tiptoe, silencing her with a kiss that's both chaste and lingering. 'You really are incredibly sweet. A year ago, it never would have occurred to me that a woman might be the most perfect gentleman I could meet.'

It's Ava who looks away first, though she doesn't drop Jean's hand. 'How about we spend the rest of the afternoon on the beach?'

—

Cramond is every bit the haven Rhona promised; quieter than Portobello yet just as beautiful. Though the glorious weather draws out tourists, Jean and Ava are able to set out their towels on the sand and sunbathe in relative seclusion day after day. They share decadent packed lunches, a hefty bottle of SPF50, and a settled kind of slowness Jean never imagined herself capable of enjoying. Side by side they listen to children's laughter, the gulls' pealing cries, the steady hush of ocean against shore. It's easy being silent with Ava – and should Jean's mind wander south to London's eternal machinations, the subtle brush of her fingertips against Jean's ankle is enough to anchor her here in the present.

Conversation flows easily as the River Almond into the North Sea. As they watch a boy construct a sandcastle, Jean shares her snatches of memory about a holiday to

Blackpool with her parents – her mother's hair rippling in the breeze, Dad lifting her and Bridget onto the back of a donkey, her absolute wonder at those twinkling lights against the ink-black sky.

When the tide permits, they hike across Cramond Causeway, the watery sand a perfect mirror for the sky above. And the path before them stretches out into blue infinity. Here, in the liminal space between land and sea, Ava opens up about Ephraim, the gentle giant of a man who had thrown Ava up in the air and caught her every time.

As a child uncertain of her place in the world, often lonely because she hadn't fit neatly into one group or another, Ephraim's love had been a sanctuary. He was the first one Ava came out to, before even Aaliyah, aged twelve. And he'd died three weeks later after getting into a fight with a group of white boys who'd pelted him with slurs. The police had taken Ephraim alone into custody after breaking it up, ignoring his complaints of a headache, locking him in a cell overnight. In the morning they'd found his body, still warm.

Ava's eyes remain fixed on the horizon as she recounts the tale, curls rippling round her face. Her pace does not slow. Overt comfort would not be welcome. But Jean links their fingers, lengthening her strides to fall into step beside Ava. They pass a family of walkers, exchanging cursory greetings – and even then, Jean doesn't let go, though she feels it in her stomach when the father's eyes dip to their joined hands; feels it long after he's a speck in the distance.

'I could say all that useless shit about how sorry I am,' Jean says, breathless. 'What a terrible tragedy. But the truth is nothing ever fixes a loss like that. You just spend the rest of your life walking round with this gaping wound. An empty space where they should be.'

Ava slows then, a pace more in keeping with the natural span of Jean's footsteps. 'I know it won't bring him back, the CJC. But maybe other people can escape that empty space for a bit longer.'

Jean shares a confession too, out on the island, where wild heather grows, and such things feel possible. 'I never had a relationship like this, in my personal or professional life. Even my marriage was largely transactional – I gave Henry what I thought he wanted and played the role of wife, and in return my life got closer to the conventional markers of success.' Jean shakes her head, wind whipping at her hair. 'But with you? It's so different to anything I've ever known.'

Ava doesn't say anything then. Just lets her hand brush across Jean's on its way to the picnic basket. And Jean lets herself bask in the sun, the sea air, this perfect moment.

—

It might be summer, but it is still Scotland – and of course the weather doesn't hold. They wake up to the sound of raindrops pattering against the windows, the musical gurgle of water spilling down the gutter. Jean opens the blinds and finds the beach utterly deserted, save for a lone dog walker wrapped in a mac.

'Well.' Ava rolls over onto her stomach, squinting out the window. 'What's on the schedule when it's raining?'

The water's dull grey, cloud so low that Jean can't even make out the little island, let alone the lush greens of the opposite shore. But nothing about the misting rain feels oppressive; it cocoons around them like a blanket. 'I want to go swimming.'

'What?'

'In the sea. Let's do that today.'

A slow grin spreads across Ava's face, carving a dimple into the swell of her cheek. 'You're a wild woman, Jean Howard. I could tell from the moment we met.'

Jean laughs, incredulous. 'I'm not wild – it's perfectly logical. If we go outside, we're going to get wet no matter what we do. So, it might as well be swimming.'

'Wild swimming for a wild woman,' Ava says as she retrieves her tankini.

And Jean has to turn away from those long golden limbs as she shimmies into the lycra set. She pulls on her own swimsuit in the bathroom – a traditional cut, textured across her stomach, with in-built cups for added support around the bust. She'd bought it almost five years ago for a trip to Mandalay, and it's tighter now, but that can't be helped. A bathing suit had never been high on her list of priorities. Yet this negligence pays off as she pads back into the bedroom.

'Should we take our towels, or will they just get we—' Ava's jaw hangs open as she takes in the sight of Jean's body poured into her one-piece. 'Oh my days. Just as well we're going wild swimming, otherwise I'd need a cold shower.'

Jean swats her with the towel before wrapping it around herself. 'Yes to the towels – we can put them in a bag to keep them dry-ish. But it'll be freezing when we get out, and I'm not showing my cellulite to every passing dog walker.'

Ava pauses midway through knotting her hair into a pineapple. 'I don't think anyone who catches sight of you in that swimsuit is going to be thinking about cellulite. It doesn't inspire a single thought that I can articulate without being sent straight to horny jail.'

'You're ridiculous,' Jean says. And yet it's impossible to entirely scrub the smile from her face. 'Come on.'

They jog down the beach holding hands, skirting stones and seaweed. The rain is cool against her cheeks, the sand even more so underfoot – and as they draw closer it occurs to Jean that the ocean will be glacial. Scotland in July is still ultimately Scotland. Yet Ava is undeterred. She stuffs her towel into the bag and sprints into the water, shrieking as she splashes up to her knees, thighs, waist. Then Ava dives beneath the water and Jean doesn't breathe until she surfaces, gasping as water streams down her face.

'G-get in! It's amazing.'

'That might be more convincing if your teeth weren't chattering.' Still, Jean folds her towel up into a square. Kicks off her sandals. Tiptoes across the shoreline.

Her toes go numb as Jean steps deeper into the water, chill climbing her calves, and it's the opposite of the baths she'd taken to scrub away any trace of Will. Jean slows to a standstill, frozen stiff. Even now, even here, she can't escape the memory of him. The old bastard would have laughed himself silly to know that Marianne had turned on her; that even from the grave he can reach far enough into Jean's life to punish her.

But then Ava's there, lacing her icy fingers through Jean's warm ones, walking backwards as she guides Jean into the water. She's right there as Jean throws herself into an ungainly breaststroke, cheering as if she were witnessing Diana Nyad swimming from Cuba to Florida.

Whether it's her body acclimatising to the ocean, or simply the irresistible effect that Ava has upon her, Jean no longer feels the cold. She swims parallel to the shore, gliding through the water, sure now of her own strength. Ava follows, dipping below the softly rippling waves;

surfacing before Jean, laughing and drinking in the crisp air.

Vitality has always shimmered just beneath Ava's skin, sparkled bright in her eyes – but with her curls plastered to her face, cheeks pink with cold, Jean has never seen anyone so gloriously alive.

Jean swims to her, treading water as she pulls Ava close.

'What are you doing?' Ava's breath is hot against Jean's cheek, minty fresh from her toothpaste.

'Being wild.' Jean pulls her close for a kiss, tasting salt on Ava's lips.

It's too brief, not enough, their legs cycling beneath the surface. Jean turns away from the wonder in Ava's eyes and swims back to shore, leading the way back to their bungalow on trembling legs. But even after they're inside and out of the rain, warmed by a shower and towelled dry, Jean's body doesn't still.

She goes to Ava, fishing in the drawer for a clean t-shirt, and stills her searching hand. Wordless, Jean leads her to the bed. And there can be no mistaking her meaning.

Obedient, Ava sits down on the mattress, But, when those hands wander, skimming the inside of Jean's bare thigh, she stops them. 'Not yet.'

A question forms on Ava's lips, but Jean eases her back down against the mattress. Leans down to kiss Ava breathless, rolling a nipple between her fingertips until Ava's straining up towards her.

Jean kisses her slender neck, nipping at Ava's pulse point. Nuzzles at the hollow between her breasts. Though Ava savouring her curves has softened Jean's perception of her own body into something resembling acceptance, something about these pert little tits – the way the swell of them fits perfectly moulded to the curve of Jean's palm

– wakes the animal part of her brain. At first Jean had put her interest in small breasts down to feminine jealousy, the grass always being greener on the other side. But Jean groans as the bud of a nipple furls tight between her lips, Ava's desire waking her own.

Jean grinds against Ava's leg as she shimmies down the bed, craving firm pressure against her clit. But there's one thing Jean craves more than her own pleasure – Ava realises it too as Jean reverses further still down the mattress, pulling the damp slip of Ava's underwear away with her.

A trembling hand cups Jean's cheek, tilting her face up to look at Ava. 'Are you sure?'

'Yes.' Jean's voice is husky but certain. 'I want to taste you.'

In answer Ava parts her thighs, revealing a flash of pink between her wiry curls.

Jean lowers her head, breathing in musk as she traces the folds of Ava's sex with her tongue. Ava shudders the moment she makes contact, parting to the gentlest probing. Her cunt is impossibly hot, slippery against Jean's mouth and cheeks and nose. But the knowledge that all this secret slickness is just for her spurs Jean on, her tongue searching out every last drop.

Ava tastes briney and fresh as the ocean, smooth as an oyster against Jean's lips. She cries out as the point of Jean's tongue darts across that perfect pink pearl. What Jean lacks in experience, she makes up for with enthusiasm, or tries to; when Ava's stomach jerks as she sucks in a breath, when her thighs tremble, Jean takes it as sign she's moving in the right direction, lapping until her tongue grows numb.

In the end it takes her mouth and her fingers working in tandem to get Ava there, rubbing frantic circles round Ava's clit while her tongue delves inside. But get there

Ava does, clenching tight and shuddering, thighs locking Jean's mouth flush against her. It is messy. It is primal. And it is utterly glorious.

Jean pulls back, gasping for air and wiping her face clean. And Ava, chest heaving with the force of her orgasm, looks up at Jean with a fresh, dazed sort of wonder.

Chapter Twenty-Seven

One week bleeds into two – Peter is delighted for her to continue holidaying. And her words are only halfway out when Ava, who has made no mention of heading home, agrees they may as well stay a full fortnight. The Baird family's generosity is easily supplemented by a trip to the Co-op, their clothes laundered in the washing machine and dried in bright sunshine. The weather, that fickle temptress, picks up just when Jean accepts summer is over. Sweating and laughing they climb Arthur's Seat, Ava snapping a picture of them pink-cheeked at the summit.

In fact, true to Millennial form, she has documented almost the entirety of their trip. Amidst the nature shots and selfies, there are candid photos Jean hadn't been aware of her taking until Ava messages them. Jean from behind, gazing at the island, hair gleaming and rippling like fire. Jean lying on her front atop a towel – though her eyes are concealed by dark lenses, she wears an enigmatic little smile as she reads her book. Jean laughing as the champagne fizzes open, eyes still wide from the cork popping – a sound that's always louder than she expects.

She tries to sneak a few photos in retaliation, but Ava always catches her, giggling or beaming at the camera while she poses. The only time Jean manages to capture her unawares is when Ava sleeps, a curl peeping out from beneath her bonnet, one hand tucked under her cheek like a child. But that photo feels too personal to share, even with its subject, so Jean keeps it to herself.

The days stack up, one adventure after another. And Jean doesn't recognise herself when she looks in the mirror – this carefree woman, tanned and freckled and always smiling.

On the night before their last day, Jean makes reservations at a restaurant Alasdair had recommended for its seafood, caught fresh and local – rather swanky for a communist, though Jean had refrained from saying so. Jean decides it's now or never for the dress. She had bought it spontaneously in the January sale, yet never worn it – with the vivid henna red of her hair, it had felt too much, the silky material shining bright as a ruby.

Ignoring her misgivings, she wiggles into the sheath, zipping it up the side and applying a smoky lavender eyeshadow. With her lips pillar box red and hair brushed smooth round her shoulders, there's even a touch of pin-up glamour. Before she can doubt herself, Jean retrieves her clutch and steps out into the evening sun.

Ava turns as the door swings shut behind her. And those dark eyes pop round as saucers as she takes in Jean's ensemble, scanning her from head to toe. 'Holy shit. Did you… dress up as…?'

'Jessica Rabbit.' She twirls, enjoying Ava's newfound inability to close her jaw. 'Minus the sequins and improbable anatomy.'

'I… like this version way better.'

'You do?' Jean bites the inside of her lip.

'Oh yeah.' Ava steps closer, tracing the contour of Jean's hipbone through the thin material. 'As a kid it didn't occur to me that it was problematic, that glorification of unrealistic female beauty standards. I was also quite a few years off working out just how much I enjoy real curves. And, well…'

A pulse hammers against Jean's throat. Her voice is scarcely more than a whisper. 'What?'

Ava tucks a lock of hair behind Jean's ear, fingertips brushing against the lobe. And though her cheeks colour, she looks Jean dead in the eye: 'The reality of you is so much better than any fantasy, Jean Howard.'

Jean stands up on tiptoe, no mean feat in these heels, pressing a kiss to Ava's lips. She sighs as Ava's arms wrap around her back, half steadying and half claiming, then Ava's tongue slips into her mouth. Jean's fingers knot in Ava's hair, then somehow she's pressed between Ava and the door and they're tumbling back inside.

Of course, Ava doesn't let her fall. No, Ava scoops Jean up as if she weighs nothing more than a bag of feathers and carries her through to the bedroom, stumbling only when Jean's lips find her neck. Ever so gentle, she sets Jean down on their unmade bed.

But Ava doesn't join her, scrubbing away the lipstick smeared across her mouth. She's breathing hard. 'Fuck, I want you so much. But what about dinner?'

'Screw dinner,' Jean says, deadly serious. 'I need you to go and fetch that… item from your bag and get in this bed with me. Right now.'

Ava's lips twitch, a devilish glint in her eyes. 'You know when you say *item*, it sounds way dirtier than asking me to get the strap, right? Same with *arrangement* instead of fuck buddies.'

Jean's cheeks are surely a perfect match for her dress and hair, hot enough to fry an egg on. 'Less talking, more doing.'

'Yes ma'am,' Ava says, divesting of her clothes in record time. She's never shy about her body, never flaunting but never trying to hide it either, and the sight of all that smooth brown skin has Jean chewing on her lip, the sheets knotted tight beneath her fingers.

Then Ava's buckling the harness around her hips, and it's just as well Jean's draped across the bed because there's no way her knees could support her.

Ava grins as she approaches, so sure of the effect she has on Jean. But she doesn't pounce or pull at Jean's clothes. The mattress shifts as she climbs onto the bed, careful not to lean on Jean's dress or hair as she draws near. Then Ava cups Jean's cheek as if she's holding something rare and precious, leaning down to kiss her. Between them the dildo presses firm against Jean's belly. And Jean melts against her, the sweetest surrender; gives herself over to what Ava has planned, a passion all the more urgent for its restraint.

Ava's hands trace the topography of Jean's body, sliding over the silk like water. Between the whisper of her dress and Ava's caress, Jean's practically purring her contentment. The way Ava's peppering tiny kisses across her face, she feels not simply desired, but wanted. Cherished.

Yet when Jean slides her hands down from those strong shoulders to the fastening of Ava's sports bra, eager to do some exploring of her own, Ava pulls back. She takes Jean's hands, kisses both palms, and sets them down on the mattress either side of Jean's head.

'You don't want…?'

Ava shakes her head, thumb caressing the tender hollow of Jean's injured wrist. 'I don't want anything distracting me from how beautiful you look in that dress, or what I'm about to do to you while you're wearing it. Is that alright?'

Jean nods, breath quickening. And Ava's eyes are drawn irresistibly towards the swell of her breasts. Jean's nipples peak the smooth fabric, her desire apparent, but still Ava will not be rushed. She nuzzles at Jean's armpit, a place its owner had never previously considered to have any great erotic potential – but want throbs low and persistent in her belly. Ava feels it too, pupil and iris indistinguishable as she unzips the dress just a fraction, knuckles brushing against bare skin.

The dress puckers at Jean's chest; just enough that she can reach in to cup a breast. Ava flicks at a nipple, catching the tender bud with the edge of her thumbnail until Jean's breath is ragged. Anticipation sharpens to a dull ache between her thighs.

She shifts on the bed, wrapping her legs tight around Ava's waist, only the thin scrap of Jean's underwear keeping the dildo from slipping inside her. The pressure is an exquisite torture. As Jean rocks her hips, Ava smiles against her mouth. Says: 'Easy. I've got you.'

Then Ava's reaching between them – not to dispose of Jean's underwear, but rather push it to one side. Running a testing finger through Jean's slickness.

Jean gasps, parting to the touch, and Ava slips that finger into her mouth. Before Jean can complain at the loss of contact, Ava's shifting. Sliding home, deep inside her. Jean cries out, lips coated in the taste of her own desire. Ava's hips undulate, so slow and steady that Jean is sure she'll go mad with it. And yet it's a relentless pleasure, one thrust melting liquid smooth into the next until Jean's quivering in Ava's arms.

And all the while Ava watches her, drinking in every flicker and spasm that crosses Jean's face. Stroking her hair, her back, her thighs with the dress rucked up round them. And Jean couldn't move even if she wanted to, caught on this unbearable edge of ecstasy.

Passivity has never appealed to Jean. In or out of the bedroom, she has no interest in being dominated. But the way Ava's touching her, gliding in and out of her, is infinitely closer to worship. Jean grips at her shoulder, the pressure mounting to an intolerable high.

And in the moment before she comes, it occurs to Jean: Ava isn't taking her. Ava isn't dicking her down. Ava isn't even fucking her. *She's making love to me.*

Then orgasm obliterates every coherent thought. There's only Ava's arms around her, Ava's lips brushing against her ear as she whispers: 'You're so perfect when you lose control.'

Ava doesn't let up even as Jean shudders; forehead shining with effort, she draws out Jean's climax with every stroke. Ava bites her lip until blood beads on the skin, a tremor running through her shoulders. Still she maintains that perfect rhythm, driving into Jean to the very hilt.

Only as her thigh twitches beneath Ava's grasp does Jean understand that she's coming again, coming apart at the very seams. And this time she is taking Ava with her. Those dark eyes roll back in her head until Jean glimpses the whites, a spasm running through her spine. And in that moment Jean can't tell where her own body ends, where Ava's begins.

Even through her own orgasm, Ava's control is masterful. She braces herself against the mattress, breath coming hot and fast against Jean's neck. And when she recovers, her first thought is tending to Jean.

'There.' Ava kisses her parted lips. 'Wasn't that divine?'

Jean nods, unable to speak past the lump in her throat.

'What's wrong?' Ava's thumb wipes across her cheek. 'Did I hurt you?'

'No! No.' Jean traces the line of Ava's collarbone, slippery with sweat. 'You were so incredibly gentle. And nobody's ever – I haven't... It's never been quite like this for me. None of it.'

Ava ducks her head to kiss Jean. 'Me neither.'

She eases out from between Jean's legs then, missing the look of surprise that Jean's altogether too raw to disguise, Ava unbuckles the straps, dropping harness and dildo over the side of the bed, and pulls Jean into her arms.

—

It's dark when Jean wakes, sticky thighed and supple boned. Ava's arms are wrapped around her, mouth still pressed to Jean's temple as if she'd dropped a kiss there in the moments sleep took hold. And Jean wishes that she could stay here in this bed, in this woman's arms, for all eternity. But even now the clock is ticking. Another night and they'll be boarding the train back to London, back to busy lives and expectations.

She could propose a third week – the Bairds are still in New York, and Ava would certainly say yes, though surely there's work she ought to be doing. But even if she agreed, what after that? It would only be delaying the inevitable. A return to Jean's quiet home, her empty bed, with only stolen nights to look forward to. A life where she and Ava make no sense by day.

Jean's lungs pull tight. Though the window's open, there's not enough air lying among the shadows. She rolls from the bed, retrieving her coverup shirt from the chair, and pads through the darkened house. Opens the patio doors to the tiny back garden, where she had sipped champagne while Ava repainted her toes, taking exquisite care.

She lowers herself into the chair, gulping at the cool night air. But even then, there isn't enough of it. Hot tears spill down Jean's cheeks to splash against the glass table. She presses a hand to her mouth, not wanting to risk disturbing Ava.

Still, minutes or hours later, she appears – wrapped in a jumper and still yawning. 'Hey. I woke up and you weren't there – is everything okay?'

'Fine,' Jean says, though it's a transparent lie.

'Your legs are freezing.' Ava disappears back inside and returns with a woollen blanket from the sofa, tucking it round Jean's bare thighs. The tenderness of it pierces Jean's heart. 'What's the matter?'

Jean blinks, gazing up at the sky. The moon blurs as a tear rolls down her cheek. 'Do you ever think about all those infinite galaxies out there? About how there could be countless parallel worlds in them, each with some version of you?'

'Not really. I was never good at science.'

'I wasn't either, but it keeps coming back to me.' Jean folds both arms around herself, hugging the blanket. 'What if there's a world where my parents never died, and Bridget went off to fashion school to live her dream? Or a world where I hadn't betrayed Marianne.'

'Jean...' There's a pleading in her voice, but Jean ignores it, staring at the pinpricks of glimmering light piercing through the inky darkness. The stars are so much brighter here, without London's light pollution.

'Maybe Bridget would be the next Vivienne Westwood. Maybe Mari would have my job, and we'd still be friends. Maybe I wouldn't even have gone into law in the first place.' Jean laughs, fresh tears brimming. 'Perhaps in another world you and I could have...'

'What?'

'It doesn't matter. It's stupid, and it doesn't fit into this one.'

'What, Jean?' Ava's voice is ragged, the words tearing from her. A warm hand covers Jean's, squeezing tight. 'Tell me.'

'Maybe you and I could have been like this on ordinary days too. Maybe we could have more than nights and holidays and stolen moments.' Jean's cheek itches with the salt, and she scrubs the back of her hand across it. All the while Ava stares at her, dumbfounded. 'Never mind – I'm being stupid. It's all the sun, or maybe I didn't drink enough water. Forget it.'

'Why is that stupid?' Ava's very still then, only her curls rippling in the breeze.

'Because my life, my career, everything that I've worked for... I became the person that I needed to be to get this far.'

'None of that stops being possible just because you're with a woman. Discrimination's illegal, and we have rights enshrined in law.'

'You and I both know that social norms take years to catch up. It would still mark me out as... as... different.' Jean shakes her head, adamant. 'No. You'll find a connection like this with someone else. Someone who's out, someone closer to your own age.'

Ava looks at her like she's speaking Martian. 'No. I won't.'

'Of course you will, Ava – I'm not saying this to be cruel. You are charming and considerate and an incredible lover. Beautiful, too. It should be the easiest thing in the world.'

'Sure, I can pick up women. I *did* pick up women. But do you really think this kind of thing happens often?' Ava shakes her head, curls springing free from her ponytail. But she doesn't stop to pick up the fallen elastic. 'I meant what I said, Jean – it's never been like this for me either. Not once. What we have, it's exceptional.'

'We're *friends*. Friends who also fuck. It's good, I admit it, but there's nothing rare or special about that.' If there is, and Jean has lured Ava in anyway, she's guilty of all that Aaliyah had accused her and much worse besides. The knowledge is a hook through her heart, weighing it down with shame.

'Friends who make love and go on romantic holidays? Friends who share things they've never told anyone else and trust each other with their deepest, darkest truths? Friends who spend every possible night together?' Ava stares at her, jaw tight. 'You're a smart woman, Jean. Is that really what you think fuck buddies do?'

'It's not like I've ever done this before!' Jean pushes the hair back from her forehead. 'There was my marriage to Henry. There were hook-ups with forgettable men. And then there was you. I'd never – I've never had anyone or anything I could compare this to.'

'Me neither. I've done casual before, Jean, and this isn't it. It never was.'

'But you agreed! Every time I said casual was all I could offer you, you agreed.'

Ava spreads her arms wide, as if the answer is obvious, floating in the air between them. 'I was waiting for you to figure it out on your own! I thought that if I gave you enough space, enough time, then—'

'What?' Jean scoffs. 'That I'd tell everyone "*I'm a lesbian, surprise!*" and we'd live happily ever after?'

Ava doesn't laugh. 'Something like that. Yes.'

'Oh, be serious.'

'I am!' Ava's voice echoes through the stillness of the night. She leans forward, speaking lower, faster. 'I *am*. People come out at all different stages of life, Jean, don't you see? And with women it's particularly common to come out during middle age—'

'NO!' Jean stands, heart pounding, and the blanket falls away. 'I can't. Not now, not ever. I don't want anyone to look at me and think...'

'What? That you're capable of having romantic and sexual feelings for women?' Ava rounds the table, coming close enough that Jean has no choice but to look her in the eye. 'That doesn't make you any less worthy as a human being. It doesn't make you any less brilliant or capable as a lawyer.'

'It might as well. You know nothing – nothing at all – about what it's like in the corporate world. The sacrifices it takes. Or how little room there is for any kind of difference. So don't you dare try and tell me that it wouldn't matter.'

'But is it worth it? Living a lie for the rest of your life so you can keep on fitting the image of what people expect you to be?' Ava's mouth pulls to one side, as if she's incapable of imagining such an existence. 'Wouldn't you rather stop pretending?'

Jean's breath catches, and Ava presses her advantage. 'You've been happy these last two weeks. Properly happy. And on all the nights you've stayed with me. Look me in the eye and tell me that doesn't matter.'

'Who isn't happy when they're getting regular orgasms?'

Ava's mouth twists. 'No. Don't do that. Do not pretend like it's only a sex thi—'

'And what does being happy have to do with anything?' Jean shakes her head, incredulous. 'Adults don't make decisions based on happiness alone. I haven't spent all these years working towards becoming managing partner so that I could be happy.'

Ava's expression verges dangerously close to pity. 'Then why did you?'

The question knocks Jean off course, flooding her with uncertainty. Why *has* she travelled so far down this path? There's no joy in the thought of returning to her corner office, none of the excitement she's found in helping Ava prepare for her charity launch. With Marianne rejecting her offer in such a spectacular fashion, the old dream of them taking the firm together is well and truly dead. 'All that, what you're talking about, it's so fragile. It could be taken away at any moment. I wanted something solid; something that lasts.'

Ava steps closer then, voice unbearably soft. 'The only time you've ever come truly alive while describing that job is talking about the hours you spent with Kate. I think she was what you wanted, far more than anything to do with the firm.'

'No.' Jean backs away, shivering in the cool night air. 'That's not true. Or why would I have chosen my career over her?'

'Because you were scared. Because you were traumatised. Because we live in a world more likely to punish women who are victimised than the men who abuse them.' There's no judgement in Ava's eyes, even now. Only an understanding that leaves Jean feeling naked, though her shirt skims her knees. 'You don't have to spend the rest of your life in penance for that decision. We could be together. And nobody needs to know until you're good and ready.'

Jean places a steadying hand against the table's glass, cool beneath her palm. Aaliyah was right – of course she was. Jean had been a fool not to see it, when Ava has spent all these months drawing closer. *Or maybe*, says the sly voice in her head, *you didn't want to see. You wanted to have your cake and eat it too.* 'Ava, I am telling you, that is not going to happen.'

'Just consider your options – that's all I'm asking. Nothing about your life has to change.' Ava holds up both hands and speaks slowly, as if she's come face to face with a wild animal. 'We could have something solid, Jean. I know that I'm not the person you planned on being with. But if you jump, I *will* catch you.'

It's too much. Jean tugs at her collar, gasping for air. Ava reaches for her shoulder, but Jean pulls away as if scalded by her touch. 'I don't want that life with you,' Jean hisses. 'I want the one I'm living now. And what the hell gives you the right to judge me for that?'

'I'm no—'

'You think there's some kind of virtue in making life as hard for yourself as you possibly can?' Jean slams her hand against the table, palm stinging as the glass shudders. 'There's not. There is, however, a lot to be said for making the most of the cards you've been dealt.'

Ava's hand, still reaching towards Jean, withdraws. Her voice wary. 'What are you saying?'

Now it's Jean who advances, finger pointing in accusation. 'That you could blend in if you wanted to. You could have done anything at all if you had, instead of limiting your own potential.'

Ava goes deathly pale, white as the moon's impassive face as it looks down upon them. 'I don't... That's not...'

'You tell me that I'm scared because I don't live what you consider an *authentic truth*.' Jean injects real venom into those two words. 'But I think you're the coward, too afraid ever to find out just how far you could have gone if you'd really tried.'

'Fuck you, Jean.'

'I wish you would, instead of going all touchy-feely on me.' Instead of slipping past every defence to claim some part of Jean that she had long since locked away.

The words are sharp enough to cut Ava's knees out from under her; she slumps into Jean's recently vacated chair. 'Who are you?' Tears spill down Ava's cheeks as she searches Jean's face. 'Because I don't know this woman at all.'

'That's exactly my point! This is who I've always been.' Jean slams a hand against her breast, and something cracks beneath the muscle and sinew. 'This is who I will always be. You don't know me, Ava. At all. The person you're asking to be with you? She doesn't exist.'

Chapter Twenty-Eight

But Jean doesn't recognise herself either, in the morning. That ever-smiling, freckled woman has vanished from the mirror; only a tired shadow remaining. She'd woken alone in their bed, the air impossibly still, and known even before checking Ava's drawers that all her things would be gone. Though Jean had waited until dawn spilled through the curtains, casting a pale glow over their bedroom, still Ava hadn't joined her. And Jean's eyes, puffy and sore from crying, had drifted shut. She must have packed in silence while Jean slept. There isn't a note or a text – not that Jean expects either. After all, what's left to say?

Numb, she packs her things and tidies the house. There's no point in lingering – though the sun's still bright in the sky, Jean can't feel the warmth. Scrubbing down the kitchen and bathroom at least gives her something to do. Jean calls an Uber, locks the Baird family's cottage, and tucks the key back into its safe.

The journey back to London passes in a similar blur, Jean's chest knotting tighter with every passing mile. There is no reason now to look up from her book and smile. Nobody now to twine their ankle round hers like a cat.

She goes back to work the next day, determined to prove Ava wrong, to fill the emptiness that had plagued her with the firm's hustle and bustle. To show all who had doubted it that Marianne's ghost has not defeated her.

Helen greets Jean in the lobby, all business as if she'd never been away, which makes it easier to sink back into DDH's routine. But there's a bouquet on her desk – chrysanthemums, freesias, birds of paradise in full bloom. An elaborate arrangement with a discreet card, signed personally by Minerva's CEO. Jean drops it into the recycling bin. 'Get rid of those.'

'Ms Howard…?'

Jean sighs. 'Take them home if you want, Helen. Just get those flowers out of my sight. And open a window.'

Helen does as she's bid, carrying the arrangement out into a corner of the reception area. But even after she returns, Helen stares whenever she thinks Jean's not looking. It's impossible to settle into the Priestley tribunal she is preparing for in the face of such concern.

And she's almost relieved when Peter arrives in the afternoon, fresh from the golf course, a shrink-wrapped charcuterie board for them to share for lunch. Helen slips from the room, and he launches into the update Jean has really been waiting for – the one neither of them wants committed to paper.

Marianne has been suspended. Caught in that strange limbo between joblessness and gainful employment. 'They're waiting,' he says. 'To see if we'll take any further action against her or Minerva, since she was there representing them.'

'No, I—' Jean shakes her head. 'No.'

'I didn't think so.' He clears his throat. 'You know, I was glad that you switched off so completely on your holiday. That you didn't take your laptop or your work phone. Did you have a good time?'

Jean nods, unable to swallow her cracker, hoping her tan and freckles will speak for themselves.

But Peter doesn't appear entirely convinced. He squeezes Jean's shoulder. 'My door's always open to you, Jeanie. You know that, don't you?'

Again, Jean nods. And he leaves her to it. Peter, who has supported her through thick and thin. There is, Jean realises, a good chance that he'd understand – be delighted, even – if she'd come to him with news of a female partner. But Peter is not the only one who'd have an opinion. Together, a pack of hyenas may bring down a lion. And Jean cannot repay his trust by feeding DDH back through the rumour mill hot on the heels of their last scandal, or risk rebranding herself at a time when it's more important than ever to project the image of stability.

She just about manages it too, reining in Edward, who had grown too bold in her absence, redirecting those left floundering after the Leonides contract fell through to other briefs and projects.

Jean steps up her training regimen, keen to burn off the extra pounds she'd gained luxuriating with Ava. Every day she works late, nothing now to lure her from the office. By the time she gets home, she has no spare energy to spend dwelling on her bed's emptiness.

And yet, though nobody in her life had known what Ava was to her, somehow they all find ways to remind Jean of what she has lost. Bernard calls one evening, friendly as ever, asking how they'd enjoyed *Hamilton*. And Jean's overwhelmed by the memory of Ava's fingers linked with hers in the dark; of Ava attempting to sing every single part as she'd performed the musical in her shower, mostly succeeding.

At brunch, Naomi and Cora push her for more salacious details about Aiden, ignoring Jean's reticence and Imogen's attempts to redirect the conversation.

'Really, Jean.' Naomi twirls her cocktail glass, the margarita sloshing against the sides but never quite spilling over. 'A beach holiday, a toyboy lover, and a promotion on the horizon – you could spread the joy a little.'

'Work's busy, is all. There's lots to do before the handover – but I'm fine.'

'Are you?' Cora's dark eyes are alert. 'You don't seem happy about much at all, lately.'

'Did things end with Aiden? Is that what's got you down?' Naomi's hand covers her wrist.

'You two need to stop,' Imogen says, an edge of warning in her voice. 'Whatever it is, Jean can tell us in her own time.'

'Nonsense.' Cora drains her drink, gesturing to the waiter for another. 'What are girlfriends for, if not sharing your problems?'

Laughter bubbles up Jean's throat. Even before offering to be her girlfriend, Ava had been there whenever she needed her. Listened when Jean wanted to talk. Held Jean when she wasn't ready to speak. Nobody since Mari has made her feel so seen, and even then, Mari had never been safe the way Ava is. 'You're right,' Jean says, realising all three of them are still watching her. 'It ended the day I came back from Edinburgh, and I've felt lost ever since.'

'I'm sorry, Jean. It can be difficult when these things end. But let's face it, you went in knowing that it was never going to last.'

'Jesus, Naomi.' Imogen gets into it with the two of them, distracting Naomi and Cora long enough for Jean to try and gather her thoughts. But the back and forth between them rattles round her skull like a pinball, knocking the last of her doubts loose.

'It could have,' Jean whispers.

'You always think that you know best, that you're the moral arbiter of our little group. But—'

'It could have.' Too late the conviction comes.

Cora and Naomi exchange a glance. 'Darling—'

'I'm serious. If you want the whole sordid story, you're welcome to it. But there's one vital piece of information you need to know before we go any further.' Jean's hand trembles as she lifts her cocktail glass, half the margarita spilling out the corner of her mouth. She reaches for a napkin and dabs at her chin while her three oldest friends stare. 'There never was any Aiden. I panicked and made up a cover story, because I was embarrassed about the truth.'

Cora's Botoxed brow barely wrinkles, though she frowns. 'What?'

'Then who…?' Naomi blinks slowly. 'Then who were you having it off with? Who was he?'

Imogen cuts her a glare. 'Jean might have an easier time telling us who they were if you didn't keep interrupting her.'

'They? Were there multiple somebodies? Was this a polyamory situation, or an orgy?'

Jean has to look away from Naomi's searching gaze. She trails her fingertip across a scratch in the wooden tabletop. 'Neither. The truth is, she is a woman. Her name is Ava. She came to Edinburgh with me.'

Naomi's laughter is sharp and clear as broken glass, cutting Jean to ribbons. 'You're joking, right? She is joking?'

A moment later Naomi gives a sharp gasp, and Jean's almost certain Imogen kicked her underneath the table.

'Ava... as in that woman from the hospital?' Cora's brows draw together as, at last, the pieces fall into place.

'It's not a joke. It started as a hook-up, and became...' Jean sniffs. Takes a deep breath. Her composure, her dignity, might be all that she has left by the end of this. She grasps the soggy napkin, twisting and tearing it to shreds in her lap. 'I don't have the words to describe it. What we were to each other. It was so unlike anything I've ever known.'

'Bloody hell!' Cora sinks back against her seat, and even without looking, Jean can picture her incredulous expression. 'That's why she was so sore about the whole Aiden situation. But it can't be serious, can it? You were married to Henry, for goodness' sake.'

But Ginny cuts through this line of enquiry, reaching under the table to interrupt the napkin shredding as she takes Jean's hand. 'Would you like to tell us about her? Ava?'

A crack runs through Jean's voice, and she rushes to get the words out, knowing it's only a matter of time before her throat completely splinters under their weight. The subtle pressure of Imogen's fingers is the only thing holding her together. 'She was falling in love with me. But I was too much of a coward to admit that I felt the same way. I said things. Stupid, unforgivable things. And she left me.'

Imogen passes her a dry napkin, and Jean presses it to her eyes, burning like she's run through tear gas.

'But...' Cora drums her fingernails on the table. 'You're not a lesbian now, are you?'

Jean's still fumbling for an answer when Naomi speaks. 'Don't be ridiculous. Nobody magically wakes up gay.

Certainly not at our age. Whatever this is, it's bound to pass.'

Jean grabs her handbag and bolts from the table as a fresh round of debate kicks off, unable to stomach witnessing her own vivisection. And on the street, nobody gives her wild eyes or smeared make-up a second glance – the beauty of London's anonymity.

She ducks between meandering tourists and striding locals, almost at the tube station when an arm closes tight around her elbow. Jean jerks back, clinging to her handbag.

But instead of a desperate man she comes face to face with Imogen, pink-cheeked and breathing hard. 'I called you,' she says, still panting. 'But I don't think you heard. I stayed to give Naomi and Cora a piece of my mind, and I'm not fit enough to run and yell at the same time.'

'I think Grant's still accepting clients.'

'I think I'd rather step in front of a bus than go to the gym.' Imogen steps closer, ignoring the commuter who swears at her. 'You're one of the only people in this world I'd voluntarily run anywhere for, Jean Howard. And don't you forget it.'

Then she launches herself at Jean, wrapping both arms around her. And Jean doesn't care that her mouth's full of silky blonde hair, or that with this fresh round of tears she likely resembles Pennywise. She doesn't even care about the spectacle they're making. It's good to simply be held.

Imogen insists on getting the tube with her. But instead of heading home, they take a detour round Kensington Gardens, making the most of early autumn sun. The leaves on the trees are just beginning to yellow, the elaborate arrangements of flowers losing their bloom – yet there is beauty in the day, in Imogen's gentle understanding, and Jean wouldn't wish for a single thing about it to be different. Except for the promise of knowing she'd see Ava again.

It's a relief, opening up to Imogen. Voicing those secret, soaring joys and her deepest buried fears. Her friend listens without judgement to the whole story as they stroll through the park, asking the occasional question and nodding while Jean clarifies.

Ginny is quite delighted by what little Jean shares of their sex life, and utterly charmed by how persistently Ava had attempted to elevate their relationship beyond the physical. She throws back her head and laughs at Ava's transparent jealousy over Bernard. 'Oh, Jean. It sounds like she's head over heels.'

'Maybe once. Not anymore.' It's easier to say it while they're walking, while she doesn't have to look into Imogen's eyes. She describes the holiday; how she'd felt like another person entirely, enlivened by the sea air and Ava's heady affection. How perfect it had been until that final night.

As Jean recounts that argument – their first and last – Imogen guides her to sit on a nearby bench, producing an unopened bottle of water from her bag. Jean downs half of it in a few gulps, dehydrated from the killer combination of day drinking and tears.

Ginny rubs Jean's shoulder, steady and firm. 'But did you apologise to her afterwards? Have you tried to make things right?'

Jean can only shake her head, watching a pair of swans glide majestically across the pond, a perfect trail of ripples expanding in their wake.

'Oh, Jean!' Ginny's voice startles even the fearless London pigeons from an overhead tree. 'Why the hell not?'

'Because. Naomi's right – it would be ridiculous coming out at my age. I can't just change everything about who I am. And the timing couldn't be worse for the firm.' Jean sighs, leaning against Ginny. 'Plus, she could be much happier with someone far less complicated. A woman that's out and proud, young... not a closeted older woman cripped by Catholic guilt.'

'Maybe it's not a change. Maybe it's who you've been all along.' Imogen toys with the gold links of her necklace, running the chain between her fingertips. 'I sometimes wondered about you and Marianne. It used to make me jealous, how much you adored her.'

Jean's head snaps up. It had never occurred to her that any of her friends might have perceived Marianne as a rival. 'Ginny...'

'Then I thought, maybe it's a different kind of love. You took the divorce in your stride, but losing Marianne – it dimmed something in you. Something that hasn't been bright and alive until this year.' Imogen twists then, giving Jean no choice but to look at her. 'Sure, Ava could have someone else. But she still chose you – even knowing this was new territory for you, even when you were in complete and utter denial about how much you wanted her. Ava could have walked away at any point, but she chose you instead.'

Jean slumps back against the bench, impossibly weary. All those years regretting what she did to Marianne, only to make the same mistake twice. She blinks, forcing herself to concentrate on a cloud in the shape of a seahorse, complete with curling tail. She can't remember now whether it had been Bridget or their mother who'd lain blankets out on the grass so they could look up and find all manner of fantastical creatures riding across the sky. 'If I do this, if I start telling people that I'm a lesbian, it'll be the end for me and Bridget. She'll never accept it.'

'You don't have to make any big announcements to your sister. It's not mandatory.' Imogen takes her hand. 'But I am grateful that you trusted me enough to let me know.'

Jean squeezes back, tight enough that her bones grind against Ginny's. 'I'm not sure Cora or Naomi feel the same way.'

In typical Imogen fashion, she mulls it over, not rushing in with meaningless assurances. 'They were shocked,' Ginny says. 'And they were idiots – that I don't dispute. But Cora and Naomi both care about you. And I think they'll come around.'

It's difficult to share her optimism – even now, the echo of Naomi's laughter rings loud. 'And if they don't?'

Imogen considers, the breeze rippling through her hair. Her smile is warmer than the noonday sun. 'Then it's us against the world.'

Chapter Twenty-Nine

Afterwards, Jean's world doesn't end with that coming out. The days continue to pass one by one. And, as the shock wears off, Jean realises she can breathe a little easier. Imogen hasn't rejected her. Imogen has carried on loving her, if the steady stream of phone calls and invitations are any indication. And though Jean wishes Ginny would just let her wallow, she's grateful too.

There's even a present. It arrives in a discreet cardboard box: an anthology of writing from men and women that, for all manner of reasons, came out in mid to later life. At first Jean tries to ignore the book, stuffing it in an anonymous corner of her shelves. But the rainbow spine catches her eye every time she steps into her home office. While she's poring over the Priestley case documents, highlighting and underlining, it's there in the corner of Jean's vision.

Even during her days at the office, an entirely rainbow-free space, it weighs on Jean's mind. A constant source of temptation, just like Ava had been. So, when she gets home, she kicks off her shoes, pours a glass of wine, and curls up with the book in her armchair.

The essays are honest – terrifyingly so – and completely heartfelt. And though the lives of the contributors couldn't be more different – a primary school teacher and an army general, a civil servant and a comedian Jean's never heard of – their stories are all the same in one key respect. Not one among them regrets coming out. They write of it as a weight lifted; the ability to breathe.

Even after she turns the last page of the final chapter, Jean hungers for more such stories. She finds the memoir of a Jewish housewife who realised she was gay after being captivated by a painting of a woman's naked body. A blog post from a romance author whom, after twenty years of marriage to a man and two children, knew beyond a shadow of a doubt that she was a lesbian. All her subsequent releases have been sapphic, and Jean downloads them onto her Kindle, more discreet than old-fashioned paperbacks. If lesbianism is at odds with the image she presents to the world, Mills and Boon is its very antithesis.

And yet, Jean is forced to admit, they are good stories. Compelling, well-written... and rather sexy. She breezes through the novels at night, and becomes reacquainted with her vibrator. But though her intentions start out strong, it's never the characters Jean pictures as she bucks and trembles. The sweeping emotions call Ava to mind too. Before her, Jean would have written it all off as hyperbole used to sell books in much the same way Valentine's Day is used to hawk cards. Now, though, she's familiar with the yearning. The laughter. The way her entire world seems brighter when shared with the right person.

But the relentless optimism is where these stories lose Jean. A character makes a dreadful mistake, often around the seventy-five per cent mark. And by the end they are forgiven, back in the arms of their beloved, love having conquered all. Real life has never offered Jean such an abundance of second chances.

There are wild moments when she considers calling Ava. If this were one of her covert romance reads, then Jean would race across the city and implore Ava to take her back. But what on earth would she say? What possible combination of words could have the power to repair things between them?

Jean picks up a pen, jotting down options and scribbling them out. Rejecting the trite, the easy refuge of justifications, the self-serving. It takes Jean several evenings to produce something she doesn't entirely hate. And in the end, she settles on unvarnished honesty:

> *Dear Ava,*
>
> *I know that I'm probably the last person you want to hear from. And if you throw this into the rubbish (or recycling) then I completely understand. But – on the off chance you're still reading – I would like to apologise. Without reservation. I'm so sorry for those awful things I said to you. Not one of them was true. For what it's worth, and I imagine very little, the work you do is courageous and necessary. It has changed, and will continue to change, people's lives for the better. It would be impossible to put a price on it all. And I should never have implied that your work, or that of your sector, is limited to monetary value alone.*
>
> *Having been raised with your mother's faith, you will be familiar with St Peter as heaven's gatekeeper. And though it's been a long time since I left the church, it's an image I find myself coming back to. Of the two of us, you are a far likelier candidate for entry. I was eighteen years old when you were born – already an adult in the law's*

eyes, if not quite reality. But you have long since outstripped me in the good you have managed to achieve within your lifetime.

If we were up against each other in court, you'd use what I said to you that night as evidence against this claim. And I'd have very little defence, except to say this. You came so close to the truth – to my truth, one I've spent decades burying – and it scared me. I don't say that to excuse my actions. I could, and should, have handled it better. Given you even a fraction of the grace you have extended to me.

As well as an apology, I owe you something else. You have the right to know that the months we spent together were the happiest I've ever been. And loving you is the truest thing that I have ever felt – I was a coward and a fool to deny it. To deny you.

I wish you nothing but the best with launching the CJC, and whatever comes next.
With much love,
Jean

On her way to work she has Bogdan stop beside a post box while she nips out to send the letter, the driver behind tooting his horn and making eloquent use of gestures all the while. But Jean feels better – lighter than the day she'd made her First Confession – for having sent it. For trying to make amends.

—

Text had always been Ava's preferred method of communication, or perhaps the only one she'd trusted Jean would allow her in the beginning. And yet, though Jean receives a steady string of messages – Ginny with the news that Amelia Hawthorne has lost her licence, and an unspoken reminder of her affection; Naomi and Cora with apologies sent within minutes of each other, leading Jean to suspect they'd met up to discuss an approach – not one is from her. Not, Jean reminds herself, that she'd expected a response.

It's easy putting her personal phone out of reach, if not out of mind, while she throws herself into the tribunal. Valerie Priestley and her IT company stand accused of wrongful dismissal by seven female employees, all with small children, all of whom had been fired within a year after their maternity leave ended.

It's an uphill battle, defending the indefensible – one that takes Jean's utmost concentration. She resists the urge to ask Valerie how she could have been so stupid, following the same predictable pattern of behaviour every time. Though her reasoning changed – poor timekeeping, low performance, a role becoming obsolete – the timeline remained identical. Instead, Jean has her team pulling information that can work in their favour: Valerie's trio of Women in Business awards, the money she has donated to women's refuges and scholarships for girls in STEM, viral videos from her company's Take-Your-Daughter-to-Work Day.

It would be a home run for Lawson and Pierce, the opposing side in the case, if Valerie didn't have DDH money. Carl quickly strikes gold digging through the dregs of the dismissed women's lives. The ringleader of the posse, fired officially for the dip in her performance, attends weekly Alcoholics Anonymous meetings in her local church hall.

Jean feels grubby as she picks through his findings. Matters are complicated even further by the fact her ex-husband, always so moral, is heading up this case on behalf of the women. It doesn't matter, or at least it shouldn't – Alexander's the one who will face Henry across the negotiating table, and in the courtroom. And the divorce had been straightforward, a neat division of assets uncontested by either party. Henry had tried to be generous, ashamed of his outburst towards the end. And Jean had remained fair, guilty over her relief at being free from all the love Henry had tried to give her.

Their paths haven't crossed since they signed the papers. Which is why Peter is nothing short of astounded when Jean proposes she visit L&P's office for this preliminary round of settlement discussions. But he doesn't argue; just gives Jean the afternoon off.

—

Henry's eyes go wide at the sight of her. He's always had the most dreadful poker face, always worn his heart on his sleeve – likely why he's never risen beyond senior associate. And certainly it was a factor in their marriage failing. Whereas Jean's ambition had grown with every passing year, Henry's had waned. While Jean climbed higher still in DDH, Henry moved to a smaller family-friendly firm, married a music teacher, and took full paternity leave for all three of his children. By all accounts Henry is happy in his new life. And yet he's gracious at this unexpected reminder of the old, rising to shake Jean's hand.

'Henry,' she says. 'You're looking well.'

And it's true – fatherhood suits Henry. The kids have kept him active enough to avoid middle-age spread and, though his sandy hair is undeniably greying, the lines he's acquired since their last meeting suggest a life filled with laughter.

To his credit, Henry doesn't return the compliment. He's kind, but honest too – and Jean's grateful for the lack of pretence. 'Jean – I wasn't expecting you, but it's good to see you again. Really.'

Her eyes prickle at his sincerity, and Henry squeezes before letting go.

'Yes, well.' Jean clears her throat. 'Rhona Baird is one of our more promising junior associates, and she'll be taking the lead today.'

Rhona looks almost as shocked as Henry, though she recovers quickly, stepping forward to shake hands with him and the young brunette from L&P.

'That's a great idea,' Henry says. 'Hannah, why don't you take point too?'

The junior associates launch into it, haltingly at first. Going over red lines, potential concessions, and the grey area in between. Rhona looks to Jean after every other sentence, as if searching for approval. Only once does Jean have to intercede, when Rhona comes perilously close to admitting wrongdoing on their client's part, Henry's half-smile just visible behind his hand. But the rest of the time Jean busies herself with taking notes, Henry doing the same. And gradually their underlings grow used to this role reversal. Rhona sits up straighter, parrying every one of Hannah's attacks, and Jean's pride is absolute.

–

Afterwards, Rhona returns to the office, a spring in her step. Hannah too disappears, still glowing from Henry's praise. Then there's just the two of them, and the room's as quiet as their house – newly Jean's – had felt after the divorce. And with Henry loading up his briefcase, she might not get another shot. Jean steps closer, pulse pounding at her throat so hard she's nauseated.

'Did you ever wonder… about me?'

Though he puts down the papers to give Jean his full attention, she can't meet Henry's gaze. Keeps her eyes fixed on the silken knot of his tie. 'When we got divorced. I keep coming back to what you said, about how it felt like being married to a widow. Did you think that maybe I might be… might be a—'

But Jean can't get so much as a whisper past the lump in her throat, solid as a golf ball. Hot tears slide down her cheeks. And she covers her face, mortified. Her emotions have never been far from the surface since Ava left, the blank professional mask lying in tatters at her feet.

Through the gaps in her fingers Jean watches as Henry darts past her, slides the 'Meeting in Progress' sign back in place, and closes the door. Then it's Jean's turn to be astonished as he wraps both arms around her. She's too stunned to do anything but cry while Henry strokes her back. Jean sobs until there's nothing left. Afterwards, though the pressure behind her eyes warns of a headache, she feels better for it. Henry passes her the handkerchief from his breast pocket, and Jean dabs at her face – her make-up is beyond saving now – and blows her nose.

'I'm sorry,' Jean says, thickly. 'I don't know what I was thinking.'

Henry shrugs. 'Maybe you weren't thinking. Maybe you needed to feel something. Either way, don't be sorry.'

For all she'd hated Henry's psychoanalysis during their marriage, the words wrap around her like a thick down quilt. 'Thank you.'

'And I'm sorry, by the way. That comment wasn't my finest moment.'

Jean shrugs away his remorse. 'Even so, there might have been some truth in it. God, did I make a mess of things.'

'Well...' Henry puts his hands in his pockets. 'No problem ever seems quite so bad after a square meal. How about we get some lunch and talk properly?'

They go to a steak joint Henry favours, where the waiters greet him by name and guide the pair of them to a comfortable leather booth. Over the bread basket Jean asks about his life, genuinely curious. Imogen's given her updates over the years about Henry's engagement, his wedding, the pregnancies and births. And Jean felt relief at escaping that tightening domestic noose even as she'd missed Henry's companionship from the early days, a friend that fully supported her ambitions. The two warring emotions had almost cancelled one another out, leaving Jean strangely numb as she'd listened. But now Henry opens up to her, cautiously at first, then easing into stories about his life as Jean continues to ask about it.

Henry clears his throat. 'Having kids myself made me realise something about our marriage. I love all my children dearly, but it's incredibly hard work. Being a parent. It changes everything. And nobody should have to do it if they're not completely certain.'

Jean can only stare. This quiet, careful conversation is a world apart from their worst arguments, when Henry – a vein popping in his forehead – had called her unfeeling, unnatural.

When she doesn't speak, Henry continues. 'I've wanted to apologise, over the years. About the guilt and the pressure. I wasn't fair to you.'

'No. You weren't.' Jean sips her martini, and it takes everything to keep her hand from shaking as she sets it down. 'I told you from the beginning that I never wanted kids. And you said that was fine. But then you spent our marriage punishing me for it. Why?'

'Because I loved you. And I could feel you slipping away from me every day. I thought a child would bring us closer.' Henry's smile is sad. 'And I know now it was a terrible idea. That you'd have resented me, and rightly so. I didn't have healthy reasons for wanting to start a family – not back then.'

'What changed?'

'I did a lot of soul-searching. After the divorce. And therapy.'

Jean's still puzzling that one out when the waiter sets their plates down. Sizzling steaks, fresh salad and steaming hot chips – food had been the last thing on her mind. And yet it smells so delicious that she can't resist tucking in. The steak is done to medium-rare perfection, practically melting against her tongue. Henry too carves into his steak, the food creating a natural armistice.

'What about you?' Henry asks between bites. 'What's new in your life? How have you been?'

'I've been thinking a lot. About what you said just before the divorce; that we both deserved more.' Jean pauses until Henry nods. 'And you seem to have found it, but I – Henry, what did you mean?'

'Jean...' He reaches across the table, attempting to cover her hand. But she pulls away.

'No, tell me. *Please.*' Jean despises her own voice, tight with desperation. 'You were enough for me. Why wasn't I enough for you?'

Henry's expression grows pained. He's silent for a long moment, sprinkling salt on his chips. Until, at last, he says: 'I wanted to be more than *enough*. You were so much more than enough to me. I was mad for you, Jean. And I wanted you so much that at first it didn't matter if I loved you more than you loved me. But you were alive at work in a way you never were with me. As time went on, it felt like you were going through the motions.'

'In what way?' Jean has her suspicions, but she needs to hear him say it.

'Do you remember we went almost a year without having sex? I stopped initiating, because I realised it was always me. And I waited.' Henry looks down, fidgeting with the strap of his watch. 'But you didn't seem to notice anything was missing from our marriage. Then when I suggested couple's therapy, you took me to bed. And I was thrilled until I realised.'

'What?'

'It was always Wednesdays in the morning or Fridays in the evening. You'd planned it.'

Jean sits up straighter, martini forgotten. 'And that's a bad thing?'

Henry takes a deep breath, and Jean can see him reaching for calm. 'I didn't want to be a task slotted in your diary. I wanted the kind of passion that defies a schedule; for you to crave me the way I needed you.'

'You complained that I didn't have sex with you, then you complained when I made time for it. What else did you want?' But even as the words leave her mouth, Jean understands. Her need for Ava had defied all reason or planning, a tsunami that washed away every boundary Jean had erected to protect her heart. She'd fallen for Ava, craving her body and spirit. Though Jean had loved Henry dearly as a friend, considered him family well before swapping rings, she'd never felt any kind of sweeping passion for him. Nor any passion at all.

Henry sees the realisation dawn. Gives Jean a little time to mull it over. Then, ever so gently, says: 'Did you ever find it with anyone else? I hoped that you would.'

'I did,' Jean breathes, barely audible over the restaurant's hum of chatter. 'But I screwed it up and it's over now.'

Henry nods sagely. 'Would you like to tell me about them?'

Them. He says the word so casually, as if the sex of Jean's hypothetical lover scarcely matters. As if the idea of Jean being with a woman were of no significance. And this is what gives Jean the courage to speak. 'I met someone. At a bar.'

'Oh yes?'

'Yes. I was stood up for a date.' She tells him about Ava between mouthfuls. Everything they'd had, what could have been, and how it all slipped through her fingers.

And Henry listens without judgement or surprise – he wouldn't be able to hide either from her, even after all these years.

'You were right,' he says, when the waiter goes to fetch them coffee. 'I did wonder about you and Marianne. At the time I was trying to provoke a reaction, but in recent years...'

'What?'

'My son. Lucas. He hasn't said anything about his sexuality to me or his mother.' Henry steeples his fingers. 'Let's just say that we're alive to the possibility he might be gay.

I've been doing research, just in case – I want to be able to support him through whatever difficulties he might face. And some details made me think of you.'

'How would you feel about it, if I were a lesbian?'

'I... I would want the same things I've always hoped for you,' Henry says, carefully. 'I'd hope you'd be happy.'

Happiness, again. He's more like Ava than he could possibly know.

'You wouldn't resent me, for having married you?' This time it's Jean who reaches across the table. 'I really did love you, Henry. If I could have been in love with any man, it would have been you. I just hadn't realised there was a difference between that kind of love, and...'

Henry takes her hand, his smile tinged with sadness. 'I don't regret the time we spent together. We were good friends once, with so much laughter. And if our marriage hadn't ended when it did, I wouldn't have gone to L&P, wouldn't have met Nina. My children would likely never have been born.' He looks at Jean then, earnest. 'But even if I wasn't glad for you, there's no sense in letting other people's opinions keep you from what makes you happy.'

Jean blinks. 'I... will keep that in mind. Thank you for this, Henry. I've missed your friendship.'

'Me too.' He gestures to the waiter for their bill. 'Actually, on that note, I'm delighted that you're a lesbian.'

Jean laughs loud enough that the nearest table turns to stare, ribs aching with the force of it. She'd forgotten Henry's gift for the unexpected. 'Why?'

'Because Nina won't have any suspicions if we do become friends again.'

They part with firm plans for Jean to come over and meet his family. Jean's still smiling when she gets home, picking up the bundle of post from her doormat. There's another book waiting – the memoir of a Christian mommy blogger turned gay rights activist. Plus, the usual assortment of bills, communications from her local councillor and coupons for nearby takeaways. And a creamy envelope, her name written in a familiar looping hand.

Jean can't breathe as she opens it. Even her heart comes to a standstill inside her chest. But there's no letter. Only a solid invitation card listing the date and venue for the CJC's launch event, with her name written in that same flowing script. Nothing else inside the envelope.

If it had come to the office, Jean would have suspected Ava meant for Peter to attend instead – he's been an enthusiastic supporter of the CJC since she'd mentioned it, signing up personally to represent clients and encouraging various senior associates to do the same. But the invitation has her name, it was delivered to her home. And though Ava has said nothing directly, Jean can't help but hope there's a message in it.

Chapter Thirty

The venue isn't difficult to find, a five-minute walk from Waterloo Station. The building has a beautiful exterior, cheerful yellow panels and broad windows. From the website Jean had learned that it's run as part of a social enterprise – and that ethos can be felt the moment she steps inside the foyer, where a magnificent ficus tree stretches up towards the glass ceiling. Children's laughter echoes down from the upper floor, where signage indicates there's a nursery. Beside it there's a printout emblazoned with the Colourblind Justice Caucus logo with a downward arrow.

A lift ride later, she queues for the registration table, alone amidst clusters of people she recognises from the party. Nobody else within her line of sight has a solid card invitation – they display either phones or paper printouts to the women manning the desk. And when Jean reaches the front of the line, a girl with tight sisterlocks hops to her feet.

'Oooh,' she says, coming round the table. 'You're at the Crenshawe table. Come with me.'

Jean follows her along the corridor. 'Is that a good thing?'

'It's Ms Harris – Ava's – personal table.' The girl turns back, smiling sheepishly. 'I'm Beth, her assistant. And I'm still getting used to using her first name. Too many years in corporate.'

Beth keeps up this excited flow of chatter all the way, which is just as well because Jean's mouth goes dry as they step into the main hall. The space is filled with round tables dotted with a smattering of people – the majority are still lining up to register. Only the leftmost table by the stage is almost entirely full, and it just so happens to be the one Beth is leading her towards.

There's no sign of Ava at the table, nor elsewhere in the hall. But Aaliyah sits by Simon in an elegant shell pink dress suit, pausing mid-sentence as she catches sight of Jean. Laila's there too, resplendent in a gold-stitched sari, bangles chiming as she stands to kiss Jean's cheek.

Ava's parents are just as effusive. Chibundo pulls Jean close for a sweetly perfumed hug, which she returns, realising that Ava has neglected to tell her parents about their split. Even Alasdair – a bowtie his only concession to the occasion – seems pleased to see her again. 'Comrade Howard! Glad you could join us.'

'I'm glad to be here,' Jean says, meaning it. 'And honoured that Ava has seated me with all of you.'

'Mhmm.' Aaliyah doesn't look up from her phone.

Simon winces as he meets her gaze, with a subtle shrug as if to say *You know how it is...* And Jean does – any overt friendliness on his part will lead to marital strife. After the divorce she'd missed it, having an automatic ally at every family event.

Jean can't resist another quick scan of the room, searching out warm brown eyes and an easy smile – but still no Ava, though the hall is filling. She looks back in time to catch Chibundo frowning at her firstborn, a reprimand taking shape on her lips. But – before she can speak – Jean introduces herself to the only person at the table she hasn't yet met: a slender woman with deep mahogany skin, sharp cheekbones, eyes cat-like in both shape and intelligence.

'You're Kelani Griffith.' Jean shakes her hand. 'Pleasure to meet you – I'm Jean Howard. And I've never seen Ava more excited than when you agreed to join her board.'

Only as the words leave her mouth does Jean realise, they aren't strictly true. Ava had been just as buoyant the first time she'd been permitted to go down on Jean... but that's not an anecdote she can share in polite company.

Kelani grins, exposing perfect white teeth. 'Jean! Ava's told me so much about you. I gather you've been a huge help behind the scenes.'

'It was nothing.' Jean takes the place marked out by her name card, in between Kelani and Ava's empty chair, conscious of Aaliyah's gaze cutting into her. 'Truth be told, I enjoyed the distraction from my usual work. Everything Ava wanted, everything she needed, it was easy enough to give her.'

Aaliyah's lip curls. 'Everything?'

Jean's eyelid twitches, but Kelani continues as if there has been no interruption to their conversation. 'Well,' she says, expression thoughtful, 'maybe you should do it more often.'

'What?' Jean's laughter rings too loud, too bright in her own ears. 'Helping out my friends?'

'Consultancy work for charities and non-profits. You have a gift for it.' At Jean's stunned expression Kelani simply shrugs. 'Just a thought.'

But it stays with her long after a trio of adoring young women appear to interrupt the conversation, requesting selfies with Kelani. She autographs copies of her book, personalising each one as the hall fills.

Then – at last – Ava appears in another of her bold, funky suits, this one a deep plum that complements her tawny skin. As she exchanges hugs with her family, Jean realises that her hair is different – a short bob shaved in at the nape. The sharp definition suits her, emphasising high cheekbones, the length of Ava's slender neck.

Ava kisses Kelani's cheek, the pair of them buzzing with excitement. Then she's face to face with Jean, and any possible plan of action vanishes as she catches the distinctive notes of Ava's cologne. Longing pierces Jean's breast. More than anything she wants to pull Ava close, to beg her forgiveness – but it's impossible in this room, packed full of people, under Aaliyah's fierce scrutiny. And besides, the last thing she wants is to weigh Ava down with added worry when it's her time to soar.

Ava too freezes, though her eyes are in constant motion. Her arms flutter by her sides, like she'd considered embracing Jean and thought better of it. 'You came,' is all she says, half wondering. As if there had ever been any question of it.

'Of course.' The words thrum with everything still unsaid.

Ava steps closer – whether towards Jean or her own seat remains uncertain, because Beth materialises at her side, whisking Ava and Kelani off to wait by the stage, where the CJC logo is projected onto the screen behind a podium. And Jean, weak-legged, sinks back into her chair.

Kelani, the star turn, goes first. She describes the thousands of requests that find their way into her inbox every single year, the struggle of wading through them all even with an assistant – and how Ava's proposal for the CJC had stood out right away. That her vision for the law and her passion for racial justice had aligned perfectly with Kelani's own.

'But there's only one person who should be up here telling you about the Colourblind Justice Caucus,' Kelani says. 'Our founder and CEO, Ava Kehinde Harris.'

Ava mounts the stage to much applause. Amari whistles, drawing Jean's gaze to the ACWRC table. Then she's standing at the podium, eyes sparkling in the spotlight as she takes in the crowd; the hundreds of people brought together by her vision of what could be.

She's less polished than Kelani, who has spent the last two and a half decades speaking in increasingly busy lecture halls and theatres around the world, but better than Jean will ever be for her raw honesty. Utterly heartfelt as she describes the loss of Ephraim; how it had shaped the trajectory of her life. And Jean's pulled back to that midpoint on the Cramond Causeway, when Ava had shared her devastation in personal terms.

Here and now, Ava's voice cracks under the weight of offering her grief up to colleagues and strangers. Jean's heart walks a tightrope of pride and fear as Ava falls silent, taking several moments to gather herself. But then she's talking about the CJC's aim of sparing other families that pain, and the room lights up with spontaneous applause. Chibundo buries her face in Alasdair's shoulder, and he holds his wife tight.

Laila's cheeks glimmer with silent tears – Jean retrieves a packet of tissues from her clutch and presses it into her hand while Ava carries on speaking.

'It's a strange thing to say at the birth of a new organisation. But in the end, I'd love nothing more than for us to become obsolete.' A rueful smile. Then Ava's thanking her newly formed team, her friends and family – Jean's heart stutters at the sound of her own name on Ava's lips – and every last person who has shown up to help launch the CJC.

The applause is rapturous, Ava's path back to their table slow and meandering. But wherever she goes in the room, Jean is conscious of her, an invisible string knotted behind her ribs, pulling taut whenever their eyes meet. The main course has been served by the time Ava sits down, bright-eyed and restless. And though the food is sumptuous, Jean can scarcely touch it, her throat too tight to swallow.

Throughout the afternoon Ava is close enough that Jean could cup her face, tracing it from cheekbone to jaw, yet remote as the sun while shining just as brightly. Jean isn't alone in hoping for a quiet word with Ava – the entire hall is packed with people longing for the same thing. Ready to pledge their support, or simply eager to witness Ava's sparkle up close.

There are drinks afterwards on the rooftop terrace – it's mild for early October, and a perfect opportunity for Ava's team to mingle with those likely to donate time and resources. Jean's glass of prosecco is purely ornamental, fizz an impossibility with her stomach roiling.

But Imogen finds her among the throng, keeping up a one-sided flow of conversation that requires little from Jean and discourages others from interrupting. Still, Elizabeth Granger can't resist saying hello – though she'd performed well at the first interview, it never hurts to exchange pleasantries with one's prospective employer. Jean can scarcely concentrate on her greeting, eyes drawn towards Ava standing side-on with the adjacent cluster of people.

'I wondered whether I'd see you here, Jean,' Elizabeth says. 'But you weren't sat with Peter at lunch.'

'Oh, I'm not representing the firm today.' Jean clears her throat. 'Actually, I'm here to support Ava in a personal capacity.'

Elizabeth's lips part, surprise plainly written across her features. But Jean is saved from having to formulate a response by the arrival of Ava herself, all smiles and handshakes, though she doesn't meet Jean's eye. And as Ginny makes introductions between Ava and Elizabeth, Jean can't help but wonder whether she has made a spectacular blunder. A suspicion sharpened by the way Ava still refuses to look at her; by the narrowing space between Imogen's brows as she notices.

Only Elizabeth appears oblivious to the tension, charmed into volunteering her services. And as Ava waves Beth over to take note of her details, Jean makes her escape, setting her untouched glass down on a table and disappearing down the stairs as fast as her heels will allow – which isn't very.

Peter catches her in the stairwell, wearing the worried look that is in danger of becoming habitual during their conversations. 'I hadn't realised you were going to be here, or we could have come along together.'

'I'm sorry,' Jean says, her skin too tight. 'Look, I'll explain everything later. But I need to go befo—'

'Jean!' Her name echoes against the walls as Ava gallops down the stairs, significantly faster in pristine white trainers. 'I was hoping we could have a word… if that's alright, Mr Dennings?'

'Peter, please. Or I'll have no choice but to call you Ms Harris,' he says with good humour. 'And it's no problem at all – I was on my way to enjoy more of your excellent prosecco.'

They watch him ascend the staircase. Only when they're alone does Jean dare to speak, words tripping over Ava's. 'Sorry, I shouldn't have assumed th—'

'Sorry! I kept hoping there'd be a gap, and—' Ava breaks off, smile rueful. Now her eyes meet Jean's without a trace of hesitation. 'You go first.'

'I'm sorry.' Jean wipes her palms against her skirt, thighs tense beneath the tweed. 'If I misspoke. With Elizabeth. It was good of you to invite me. And I shouldn't have read more into it.'

Ava steps closer, into Jean's space, voice low and urgent. 'No, I – I wanted you here. I thought we could find a quiet moment to talk. But I haven't had a second to myself all day, and I knew that if I looked at you while Elizabeth was there then I wouldn't be able to concentrate on a word she wa—'

Laughter echoes from the top of the stairs, heels clicking against stone. And Jean could scream at the interruption. But before she can draw breath Ava's fingers close around her wrist, and together they're dashing down the steps, Ava's thumb pressed to her pulse. And Jean follows, heart slamming against her sternum.

But downstairs Ava's guests linger, queuing for the toilets or meandering around the cloakroom. Ava searches their immediate surroundings, a frantic gleam in her eye. Then she's bundling Jean through a discreet door.

The stationery cupboard is brighter than the room Jean had forced Ava into, and mercifully mildew-free, but no bigger. As the overhead light flickers on, they have no choice but to stand face to face between flip charts and shelves bearing all manner of office supplies.

'Well.' Ava runs a hand through her hair, taking in the boxes of staplers and marker pens, the hefty stack of printer paper. 'I guess closets are becoming our thing.'

The tension ebbs from Jean as she laughs. It's still there, the strange and logic-defying pull between them. 'Actually, less so for me. I told my three oldest friends… that I'm a lesbian.'

Ava's eyes are round as pennies. 'Fucking hell. Well done, you. How did it go?'

'Imogen was great about it.' Jean plucks an errant dot of Blu Tack from a nearby shelf, rolling it between thumb and forefinger. 'Naomi and Cora were shocked. They had doubts at first. But I think they'll come round.'

Ava's hand finds the crook of Jean's elbow. 'You know I never expected you to do that. I'd have waited until you were ready.'

'I know.' The Blu Tack is soft as fresh clay as Jean presses her thumbnail inside the ball. 'But I had to, whether or not you and I… It was suffocating. I hadn't realised how much until I spoke to Henry. He was wonderful about it.'

Ava's brow creases. 'Your ex-husband?'

Jean nods. 'A friend, too. I told him all about you; about what we had. And what a fool I'd been to let you go.'

'Jean…' Ava's expression softens.

'This is going to sound crazy, but bear with me.' Jean clasps the Blu Tack tight in her fist. 'Henry and his wife have invited us over for dinner. If you'd be interested.'

Ava's head tilts, curls grazing her cheek. 'You want to have a dinner party with your ex-husband and your fuck buddy? That's a bold choice. I was right about one thing, Jellybean – you're a wild woman.'

Elation fizzes through Jean's veins, sudden as the first gush of bubbles from a bottle, at the sound of that stupid nickname. It's not an outright acceptance, but it's not a refusal either. 'Actually, I was hoping to have a dinner party with my friends. And maybe... maybe even my girlfriend. Or partner. Whatever you want to be. Mainly I was hoping that you could be part of my life, the way you let me be part of yours.'

Ava looks at her for a long moment, expression inscrutable. Then the ball of Blu Tack falls from between Jean's fingers as Ava pulls her close. She tilts her mouth up towards Ava's and they're kissing, slow and deep. Even when Jean's lungs burn for oxygen she can't bear to pull away. The perfect glide of tongues leaves Jean's knees weak, and she clings to Ava's shoulders, tangles her fingers in Ava's hair.

All the while Ava's hands skim across her back, her hips, featherlight – as though she can scarcely believe that Jean is within her grasp. Even when they're forced to come up for air, panting heavily, Ava holds her close.

'You should go back upstairs,' Jean says, though her arms remain locked around Ava's waist. 'They'll all be wondering where you've got to.'

'I got Kelani to do an impromptu Q&A session. They'll be okay for a while yet.'

Jean pulls back just far enough to look her in the eye. 'Ava, this is your big day. You should make the most of it. And I'll come back upstairs with you, of course I will, but I don't want our thing to distract people from your work.'

Ava's smile is lop-sided. 'My girlfriend's pretty sweet.'

'It happens on occasion.' Still giddy from their kisses, it takes a moment for the full weight of Ava's words to hit her. 'Your girlfriend?'

Ava kisses the question from her lips. 'My girlfriend.'

'Are you sure?'

Ava's breath ruffles Jean's hair as she huffs a laugh. 'What, are you trying to talk me out of it now? After you seduced me in a stationery cupboard?'

'I just want you to be positive.' Jean clutches Ava's lapels, desperate to make her see. 'I don't think I'll ever be able to tell Bridget. Speaking of sisters, Aaliyah's not going to be thrilled either. And by the time you're forty I'll be pushing sixty – doesn't any of that bother you?'

'Hey.' Ava kisses Jean's forehead until the frown melts away. 'I told you: I never expected you to tell everyone. It's up to you whether you come out to Bridget. And if you never do, that's fine. I promise.'

'And your sister?'

Ava sighs, searching for the right words, though her grip on Jean never loosens. 'Al was sick of watching me get my heart stomped on – there have been a couple of times when I've fallen for a straight woman, and it's ended badly. Not,' Ava says, hurriedly, 'that that's what this is. And once she sees that, once she knows we're both serious, she'll come around. I'll have a proper talk with her later. Don't worry.'

Jean nods, forehead tucked beneath Ava's neck. 'And the other thing?'

'Your age never bothered me,' Ava says, without hesitation.

'Yes, but it mattered less when we were just hooking up. Now we're trying to build…' *A life. A life, together.* The possibility is so vast, so perfect, that Jean can't fit her mouth around it. 'Something real.'

Still Ava doesn't share her panic. 'I've never met anyone quite like you, Jean Howard.' Her hand cups Jean's chin, tipping it up until their eyes meet. 'Not before and not now. Not in my entire life. I love you exactly the way you are. And I wouldn't change one single thing about you – not even when you go Full Glenn on me.'

Oh.

'And, well...'

'What?'

'It's not like I'm trying to get you pregnant. So, what does it matter?'

For a long moment Jean can only stare at her, incredulous. Then the laughter's pouring out of her, impossibly loud in the tiny room. Ava slumps against her, wheezing. And only the lack of space to fall keeps them both upright, entwined around one another for support.

This is how Beth finds them, clearing her throat until they take notice, still giggling like naughty schoolgirls.

'Ms Harris – Ava.' Beth lingers in the doorway, lips twitching as she takes in their mussed hair; Jean's lipstick smudged bright around Ava's mouth. And Jean waits for the shame to hit her, the embarrassment of being caught *in flagrante delicto*, but there's only the reassuring warmth of Ava's hand against her back. 'We have a prospective donor waiting upstairs. Shall I say you'll be five minutes?'

'Yes,' Ava says. 'Thank you, Beth.'

The moment the door closes, they dissolve into fresh giggles, Jean smoothing Ava's curls. She retrieves a comb from her clutch to fix her own hair, wiping their mouths clean with an anti-bacterial wipe that nips at Jean's swollen lips. And Jean applies a fresh coat of lipstick while Ava waits, blushing at the tender look in her eyes.

Then Ava takes her hand, and they step out into the open.

Chapter Thirty-One

Even Aaliyah thaws over time, as Jean keeps showing up at Ava's side. There for Theo's violin recital, Evie's fifth birthday party, and fortnightly dinners at the Harris-Emmanuel family home. The first time Aaliyah offers Jean a refill of wine, the glass nearly slips from between her fingers, though she quickly recovers herself. Ava squeezes her leg under the table, which does nothing to calm Jean's racing pulse.

They carry on this way until, after Theo's school nativity play, he asks: 'Why is Jean here?'

Ava's gloved hand closes around Jean's as they cross the frosty carpark.

'To see you being a shepherd,' Aaliyah says, swift to fill the awkward silence. And, hissed in a white puff of air: *'Don't be rude.'*

Theo tugs the dishtowel from his head, indignant in the way of the falsely accused. 'If I'm being rude then you need to give Nanny C trouble too, because I heard her asking Grandpa the same thing.'

Simon gives a high-pitched giggle, which dies on the pointy end of his mother-in-law's stare. They linger by Aaliyah's Range Rover in an uncomfortable silence that threatens to stretch on all night, until Jean steps forward. Looks the boy in the eye. 'I'm here because I'm Ava's girlfriend. And because I wanted to support you.'

Aaliyah and Chibundo exchange a glance. And Ava grins down at the sparkling tarmac.

'Hmm.' Theo's eyes narrow, and Jean's mouth goes dry. 'Does that mean you're allowed to decide if we go to McDonald's?'

'Oh, please! Please!' Evie hops up and down on the spot, sleepiness shed in an instant.

Ava laughs, wrapping one arm around her nephew's shoulder and looping the other round Jean's waist. 'Sure it does.'

'I think,' Alasdair says, 'given the occasion, we could ignore their business practices. Just this once.'

And just like that, over fries and milkshakes, Jean is absorbed into the Harris family fold.

—

It's Jean's own friends who pose the greatest challenge. Imogen suggests meeting for drinks – something non-committal and, in theory, relaxed enough that Jean won't get overly stressed at the prospect of Cora and Naomi seeing her with Ava. She's too anxious to eat beforehand; a rookie mistake.

Ginny is easy with Ava, effortlessly charming. But Naomi tries too hard, overcompensating after the disaster of Jean's coming out. And Cora is her usual unassailable self, more immune to embarrassment than a duck's back to water. Even Aaliyah's censure was easier to bear than having every gesture between them scrutinised by Naomi, or Cora's probing questions. Jean's first martini melts into her fourth, only Ava's concerned gaze keeping her from a fifth, and she knows at least part of the evening's strangeness is due to her own inebriation.

Ava holds Jean in the taxi home as the streets swim by, hushing her every time she tries to apologise and paying the driver before Jean can successfully co-ordinate the zip on her handbag. Inside she gets Jean to down a pint of water; makes a ham and cheese sandwich spread thick with mustard, just the way she likes it. Whether it's the food lining her stomach or the comfort of being squarely back on her own turf, safe with Ava, Jean feels better for it.

Upstairs Jean collapses onto the mattress, her ceiling sliding gently in and out of focus. 'This wasn't,' she says, as Ava crawls in beside her, 'how I'd planned on getting you back into my bed.'

Ava's lips brush against her temple, curved upwards into a smile. 'Go to sleep, Jellybean.'

And though her head and stomach pulse in the morning, and her neck prickles every time she remembers the awkwardness with Cora and Naomi, Jean's resolve doesn't waver.

Throughout the week Peter double and triple checks that she's sure about their plan. Jean bristles at this smothering, until it truly hits her: their days of working together are running out. Ten, nine, seven... A week from now there will be no impromptu lunches, no sounding board, none of that relentless optimism. No more safety net as Jean flies higher than ever before. But every day in the office only serves to solidify Jean's certainty – there are other possibilities, other ways of being. The cake is ordered, the handover date marked in the company calendars. She has Helen messenger an invitation to Ava's office; if anyone is to witness her final, glorious leap at DDH, it should be her partner.

Jean changes into her crushed velvet blazer dress in her private office bathroom, a final check, dabbing fresh perfume at her neck, her wrists, and – after a moment's deliberation – between her breasts. Though Helen offers, Jean goes down to the lobby and greets Ava in person. She's dressed up for the occasion, in a crisp white shirt and high-waisted grey slacks that emphasise the curve of her hips; the length of her legs. Ava could almost blend in at the firm, were it not for her chunky silver rings and the bold orange scarf knotted through her updo. Even in this place, she could not be more perfectly herself.

And through her eyes, Jean sees DDH as if for the first time: the polished marble floors, the airy expanse of the reception, the steady stream of water splashing in the fountain. But, above all things, Ava is the truest measure of her wealth. *My cup*, Jean thinks, *runneth over*.

When Ava catches sight of her, she approaches at a trot, only to slow at the last moment. Uncertain of protocol. Unsure of Jean. But that's easily remedied. Jean stands up on tiptoe, not bothering to check who might be passing, and presses a kiss on the corner of Ava's mouth.

Though it's a chaste enough greeting, Ava's eyebrows climb, her eyes round as saucers. 'Jean?'

'Ava?' Jean takes her hand, still limp with surprise, and pulls Ava towards the lifts. 'Come on – let's go upstairs. Peter's wife is due to arrive any second, and she's not pleased with me.'

In the lift Ava still wears that same stunned expression. 'I'm fine with PDA,' she says. 'And I couldn't be prouder that you're my girlfriend. But Jean, you were so afraid of your colleagues finding out. What it might mean for your career. You don't have to come out to them, especially not today of all days. I'm fine keeping it ambiguous.'

'I'm not.' Jean turns to face her, looking Ava in the eye. 'I've spent my entire adult life making decisions based on what other people might think, and it made me miserable. These last couple of months... I can't remember ever feeling so free, so alive. Alright?'

'Alright.' Ava grins. 'Knock them dead, my wild woman.'

Jean laughs as the doors slide open. Already the break room is buzzing with activity. Gold and silver balloons bob in the air among clusters of people. Emily stands on a chair, pinning the final *Congratulations!* banner in place.

Alexander is the first to approach her, always with an eye for an opportunity. 'Big day for you, Ms Howard.'

Jean's smile grows demure. 'A big day for the firm, Alexander. And I'd like you to meet my partner, Ava.' His expression doesn't flicker as the two of them shake hands – perhaps Jean has misjudged him. 'Alexander's one of our senior associates.'

'Hi!' Ava beams, though her knuckles pale with the force required to return Alexander's death grip. 'Pleasure to meet you.'

'Likewise.' Alexander looks between them, lowering his voice. 'So, you and Ms Howard have gone into business? Always a good idea to diversify the portfolio.'

Jean stares, slack jawed. *Of all the possible responses...* Alexander saunters off to have a word with Peter, utterly oblivious. And though Ava covers her mouth, there is no disguising the shake of her shoulders.

She spies Elizabeth lingering in the corner, Dale discreetly adjusting a shoulder pad in her jacket – he is perhaps the least resentful trailing spouse Jean has yet encountered, perfectly content running his web design business from home while Elizabeth takes the legal world by storm. And after today her position will be unassailable.

Jean guides Ava through the throngs, accepting thanks from assorted underlings, and exchanging air kisses with Elizabeth.

'I know you're already well acquainted with Elizabeth, but this is her husband, Dale.' Jean takes a breath. Keeps her tone light, as if remarking upon the weather. 'And this is my girlfriend, Ava.'

'Oh, how lovely,' Elizabeth says, 'that you brought a friend along for moral support.'

With the muscle in Ava's cheek working overtime, her mouth clamped firmly shut, it's on Jean alone to rescue this attempt at coming out. 'Actually, we're... Ava's my—'

'Jean!' Peter's hand clamps around her shoulder, and it's a relief to turn her back on the temptation to start a sentence with *for fuck's sake*. 'Everyone's here now, so we should make a start on the speeches. The sooner we do, the sooner they can bring out the cake.'

'Right.' Over his shoulder Jean spies Caroline, gaze sullen as she sips champagne on the other side of the room. 'Thank you. For everything.'

Peter's smile grows fond. 'Don't mention it. And Ava, I'm very glad you could join us here today. Trust me when I say you wouldn't want to miss this.'

Jean lifts two flutes of champagne from a passing tray and hands one to Ava. The crystal grows slippery against her fingers as Jean approaches the raised platform. And a hush falls over the room as heads turn to track her progress. With every eye upon her, Jean speaks.

'For the last thirty years, DDH has been the epicentre of my universe. From my first day as an intern, every decision that I've made has ultimately been about this firm.' Jean scans the sea of faces turned up towards her – Hugo and Rhona by the canapé table, Carl watching from the side of the room, Peter gazing at her with unabashed pride. 'In that time, I've had the immense privilege of watching us grow, watching all of you build us into titans of the legal world. And I am so incredibly proud of what we have achieved together.'

Applause blazes through the room. Even now she could wrap up there, return to the original plan. 'I know that many of you came here today with the expectation that we'd be announcing Peter's retirement along with my promotion to managing partner. That I would oversee the firm for the foreseeable future. But this last year has made it clear to me that it's time for new adventures, fresh challenges.'

Murmurs ripple through the crowd. Even from this distance, Jean can make out the frown creasing Rhona's forehead. 'This is a significant change in plan. And all of you deserve an explanation. There is not one single reason, but there is a significant one. It's possible that you may have heard recent rumours on the subject after my... confrontation with Kate Brennan.'

The murmurs rise to a dull hum of chatter. With a shaking hand, Jean lifts the knife lying by the cake and taps it against her glass. 'I know that I'm giving you a lot to talk about, but this next part is rather difficult, and I'd thank you all to be quiet.' The room falls silent once more. Ava inches forward to stand at the edge of the platform – ready, as she had promised, to catch Jean in more ways than one.

'Certain allegations were made against our founder, William Decker. And I regret to inform you that they were true. And just as much, perhaps eve—' Jean clears her throat, and it helps that all the faces before her blur. 'Even more so, I regret not speaking up about what happened to us all those years ago when Marianne... Kate did. I was so concerned with my career, my reputation... And now I'd like to find out how life would look if I put those worries down.'

Ava steps forward, pressing a tissue into Jean's hand. But she doesn't retreat, staying on the half-step between the platform and the ground. And Jean draws strength from her closeness, enough to blow her nose and keep going.

'I don't know what I'm going to do in this next chapter of my life – that's a shock for me too. It's the first time in forty years I haven't had some kind of plan in place.' A few people laugh. And even Caroline's glare has softened. 'But I do know that you'll be in very capable hands. Peter has been at the forefront of every positive change in the direction and culture of this firm in the time I've been here. I've been proud to call him a colleague, and I remain proud to call him a friend. And nobody could fill my shoes more ably than Elizabeth Granger – I'm thrilled to welcome her to the DDH family.'

Elizabeth tries and fails to look modest at the applause. And Peter dabs at his cheeks with an immaculate white handkerchief, Caroline stroking his shoulder.

'And while I'm dropping bombshells left, right, and centre, I would like to thank the woman I love. The woman I want to spend the rest of my life with.' Their eyes meet, and Ava almost slips from the little step in shock. Jean rests a steadying hand on her shoulder. 'Ava Harris. Without her support, none of these realisations or decisions would have been possible.'

With a final round of thanks to the team, Jean steps from the platform, shaking like a leaf. Over thunderous applause Ava pulls her close, lips brushing Jean's ear as she says: 'I'm so fucking proud of you, Jean.'

She doesn't let go while Peter and Elizabeth speak, an arm wrapped tight around Jean's shoulder. And this gentle pressure is enough to slow her heart's erratic gallop to a steady beat. Even afterwards – through the cake, congratulations and well wishes – Ava stays close, the back of her hand brushing against Jean's. And she wouldn't have it any other way.

Chapter Thirty-Two

Even though Jean's cheeks ache, she can't stop beaming as she steps out into the cool night air. In the run up to Christmas, London is at its most beautiful, lights sparkling from shop windows and dangling in glittering strings between buildings. She and Ava spend the taxi ride pointing decorations out to each other, breath misting the windows.

Strata is stuffed to the gills, the usual Friday night pre-gaming supplemented by obscenely early Christmas parties, identifiable by festive jumpers and Santa hats and glowing jewellery. Their booth is an oasis of calm, and Jean's glad she had the foresight to book it.

In typical Ava fashion, she insists on braving the crowded bar. And Jean takes off her coat, humming along to Bing Crosby – a tune her mother always loved.

Sooner than Jean would have imagined possible, Ava returns with a dirty martini, a mojito, and a question. 'You okay? That was big, what you did there.'

'Yes.' Jean strokes Ava's cheek until the concern melts away. 'Better than ever.'

'Good.' Their feet find each other under the table. 'So, what did Rhona want to talk about?'

'She asked to come and work for me.' Jean sips her martini, tart and cool and delicious. 'I said yes.'

Ava frowns, concerned. 'It's not that Rhona isn't great, but do you think taking on employees off the bat is a good idea? Do you want me to help you look up grants and stuff?'

'No.' Jean laughs, resting a hand on her wrist. 'I appreciate the offer, but I don't need grants to afford her or Helen. I don't technically need to work at all. But this is something I have to do.'

Over shared wings and fries Jean launches into her plans, her goals. The layers of possibility that have been building in her mind, taking shape ever since Kelani's comment. And with every word it feels more achievable.

The baskets are empty, her stomach full, before Jean realises just how much she's talking. 'Sorry. I meant to ask about your day, but I've completely monopolised the conversation.'

Ava shakes her head, smile fond. 'Don't apologise. It's nice seeing you like this. Properly excited.'

In the face of such sincere support, Jean feels able to voice a doubt that has niggled at her along with the hope. 'Do you… think I'll be alright at this? I mean, what do I know about charities?'

'More than most people.' Ava squeezes her hand. 'And besides, I think you'll be sensational.'

'Really?'

'Of course! I'm happy to provide a glowing testimonial – about your consultancy skills.' Ava winks. 'And your sex acquaintance ones.'

Jean rolls her eyes. 'You're never going to let me live that down, are you?'

'Nope!' Ava's eyes sparkle with mischief as she sips her mojito.

All the same, Jean feels compelled to clarify. To shut down the slightest ambiguity or doubt. 'You know that you're so much more than a sex acquaintance to me, don't you? I really do love you.'

Ava's attempts to wave the words off are undercut by the pretty flush warming her cheeks. 'Yeah,' she says, not quite looking at Jean. 'I picked up on that when you told your entire office that you want to spend the rest of your life with me. Baller move, by the way.'

'It just slipped out.' Jean lifts the stick impaling her olive, stirring it round her glass. 'But it felt right. At the time.'

'Did you mean it?' Ava's whisper is scarcely audible above the hubbub of chatter and Annie Lennox's unearthly voice. But in the last year Jean has become finely attuned to this woman, every shift in expression and tone. And it's not disapproval nor even displeasure that keeps her from looking at Jean, but rather nerves.

It's Jean's turn now to be brave, to set aside her fears and speak up. 'I did. I meant every word.'

'Okay. Then I would like that too.' Their eyes meet, and Ava bites her lip. 'I'd love it, actually. Being with you long-term.'

Jean's heart contracts, but her voice remains steady. 'Well, we renegotiated the terms of our relationship before. Should we do it again?'

Ava's looking at her – really looking at her – as if nothing else exists but Jean. 'What sort of thing did you have in mind?'

'Hmm. I was thinking along traditional lines – or traditional as it gets with a lesbian couple.' Jean reaches across the table and takes Ava's hand in hers, uncertain whose fingers are the origin of their trembling. 'In sickness and in health, for richer or poorer, 'til death do us part. I'll gladly love and honour you, but I do have major reservations about obeying you.'

'We could scratch that particular clause – I'm not wild about it either.' Ava's thumb whispers across the back of her hand, smooth and natural as an ocean caressing the shore. 'Do you really want to get married?'

'Well, yes. With you I do.' The possibility hadn't occurred to Jean until meeting Ava, that she might ever willingly call herself wife again. So many things hadn't. But now Jean can't imagine a sweeter string of tomorrows, bright and optimistic as the Christmas lights. 'In the not-too-distant future.'

'That settles what we're getting each other for Christmas: rings.' Ava leans across the table, her kiss full of urgent promise. 'Now let's go home. I want to celebrate with my beautiful fiancée.'

A Letter from Lou

Hello,

In much the same way that Jean wasn't planning to have a relationship with another woman, *Strap In* isn't the book I'd planned to write for my debut novel – but ultimately it worked out for the best. Jean learned how to live and love authentically, and I wrote a story that came directly from the heart.

It was always my intention to create lesbian romance, because this is what excites me most, both as a reader and a writer. But I'd originally intended a Dual POV romance featuring both a woman of colour and a white woman as protagonists. I wanted to depict an interracial relationship in a way that felt more truthful and realistic than the colour-blind stories written by white authors. While working out the details, I went on one of Rachel Kramer Bussel's excellent workshops on writing sex scenes. For one of the exercises, she gave us the prompt of food or drink – and instantly I had Jean and her martini in mind.

Ava quickly followed, her confidence and knowing – not to mention her androgynous charm – the kryptonite to Jean's repression. Only the more I got to know Ava, the clearer it became that she knew exactly who she was and what she wanted; being so fully self-realised, she had no need of the growth arc that is the engine driving a novel forward. Jean, on the other hand, had a long road to travel from hole-hearted to wholehearted – how Gwen Hayes describes the romance arc. What was initially planned as a short story soon blossomed into a novel – I wrote the first draft over forty-six feverish days and nights.

And though I hadn't planned to write a novel solely with a white protagonist, there was a rightness to Jean's story that made me certain this was the right path, both in terms of my creativity and my commitment to expanding the range of women found in lesbian romance. Though lots of women only realise they're lesbian or bisexual in mid to later life, the vast majority of coming out narratives are centred around teens or young adults.

I hate the term 'late-blooming lesbians', because it implies that any woman who doesn't know she's gay from her youth is running behind schedule. In reality there are a whole host of social, cultural, and political factors that stand in the way of this realisation. Partly it can take time because of sexist cultural narratives that frame women as inherently less sexual than men, which lead to women in heterosexual unions not questioning why their desire is low. But also because so many women grow up being bombarded from early girlhood with the idea they'll marry a man and have his children – even when that plan doesn't fit with our desires or dreams.

When I was a little girl, my grandfather outlined his plan for my life: I'd stay in school, go to university, get a job, find a husband, then have children. In that order. And given he always knew the answers to my maths homework, and could drive around Britain without getting lost, it didn't occur to me to question his wisdom. At home, at church, at my Catholic primary school, straight life was presented as the only path – what Adrienne Rich called compulsory heterosexuality. And even though the thought of having a husband filled me with dread, even though I have a lesbian mother, even though I spent my adolescence thirsting over Meryl Streep as Miranda Priestly, I was nineteen before the lesbian penny – or pink pound – fully dropped.

For context, I was watching *Orange is the New Black* on Netflix, thinking that it would be entirely worth going to jail if I could have a prison wife instead of the dreaded hypothetical husband. Only as I contemplated potential non-violent crimes that would enable me to swap liberty for a shot at love did it occur to me: *I don't need to go to prison to be with a woman...* Thus began a life-altering epiphany.

And sure, it's funny. But the fact young Lou thought 'I should go to prison!' before 'I'm a lesbian!' is also proof of how deeply compulsory heterosexuality runs through society. I figured my lesbianism out at nineteen. Jean takes nearly three times as long. Some women take longer still. And they're just as valid, just as worthy of representation, as the lesbians who figure it out in childhood.

Strap In is my love letter to the women who come out in mid or later life, because sapphic community wouldn't be the same without you in it. And I hope that Jean's story will inspire readers from every background to seize the day, regardless of your age, because it's never too late to follow your heart.

With love,

Lou x

Acknowledgements

Thanks go first and foremost to my grandmother. This book quite literally wouldn't exist if you hadn't been generous enough to give me the space, time and security needed to transform my earliest, dearest wish into reality. Thank you from the bottom of my heart. I love you now and always.

Thanks to my mum for a lifetime of support – all our early trips to the library planted the seeds for this story. Every time someone borrows this book from their local library, know that your encouragement made it happen. And thanks to my stepmum, who rooted for me the second I revealed this plan. I'm glad you two found your own Happily Ever After together.

Thanks to Becky Thomas for being my dream agent, steadfast with sharp instincts – I feel endlessly blessed to have you in my corner, championing the books of my heart. You're a star. And I hope the same light you bring to others is revisited on you tenfold.

And thank you to Hera for making every stage of the publication journey a joy; in particular, to Jennie Ayres for being my dream editor. From our first meeting at the Romantic Novelists' Association conference, I knew that you got not only these characters and their story, but the yearning I felt to broaden the variety of women found in the pages of lesbian romance. I'm ecstatic to have found such a perfect home for my stories.

Thanks are also due to Lindsey Harrad for a brilliant and thorough copyedit, and Vicki Vrint for being eagle-eyed with the proofread; also to Rachel Lawston for giving this book such a gorgeous cover, fully capturing Ava's top energy and the way Jean can't help lighting up around her.

Thanks to RD, whose feedback for my early work transformed me as a writer and whose friendship vastly improved me as a person. And TG, our Fairy Squad Mother, who cured my not-like-other-girls-itis and made me realise how much I love the tropes and genre conventions of romance. You two are the best friends imaginable, and I can't wait to read your books.

It would be impossible for me to write a lesbian book without thanking LK, who has always been generous and intentional in connecting me with a world of lesbian culture – meeting you was one of my life's greatest blessings.

Also, shoutout to Lucy Ribchester for being a stellar crit partner and outstanding friend. Thank you so much for being a safe, constructive person with whom to share early drafts. Starting out as a novelist, it meant everything to have someone so brilliant, subversive and accomplished believe in me.

Thanks to the wonderful Catherine Tinley, for nurturing the next generation of romance writers – me included. Your advice has never yet steered me wrong, and that tip to prepare extra pitches transformed the trajectory of my career. I'll be forever grateful. Thanks are also due to all my fellow Tattlers for making writing a much less lonely job, especially the phenomenal Saoirse Morrigan.

Thanks to the Romantic Novelists' Association for being such a welcoming, inclusive community. You've supported me in growing from a New Writer into a published novelist, and we'll always have the *Nutbush*!

Thanks to Jae for all you do to uplift a broad range of sapphic authors – I hope to pay forward everything you've been kind enough to do for me.

D and BG, who have supported my ambitions in every iteration, and had me to stay when I met my agent – my love and thanks, always. Also to CW, for truly being a great aunt ♥.

S, LM, and K – thank you all for understanding when I needed to disappear into the writer bunker. Sisters for life.

Thanks to Sacha Black and Rachael Herron, whose writing podcasts kept me sane and motivated on the walks I'd take to untangle this story. I'm a proud rebel with ink in my veins.

And thank you to my local librarians for providing books, community and some much-needed calm during the frenzy of drafting. Every single day, you all work magic.

Lastly, but by no means least, thank **you** for taking the time to read this story. Whether you bought a copy or borrowed it from your local library, whatever format you've chosen to read in, it means the world that you chose to spend time in this story.

Lou's playlist

- 'No Homo', by Lambrini Girls
- 'Tranquillity Base Hotel & Casino', by Arctic Monkeys
- 'Solitaire', by Marina
- 'Nameless, Faceless', by Courtney Barnett
- 'Ministry', by Karen O & Danger Mouse
- 'Beauty of Uncertainty', by KT Tunstall
- 'Longing,' by Gustavo Santaolalla
- 'Kiss My Feet', by Laura Mvula
- 'West End Girls', by Pet Shop Boys
- 'Wait for It', by Leslie Odom Jr. and Original Broadway Cast of Hamilton
- 'Say Yes to Heaven', by Lana Del Rey
- 'Pandora's Box', by Marina
- 'You Know I'm No Good', by Amy Winehouse
- B'lind Valentine', by Metric
- Justice, by Martha Wainwright
- 'Somebody That I Used to Know', by Goyte (dedicated to Marianne!)
- 'Big Exit', by PJ Harvey
- 'Need a Little Time', by Courtney Barnett
- 'Life Is Hard', by Edward Sharpe and the Magnetic Zeros
- 'Universe & U', by KT Tunstall